THE SCENTED SWORD

'My sword,' Richelieu snapped, close at hand. She lunged in his direction, and he gave a startled gasp and obviously threw himself to one side. 'The candle,' he called. 'For God's sake light the candle.'

Geneviève listened to the sound of a door close.

'Only a girl, lads,' Richelieu was saying. 'Claude, are you there? Light the candle, man. Only a girl.'

Geneviève remained still, slowly inhaling and expelling her breath, keeping her body in balance, her sword at her side, as she had no intention of giving her position away until she had to. Her fear was entirely past, and in fact had been replaced by a mood of exultant fury. She was quite looking forward to the coming brawl. Her very first, in earnest. She never doubted she would triumph.

THE SCENTED SWORD

Alison York

Star

A STAR BOOK

published by
the Paperback Division of
W. H. ALLEN & Co. Ltd

A Star Book
Published in 1980
by the Paperback Division of
W. H. Allen & Co. Ltd
A Howard and Wyndham Company
44 Hill Street, London W1X 8LB

First published in Great Britain by
W. H. Allen & Co. Ltd, 1980

Copyright © Alison York, 1980

Printed in Great Britain by
Hunt Barnard Printing Ltd., Aylesbury, Bucks.

ISBN 0 352 30706 4

Chapter One

The clanging of the bell echoed through the bedchamber, and Charles d'Éon was immediately awake, dragging back the drapes to leap from his bed, white nightshirt fluttering as he ran to the open window to watch the *péniche* gliding slowly through the water, still moving although the horse on the tow path had stopped, and like its master was regarding the closed lock gate with censorious concern.

Charles inhaled, filling his lungs with the cool spring air drifting down to Tonnerre from the mountains of the Côte d'Or. His window, at the back of the house, faced the rising sun, and the canal. He adored the canal, although only once in his thirteen years had he even been allowed to stand on its bank and look down into its turgid brown depths. Canals were not for an Éon de Beaumont. The last Éon de Beaumont, as he was reminded often enough. But the canal promised all the wide world that lay beyond his window, and into which he had never been allowed to venture. It came from Sens, and before that, from Paris itself; the great city was only a hundred miles away. And it was going south, carrying its traffic with it until it ended in the rushing Rhône, with only the Mediterranean to halt it after that. Would he ever see the Mediterranean? For all Great Uncle Henri's oft repeated reminders that he would shortly be away to Paris to complete his schooling, Charles doubted he would ever see anywhere else. Tonnerre was a prison. A most delightful prison, to be sure, but one none the less.

The door opened. Tante Marie was the only servant allowed in Charles' bedroom. It was a symptom of the seclusion in which he lived, the cosseting he endured. Mama said it was because he was the very last Éon de Beaumont. Not even Papa had the full title; it belonged to *him* because he was Great Uncle Henri's godchild. Therefore he could be exposed to no harmful influences. Even the footmen and the gardeners were not to be romped with. What harm could *they* do? He sometimes wondered if he suffered from some dread disease, which would permit no risk of injury.

'Drink your chocolate,' Tante Marie recommended. 'And stop dreaming out of the window. Dreaming is for girls, and you are a boy.'

Tante Marie was always stressing this point. She was very old. She had been Papa's nurse as a young woman, and had been Pierre's nurse as well, for the brief year Pierre had lived. Oh, unhappy Pierre. *Had* Pierre lived, he would have been the Beaumont heir, and Charlie might have been allowed to go his own way. But of course it was Pierre's untimely death that had caused so much concern about his own health.

He sipped his chocolate – so hot it burned his mouth – and peered at himself in the mirror while Tante Marie filled the china basin from the ewer she had placed outside the door. He licked his lips to remove the last of the scalding liquid, smiled at himself. It was a secret smile. He was beautiful. It was an absurd word to use about a boy, but the Countess, when last she had stopped in Tonnerre on her way from Clermont Ferrand to Bordeaux, and he had been presented in his best satin suit, had cried, 'Oh, but what a beautiful child.' And undoubtedly she had been right. He could tell that by looking around him. Tante Marie did not count, because her nose was too big and her face was a mass of wrinkles and besides, she smelt of garlic. But Mama was a lovely woman, still. And Papa was a handsome man. Their combined looks had come together in his own elegant features, his high forehead and his wide-set amber eyes, his straight, short nose and his flat mouth, the dimples in his cheeks and the point to his chin, the whole enhanced by the straight yellow hair which rested on his shoulders. I am beautiful, he thought. I am the most beautiful thing I have ever seen.

He was a prince, bound to rescue princesses, and Monsieur Lannes was coming today, to make sure he was able to fight the world, if need be. He adored Monsieur Lannes. He thought he loved him as much as he loved Papa.

He threw his nightshirt on the floor, washed his face – he had never been ashamed to be naked in front of Tante Marie – and dragged on his clothes, while the nurse leaned against the door and watched him. She always did this while he dressed, guarded the door like a soldier, refusing admission to anyone save

Mama. No doubt she was afraid he would catch a chill. They were all afraid, afraid, afraid. But today Monsieur Lannes was coming. Charles d'Éon paused, slowly sitting on the bed, shoe in hand. It was quite inexplicable, really; Monsieur Lannes came to teach him swordsmanship. Even with discs on the ends of their rapiers there was the possibility of injury, certainly of a bruise as they tumbled about the rose garden. But Monsieur Lannes came twice in every week, and when they had finished their swordplay, it was time for his riding lesson, round and round the paddock and over the jump, always with a risk of falling off. Yet he was not permitted to romp with the servants, not allowed a single friend of his own age, although often enough he clung to the garden railings and watched the schoolboys of Tonnerre trooping off to their lessons.

He would never understand the ways of parents.

But Monsieur Lannes *was* coming. Charles tumbled down the stairs, leaving Tante Marie far behind. At the bottom, Madame Louvanne, his governess, waited, her hands clasped primly in front of her. Madame Louvanne lived in the town, and walked up to the house by the canal every day. She taught him Latin and arithmetic, and read him the classics. She was his only contact with the outside world, save for Monsieur Lannes, his only source of gossip, for Monsieur Lannes never gossiped. Madame Louvanne would tell him about Paris, and the King, and how the war was going, what the great Prussian Frederick would be doing next as he sought, with French aid, to dispossess the young Empress, Maria Theresa, of her throne. This was the world of men and affairs, the world Charles sometimes doubted he would ever see. But madame was an unsatisfactory playmate. *Her* world was governed by propriety, and by time. 'Young gentlemen never run downstairs,' she said, and immediately proceeded to contradict herself. 'You are late for breakfast.'

'I was watching a barge,' Charles explained. He had a curiously gentle voice, a low contralto which sometimes surprised even himself. 'When I grow up, I am going to be a bargee.'

'What nonsense,' Madam Louvanne remarked, walking in front of him to the breakfast room, where the glass windows opened on to the terrace. 'What nonsense.'

'I am,' Charles explained. He hated being opposed, at least quite so carelessly. 'I am.' He paused in the doorway, his face crumpling as an agonising pain struck at the pit of his stomach,

3

seeming to penetrate until it reached the small of his back. It was a pain he had never felt before. Indeed, as he doubled up and sank to his knees, he realised that if this was pain, he had never *ever* felt it before. Yet his brain, seething away as he clutched himself and moaned, reminded him that he had expected something of this nature. All yesterday he had felt strangely tired, strangely lacking in energy, strangely anticipatory of something terrible about to happen to his life.

There were people around him. Jules the butler, holding his shoulders and trying to raise him; Madame Louvanne, standing immediately before him and repeating, 'Charles,' over and over again; Tante Marie saying, 'Oh, my God.' And suddenly and most surprising of all, Mama, standing beside Madame Louvanne and gazing at Tante Marie, her face pale.

The cramp passed, and he raised his head, discovered himself on his feet, held there by Jules, who had passed an arm round his waist.

'A surgeon,' Madame Louvanne was saying. 'We must send for the surgeon.'

'No,' Mama said, quite definitely. 'It is nothing more than a fit. But you must go to bed, Charles.'

He shook his head. 'I am all right.'

'Obey your mother,' Tante Marie said. 'You must go to bed. Come along now.'

'I am all right,' Charles insisted, feeling his cheeks burning with a mixture of anger and embarrassment, increased by the sudden start of tears to his eyes. This was his greatest bane, this tendency to weep when angered. Not that it softened his resolution in any way. They would rob him of his practice with Monsieur Lannes; it was the only part of the week he looked forward to.

'Well, you certainly cannot fence today,' Tante Marie declared, reading his mind. 'I will send Monsieur Lannes away.'

'You'll not!' Charles shouted. 'You'll not!' He wriggled free of Jules' arm, darted past them, and down the next flight of stairs to the basement.

'You come back here,' shouted Tante Marie, starting after him.

'Well,' declared Madame Louvanne.

'I'll speak with Monsieur d'Éon,' Mama declared. Then they were out of earshot, and he was tumbling along the corridor towards the gunroom, where the swords were kept. He panted, and his leather shoes slipped on the parquet flooring, while the maids emerged from the pantry to gape at him, but a moment later he was closing the heavy oaken door behind him, and leaning against it, smiling at Monsieur Lannes. 'Here I am.'

The fencing master belied his profession; he was a short, heavy set man, with large, friendly features. He dressed all in brown, and looked nothing so much as a genial country merchant. But to him a sword was but an extension of his fingers. Now he allowed his soft brown eyes to envelope the boy. 'And weeping?'

'It is nothing.' Charles took off his coat, but left his doublet in place; no matter how warm the exercise, Father had told him he must never remove his doublet. 'I had a pain, and they would stop me fencing.'

'A pain?' Lannes came closer. 'Where?'

Charles smiled at him. 'A tummy ache, monsieur. Nothing more serious than that.'

'A tummy ache can be very serious indeed, Charles.'

'Not mine. It was over in a moment. It was something I ate. Aimée's cooking. Please let us commence, monsieur.'

'If you are sure.' Lannes took down the two rapiers, opened the outer door, which led directly into the sunken rose garden. 'You must tell me if you feel the slightest fatigue.'

'Oh, bah.' Charles hurried in front of him, expecting to hear his father's voice calling out to him to come back inside. He took his place in the centre of the small lawn, settled his feet, crooked his left arm and presented the sword with his right, haft held lightly but yet firmly, as he had been taught, point moving gently from side to side. Lannes took his position opposite, raised his weapon. 'Salute.'

Charles obeyed, bringing the hilt up to his lips, while his heels came together. Lannes did the same, then their points touched. 'On guard.'

The older man came forward quickly, blade flickering with such speed it was almost invisible. But Charles had been well taught. A quick spring backwards and a downwards cut of his own sword deflected the lunge, and he was immediately returning the onslaught, only to be parried in turn. Their blades clashed, and slid along each other's lengths until the guards themselves smashed against each other; the jar went right up Charles' arm, but immediately he was disengaging himself and jumping away before Lannes could push him with superior strength.

Panting, he regained his ground and settled his feet, while Lannes smiled in approbation. But suddenly Charles was aware that something was the matter. The pain was back, not as severe as before, but grinding into his belly, and there was a sudden feeling of weakness, accompanied by a trickle of liquid down the inside of his right thigh. It could only be blood. His sword point drooped. Had he been hurt? It was not possible. He had felt nothing, and beside, Monsieur Lannes would never be so careless.

Lannes' face was a picture of distress. 'Charles?' he inquired, lowering his point in turn. 'You are hurt?'

'No, monsieur. No.' I cannot be hurt, he thought. I cannot. 'Have at you, monsieur. Have at you.'

'Stop that!' came the shout. Charles, already thrusting forward, hesitated, and Lannes stepped backwards out of range. Their heads turned to gaze at the doorway, at the face of Guillaume d'Éon peering at them. 'Stop it, I say.'

Charles wondered if he was going to be whipped. It was several months since Father had last whipped him, but he sounded very angry indeed. And what would he say, what would he do, when he discovered the blood on his leg?'

'You'll join me, Monsieur Lannes,' d'Éon said. 'And you, Charles, your mother wishes to speak with you. Go to your bedchamber immediately.'

Charles sucked his lower lip under his teeth for a moment. He was going to be punished, after all. But not with a whipping. With a day locked in his room, no doubt, and bread and water for dinner. But there was no help for it.

'You'll excuse me, monsieur,' he said.

Lannes winked at him. 'I'll make your peace with your father, Charles. You have my word. Come along now.'

He took the sword from his pupil's hand, tucked both the blades under his arm, ushered him towards the door.

'Off you go,' Father said. Strangely, he did not look very angry, merely anxious.

'Yes, Papa.' Charles hurried down the gunroom, frowned; Papa had had one of the footmen place a tray, with a decanter of wine and two glasses, on the table. Charles went through the inner door, and there hesitated, leaning against it from the outside.

'Hot work, on a hot day,' said Monsieur d'Éon. 'You'll take a glass?'

Charles listened to the sound of wine gurgling from the decanter.

'How does the boy fare?'

'Your son fights like a madman, monsieur,' Lannes said. There was a brief silence, and Charles could imagine him draining his glass. Once again there came the gurgle of the liquid. 'In all my years, the one advice I have given my pupils, apart from teaching them the correct passes, is to remain cool, at all times. Charles delivers each lunge with *passion*, as if it were to be his last. And yet I swear it affects his ability not the slightest. And today I would suppose him not at his best, as he tells me he is not feeling well. I will tell you this, monsieur. When you asked me to teach so young a child, I was appalled. You will remember what I said. But now, monsieur, why, give me another six months with him and he will be the finest swordsman in the kingdom.' He sighed. 'What he will do with such a skill, at so early an age . . .'

'I doubt the problem will concern you, Monsieur Lannes,' Papa said. 'You have just given Charles his last lesson.'

'Last lesson? But monsieur . . .'

'Have you not just said he is as good a swordsman as any in the kingdom?'

'Well, monsieur . . .' Lannes finished his third glass. 'He is very good. Oh, very very good. But equal to any in the kingdom . . . another six months . . .'

'It may be possible, at some future time,' d'Éon said. 'But Charles is thirteen, as you keep reminding me. It is time for him to pursue his studies in Paris. It is all arranged.'

'He mentioned naught of it to me, monsieur.'

'He does not yet know my decision,' d'Éon said. 'What *did* he say to you, this morning?'

Another brief hesitation. 'Good day to you, monsieur, as I remember. Shall we set to? Words like that. Your son is not given much to speaking.'

'Indeed he is not,' Papa said, and from his tone it occurred to Charles that he was relieved. 'Well, Monsieur Lannes, it has been a pleasure having you in my house. You will do me the honour of rendering your account as soon as possible.'

'May I not say goodbye to Charles, monsieur? I count him my finest pupil.'

'Not today, monsieur. It may be possible for you to see him again before he departs.'

Charles heard their feet on the floor as they approached the door. He ran for the stairs, and suddenly lost all the strength in his legs, while the pain was back, gnawing at his belly. He fell to his knees, and knew that blood was pouring out of his body and down his legs, soaking his breeches.

'Charles?' Papa stood above him.

'My God! He is ill, monsieur,' Lannes said. 'I was sure of it. Let me fetch the surgeon.'

'No,' Papa said. 'No, he is not ill. I will attend to him. My thanks, monsieur.' To Charles' surprise his father stooped, gently turned him, thrust one arm under his knees while the other went around his shoulders, and lifted him from the ground. He had not supposed Papa could be so strong, or so tender, when he had imagined him angry.

The pain was fading. He managed a smile. 'I am sorry, monsieur. My tummy-ache.'

Lannes took his hand between both of his. 'Your father informs me that our lessons are at an end, at least for the moment.'

Guillaume d'Éon gave him a squeeze. 'There are more important things in this world than sword-play, eh Charles?'

'Then I must say goodbye, monsieur,' Charles said. 'Am I proficient?'

Lannes gave the fingers a last squeeze. 'You would give even Shirér a fight, I promise you.'

'Shirér?'

'Monsieur Shirér is the first swordsman in France,' Papa said in a reverent tone.

'He is also very much of a bravo,' Lannes pointed out. 'Best avoided. You would destroy most men twice your age, Charles. Pray to Heaven that you only have cause to do so in your own defence. I must be away. Monsieur, your house has been a second home to me these last six months. I have been happy here. Charles, should you ever wish to practise when you are in Tonnerre, I am at your disposal, day or night. And get well again, soon, eh?'

He hurried for the door, somewhat embarrassed, Charles thought. Because *he* was being carried like a babe. 'I am all right now, Papa,' he said. 'I can walk.'

'You should not,' Papa said, for all the world as if he *knew* what was wrong. He climbed the stairs, while the maids and the footmen gazed at Charles in mingled embarrassment and surprise and dismay. Charles looked up to the top of the next flight, where Mama and Tante Marie waited, faces the picture of consternation. They knew too. Perhaps, although he could not see it, the blood had already soaked through his breeches and was dripping on the floor. But he felt all right again, only terribly tired.

Papa carried him up the next flight. Tante Marie had his bedchamber door opened, and Papa laid him on the bed. Tante Marie and Mama followed them into the room, and Mama closed the door.

'You will need water and towels,' Papa said. 'There will undoubtedly be blood.'

'I have them here,' Tante Marie said.

'Then commence. You'll take off your breeches, Charles.'

'Women's work, monsieur,' Mama protested. 'It would be best . . .'

'*My* work,' Papa said. ''Tis something which must be done, now, Louise.'

Mama hesitated. Then she nodded. Her shoulders seemed to slump, and she sat in the straight chair by the window.

'We must clean away the blood, Charles,' Papa said gently. 'And I am sure Tante Marie has a pad for you to wear, which will stop the inconvenience.'

Slowly Charles released his belt buckle. 'I . . . I do not know what has happened, Papa,' he said. 'I suddenly felt it . . . and the pain . . . am I very ill, Papa?'

The buckle was released. 'You lie there,' Tante Marie said, and raised his body to pass the towel underneath his thighs. He saw that her eyes were full of tears.

'No,' Papa said. 'You are not ill. In a very few days you will be as well as you have ever been.'

Tante Marie was easing the breeches down to his knees, and he looked at himself in horror. There was far more blood than he had supposed possible.

'Papa . . .' he wailed.

Papa stood beside his head, and held his hand. ''Tis naught to be afraid of, Charles.'

'But, Papa . . .'

''Tis an event, Charles. An event to which all women are subject. But were they not, then would the human race have perished centuries ago.'

Charles stared at his father, the words only slowly penetrating his brain, and even then, making no sense.

'Oh, Guillaume,' Mama said. It was the first time Charles had ever heard his mother address his father by name. 'Was there no other way?'

'No,' Papa said, very brusquely, as if he was trying to convince himself. 'As it has happened this way, there was no other way. Do you understand what I am telling you, Charles? You are not a boy. You are a girl. Do you understand me?'

I must be dreaming, Charles thought. How can I be a girl, when I am a boy? When I have a boy's name? When . . .

Papa seemed able to read his thoughts. 'What is your name, Charles? Say it for me, all of it.'

Charles opened his mouth, realised his throat was too dry to speak. He licked his lips, felt the gentle insistence of Tante Marie's fingers as they guided the towel over his thighs, drying the flesh.

'My name is Charles Geneviève Louise Augste André Timothée d'Éon de Beaumont,' he muttered.

'Geneviève, Louise,' Papa said. 'Have you never wondered about those names?'

'But . . .' Charles looked down at himself, at the naked thighs, the gentle down which was beginning to coat his groin. He reached for his father's hands. 'I am a boy, Papa. I have always been a boy. I *cannot* be a girl.'

Papa raised his head to look at his wife; Mama blushed with sudden alarm. 'You cannot, Guillaume. You cannot.'

'I must, Louise. Tante Marie, you'll leave the room.'

'Stuff and nonsense,' Tante Marie grumbled. 'I *was* your nurse monsieur. I know what you look like.'

Papa seemed to hesitate, then shrugged; as Marie was in the secret already, there was no point in sending her away. The secret, Charles thought. But I am not Charles. I am Geneviève. But that is impossible. I am Charles. I have always been Charles. I have always worn boys' clothing. The only playmates I have ever desired have been boys. Why, I like fencing. I am going to be a great swordsman. Monsieur Lannes has said so. Whoever heard of a great swordswoman? It is quite impossible.

'I want you to look at me,' Papa said, unbuckling his own belt.

Geneviève shut her eyes. I do not want to look at you. It will be something terrible. I refuse.

'Look at me, Charles.'

Geneviève opened her eyes. Tante Marie had shut hers, and

Mama, face still crimson, was staring out of the window. But Papa had lowered his breeches. Geneviève darted a quick glance at him, closed her eyes, and opened them again. Oh, God, she thought. Oh, God. She was not sure what she saw, what she dared see. She only knew she had never seen anything like it before, and she hated it. She closed her eyes once more.

'I am a man, Charles,' Papa was saying. She listened to the sound of his belt being fastened, and knew it was safe to open her eyes again.

'There was another way,' Mama muttered. 'Surely to God there was another way. A better way.'

'No,' Papa said. 'Do you understand now, Charles?'

I am not Charles, Geneviève thought. I am Geneviève. Oh, God, I am Geneviève. I will never hold a sword again. I am Geneviève.

'Do you understand?' Papa insisted.

'No,' she whispered.

'You understand that you are not the same as I?'

'Yes, Papa, but . . .' She bit her lip.

He nodded. 'Louise.'

'I shall not,' Mama said. 'I shall not. This is wrong. It was wrong from the very beginning. You are making it worse. You are compounding evil upon evil, Guillaume, and naught but evil can come of it.'

Papa sighed. 'Marie.'

'Me, monsieur? That is impossible.'

'You will do as you are told, Marie, or I will dismiss you my service.'

'You'll not do that, monsieur. Not now.'

Papa gazed at her for several seconds, but he knew he was beaten. 'I will summon one of the maids,' he said.

'No.' Mama got up. 'That would be to make things worse.' She stood by the bed. 'Your father is not lying to you, Charles,' she said. 'By his own reasoning he is doing the best possible. You are a woman. Your body is the same as Tante Marie's or mine. You will believe that. It is not necessary for you to compare. Do you believe that?'

Geneviève licked her lips. But she did not doubt her mother. She had never doubted her mother. 'I believe that, Mama,' she said. 'If you say it is so. But I do not understand.' She could feel the tears welling into her eyes. 'I do not see why.'

Mama looked at Papa. Who rubbed his chin, and sighed

again. 'It will be difficult,' he said, half to himself. He sat on the bed, raised the coverlet to conceal her from the waist down. 'You must understand, first of all, my position. Our position. Your future, Charles.' He attempted a smile. 'Geneviève.'

Geneviève, she thought. But I do not wish to be Geneviève. I am Charles. Oh, God, I am Charles.

Guillaume d'Éon sighed again, rubbed his chin again. 'Have you never wondered how we keep such style? This house, the servants, the horses you ride? Have you never wondered who pays for Madame Louvanne? For Monsieur Lannes?'

Geneviève gazed at him. He looked so stricken she almost felt sorry for him. 'Is it not you, Papa?'

'Oh, indeed, it is I who disburse the money. But where do I obtain so *much* money? From my practice? A country lawyer, here in Tonnerre. Do you never wonder at the lack of custom to my door?'

'I... Tante Marie told me once you had obtained an inheritance.'

'And she told you the truth. Our benefactor is your Great Uncle Henri. He is fond of you?'

'Indeed, sir. Whenever he visits he rubs my head.'

'And gives you a gold piece,' Mama said.

'He does, Mama.'

'He loves you dearly, Geneviève. As the heir to the family fortunes,' Papa said. 'Shall I tell you of that fortune? Your Great Uncle Henri, my uncle, was my father's only brother. He prospered in business, while my father did not. Indeed, the two brothers quarrelled, and my father took himself off to the wars, and eventually perished, fighting the English, as you know. But Uncle Henri prospered only financially. Both of his wives died in childbirth, and with them his hopes for an heir. Thus, despite himself, he must in the end turn to me. But because I had sided with my father in the quarrel, he would not have me. My son, he told me, should inherit his all, and indeed should be granted an income from birth, of which I would have the use, provided I agreed to his decisions in all things concerning the boy's upbringing. My son, he insisted, not my daughter. His heir had to inherit the name he had gained for his use, d'Éon de Beaumont. After much consideration, in which your mother shared, I agreed, as she was then pregnant. And indeed, she gave birth to a son, as required. But your brother Pierre died before your own birth.'

'I know that, Papa,' Geneviève said. 'Then...'

'Exactly, my dear girl. Pierre was dead, and you were born, a girl. My fortune, our fortune, *your* fortune, was destroyed at a stroke, for the physician assured me that for your mother to bear a third child would be to risk her life and the babe's. What would you have me do?'

Geneviève bit her lip again. 'I am sure you acted for the best, Papa.' But I hate you for it, she thought. I hate you for making me what I am, neither one thing nor the other.

'I supposed so,' Guillaume d'Éon said. 'God knows, I supposed so. Your birth was premature. No one was present save your mother and Tante Marie and myself. Thus we gave out that we had again been blessed with a son. You are so entered in the parish register. And your great uncle was overjoyed at this stroke of good fortune where he had expected only dismal failure.'

Geneviève's head fell back on to the pillows.

'We thought it could be done, Geneviève,' Mama said. 'It was that or poverty.'

'And it was simple enough in the beginning.' Papa took her hand into his. 'And even more recently. Uncle Henri was quite happy that you should remain at home with a governess rather than attend the village school. The family d'Éon bears a long and famous name, however much we may have slipped down the scale in recent years. But he was determined that at the age of fourteen you must attend the Mazarin College in Paris. There was a problem. We put our trust in Uncle Henri's great age. Perhaps he would die before you reached puberty, before you reached fourteen. Then you would have inherited his fortune, and we could have told you the truth.'

'But he did not die,' Mama said, bitterly.

Papa nodded. 'Yet was I prepared to face even that possibility. Hence Monsieur Lannes.'

'But that is what I understand least of all, Papa.' Geneviève squeezed the fingers holding hers. 'You say what has happened today is the fate of every woman. Therefore it had to happen to me soon enough. Thus why teach me to act the man so completely?'

'Because you must continue to act the man,' Guillaume d'Éon explained.

Geneviève frowned at him. 'Papa?'

'You cannot,' Mama said. 'It would be criminal. We gambled. We gambled on an old man's life, and cruelly deceived him as well as our own daughter. We did a terrible thing, and it has failed. We deserve to be punished. We cannot risk this subterfuge a day longer.'

'In the name of God,' Guillaume d'Éon shouted. 'Would you have me begging on the streets? In prison for debt? Sent to the galleys? Is that what you wish?'

'It would be preferable to destroying my daughter.'

'What stuff and nonsense.' He released Geneviève's hand, got up, paced the room. 'Uncle Henri is seventy-four years old. He cannot possibly live more than another few months. All Geneviève has to do is play the man for a short while longer, and all will be well.' He stopped by the bed. 'Believe me, my dear child, I understand the difficulty. The burden is entirely upon you now that you know the truth. But you can do it, Geneviève. You have but to continue as you have done for the past thirteen years.'

'God give me patience,' Mama cried. 'She has but to continue? You are sending her to Paris, to school. A school entirely inhabited by priests and boys.'

'I have considered that,' Papa said. 'I have written letters to the Prior, and to Uncle Henri, explaining that Charles is a delicate boy much given to private study, and insisting that he be allowed a private cell. The Prior has agreed.'

'And you think that will suffice?' Mama demanded. 'What of the privy?'

'Charles will have to exercise some self control. Should he confine himself to the pot in his room all will be well.'

'And her period?'

'He is a delicate boy, as I have said. This is well understood. So once a month he will take to his bed for a day or so.'

'And the pads?'

'For Heaven's sake, Louise, there are risks to everything. Charles will have to get rid of the pads. She is an intelligent girl.'

Mama sighed. 'What of boyish pranks? Do not pretend to me you have forgotten them.'

'Ah,' Papa said. 'That too I have considered most seriously. Thus Monsieur Lannes. Charles will be independent and hot tempered, at least to his fellows. He will be quick to take offence, and he will return a blow with a blow. Soon enough, indeed, he will return a blow with a drawn sword.'

'My God.' Mama collapsed back into her chair. 'You would make my daughter into an assassin.'

14

'He will need to give those who would annoy him but one sharp lesson, believe me.'

'You are mad,' Mama said. 'Mad. And suppose Uncle Henri does not die, this year or next? Geneviève is of this day a woman. She will soon enough take on a woman's characteristics. Has she not already grown breasts? Have you not, girl?'

'I . . .' Geneviève stared at her mother in horror. Certainly her chest had grown more fleshy over the past year. But she had supposed she might be getting fat.

'Oh, nonsense,' Papa said. 'A shirt, followed by a doublet, followed by a coat, would flatten the chest of a Vallière. You are creating difficulties, madame, where none should exist. It is a subterfuge we practise, but to a good end. Our own prosperity, and more, the continuance of the d'Eon into history. Were Uncle Henri not such a crabbed fool, were he willing to recognise that a female heir is as valid as a male, then none of this need have happened. The fault lies with him. My conscience is clear.'

There was a moment's silence. Then Tante Marie spoke for the first time. 'She will need a servant. *He* will need a servant. He cannot hope to attend school, and carry off such a plan, without a trustworthy servant.'

'By God you are right.' Guillaume d'Éon slapped his hands together. 'A manservant. Jules. Jules has been in my service for twenty years. There can be no one more trustworthy than that.'

'Jules is a butler, not a valet,' Tante Marie objected.

'He will *learn* to be a valet, when the situation is put to him.'

'You will admit Jules to the secret?' Mama demanded. 'Why not shout it from the window?'

'Jules is trustworthy,' Papa insisted. 'He will share in our fortune, should we prosper. And equally will he share in our catastrophe, should we fail. You may leave Jules to me.'

'Leave Jules to you,' Louise d'Éon said contemptuously. Oh, we may leave everything to you, monsieur, as you have arranged everything since this poor child's birth. But you have forgotten one vital thing, one point, monsieur, without which your entire foul scheme falls to the ground.'

'God give me patience,' Guillaume d'Éon begged at large. 'One would suppose you loathe the silks you wear, madame, the house you enjoy, the food you eat and the wine you drink. But come along, tell me of this vital matter.'

Louise d'Éon pointed at the bed. 'You have forgotten the

acquiescence of Charles, monsieur, without which your schemes are as nothing.'

'Charles?' Papa turned to the bed. 'Geneviève? Oh, indeed, your mother is right. But would you give up all of this for a hovel? I ask a continuing subterfuge of you, for perhaps two years. Not a moment longer than that, I promise you.'

Geneviève gazed at him for some seconds, then looked at her mother. *She* would not speak, but she begged with her eyes. She *would* rather have us starve in a hovel than permit this crime to continue, Geneviève thought. She is a good woman. And thus Papa is a bad man. So what am I? I am Charles d'Éon de Beaumont, heir to a fortune. No, no. I am Geneviève d'Éon, a sorely confused maiden who must continue upon such a damnable path. But only for two years. And what is the alternative? I do not wish to be a woman. Never, never, never. I am Charles d'Éon de Beaumont. So I have no monstrosity hanging between my legs, and I am subject to monthly attacks of blood. There can be no other difference, and are either important? Compared with wealth, and the power that comes with wealth? I am Charles d'Éon de Beaumont.

She smiled at her father. 'I am Charles d'Éon de Beaumont,' she said. 'After all, Papa, it is but for two years.'

Two years. Could anyone suppose that such a miserable old man, for so she now considered her great uncle, could possibly live that long? Could possibly live for *four* years? There was an absurdity. Four years. The doddering old fool was all but eighty.

And Charles d'Éon de Beaumont was past seventeen, and existed on the brink of catastrophe. Geneviève tested the water with her finger, wrapping her undressing robe closer about her. 'That will do, thank you, Jules. You may leave me.'

'Of course, monsieur.' Jules gave a brief bow. Four years ago she had permitted him to scrub her back. But then she had been a shapeless adolescent. Now she was too much of a woman, and he must seek the odd surreptitious look, the apparently careless caress. He would do more, if he could. If he dared. But on two counts, avarice and fear, he dared not.

She shot the bolt, turning the little cell into a private world. Only a fortnight ago she had forgotten, and after a moment, allowing her sufficient time to sit in the bath Jules had re-entered, covered in blushes at her confusion. The wretch. But he was a man, and all men were wretches. Once she had supposed only her father thus qualified. Now she knew he but typified the entire sex.

She released the robe, threw it on to the narrow cot which, with the table and stool, was the only furniture in the room; cold and damp in the winter, the cell at least had the virtue of coolness in summer. Slowly she sank into the tub, dipping first of all her bottom, holding herself there to allow her flesh to become accustomed to the heat, and then lowering herself entirely. Her legs came up, and her thighs were brushed by her nipples; it was a small tub. But was ever a girl cursed with such breasts, which swelled against her thighs as they swelled against her doublet, or with such thighs, white and slender, slipping down into perfect calves; on festive occasions it was the rule of the Mazarin College that their students cast aside their robes and don stockings and breeches, and when they did, not an inmate, friar or student, could take his gaze from Monsieur d'Éon's calves.

What did they think of her? Of him? It was not a point to be forgotten. Her first weeks here had been a constant trial. She had so looked forward to the great adventure of leaving Tonnerre at all, of getting to Paris. But the enjoyment had been spoiled by the decision of Papa to accompany her, as he accompanied her to and from Tonnerre at the beginning and end of every vacation. He was afraid she might not be able to sustain her role, without him at her side, at least at the staging posts.

But would she not have been disappointed in Paris, in any event? It was dirty and it smelt, and the buildings were dilapidated and huddled too close together. It was nothing like the city of her imagination, the city of Madame Louvanne's stories. Yet she had spent the better part of four years here now, almost regarded it as home. And she had prospered, as she had obeyed Papa to the letter, and he had been proved right – so perhaps he would be proved right in other things as well, even if had so far been proved wrong about Great Uncle Henri's imminent demise. But when her fellow pupils would have teased her, she had whipped out her poniard and threatened to cut the nearest throat. That had sent them tumbling away, and if the incident had earned her a whipping from the Prior, he had done nothing more than command her to lie across his desk, and the confiscation of her dagger had proved irrelevant thereafter; the sons of merchants and advocates and petty nobles who attended

17

the Mazarin College had decided that a boy who would use a knife so freely was not to be tangled with. Which but further confirmed her contempt for their sex, even if it also confirmed the friendless loneliness of her existence.

Even the Prior, no doubt primed by Papa with a suitable tale, had recognised that his pupil was an exceptional lad, who preferred to spend his time by himself, reading and studying. Well, that at least was no lie. Where her fellows did little more than drink wine and exchange baudy stories and baudier tales of their derring-do with village maidens, and write maudlin pieces of doggerel which they were pleased to name poetry, she had found an entire treasure trove of knowledge and opinion in the College Library, thoughts and ideas she had never supposed existed, save in the recesses of her own brain, as she delved into the poetry of Malherbe, the philosophy of Pascal's *Thoughts on Religion,* the plays of Corneille and Racine and Molière. But even these were less instructive than the fables of La Fontaine and Perrault, the historical essays of Mabillon and Bossuet and Bayle.

She had absorbed so much knowledge over the past few years and had become bold enough to write a pamphlet on the evils of the *poulette,* the tax paid by the hereditary officers of the kingdom, and which indeed enabled them to *make* their offices hereditary. Whether published or not, it had taken some of the pressure from her mind.

So then, she had achieved an equilibrium, if not happiness, in the real world which surrounded her. Her fellow pupils treated her with a contemptuous respect, even if they never invited her to take part in their riots, which invariably finished up at some disreputable tavern – not that she would have gone even if invited. And her tutors were content to humour her silent and secretive ways, because of her undoubted literary talent, her deep interest in whatever theories they propounded, her quiet behaviour in class. She had no worry in the world, save for Jules.

Jules. Thoughtfully she soaped, under her arms and across her breasts, and gave a little shiver of pleasurable disgust. She was afraid of her body, for the very reason that she was afraid of Jules – even if he should never know of it. It was a fear of admitting that she found pleasure in herself, that every time she bathed, every time she soaped between her legs, she wished to do more, wished to learn more about herself, about the Geneviève she was afraid to admit existed. But to do that would be to succumb to womanhood, to a hedonistic delight in her body, in herself, to turn inwards to such an extent that she doubted she would ever be able to look outwards again. But every time she rejected herself, every time she turned away from suspected pleasure, was she not even so withdrawing from her life as a man? Thus Jules. They shared a secret. And he would be happy to share more than that. He knew her as intimately as she knew herself, secreted her bloodstained bandages, assisted her to dress and undress. All her fears that he might betray her, either when drunk or from natural garrulity, had long disappeared. He was a faithful servant to the d'Éons, and besides, he waited for his share of Great Uncle Henri's wealth.

But he was a grown man in daily contact with a lovely young woman. And it was something she *wanted*. Just to experience it. She had never sought any intimacy with Jules. He was so *old*, at least forty. And she did not know what he looked like, what he would *be* like. She did not know what he would do to her. But she knew that she could not truly equal the men around her until she had learned the secret of their superiority, the hold they possessed over women; as she was no different to any of her fellows in any daily matter, and superior to most of them in ability, whether with the sword or with the pen, it had to be nothing more than the power of their penises. What power, she could not imagine, but it was a secret which had to be discovered, and as soon as possible. How else could she combat it, conquer it, retain her superiority? She envisaged life as a long conflict between Geneviève d'Éon and the masculine sex, a contest she was resolved to win.

But her first victim had to be chosen with care. Her schoolmates were absurdly juvenile. The friars were of course out of the question; it was a mortal sin for them even to consider consorting with women, and therefore it was, no doubt, a mortal sin for her to consider it either. No doubt it was a mortal sin for her to be living within the confines of their convent at all. But that sin was Papa's, not hers, and he would undoubtedly burn in hell in any event. It would be possible to obtain some man off the streets of Paris itself, but the thought disgusted her. What little she had seen of them suggested only dirt, and brutality; the women they had apparently mastered were little better. Besides, to approach *any* man in the guise of a woman meant revealing herself; she did not really know what she would have to do after that – to be in the power of a man was an abhorrent thought.

So that left Jules. As he knew her secret in any event she had nothing to lose there. But Jules. He was old enough to be her father. Was that necessarily a bad thing? He would at least have the experience to approach her kindly, because for this first occasion she must surrender entirely; no other way could she hope to appreciate the full force with which she had to contend. And he was certainly clean; she insisted upon that.

Fingers rattled across her door. The wretch had come back to chase her from her tub. She pushed herself up, wrapped herself in her robe, pulled the bolt, and gazed at one of her fellow pupils, a lad named Bertrand de Caillas. Who returned her stare with equal amazement as he took in her hardly concealed legs, and her even less concealed bosom, over which she hastily gathered the robe.

'How now, Master Caillas?' she demanded. 'What means this intrusion?'

'You'll pardon me, Master d'Éon,' he stammered, well aware of his senior's reputation for quick and aggressive temper. 'I come from the Prior. He requests your attendance in his office, and immediately.' His gaze rolled around the room, came back to rest on her.

'Then you may tell the good Prior that I shall attend him as soon as I am dressed,' Geneviève said. 'Now leave.'

'Of course, Master d'Éon. Of course.' Caillas backed to the door, hesitated. 'Would you not like me to assist you?'

'Out,' Geneviève commanded, and closed and bolted the door behind him. She threw her robe on the bed, towelled herself vigorously. What could the old man want at this hour? Surely she was entitled to some time of her own? She discovered she was distinctly out of humour, and the fault was Jules'. Why, had it been he at the door ... but it was not something to be considered. No doubt she had been saved from herself, and should count herself fortunate. Jules would be a mistake.

She dressed herself in her black student's gown – by far the safest of all garments as it entirely concealed her from her neck to her ankles, although to be safe she wore doublet as well as shirt, breeches, stockings and shoes beneath – crammed her black velvet hat on her head and made her way along the corridors, past Master Caillas, who was standing with a group of his fellows whispering and gossiping, glancing at her and grinning as she passed. Little wretch. She must remember to pick a quarrel with him and frighten him out of his wits in the near future.

She climbed the bare stone steps, knocked on the wooden door.

'It is open, Master d'Éon.'

His voice was stern. Geneviève found her heart pounding as she turned the handle and pushed the door in. He had found out about her pamphlets. She knew it. And he would whip her. She was in no mood to suffer a whipping, even from the Prior.

Prior de Mass was a younger son of the lesser nobility. He was tall and thin and was fond, when in a reminiscent mood, of recalling how, as a boy, he had once been presented to the Great Louis. Today however he did not appear to be in a reminiscent mood. And he was indeed holding a broadsheet, and waving it gently to and fro.

Geneviève closed the door behind her, waited.

'You are an accomplished journalist, Monsieur d'Éon,' the Prior said.

'Is it published, Monseigneur?' she cried, delighted despite her apprehension.

'You do not deny it is yours?'

'It is but an opinion, Monseigneur.'

'Indeed. A very forceful opinion, forcefully expressed. It has attracted a great deal of attention.'

'Monseigneur is too kind.'

'You are aware that anything offered from this college for publication should be submitted to me beforehand, Master d'Éon.'

Geneviève licked her lips; she could feel her shoulders breaking out in a rash of sweat. Undoubtedly he was going to whip her. 'Yes, Monseigneur.'

'Ha. You are fortunate in having an advocate. Or I would have no hesitation in punishing you.'

'An advocate, Monseigneur?' Geneviève turned her head, for the first time noticing the other man in the room. He stood in the far corner, in the shadows, and was hard to make out accurately. But he was certainly a gentleman; his clothes were of satin, and he wore a sword. And something of a fop, she estimated, as even at a distance she could smell his pommade.

'Allow me to present the Prince of Conti, Master d'Éon.'

'My lord.' Geneviève bowed, while her brain tumbled. The

21

Prince of Conti. One of the very greatest men in all the land. At the Mazarin College? And interested in her?

'Stand straight, Master d'Éon.' The Prince had a curiously soft voice, and now he came farther into the room, and Geneviève could only gape at the white bag wig, the rings on the pale fingers, the gold buttonholes and the gold buckles on his shoes. The man himself was a disappointment, for he was short and thin, and if by no means old, had curiously sharp features. Clothes apart, he made her think of a clerk. But he was the Prince of Conti, a member of one of the three greatest families in the land, an intimate of the King himself. And he was inspecting her with equal interest. 'A pretty fellow,' he said at last. 'Have you nothing better to do, Master d'Éon, than write scurrilous pamphlets?'

Geneviève felt her cheeks burn, but it was with anger at least as much as embarrassment. 'Scurrilous, my lord? My opinions are the result of much thought and equal learning.'

'Be quiet, boy,' the Prior snapped.

'No, no,' the Prince said. 'He is clearly a young man of pronounced opinions. Indeed, his literary style guarantees it. You have done well, Monseigneur, to bring him to my attention. Oh, indeed, well.'

Geneviève glanced at the Prior in surprise. She had supposed it had been the Prince who had brought the pamphlet to de Maas' attention.

'Ah, well, my lord,' the Prior said, with a sly smile, 'it is my duty, is it not, both to forward the aspirations of my pupils, and to see that France does not miss the opportunity to utilise those brains which are sharper than the average. I am sure Master d'Éon will go far, should he be pointed in the right direction.'

Geneviève licked her lips. She was aware of being at the centre of a conspiracy. But to what end?

Conti was also smiling. 'We shall have to see. But I would converse further with Master d'Éon. You'll permit him to sup with me this night, Monseigneur.' It was not a question, and the Prior dutifully bowed his head. 'He shall be returned, I do assure you, at an appropriate hour.'

'You will accompany His Highness, boy,' the Prior said. 'And obey him in all matters. You understand me? All matters?'

Geneviève found her voice. 'Of course, Monseigneur. But I am not dressed for the street.'

'You will come as you are,' the Prince said. 'If Monseigneur will permit it.'

'Of course, my lord.'

'Then you will excuse us, Monseigneur.' Conti came towards her, and she hastily opened the door. He allowed her a nod, and stepped through. She gave the Prior a hasty smile and followed, walked behind him down the stairs. The group of boys were still gathered by the outer door, and they stood to attention and bowed as the Prince passed them by, their eyes bulging as they saw Geneviève at his heels. A carriage stood at the outer gate, with a postilion waiting by the steps, the crested door already open. The Prince got in, and when Geneviève hesitated, he patted the seat. 'Come on, Master d'Éon.'

Geneviève climbed up, sat beside him. The postilion closed the door, and a moment later the carriage was rumbling over the cobbles. Geneviève had a curious feeling of release. No doubt it was mainly relief at having avoided a whipping, and beside, she felt as if she were being released from prison whenever she managed to leave the college. Too late she remembered that she had not told Jules; he would be in a state of high alarm. But no doubt he would find out where she was soon enough.

And meanwhile she was riding in a carriage, with a prince of the blood, who had invited her to supper. Why, she would be meeting his wife, and family, and . . . she stole a glance at him, found him smiling at her.

'You are a remarkably pretty boy,' he said. 'I have the honour to know your uncle, Henri d'Éon de Beaumont.'

'My great uncle, my lord.'

He wagged his finger at her. 'You must overcome this weakness for contradiction, Master d'Éon, if you are to prosper. I would rob no man of his opinions, but the wise man keeps his opinions to himself unless he is sure he will profit by expressing them. You wish to prosper?'

'Indeed, my lord.'

'I had supposed as much.' He dropped his hand over hers, gave her a gentle squeeze. 'Tell me when you were born.'

'On the second of October 1728, my lord, at Tonnerre in Burgundy.'

'Ah. So you are approaching your eighteenth birthday. Your great uncle tells me you are to be his heir.'

'That is my fortune, my lord.'

'And it is not to be sneezed at, eh? But still, it is but a *little* fortune. Would you not prosper to a still greater extent?'

'Is that possible, my lord?'

'All things are possible, Master d'Éon, to a young man of talent, and address, and ambition. You undoubtedly have talent. You certainly have address. We seek merely to establish that you also have ambition.' Again the quick squeeze of her hand.

'Indeed I have, my lord.'

'I was sure of it. Then there can be no limit to the conquests you will achieve, certainly with me to guide you. Would you have me guide you, Monsieur d'Éon?'

'My lord, I am overwhelmed. That you should wish to take the part of someone like myself . . .'

'It is my amusement, to discern talent, Charles. You do not mind if I call you Charles?'

'I am flattered, my lord.'

'You are a good lad. I am sure we shall get on famously. This is my house.'

Geneviève realised that she had forgotten to look out of the windows to discover where they were going. Now she could only gape as the carriage rolled through a pair of opened gates set in high stone pillars, the pillars themselves surmounted by representations of flying eagles; a short drive, bordered with sycamores, led to the house, a somewhat gloomy looking mansion, fronted with Doric columns. Here a dozen blue and gold liveried grooms were waiting to grasp the bridles, open the door, and roll down the step. The Prince descended, and Geneviève hurried behind, putting up her hand to straighten her hat. Now for the first time she was glad that she had not been given time to change; her own outdoor clothes would compare very badly with the wealth around her, and beneath her scholar's robe no one could tell she was not a prince herself.

The Prince was entering the front doorway, past a line of bowing flunkies, and mounting the great inner staircase. Geneviève had amost run to catch up with him, for he walked very quickly, and was given no time to admire the high ceiling, which served as a ceiling for the first floor as well, and which was painted in a magnificent design featuring mainly bare breasted girls playing at ball, or the portraits on the walls, all of sharp-featured gentlemen whom she presumed were other members of the Conti family; she could only stare at the seemingly endless row of Cupids, to either side, every one holding aloft a flaming torch.

She reached the gallery, followed the Prince a short distance to her right over the parquet flooring, every doorway guarded by a liveried footman, who bowed as their master approached, and remained bending until she too had passed them by. At the third doorway the door was opened, and she followed the Prince into a small withdrawing room, a place of elegant settees upholstered in satin, in the inevitable livery of blue and gold, of delightful clocks – there were three in the room – one a grandfather, the other two made of gold and onyx and set on little tables – and more paintings on the walls, but these were street scenes of Venice rather than portraits. The drapes at the windows were also of blue and gold, but the windows themselves stood open and allowed her a glimpse of the lawn below, bordered with flower-beds, a profusion of carnations.

Once inside the door she halted, because the Prince had also stopped, and had turned to face her. A footman stepped past her, carrying a tray on which there was a decanter of wine and two glasses. These he filled, took the tray first of all to his master, and then offered the remaining glass to Geneviève. She gazed at the Prince, who smiled at her and raised his own.

'Welcome.'

'My pleasure, my lord.' Behind her she heard the door softly close. Conti had sipped his wine, and she did also, wondering when his family would appear, and what they would think of her.

'The Monseigneur tells me you have spent four years at the College.' The Prince sat on a settee, one leg thrown carelessly over the other.

'Yes, my lord.'

He patted the seat beside him, and she obediently sat down, very straight, holding her goblet in front of her.

'And he has delayed until now to bring you to my attention. That was remiss of him.'

'I have only recently taken up writing pamphlets, my lord.'

'Ha. Ha ha. Do you like Paris?'

'No, my lord.'

'Spoken like a man. It is a dreadful place. Would you not like to return to the country?'

'Is not Paris the place for advancement, my lord?'

'Not for such as you, Master d'Éon. Charles. Your future lies

25

at the court. Versailles. That is where you must take up residence.'

'My lord, how could *I* take up residence at Versailles?'

'Would you not go there, as my protégé?'

'My lord . . . I do not know what to say.' And for the first time she was not merely being polite.

'Versailles is the heart of France. The very core of the nation. The fount of all our accomplishments. The place for someone like you. In the course of time. When do you expect your degree?'

'Perhaps in a year, my lord.'

'Admirable. I see before me a young man of remarkable gifts. You will be guided by me?'

'My lord, I could think of nothing finer.'

The prince stared at her for some seconds, and then smiled. 'Then finish your wine, and pour us each another.'

Geneviève obediently drained her goblet, as he was doing the same. The wine ration at the college was meagre, and her head did a little spin. But she found her feet steady enough as she got up and walked to the table where the decanter had been left.

'You move delightfully,' the Prince said. 'You smell delightful. And you look delightful. Everything about you is delightful. Take off that dowdy robe.'

Geneviève, already turned back to him, the decanter in her hand, hesitated in surprise.

The Prince waved his arm. 'Humour me, Charles. You *are* going to humour me, in everything, are you not?'

'Of course, my lord.' She set down the decanter, lifted the robe over her head, laid it on a chair.

'Better than I had hoped,' the Prince said. 'Slender, and yet strong, I will swear. Pour, Charles.'

Geneviève obeyed, refilled her own goblet, replaced the decanter, and had her wrist seized. The Prince was on his feet and standing immediately behind her. 'My lord?'

'Have you no feelings, my sweet Charles? Do you not *feel?*'

'My lord?' She cast a hasty glance down, for fear that her doublet had inadvertently opened. But the Prince did not seem to be interested in her breasts. His hand slid up her arm, while his other arm went round her shoulder to bring her against him.

'Oh, Charles, Charles,' he muttered. 'You are the *prettiest* boy. I could love you, I swear. I swear I shall.'

Geneviève, still engaged in raising her head, was caught by his

26

lips, which fastened on her mouth, while his tongue drove against hers before she could close her teeth. She tasted wine. Her brain tumbled. He could not know she was a girl. He could not. But what was happening was beyond her comprehension. She had never been kissed like this before, and indeed she was losing her balance, while his left hand was sliding down from her shoulders to find her bottom and give it a gentle squeeze.

But his mouth was moving, to allow him to breathe, and she could catch her own breath. 'My lord,' she gasped, and got her hands between them. For a moment they wrestled, but she was at least as strong as he, and her last thrust had him stumbling back in turn, sitting down on the settee with a thump. 'My lord?' she cried in consternation.

For just a moment his eyes glittered, and she knew she was trembling on the brink of catastrophe.

'Do you not like me, Charles?' His voice was softer than ever.

This man was her future. Far more so than Uncle Henri. She dropped to her knees. 'Like you, my lord? I adore you. I beg your forgiveness. But . . . I know nothing . . . I . . .'.

His eyes softened. 'You are a virgin?'

'Of course, my lord.'

Now he frowned. 'Even with your fellows?'

'My lord?'

Her bewilderment was so obviously genuine his face relaxed. 'My God,' he said. 'Then you are indeed a treasure, my Charles. I meant what I said, just now. I will love you. And I will guide you to the highest post in the land, will you but return that love.'

'Willingly, my lord. Oh, willingly. I will love you. I do love you, my lord.'

He leaned back. 'Then humour me, Charles. Off with your breeches, that I may feast my eyes on that supreme object. I do not doubt its beauty. Haste boy, haste. My body is on fire for you.'

'My . . .' Slowly Geneviève pushed herself to her feet.

'Haste, boy. Would you have me explode?'

And indeed his face had turned crimson, while he seemed to be having trouble with his own breeches, which he now sought to unfasten. So, for some reason which she could not understand, he wished to fondle a boy. He could not help but be the more pleased when he discovered the truth of the matter, she reflected. And was it not the very thing she had been considering this afternoon? There could hardly be a better person to start

27

with than the Prince of Conti. Geneviève released her belt buckle, slid the breeches down about her knees.

The prince gave a gasp. He had been rising, the better to free his own breeches. Now he sat down again, the garment still clinging to his thighs, leaving Geneviève unable to obtain even a glimpse of what she feared and challenged.

'My lord?' Hastily she unfastened her doublet.

The Prince seemed beyond speech. His hand came up to the point, and then fell back again. His mouth opened and closed.

Geneviève released the last button, threw the doublet from her shoulders. She began on the buttons of her shirt.

'My God,' said the Prince.

'My lord?' She kicked off her breeches, ran forward, sat beside him. 'May I assist you?'

Her hands were reaching for his waist. To her consternation he seized them and threw them away.

'Do not touch me,' he snapped. 'You . . . you are a woman.'

Geneviève finished unbuttoning her shirt. But she hesitated before taking it off. He was angry, after all, at the deception. 'I . . . I can explain, my lord.'

'A woman.' Conti was fastening his belt again, and standing as he did so. 'Masquerading as a man. That is witchcraft. By God, mademoiselle, I shall have you burned. Oh, aye, after sundry other punishments have been inflicted, you may be sure of that.'

'My lord.' Geneviève slipped off the settee and knelt, hands coming together in supplication. She could not imagine what had happened. She only knew he was powerful enough to carry out his threat. She felt almost sick with fear.

'Witchcraft,' shouted Conti. He ran to the door, pulled it open. 'To me,' he shouted. 'Your master is assailed.'

'My lord,' Geneviève cried, crawling behind him. 'Forgive the deception, my lord. It was necessary. My lord, am I not beautiful? My lord, I am as much a virgin as a woman as a man. My lord, I will love you, in every way. My lord . . .'

She reached for his hand, but he pulled away. Yet his interest was aroused. He turned, to face her, some of the terror leaving his expression. The footmen, running to assist him, stopped at the sight of his back.

'Beautiful,' he said. 'By God, you *are* beautiful.' He snapped his fingers. 'Leave us, dolts.'

The footmen obediently melted away. Geneviève wondered what they were thinking, what, indeed, they would shortly be saying to each other.

'And a virgin?' the Prince inquired.

'Oh, indeed, my lord.'

'And not a witch?'

'If you would permit me to explain . . .'

Another snap of the fingers. 'You shall explain. Remembering that your life depends upon it. But first, dress yourself.'

Geneviève frowned at him. 'You are not pleased with me, my lord?'

'I am very pleased with you. But I wish you to dress yourself, Charles. Is that your name, Charles?'

'I will tell you all, my lord.' Geneviève dragged on her clothes, fastened her buttons, told him her story.

The Prince listened, frowning in the beginning, but slowly she saw his face clear, and before the end he had refilled both of their glasses and had thrown himself back on the settee. 'By God,' he said. 'There is a tale. No one would believe it, had they not the evidence before their eyes. Drink, mademoiselle. Geneviève. A sweet name, Geneviève.'

Cautiously Geneviève sipped her wine; she had no doubt she was going to need a very clear head. 'Do you forgive me, my lord?'

A quick glance. 'Forgive you? No, no, my dear. I doubt I shall ever forgive you. Not for the deception itself. That is entirely reasonable in the circumstances you have described. But for not being a boy. My God, had you been a boy, with that face, that body . . .'

'My lord, this face, and this body, are panting for your attention.'

'Ha.' He drained his glass, got up. 'We are yoked together, as of this moment, Mademoiselle d'Éon.'

'My lord?'

'Your innocence is remarkable. But in this instance it scarce does you credit. You were represented to me at the least as being intelligent. Is that also a subterfuge?'

'I hope not, my lord.'

'Then you'll understand that not all the world is created from the same mould. God in His wisdom gave certain men, and certain women too, you may be sure of that, different tastes to the multitude. Why, what a dull world it would be if every one of

3

us preferred the colour red to any other, if we each chose claret wine as our favourite beverage, if none of us liked a good leg of mutton.'

'Indeed, sir,' she agreed, not understanding at all.

'Well, then, you will have observed that I am not as all other men. As *sufficient* other men, to be sure. You are a most beautiful woman, but you arouse in me no more feelings than pity that you should belong to a weaker sex. My pleasure comes from the feel of a male member, the soft caress of a male buttock.'

· Geneviève did not know what to say. She could feel her cheeks burning.

'You have not before come across one such as I?'

'No, my lord.'

'Aye, well, it is an eccentricity which in its time has afflicted even kings. I say afflicted, because it is not understood by the multitude at large. In most civilised societies it is harshly dealt with. Death, no less. I would hardly suppose that such a portion would be given to me, but there it is. I would scarce survive the scandal. And this is a unique occurrence, because of course where two men are involved, betrayal is hardly possible as both would suffer the same penalty.'

'My lord,' Geneviève protested, 'do not suppose that I would ever dream of betraying you, for whatever consideration.'

The Prince permitted himself a smile. 'Would you not, mademoiselle?' He held up a finger as she would have spoken again. 'But I'll not even put temptation in your way. I could, of course, call my fellows and have you strangled on the instant. No one would disbelieve any tale I might care to tell.'

'My lord.' Her hands clasped her throat.

'But that would be a waste, as I see it. Not only are you a beautiful woman, and a passionate one, apparently, and a virgin, but you have spent your entire life dressed as a man, carry off the role with great aplomb – you certainly fooled me – and are also adept with a sword, according to the Prior, and indeed, present to the world a man's demeanour when put to it. Is this true?'

'My lord, I was trained to it. You have listened to my history.'

Conti nodded. 'Well, then, it would be a waste, as I say. But even if I let you live, you are well on the way to being ruined, should your uncle ever learn of your subterfuge.'

'I am aware of that, my lord.'

'Therefore I would suggest that despite all, you throw in your lot with me.'

'Nothing would give me greater pleasure, my lord, believe me. But may I inquire to what end I should enter your employ? If you can find no pleasure in my body . . .'

'I know one who will find a great deal of pleasure in your body, and the greater pleasure if it is presented to him in the guise of a man. Oh, indeed.'

'One, sir?'

Conti laid his finger on his nose. 'One who may raise you to even greater heights than I. Will you serve me, mademoiselle?'

'My lord, I am overwhelmed. But what of the Prior?'

'You may leave the Prior to me. You may leave your family to me. No country advocate is likely to resist his son being taken under the wing of the Prince of Conti, and even if it happens to be his daughter, I am sure your father will understand the ways of the world, especially when presented in a suitable fashion, with a lining of golden livres, eh? Well, now, Mademoiselle Charles d'Éon de Beaumont, will you walk in the shadow of the Prince of Conti?'

Geneviève endeavoured to collect her thoughts. She did not suppose she had a choice. Even supposing she wished a choice. He had spoken nothing but the truth. And he was the Prince of Conti. However remarkable and presumably detestable were his habits, he was indeed the road to advancement. And what could he wish of her, save that at a suitable moment, and to some gentleman of apparently equal rank, she should yield up her virginity? Which was what she wanted to do in any event.

As for Papa and Mama, was he not right there also? And even if he was not, and they lamented the disappearance of their only daughter into the demi-monde that was French court society, did she owe them anything? Did she not hate them for the role they had thrust upon her? Well, Papa at any rate. Papa was a man. And here was a man offering her his house and his wealth and his patronage as a stepping stone to greater things. She would be a fool not to tread upon him as invited.

'It will be my great pleasure, my lord,' she said.

Chapter Two

Geneviève awoke, and listened for the sound of the chapel bell. And heard nothing. She stretched her legs, and then her arms, moving them easily beneath the cambric sheets, reaching for the furthest corner of her cot with her toes. And could not find it. There was no furthest corner in this featherdown mattress. She sighed, and moved her head on the pillow, the softest pillow she had ever known.

Clearly she was dreaming. And there was someone in her cell. In her cell? She could not see beyond the bed, for the drapes were drawn. But now they were pulled back, and she stared at Jules, who in turn stared at her. She looked down at herself, realised she was naked, and sat up, arms hugged across her breasts, legs pulled up against her groin. And as she did so, memory came flooding back. Some memory. 'Jules?'

'I have a cup of chocolate for you, monsieur.'

'Monsieur? Jules . . .' She looked past him, realised the room was bathed in light. 'What time is it?'

'Approaching noon, monsieur.'

'Noon.' Instinctively she leapt out of bed, stood there, reaching for a non-existent robe.

'Allow me, monsieur.' Jules had the garment, and now draped it around her shoulders; his fingers stroked her neck for just a moment.

Geneviève secured the robe, sat down at the table, sipped her chocolate. 'How did you get here?'

'Monsieur the Prince sent for me, early this morning. By the same messenger who informed the Prior that you would not be returning, monsieur.' He allowed himself a sly smile. 'Monsieur has fallen on her pretty feet.'

She gazed at him, full memory returning. But it was still clouded. She could remember coming here. She could remember that absurd scene with the Prince, his even more

32

absurd revelation. She could remember sitting down to supper with him, just the two of them in a vast room lit by crystal chandeliers whose candlelight had sparkled from the silver plates off which they had eaten. She could remember the Prince's conversation, which had roamed over the whole spectrum of France, a stream of anecdotes about such people as the Duc de Richelieu and the Duc d'Orléans, and even the King himself. What had he said about the King? She frowned as she tried to remember. That he was young, and handsome, and talented, and brave. Louis the Well Beloved. Even in the gutters of Paris they called him that. How he had fought against the British at Fontenoy, and soundly thrashed them, only the previous year. How since the death of Cardinal Fleury he had ruled the country himself. But how . . . her frown deepened, he had fallen into bad company. At least according to the Prince of Conti. She suspected he even included Richelieu in that category. And how . . . she drained her cup . . . how he was now taking up with a woman, Madame d'Étoiles . . . 'the fishwife' the Prince had said with a contemptuous smile . . . who would be the worst influence of all upon him.

So much court gossip had she learned in a single evening, while she had drunk more and more wine, and the room had become more and more unsteady, until, after dinner . . . she sprang to her feet.

'Monsieur?' Jules was waiting, attentively.

Geneviève chewed her lip. After supper the Prince had himself brought her in here. He had caressed her bottom as they had walked, had murmured innumerable indecencies in her ear, had been going to make love to her. She was sure of it. Despite his unnatural tendencies, he had drunk as much as she, and he . . . but she could remember nothing more. What had happened to her?

But she felt no different. And did it matter? Had she not resolved to surrender her maidenhead to the Prince? And been bitterly disappointed when he had rejected her?

But suddenly it mattered a great deal. How could she combat mankind when she did not even remember what had happened, how it had happened, what it had been like? Except that *nothing* had happened. She would have remembered.

'Monsieur?'

'Why was I not called earlier?'

'The Prince instructed me that you were to be left sleeping

33

until twelve of the clock, monsieur. The Prince is now master to us both, is he not?'

Geneviève glanced at him. Was he mocking her?

'Well, now I am called. You will lay out my clothes.'

'The Prince has requested you not to dress.'

Her heart commenced to pound all over again. 'Why not?'

Jules shrugged. 'I cannot say, monsieur. His instructions were to awaken you with a cup of chocolate at noon, and to request you to await his coming.'

Geneviève walked across the room to the window and looked out at the gardens which stretched behind the house. Last night it had all seemed so logical, so splendid. Here was one of the greatest men in the land offering to make her his protégé, and renewing the offer even after discovering that she was not as he had supposed.

But what *did* he intend for her? What had he already done to her? What scheme was roaming through his mind? For that he had a scheme could not be doubted. He might have acted out of love for her as a boy. He would never had done so out of love for her as a girl.

'Can I assist monsieur?' Jules stood at her shoulder.

The damnable thing was that she had come here prepared to be seduced. And if she had indeed been seduced, and could not remember it, her body as much as her mind still yearned for it, yearned to begin that battle with the male sex she had anticipated for four bitter years. Then why not commence it now, with Jules?

She turned. 'There is, Jules. I would . . .'

He half turned his head. 'Caution, monsieur. I hear the prince approaching.'

She bit her lip in disappointed anger, faced the door, which was at that moment opened by a footman, to admit the Prince, also wearing an undressing robe, and lacking his wig; she discovered that he was totally bald, a razor having assisted nature where necessary. His head suggested nothing so much as an egg with a beak and was utterly repulsive.

She bowed. 'My lord.'

The prince snapped his fingers. 'Leave us.'

Geneviève straightened, watched Jules disappearing through the door, which was closed behind him. The Prince held out his arms. 'You are even more beautiful in déshabille. More beautiful than I remember, my sweet Geneviève. Come to me.'

Cautiously she approached him, was folded against his chest for a moment, kissed upon both cheeks, and released. She had closed her eyes in anticipation of a kiss on the mouth such as she had enjoyed the previous night, and now opened them again in disappointment. The Prince had seated himself in the armchair by the window, legs crossed as usual. 'Did you sleep soundly?'

'Indeed, my lord.' She stood before him, hands clasped.

'Good. Good. There is much to be done. I have sent for Colonel La Passe. He will be with us for dinner.'

'Colonel La Passe, monsieur?'

'Colonel La Passe is presently in command of the De Beauffremont Regiment of Dragoons. It is not a royal regiment. That is to say, it is not commanded by one of the royal princes. But this is all to the good, from our point of view. You will be commissioned as an ensign.'

'My lord?' Geneviève cried.

'There is naught to be concerned with. La Passe is an old friend of mine. He will not expect you to attend the barracks. No indeed.'

'But my lord, I cannot be a soldier.'

'Why not? France is at war. Everyone should be a soldier. Every young man, at least. And you will look superb in your uniform. Oh, indeed.'

Geneviève's knees gave way and she sat down. 'You will send me to fight a war, my lord?'

'Ha, ha,' Conti cried. 'Not you, my sweet child. But you must be a soldier. Trust me. I know things of which you are ignorant. You are young, and you are pretty, and you have a unique secret. I seek to introduce you to court, without exposing you to intrigue and contumely which may well strip you bare.' He smiled at her. 'In more ways than one. And I happen to know that in the course of time the De Beauffremont Regiment of Dragoons must take over guard duty in the palace grounds. Not inside, you understand; the Swiss are inside. But near enough. You will be noticed, but without being attached to my party. That is important. We deal with large matters here, mademoiselle. You will let me deal the hand; your business is but to play the cards.'

Geneviève drove her hands into her hair. 'If I could understand . . .'

'In good time. You have sufficient to do. For you will not always be in uniform. No, no. My tailor is coming this morning, and he will see to your requirements. I would also like a display of your fencing skill, to be sure you truly know what you are about. But that we will save until the colonel is here, eh? As for the rest, you will spend part of each day with my secretary, learning something about court politics, and about the art of being a gentleman.' He laid his finger on his nose. 'He does not share our secret, of course. That must remain entirely a matter between you and me. But he will regard you correctly as a protégé of mine, and be eager to assist you.'

Geneviève did not know whether she was standing on her head or her heels.

'There is one matter more I would discuss,' the Prince said. 'This fellow of yours. What is his name?'

'Jules,' Geneviève said, absently.

'Jules. *He* knows our secret. Is he trustworthy?'

'He has ever been so, as he has been promised a portion of my inheritance, whenever I receive it.'

'Ah. He has been with you a long time?'

'He was my father's butler, my lord. But he has served me these four years.'

'Four years, during which you have grown to entrancing womanhood. Has he never attempted familiarity?'

'My lord?'

'You are circumspect. Yes, I can see it. You must *never* permit him, or any man, familiarity, until I give the word. Your maidenhead is your most important possession at this moment. For the rest, I see no alternative to his continuing with you. A young man must have a servant, and his servant must necessarily know all about him. Oh, indeed, no alternative. I may have to sweeten him a little. You may leave that to me.'

'My lord, I am in a whirl. My lord, last night . . . do I still *possess* a maidenhead?'

He frowned at her. 'Do you not remember last night?'

'My brain was most confoundedly fuddled, my lord.'

'Ha ha.' His frown cleared into a smile, and he leaned back in the chair. 'You will have to control your drinking. A fuddled brain is no good thing for someone in your position. Aye, you still have a maidenhead. We romped a trifle. You managed to arouse my senses to a certain level. I even contemplated assaulting your nether portals, pretending you a boy.'

'My *lord!*'

He sighed. 'You slapped my face. Do you not recall slapping my face?'

'Oh, my lord . . .' Her heart pounded and she could feel the blood rushing to her cheeks. 'I was drunk, my lord.'

'Of course. And to say truth, I am pleased with your propriety. It would never do for me to fall in love with you after all. No, no. But there is a matter concerns me.' He leaned forward. 'You do know passion? You have felt it? You have used your fingers to your best advantage?'

'My lord?' Once again her mystification was so obviously genuine he could only peer at her for some seconds before leaning back again.

'You do *know* passion? You suggested it, yesterday afternoon.'

'I . . .' Geneviève licked her lips. 'I do know passion, my lord. I think I know passion.'

'But you have never been overwhelmed by it, in your lonely convent cell?'

'I . . . my circumstances are somewhat unusual, my lord. I . . . my life has been a contradiction. I . . . I fear . . .'

'To touch even your own body. Ha ha.' The Prince got up, took a turn up and down the room. 'What's to be done, eh? What's to be done? To let someone else into our secret . . . that were too much risk. Even if she could be disposed of after.'

'Disposed of?'

He shook his head. ''Tis naught for you to worry about, my dear. No, too risky. Too risky.' He snapped his fingers. 'Books. I will give you books to read. And mind you do.'

'Yes, my lord.'

He stood above her chair, held her chin, turned up her face. 'It is strange, how things work out. When, yesterday morning, the Prior sent a messenger to me to say he had a boy who would interest me, both on account of his beauty and his intellect, I thought of nothing more than the gratification of my lust. I panted with desire for you. For lust is a terrible emotion, my dear. It takes hold of the senses and leaves no room for anything else, at least until it is assuaged. And now today I find myself thinking entirely of affairs of state. What chance sent us together, Monsieur d'Éon? And where will chance take us in the future?'

'My lord, if you would but tell me what you plan . . .'

'Time enough. Time when I am sure you are everything I take you to be. Time enough.'

Her eyes were wide as she stared at him. 'And suppose I do not prove to be what you hope?'

He smiled at her, and his eyes took on a glitter she had seen before, when she had pushed him away from her the previous night. 'Suppose you were to catch smallpox and die, my dear Geneviève? But do you spend your time considering such a catastrophe?'

'No, my lord. But . . .'

'Then do not begin now. I have every confidence in you. Now, you will tell your man Jules to furnish my tailor with samples of your clothing that suitable garments may be provided for you. He will find it odd that he is not allowed to measure you, but then there are many odd things in this world. Certain it is he will never suspect the truth of the matter. No one could possibly suspect the truth of the matter. And do not *worry*.' He bent his head, and kissed her very gently on the lips. 'It will give you lines, and that is unthinkable.'

From that moment Geneviève had scarce a moment to call her own, was worked harder than she had ever been at the Mazarin College. There was first of all her new career as a soldier. Being accepted into the regiment was apparently no problem at all – certainly not after she had delighted both the Prince and Colonel La Passe with her swordplay, which matched that of the colonel himself – but it was necessary for her to learn the rudiments of military behaviour, and so every morning between ten and twelve she was taken down to the barracks, and there introduced to the platoon which was to be her responsibility, and with the aid of a sergeant put through the drill manual, which, as even a dragoon regiment was expected occasionally to fight on horseback, included mounted manoeuvres as well.

But to her surprise she found these military matters utterly absorbing. And she was not required to wear a uniform all the while. The Prince's tailor, working entirely from the model supplied by her own clothes, produced a stream of the most fashionable and elegant garments which she delighted to wear. There were leather shoes and silk stockings, satin breeches and velvet coats, ruby rings for her fingers – it was apparently the Prince's favourite stone – cambric shirts for her back . . . Jules

38

was hardly less delighted, and would dress and undress her like a doll. But this was part of his pleasure, to allow his knuckles to brush her thighs or his hands to touch her breasts as he fastened her buttons. The while sighing and casting her longing glances.

But she could afford to be frank with Jules. 'The Prince has forbidden me to yield myself to a soul until I am so commanded,' she explained. 'And were you to remove my maidenhead, my dear Jules, he would hang you up by your wrists while he cut away your most treasured possession.'

Jules did not appear to be disturbed. 'I had not thought you ever considered the matter, monsieur.'

'And should I not? I am a woman.' It was necessary to constantly remind herself.

'Then, monsieur ...' His tongue came out and circled his lips in a most unpleasant manner ... 'There are things the Prince need never know of, here in the privacy of your bedchamber. There is a custom, of which perhaps you have never heard, which permits many a weary traveller in the more remote parts of the country to sleep in a soft bed with softer company, all with the approval of the parents of the house, and all without the slightest risk to any young lady's virginity.'

'I have no idea of what you are speaking.'

'It is called bundling, monsieur. Both parties are enveloped from the waist down, and thus left to make free with each other to their hearts' content, sure that the ultimate cannot be achieved.' Once again the tongue.

'What a revolting idea,' she said.

'I understand it is very enjoyable,' he remarked in a huff. 'And beneficial, as our master the Prince supposes it would be to your advantage to discover a certain passion. The neglected flower soon withers on its stalk.'

She chewed her lip. No doubt he was right. But the idea *was* revolting. She had no desire to make love to anyone. Certainly to any man. And how was it possible to make love to a woman? She wished only to rise above them, to crush them beneath her heel, to dismiss any lurking suggestion of masculine superiority. For this purpose she would welcome a serious affray. But a part measure, which would put her body at the disposal of the hands of a man like Jules and allow her no knowledge in return, seemed an entirely pointless exercise.

Yet he was so anxious that the possibility of taking advantage of him was there.

39

'I might consider it,' she said. 'Supposing you humour me a little.' She was, indeed, becoming a protégé of the Prince.

'Humour, you, monsieur? I would walk a hundred miles to humour you.'

'Then let me see your secret.'

'My . . . you have never seen a man before?'

'Never.' Nor was it entirely a lie. She could remember nothing of her father. She wished to remember nothing of her father.

'But . . . the Prince . . .'

'The Prince is a gentleman and regards me as a daughter.'

'Ah,' he said, clearly mystified. But he was happy enough to obey her, and left her totally dumbfounded. Never had she seen anything so hideous. Papa's had at least hung quiescent between his legs. Jules' was enormous, twice the size she either remembered or envisaged, and jutted at her like a lance. Was *that* what he would have used? God in Heaven, she thought, he would have split me from crotch to throat.

'Put it away,' she commanded. 'For God's sake, put it away.'

'Monsieur?' He was clearly even more mystified, but he did as she commanded. While Geneviève retired to bed with a headache, and some even more serious considerations. For suddenly she at last had the answer to her conundrum. Men ruled women, not by some mysterious power concealed in their penises, but by terror. Indeed she for the first time understood why her fellow students at the Mazarin College had referred to their *weapons*. How was it possible even to look upon such a repulsive object without knowing immediate fear, and to be forced to submit to its piercing thrust, as was apparently demanded by the marriage contract, was unthinkable.

Jules' ardour towards her cooled somewhat when the next part of the Prince's scheme had to be implemented. 'For depend upon it, my dear Charles,' he said, seating her in a chair while the barber surgeon waited attentively, 'no young man of quality can possess hair such as yours, or can be seen to possess hair at all, except by his intimates. Eh?' He laughed and pinched her ear, and allowed the barber full scope to clip away at the golden locks until she was reduced to a close cropped thatch. Then it was on with the tie wig and the bag wig and the pigtail wig and the plain wig, all in white . . . 'As a soldier,' the Prince explained, 'you will confine yourself to the pigtail wig,' which she discovered, was secured with an enormous blue velvet bow, for all the world as if she were indeed playing her true sex ... and all subjected to an inundation of powder, which scattered to left and right at the slightest movement.

'Oh, you are the prettiest fellow,' the Prince cried, clapping his hands. 'You look good enough to bugger. I doubt I shall be able to keep my hands off you, even now.'

But he did, and presented her with the promised library of books to study – the letters of Madame de Sévigné, the novel *Gil Blas*, Dryden's *Fables* and a good deal of Shakespeare, mainly sonnets, and above all the *Lives of Fair and Gallant Ladies* of Brantome, from which he intended she should learn something of the dissolute manners of the court. To which he added various books on medicine; these he would sometimes come to read with her, lingering over the drawings depicting the various portions of the male anatomy, but which she found quite as nauseating as the real thing. And what were the books supposed to do for her? Certainly they were amusing, and some of them quite informative. But none of them titillated her to the extent suggested by the Prince.

She could not deny that life was pleasant enough; she was doing everything she wished, within reason, and she had never been able to resist the temptations of learning. For her studies were continued, as a tutor came in every day to continue preparing her for her degree, with such success that she reached her goal within six months of leaving the college. But of course she knew she was merely marking time.

Thus she spent every day on the *qui vive,* awaiting a summons which never seemed to come; weeks became months, until she realised that a year had passed; in a scant three months she would be nineteen. She was merely stagnating, in the lap of luxury, to be sure, but nonetheless living an entirely sterile life, in every sense. Until the day she returned from her daily drill session at the dragoon barracks, flung herself from her horse and stamped into the downstairs hall, boots ringing on the marble floor, and discovered the Prince's secretary, Monsieur Rassy, waiting for her with a long face.

'Monsieur d'Éon,' he said. 'Your mother is here.'

'Mama?' It seemed impossible. 'Here, in Paris?'

'I have shown her into the library, monsieur. If you would go to her ...'

Geneviève ran up the stairs, whipped off her hat, plunged into the library. 'Mama?'

Louise d'Éon was dressed entirely in black. She had been facing the bookcases which lined the walls, now she turned, and her mouth opened in surprise. 'Charles? Charles?' She took a step forward. 'What have they done to you?'

Geneviève held her close, kissed her on each cheek. 'Done to me, Mama?'

'This uniform...' Louise d'Éon held her at arms' length. 'You have changed. When we heard that you had left the Mazarin my child, this place, this prince...'

'The Prince of Conti, Mama. There is no greater man in the land. As for the uniform, it is the Prince's wish that I serve. France is at war, Mama.'

Louise peered at her. 'He would send you off to the wars?'

'Oh, indeed not, Mama. But he feels it is best for me to appear the soldier, at the least. The Prince considers life from every possible angle.'

'He knows your secret?'

Geneviève hesitated, then gently moved her mother's hands, checked there was no one in the hall, carefully closed the door. 'He does, Mama.'

'And makes nothing of it? Are you his mistress?'

'Indeed not, Mama. The Prince is the soul of honour.' Well, she thought, at least as regards women. And can there be honour amongst men?

Once again the long stare, as if Mama was trying to make up her mind whether or not she was telling the truth. Then she shrugged. 'It is of no matter. You may take off these silly clothes, forever.'

'Mama?' Her turn to frown.

'You have not asked what brings me to Paris.'

Geneviève's heart began to pound. 'Great Uncle Henri is dead.'

Louise nodded, and sat down in one of the straight chairs arranged around the reading table. 'A week ago.'

'Then we are rich? Papa is happy?'

Louise sighed. 'Your great uncle died penniless.'

Geneviève sat also, slowly, sinking into the chair opposite. 'Mama?'

'It was all a fraud. Don't you see? Oh, no doubt we deserved it, for practising a fraud upon him. Rich? He had nothing but debts. He fooled others apart from us. He merely pretended. And dabbled in people's lives. Ruining them.'

'Oh, Mama.' Geneviève reached across the table, held her mother's hand. 'Oh, poor, poor Mama. And poor Papa. He must be very angry.'

'When your father heard the news . . .' Louise's voice was toneless . . . 'he went down to the gunroom, and shot himself.' She jerked away, pulling her hand free, gazing at Geneviève with her mouth open as if unable to believe she had actually said the words.

Geneviève said nothing. She could think of nothing to say. She was not sure she understood what was happening.

'Did you hate him very much?' Louise asked.

'I . . .' He had wanted wealth. Could she hate him for that? Was that not what she wanted for herself? She had agreed to his plan. She was still acting the role he had designed for her. *Could* she hate him for that?

'*I* hated him,' Louise said. 'I have shed not a tear. I hated him from the moment he made you come to Paris. I have not shared his bed, these five years.'

And *that* is why he killed himself, Geneviève thought. Not just because of the money. Because the plan, his plan, failed so miserably. Because he could not face both your hate and your contempt, for the rest of his life. But would it benefit either of them to tell Mama that?

'I hated him,' she said. 'But I am sorry he killed himself. It is a mortal sin.'

'All his sins were mortal,' Louise said. She leaned forward again. 'But at the least, Geneviève, my darling Geneviève, it means you are free. We have no money. Even the house is being taken in settlement of Great Uncle Henri's debts. But we can at last be honest. You and me, Geneviève. I have my needlework, and you will soon learn an equal skill. And there is a home for us with my sister, in Cherbourg. Her husband is a *successful* advocate. He has no false hopes. And then, with your looks, my darling girl, we shall soon find you a good marriage, and all will be well. We will be honest at last. Geneviève?' She had taken her daughter's hand again, now she slowly released it as she understood the expression on Geneviève's face.

I have lived as a man for near nineteen years, Geneviève thought. I have suppressed my natural instincts, lacked the companionship of friends, been forced to live an entirely unnatural life, in order to be rich at the end of it. Now you tell me I must be poor? I must live on an aunt's charity, support myself

43

by needlework, and marry some country bumpkin?

'Geneviève?'

Geneviève pushed back the chair and got up. 'I am very happy here, Mama.'

'But . . . acting the man? Playing some game? You *are* his mistress.'

'I am not,' Geneviève insisted. 'Would you have me to a midwife? You may if you wish. You'll find an intact hymen. The Prince is an . . . an eccentric. Nothing more than that. He finds my situation intriguing, but he treats me as a daughter. I have everything I wish. More than I wish. I will see that you are as rich as ever Father dreamed of, Mama.'

'You wish to continue this masquerade?'

'For as long as the prince requires it, certainly.'

'But . . . what can you hope to gain? If this prince really has your true interests at heart, should he not be displaying you as a woman, arranging for you to be married? You are nearly nineteen. You are in the prime of a young woman's life, and look at you, your hair cut away, wearing a wig, dressed as a soldier . . . it will end badly. My God, I thought it had already ended badly. But if you persist . . .'

'As you say, Mama,' Geneviève said, 'I am a full grown woman, or a full grown man, depending upon how you look at it. You will pray allow me to decide what is best for me. You do not know the Prince. I do. By doing as he wishes I anticipate a most prosperous future. Far more prosperous than any I may hope for in Cherbourg. And besides, I enjoy my life. I like being a soldier. I like wearing nice clothes. As for my hair, I can always grow it again when I am ready. I beseech you, Mama, do not press me upon this matter. Rather share in it with me. I know the Prince will be happy to support you.'

Louise d'Éon slowly stood up. 'You are unnatural,' she said. 'You are as evil as your father. You practice some new subterfuge, of which I know nothing. I will have none of it, Geneviève. This is your chance to return to respectability, to be the woman you are, to understand the beauties of being a wife and a mother. This is your *last* chance. Persist in this madness and I can have no hope for you. Nor would I wish to.'

'I am sorry, Mama. I do not wish to quarrel, but my mind is made up.'

'Your mind,' Louise d'Éon said contemptuously. 'Do you

have a mind? Are you not merely the Prince's creature, as you were your father's creature before him? Your head is turned with a dream of riches, for which you would turn nature itself inside out. I wash my hands of you.'

She marched across the room to the door. Geneviève waited. And at the door she turned.

'Geneviève. My own dear, sweet Geneviève, come to Cherbourg with me.'

The tears were rolling down Geneviève's cheeks. How she hated those tears. But they did not affect her resolution. They must never affect her resolution.

'Rather would I ask you to stay here with me, Mama.'

Louise d'Éon gazed at her for a moment, then she turned and opened the door, closed it again behind her.

'A woman of character,' the prince observed.

Geneviève turned, heart thudding. He stood in an alcove, had clearly just entered the room by a secret doorway. 'You were listening.'

'Of course. I was informed your mother was here, as I knew she had to come, eventually.'

'My lord, I am a wretched creature.'

'Quite the contrary,' he said. 'You are a woman of spirit, and decision. Indeed, you may regard yourself as having successfully passed your last examination. Well, not the *very* last, perhaps. Upon that truly depends your fortune. But at least you have this day proved yourself worthy of the opportunity to attain that fortune. My congratulations.'

'My lord?' She was, as ever, quite confounded by his involved perorations.

'Today you go to Versailles, you silly child. Your regiment is already there.'

She spent the journey, riding at the head of her platoon, over the Seine and through the village of Sèvres, in a state of euphoria. Her doubts were for the moment banished. Even her curiosity no longer afflicted her so sharply. Whatever the Prince had planned for her was about to begin, and she was content for that.

And then, Versailles. She strolled through the gardens, the formal terraces and walks, peered at the menagerie, watched some young ladies, whom she was assured were princesses, rowing themselves about the ornamental lake, entered the great courtyard, divided down the centre by a railing, beyond which none might drive who did not possess the 'honour' of Versailles. Here was where the King's guards were assembled. This month they were the De Beauffremont Dragoons, all five hundred of them, a glitter of polished accoutrements and brilliant scarlet jackets, shining black boots and waving tassels. Their duty was to guard the gate, but there was sufficient time for relaxation, and Colonel La Passe, well aware of his junior ensign's privileged position as a friend of the Prince of Conti, permitted her to investigate the château itself, early on the morning of her second day.

She made her way past the sedan park, every chair in royal blue, awaiting hiring by the various distinguished nobles who frequented the palace, thence into the great gallery, filled with silver tables and chairs arranged over several quite magnificent carpets; there were more candles here than she had ever seen in her life before – 'four thousand, monsieur,' one of the major-domos told her – while each of the seventeen windows were shrouded with white damask curtains emblazoned with the arms of France in gold. As there were also seventeen enormous mirrors, each calculated to reflect the acres of green and gold upholstery, she seemed to be surrounded by a kaleidoscope of regal colour in the midst of which her red jacket stood out like a beacon.

After this she was prepared to be disappointed, but her breath was again taken by the Salon de Diane, where the spaces between the windows were filled with orange trees in silver tubs, and where the centre of the floor was occupied by the great billiards tables at which the King himself was wont to play. Then what was she to make of the Salon d'Apollon, which was used as the throne room, and where the hangings were in the more conventional crimson and gold; here too there were silver tubbed orange trees between each window, and in addition the walls were hung with magnificent Titians and portraits by Van Dyck. The throne itself was made entirely of silver, and sat beneath a canopy suspended from rings set in the ceiling. The whole, with its majesty as well as its quite inestimable wealth, took her breath away and left her head whirling.

But guard duty itself was an exercise in breath holding. 'The Duke of Vendôme,' whispered another ensign, as they came to attention to admit a carriage through the gates. 'The Duke of Grammont.' 'The Maréchal de Villeroi.' Names she had only ever heard, every one with jewelled fingers and eyes so cold they near froze her heart. But were they not just men, she asked herself? Would not their eyes soften as they regarded an object of desire? And was it not at least likely that most of them were as unnatural as the Prince of Conti? It was necessary only to remind herself of her contempt for the entire sex. But then there was a carriage, very plain and worn, from which there looked an equally plainly dressed man; his face made Geneviève's blood freeze, for never had she seen such pointed, bitter features, rendered the more frightening by the utterly arrogant twist of his lips.

'Shirér,' whispered the guard beside her. 'Shirér the swordsman.'

Shirér, Geneviève thought. Would she ever possess his skill? Pray to God she would never need to.

There were also women. They attended court in their best finery, hair towering above them to a height of a foot and more, sustained by great wire frames, laden with powder which turned even the most raven brunette white, and decorated with the most extravagant and indeed ridiculous conceptions, clocks, represen tations of human figures, model horses, stuffed birds, while one absurd grand dame actually had a *live* parakeet, secured within a golden cage, perched on top of hers. Geneviève supposed she had never seen a more abject sight, nor was she at all attracted by the layers of paint and powder which covered every face, by the glazed expression with which these gilded harlots – every one at the very least a Countess – regarded the world.

Until on the fourth day a carriage halted at the gate, wishing to go the other way. The guard came to attention, the captain hurried forward to see the road was adequately cleared, and Geneviève found herself looking at the most elegant woman she had ever seen. Clearly out for a visit to Paris, she wore neither paint nor powder, and her hair a splendid pale brown, was mostly concealed beneath her tricorne, although to be sure the hat itself was rimmed in gold.

Her face was handsome rather than lovely, but was possessed of a most serene confidence and was dominated by her eyes, large and brown and luminous; she smiled at the guardsmen, even gazed reflectively at Geneviève's face for a moment or two as her carriage was halted. Then the gates were opened and she was rumbling down the dusty drive beyond, leaving Geneviève staring after her.

'As well you might,' remarked Colonel La Passe. 'That was the Pompadour.'

'Sir?'

'Madame d'Étoiles. The King has recently made her a present of the estate of Pompadour.'

The fishwife. Conti's sworn enemy. And the King's mistress. There was ambition.

'Now forget her,' the colonel said. 'Where the Pompadour goes, you may be sure His Majesty will soon follow. Come to attention.'

Because sure enough another carriage was rumbling down the drive, and this was quite the finest equipage Geneviève had ever seen, the sides emblazoned with the fleur de lys, in gold on a blue background, the leatherwork polished to a mirror, drawn by six magnificent white horses, with postilions a glitter in green and gold both on the seat and standing at the rear while riding behind the carriage itself was an escort of the Swiss guards, a kaleidoscope of crimson and gold with great dark bearskins, every man sporting a gigantic moustache and daring any ordinary soldier even to meet his eye.

But Geneviève had eyes only for the King. The gates had been allowed to remain open, and the carriage checked but for a moment – but in that time he looked directly at her, and she would swear raised an eyebrow. He was more attractive than she would have supposed possible, his face amiable rather than handsome; he looked far less haughty than most of his nobles. Nor was he as richly dressed, and indeed wore quite a plain cloak. And he had looked at her. Her knees felt weak.

'And raised an eyebrow,' Conti repeated. He sprawled on his settee, while Geneviève, wearing an undressing robe, paraded in front of him and told him everything she had observed during her week of guard duty – as if he had not himself observed it all a thousand times.

'But it was so . . . so magnificent,' she said. 'It made one aware of the greatness that is France, my lord. Me, at the least. I had not truly believed it, before.'

'The greatness that is France.' He sat up, leaning forward. 'Aye, it is great. It is the greatest nation in Europe. But how long shall such greatness endure? A nation's greatness, my dear girl, depends upon its wealth, and France has no wealth.'

'My lord?' That was impossible to believe, when she recalled the magnificence of Versailles.

'The government is bankrupt,' Conti said. 'The King is bankrupt. There is a remarkable thing.'

'I cannot accept that, my lord.'

'Oh, *you* will never know of it. For who would refuse to lend a king money? Yet even loans must eventually be repaid, if not by us, by our children or our grandchildren. It is the fault of those who surround him, those who advise him. Those who would call themselves his friends.'

'Are you not a friend of the King, my lord?'

'Oh, indeed. But how may I replace those of greater influence? Influence. There is the question. The King, I think, loves me dearly, as an uncle. But he knows something of my weaknesses, and he, alas, has none in *that* direction. Yet is he a man, and a man must lust. The Pompadour. There is our problem. Madame the Fishwife.'

'Why do you call her the fishwife, my lord?'

'Ha ha. It is a pun on her maiden name, which was Poisson. The King met her but two years ago, and fell in love with her immediately. Now tell me this, Geneviève. Why does a man fall in love with a woman?'

Geneviève considered. 'Because she is beautiful?'

'All women who surround a king take care to be beautiful. A man falls in love with a woman because that woman makes it plain to him that she will make him happy, and in the case of a king that happiness can only arise out of his bed, as he has sufficient other servants to see to his table and his clothes and the ordering of his house. Why, a king even has a wife to see to the continuation of his dynasty. Therefore the woman he will love can have only one thing to offer, a welcoming, a suppliant, an ever anxious and an ever accommodating pair of thighs. Do you understand me?'

'I think so, my lord.'

'Then stop perambulating and sit down. I would talk with you very seriously.'

Geneviève obeyed, seating herself beside him.

'Kings, of course, never discover such women for themselves,' he said. 'They have no such opportunities. Yet are they never short of the lovely creatures. Do you know why?'

'No, my lord.'

'Because others do the pimping. In this case the Duc de Richelieu. Pompadour is his creature. Or was. There is always a risk that one's creature may grow more powerful than oneself.

You would not make such a mistake, would you, my sweet Geneviève?'

'Me, my lord?' Her head was spinning.

'Listen. Richelieu saw to it that Madame d'Étoiles was placed in the way of the King, and he had already seen to it that she would make herself as agreeable as possible. So the King fell in love. At least, he supposes he has fallen in love. The trouble with a man like Louis is that he will continue to suppose himself in love until he is disabused of the idea, and you may be sure Pompadour will never do that. So for as long as she shares the royal bed she will continue to influence the King, and through her Richelieu and his cronies will continue to influence the King, to the advantage of themselves and the disadvantage of France. But there are even greater problems for those who would save the country. For power, of that nature, is self perpetuating. Versailles is the centre of every government department; they spread away from it like a spider's web. That was the Great Louis' doing. No doubt it makes for efficiency, although sometimes I doubt even that. What it does make for is the accumulation of power in only a few pairs of hands. How may I speak privily with the King? Only by applying to his valet, Bertrand, for the right to be first noticed at the levée. And Bertrand, you may be sure, is by now the Pompadour's creature. My request would be approved by her, or not. Now, even this newly-fledged royal mistress might think twice about refusing an audience to the Prince of Conti, sure as she is that while the King might listen indulgently to his uncle, he would never take his advice. But were the Prince of Conti to wish to introduce a young woman to His Majesty, and were that young woman to be of even greater beauty and greater accomplishments and greater willingness than herself, the Pompadour would scarce agree, and if she did, you may be sure a vial of poison would immediately be prepared to introduce into that young lady's next goblet of wine.'

'My lord?' Geneviève clasped both hands to her throat.

'Oh, do not mistake what we are about. These are high stakes at which we toss. A life here and there is nothing. No, no, it is only possible for us to gain our ends by subterfuge, and to those ends we are already working. Your regiment has now completed three of its four weeks' term of duty at the Palace. At the end of next week it will be required to join the army of Marshal Saxe in Holland.'

'My lord?' Geneviève's voice rose to a squeak.

'Oh, stop mewing. *You* will certainly not be sent to some distant campaign, even if we fail. You have too many secrets.'

Geneviève bit her lip; she was not sure whether what he had just said was reassuring or not.

'The point is, His Majesty always holds a small levée exclusively for the officers of his guard regiment when they relinquish their task. He is fond of supposing himself a soldier, and a solider's soldier. Well, to be sure, he campaigned at Fontenoy and might have done more but for his illness. So there you have it. In complete innocence, the officers of the De Beauffremont Dragoons will find themselves closeted with their King, on Monday next. Nothing could be better, in fact, because Richelieu is at his country house recovering from the pox.'

'And His Majesty will notice me?'

'He has already noticed you, my dear girl. I had an audience with him but a week ago, and mentioned your name to him, as a young man of most remarkable gifts.' He smiled. 'Pompadour was at his side, and she merely looked bored. I may seek advancement for whichever of my young male friends I choose, and remain only an object of contempt.'

Without thinking Geneviève scratched her head, dislodging her wig to do so. 'But, my lord, introduced to His Majesty as a man, I do not see . . .'

'A young man of quite exceptional qualities. His Majesty has promised me to give you a private audience. He has sense enough to wish to seek out talent. Well, your talent may not be quite what he is expecting, but he will still be delighted.'

'Are you sure, my lord? With my hair cropped . . .'

'That will delight him even more. As I keep reminding you, His Majesty is a man, and what is more, a king, and kings, being granted from childhood the gratification of their every wish, are more easily bored than most. Now it is His Majesty's misfortune that he regards sodomy with abhorrence, and thus at a stroke has eliminated from his life one entire half of the game of love. Making do, as he must, with only the pallid remnants as supplied by the ladies of the court, he is, believe me, unutterably bored. He is even somewhat bored with the Pompadour, as she has had the royal bed to herself for just on two years. Especially as he has a weakness for the vulgar, and even occasionally sends for a whore from the streets of Paris to satisfy an obscene wish.

Oh, to *displace* the fishwife will be a difficult task, to be sure, yet it can be done. Here is a king, fondly imagining himself to be a soldier, closeting himself with a young soldier who suddenly reveals herself to be a young woman, a young woman of exceptional beauty, a young woman with a cropped head, which is different to any other woman he will ever have seen, a young woman who is a virgin, and there will be an unusual event in this court of ours, and a young woman who will be absolutely brimming with passion, who will not only grant his every wish, but implement it with whichever portion of her body he may desire.' He paused, and frowned at her expression. 'You will *be* that passionate?'

Geneviève had removed her wig entirely, and was absently fanning herself with it. He means to prostitute me, to the King, she thought. That has been his entire intention since I came to live here. But have I not known that all along, without ever suspecting the level at which I should commence? And if the Prince of Conti can bring me wealth and power, cannot the King bring me even more? Why, he might grant *me* an estate, earn me the right to be known by but a single name, have all heads turning as I pass. As to the subterfuge, is subterfuge not my business, as it has been my business all of my life? Certainly it was a logical process as Conti has just explained it.

So then, will I be passionate? Will I submit, to whatever indignities he may choose to practice upon me? The King had not much looked like a man who would practice indignities, upon anyone. He had, indeed, looked a thoughtful, friendly, even a *nice* man. But he would wish to assault her with that dreadful object Jules had revealed to her. Would she not scream, or faint? Yet it had to be experienced, eventually, and if so, why not from a king? The King. Her King. How could anyone, and especially Geneviève d'Éon be so fortunate? Why, simply because all her life to this moment had been a misfortune, thanks to the overweaning ambition of her father.

As the King's mistress, even Mama might forgive her. Mama *would* forgive her.

She smiled at the Prince. 'I will be passionate, my lord.'

The King came slowly down the line of officers, speaking with every one. A few paces behind, Madame d'Étoiles followed, also bestowing a smile and a remark to each young man. Geneviève, as the most junior ensign in the regiment, was at the very end, and could only wait, taking some comfort from the presence of the Prince of Conti, for he, together with a number of other great nobles and princes of the royal blood, were gathered in a group in the centre of the Salon, occasionally moving forward to introduce the monarch to their own particular protégé. It was a relief to note that the prince apparently had no other favourite in the regiment, but it was disconcerting to observe that he seldom even glanced at her, was engaged in a most animated conversation with his immediate neighbour. It was all part of the plot, she told herself. But her knees touched with anxiety as the King reached the boy beside her.

And here he was. Geneviève bowed, as instructed. 'Lieutenant Charles d'Éon de Beaumont, Sire.'

'D'Éon de Beaumont,' Louis remarked. His voice was quiet, his demeanour disinterested. 'A gentleman of that name recently died.'

'My great uncle, Sire.'

'This is the young man of whom I spoke, Sire.' Conti had crossed the room, stood beside the King.

'Ah. The boy of talent. Unusual talent, you said, Uncle François.'

'And should he not have unusual talents, as he is the protégé of the Prince of Conti?' The Pompadour had also come up, and now she glanced back over the assembly, inviting them to laugh with her, which several did.

Geneviève flushed to the edge of her wig, but Conti did not seem the least put out. 'Indeed, madame, I am seldom interested in ordinary young men. Lieutenant d'Éon, now, in addition to all his other accomplishments, is a most adept fisherman. Why, he can pull them out of the water with the greatest of ease.'

'Ha ha,' said the King. 'Ha ha. Ha ha ha . . .' He glanced at his mistress, and stopped laughing. 'How droll.'

The Pompadour said nothing, but after a glance at Conti which would have shrivelled a lesser man, she gave a similar stare to Geneviève, who for a moment felt suitably abashed. But why should I be afraid of her, she asked herself? She is nothing but a royal whore, as is my intended portion. We are equals, and surely my family is superior to hers. She tilted her chin, and the Pompadour flushed.

As Conti had observed. 'But fishing is the very least of Lieutenant d'Éon's accomplishments, Sire,' he said. 'He is a man of quite spectacular parts. Should you but care to grant him an audience . . .'

'And why not?' the King inquired at large. 'He is at the least a handsome fellow.'

'Too pretty by half, Sire,' the Pompadour remarked. 'One should beware of pretty fellows, especially when they are well-connected.'

'Five minutes, Sire.' Conti kept his voice low. 'Lieutenant d'Éon possesses one especial talent which places him above all other men.'

The King frowned at him. 'This sounds very like witchcraft.'

Conti smiled. 'No, no, Sire. There is nothing unnatural . . .' He paused to glance at the Pompadour. 'In this young man's abilities.'

'Then why should he not display them to the assembled room?'

'Because, Sire, it occurs to me that you might be able to put this particular talent to your own best use, especially if it is a secret between you and the lad.'

'And yourself,' Louis remarked.

The Prince bowed. 'Indeed, Sire. If, on the other hand, you find the talent worthless, why then by all means have the lieutenant display it to the assembled company.'

Geneviève gave her mentor a startled glance. She would not put it past him to recoup his reputation, should the King not react favourably, by making a public display of her sex.

'You are a superb entrepreneur, Uncle François. Ah, well, I am in the mood to be amused. Let us enter the antechamber. Will you come, my dear?' He offered the Pompadour his arm.

Oh, Lord, Geneviève thought; here disappears all our hopes. But she had reckoned without the Prince.

'This is masculine business, Sire. I fear its secret should be revealed to no one not of our sex.'

'Say you so?'

'What nonsense,' the Pompadour declared. ''Tis a trick to obtain a private audience, Sire.'

'And why should my own uncle not desire a private audience, madame?'

'With a *boy*?' the Pompadour inquired.

But she had made a mistake. 'Madame, sometimes your humour is *too* reminiscent of the fish market,' Louis snapped, and turned to walk to the antechamber, the doors of which were already being opened. Conti gave the Pompadour a smile, and then Geneviève a hasty nod. She in turn looked at her colonel, but La Passe also nodded, and so she marched across the room, heart thumping, terribly aware that everyone was watching her, but even more aware that she was approaching the most important moment of her life. Failure now would mean disaster, for Conti would discard her like a worn out glove. Success . . . but she dared not think of success. She only knew that the Prince was at her elbow, that she was through the doorway and into the small chamber, and that the Prince was closing the doors behind her.

There was a table, four straight chairs, and two settees against the walls, which were hung with the usual priceless paintings. Furniture apart, the room was empty save for the inevitable pair of footmen who hastily bowed and departed as Conti snapped his fingers.

The King stood in the centre of the room, facing the door. 'Well?' he demanded. 'Be quick about it, monsieur. And be good. Oh, indeed, be good. Be sure the Pompadour will make me suffer for flouting her.'

Geneviève glanced at the Prince.

'You may commence, Charles,' Conti said.

He had coached her in exactly what she must do, at least in the beginning. 'Be slow,' he had told her time and again. 'No haste, and no anxiety. And never take your gaze from his face.'

She stared into those pale eyes, that impatient expression, while she slowly unbuckled her sword belt, and laid it on the table. Then, with equal care, she removed her wig. Her heart, which had slowed as she entered the room, was commencing to pound, for the King was beginning to frown, but less in anger at the moment, than bewilderment.

Slowly she released the buttons of her jacket, sliding her hand down the front. She reached the last button, watched the King's frown deepen as she shrugged the coat from her shoulders, leaving vest and shirt exposed.

'Conti?' Louis' voice was harsh. 'What absurdity is this?'

'Patience, Sire, for a moment longer,' the Prince begged. 'Have I ever failed to amuse Your Majesty? Continue, Charles.'

But Geneviève had seen the danger signals, and released her vest more quickly, laying it on top of the jacket, while the King's frown returned, but this time it was an interested if still bewilderment frown: her shirt was cambric, and it was possible to discern that there were breasts beneath.

'May I sit, Your Majesty?' She kept her voice low, and even.

Louis' tongue came out, for just a moment, touched his upper lip, and was withdrawn again. He nodded.

Geneviève sat on one of the chairs, drew off each boot in turn. She took off her garters, rolled down her stockings, left them on the floor, and wriggled her toes.

'By God,' said the King.

Geneviève stood up, released her belt, slowly slid the breeches down past her thighs. The shirt came well below her crotch, but no one could any longer doubt he was looking at a woman. She stepped out of the breeches, stood straight.

'Does the lieutenant please you, Sire?' Conti asked.

The King's head turned, slowly, and then came straight again.

'The shirt,' he said, his voice thick.

'Humour His Majesty, Charles.'

Geneviève unbuttoned the shirt, moving now with haste. It fell open and she heard the King catch his breath. A shrug of her shoulders removed the garment altogether, and she laid it on top of her other clothes, inhaling as she did so to fill her lungs to their greatest capacity.

'What is the meaning of this?' the King demanded.

Geneviève remained standing absolutely still, as Conti had instructed, breathing slowly and evenly, praying that the uneasy surging of her heart was not visible.

'Meaning, Sire?' Conti came closer. 'Why, Sire, you have here but a girl. But is she not the most beautiful creature you have ever seen?'

'Beautiful,' the King muttered. Slowly he came across the room, until he was standing immediately in front of her. His hand came out, touched her shoulder, slid down her arm to the elbow, then fell away. 'But dressed as a man?'

'Circumstances have made it so, Sire. And she can play the man, too. She handles a sword or commands the use of a pistol with the best. And she wishes only to serve Your Majesty, in whatever guise you may decide.'

The King continued to stare at Geneviève. Then his hand came out again, gently took her left nipple between thumb and forefinger; it was hard enough in any event as the room was cool, but now she thought it would burst with swelling. 'By God,' he said again. 'She is *yours*, Uncle François?'

'On the contrary, Sire. She is yours.'

'But you have had the use of her.'

'I, Sire? My God, no. She is as virginal as the day she was born.'

The King released the nipple. 'Speak,' he said.

'I wish only to serve Your Majesty,' Geneviève said.

'A lovely voice, to go with a lovely body,' the King said. 'Oh, you are a clever rogue, Uncle François. But the Pompadour would never stand for it.'

'How would she know, Sire? Suppose . . . let us suppose you were so attracted by the talents of this young man that you made him an aide-de-camp? No one would ever discern his true sex, believe me, as he has successfully continued this disguise all of his life. And what *pleasure* you could have.'

The King allowed him another quick glance. '*Pleasure?* Does the creature know aught of pleasure?'

'Your Majesty has but to command,' Conti said.

The King gazed at Geneviève again for a moment, then quite without warning he seized her pubic bush. She had not observed the movement of his hand, as she had been looking into his eyes and nowhere else, and she was taken by surprise, as much by the force of the blow, which winded her, as by its nature, for while he closed his hand on her entire groin, it seemed, his forefinger went further, probing between her legs, reaching for those regions she had never investigated even for herself.

She gasped, but remained still. He is but a man, she reminded herself, a contemptible creature who seeks to impose his will upon me. I will rise above him, as I will rise above all men, the moment he has displayed his full armoury.

'Kiss me,' the King commanded, moving his finger to and fro.

She hesitated for a moment, then took his face between her hands and kissed him on the mouth, allowing her tongue to roll gently round his lips before seeking a way past his teeth. My God, she thought, suppose he bites me? But instead his other arm went round her in turn, hugging her close, while the constantly moving finger had her suddenly aware of a fear that he would stop, before . . . but she knew nothing of what to expect.

The King's mouth moved away. 'Sometimes,' he muttered against her ear, 'I wish to hurt, and hurt, and hurt.'

The grip on her groin tightened, the finger was hurting as

much as it was arousing, and yet, it was arousing. She gazed at Conti over the King's shoulder, saw his mouth moving. 'Passion,' he was whispering. 'Show passion.'

Show passion. But suddenly, and quite without warning, it was no longer necessary to act. Her groin seemed to explode, and the explosion spread outwards into her belly and thence her breast to encompass her brain. Her knees gave way, and she almost fell, was sustained only by the King's hand, but the hand itself was being withdrawn, and so she clung to his shoulders until her strength returned, and he brought his mouth back in front for another kiss, before pushing her away.

She leaned against the table, reaching for breath, aware that her face was flaming, aware that he must be able to hear the pounding of her heart, aware more than anything else that men had a weapon of which she had never dreamed, a weapon which was going to require much more resistance than a mere penis.

But that too had to be encountered. For the King was taking off his jacket. 'Leave us, Conti,' he said. 'Leave us. Tell them I will rejoin the levée in half an hour. Leave us.'

The Prince bowed, allowed Geneviève but a single quick smile of triumph, and left the room.

Chapter Three

The door had barely closed when Louis seized Geneviève once again. His hands went round her back, and she was plucked from against the table and hugged against him. She searched for his lips, but now he was more intent on satisfying himself and seemed to be trying to tear her buttocks apart, squeezing and pulling, while his fingers went between. His face had fallen to her breasts, and he was sucking and licking at her nipples, so hard that she thought he would draw blood. She clung to his head and attempted to stop herself over-balancing. God in Heaven, she thought, as the first renewed surge of passion seeped through her groin; I must not surrender as easily as before. This lecherous king will make me his slave.

She shuddered, and her knees gave way. This time there was nothing to hold on to, save the king's head, and as she tumbled forward he fell backwards until he was sitting. Over his face she went, thrusting her hands in front of herself to stop crashing into the floor, but still hitting it with a considerable thump which had her twisting her head to look at the door, expecting it to burst open and expose them to the gaze of the crowd in the adjoining room – and what a sight it would be, the King of France seated on the floor with a naked girl draped over his shoulder.

But no doubt the courtiers of Versailles were used to such antics, or they were assuming it was part of the remarkable prowess she was displaying. The door remained closed, and she managed to roll away from him, sitting herself on the cold parquet, still panting for breath, still overwhelmed by the suddenness and completeness of her surrender.

'You are magnificent,' the King said. 'You are obsessed with a desire for love, my dear . . .' He smiled at her. 'What is your real name?'

'Geneviève, Your Majesty.'

'D'Éon?'

'Yes, Your Majesty.'

'Geneviève d'Éon de Beaumont. You are a treasure.' He scrambled to his feet, began undressing. 'Assist me.'

Another new experience, to be undressing a man. But at least she was familiar with what she was encountering, in form if not in substance. She had not supposed such magnificent clothes could be made, and her wonder only grew as she approached his smalls, every one in cambric of the finest quality. She knelt to remove his shoes and stockings, and then, as he had ceased to do anything himself and was merely standing there, she released his breeches and slipped them down to his ankles. And with a great effort controlled a shudder. Younger than Jules' certainly, but none the less huge and erect, seeming to jump at her, and to throb with the blood pulsing into it.

'Does it please you?'

'Your Majesty, I . . . I am overwhelmed.'

'Then show it. Hug me. Kiss me. Love me.'

Love that? Geneviève thought. May God have mercy on my soul. But there was nothing for it, and he was at the least delightfully clean from the powders and pomades with which he had been annointed. She kissed it, and as he moved with pleasure and held her head in turn, took it into her mouth, which but seemed to increase his delight.

'Bite me,' he whispered. 'Bite me.'

It seemed incredible that he should wish such punishment, but she gave him a gentle nip, and his entire body rocked.

'Oh, wretched girl,' he sighed. 'Terrible maiden, to cause a man so much pain. Again, bitch, again.'

She obeyed, and nearly choked as his jerk sent him half down her throat. Then he was away, she had rocked back on her heels, and he was gesturing her up.

'Haste, girl, haste. I will have your maidenhead now. Haste.'

As she got to her feet, he seized her arm and jerked her towards the nearest settee. She fell over it, rolled on her back, and he was kneeling above her, pushing her knees apart. His face was as suffused as his penis, and he was panting, his chest surging. Here then, she thought, is what I have feared and wanted all of my life. It will hurt me, and I will hate him, and then I shall conquer him. Because there it was, a light touch at first, followed by a consuming thrust, which had her jerking in pain, followed by a rapid sawing up and down, while he gasped and dribbled saliva out of his mouth and she supposed him the most disgusting object she had ever seen until she recalled that he was but a man, and all men must look alike at these moments.

But then she was lost in her own passion, suddenly swelling upwards from between her legs as she had felt earlier, reducing her to an equal gasping, leaving her awaiting only the climax, and aware of a mounting anger as she felt the warmth of his own orgasm gushing into her, when the humping ceased and he lay on her chest, crushing her beneath his weight, with her body still a seethe of unsatisfied desire.

'By God,' he whispered. 'By God. I have not felt such a surge in years. By God. How old are you, girl?'

'Eighteen, Your Majesty,' she gasped. She did not suppose she could ask a king to move.

'Eighteen,' he murmured. 'Geneviève, my Geneviève.'

His body was absolutely flaccid, its weight redoubled, pinning her to the settee. Between her legs was no less flaccid, and his eyes were half closed. Here was vulnerability. But was she not equally vulnerable? If he had been able to do with his penis what he had earlier accomplished with his finger, would she not also be lying here, incapable of movement or even thought? Yet her temporary advantage should be taken care of. 'Have I pleased Your Majesty?'

He kissed her ear. 'You have pleased me.'

'Then may I stay at your side? I desire only to serve.'

Now his head moved, and a moment later he pushed himself up. She could breathe again. But now she did not want to. Had she been too bold?

'You are Conti's creature.'

'Sire, I . . .'

'Do not trouble to deny it, my dear. I am not accusing you. I am making a point. Would you transfer your allegiance from him to me?'

A trap. She was sure of it. She gained time by sitting up, throwing one leg over the other in what she hoped was an attractive movement.

'The Prince of Conti is my benefactor, Your Majesty. I cannot be otherwise than eternally grateful to him. But it was also his wish that I should serve Your Majesty. And he gave me to understand that should I accomplish such an ambition, then I was to regard myself as yours, in every way.'

He stood immediately in front of her, placed his hands on her head to tilt it back so that he could look into her eyes. 'You are a shrewd child. As Conti is a shrewd uncle. And yet I think it would be no bad thing to have a slight counterpoise, especially as it can be accomplished privily. You will understand that I will not recognise you as a mistress?'

'I wish only to serve,' she assured him.

He nodded. 'And you will do so, as a special aide-de-camp. You will have an apartment within the palace, and you will be at my side, always. But your sex must remain a secret between the three of us . . .' He frowned. 'What of personal attendants?'

'I have a man, Your Majesty.'

'A man, by God.'

'Who was my father's servant before mine, and has known the secret of my sex since my birth,' she lied.

'Hum. A secret shared between four is very seldom a secret for very long.'

'The secret has been kept between three for a long time, Sire. *You* are the recent addition.'

He frowned at her, and then smiled, took her hands and raised her to her feet. 'There will have to be five; my valet Bertrand.'

'Sire?' she cried, recalling how the Prince had referred to Bertrand as Pompadour's creature.

'He is entirely trustworthy, in my affairs, and he will have to know. I want you near me, at all times. Nothing more than that.

5

Mark me well, Geneviève. No intrigues. No reporting back to the Prince. No quarrelling with Richelieu, or with Madame de Pompadour.'

'And will she not quarrel with me, Your Majesty?'

'Not while you play the man. This is your charge. Fail me in this, and I shall give you to her. She would like that, and you would not.'

She kept her face still and her voice even. 'I understand, Your Majesty.'

'Then put out your tongue.'

She hesitated, then obeyed, and he touched it with his own.

'Now help me dress; we have been absent from the levée for too long as it is.'

So what have I accomplished, she wondered? I have lost my virginity, which was part of my plan. And to a king. I have learned that I possess a weakness, but one which is common to both men and women, and therefore, if I can control it, I will be the stronger for it. I have achieved my master's immediate goal, and am therefore well placed in his esteem. I have certainly a more prosperous existence than ever before, with quarters in Versailles itself, with no military duties to attend to – she was not even present when her regiment marched off to the wars – with all I can eat and drink and ample funds for living the life of which I have always dreamed.

Save that she could not live that life, but must persist in her subterfuge. Did she regret that? Would she ever know how to act the woman, how to simper and submit, rather than to hate? Because if to achieve a way of life where she could stop hating was *her* goal, she was no nearer that accomplishment. She had gained not a single friend, for neither the King nor the Prince could be so considered; the one was amused by her, the other regarded her as useful. For the rest, while the ordinary courtiers accepted her as a rather mysterious new attachment of the King's, she had neither the birth nor the wealth to interest the men in any way, and if several of the women were obviously attracted by her looks, she dared not risk encouraging any of them. Besides, they were all creatures of the Pompadour, and *she* clearly regarded her master's new toy with the utmost contempt. Which was all to the good. But it left her with only Jules to confide in, and how could anyone confide in Jules? He was no longer even a mystery and a temptation. He would be exactly like the King, as every man would be exactly like the King. There was nothing to be learned from him, and he was no object to be conquered. Because she knew now that to rise above mankind must depend far more upon her brain than upon any physical abilities, or even upon her beauty. There were, as the Prince had truly said, too many beauties at court.

But there were too many acute brains as well, and backed by wealth and power. How could a mere eighteen-year-old girl-playing-boy hope to equal such, much less rise above them? For the first time in her life she wondered if she had not attempted to climb too high, if a quiet home and a fat middle-aged husband in Cherbourg might not have been the wiser course.

In fact, she had very little time *to* brood on the difficulties of her position. She had never supposed it could be possible to be so busy doing so very little. She was allowed her nights to herself, as long as the King was either tired or sleeping with the Pompadour. But often enough, when he left his mistress's bed and returned to his own, he was unsatisfied, and would send Bertrand to fetch her. Then for an hour or two she must submit to his peculiar fancies, which consisted of everything he dared not do to the Pompadour, who was, it appeared, a very proper lady. Therefore it was Geneviève's duty sometimes to be spanked with the flat of his hand, sometimes to be entered as if she were a dog, sometimes to use the pot before him, and sometimes merely to walk up and down the room, while he sat on the edge of the bed and watched her. Her body, such a strange mixture of hard muscles and budding femininity, clearly attracted him as no other woman had ever done. As for being humiliated by his outrageous demands, she thought nothing of them. She regarded her beauty as a weapon, and if she was having to use it as a bludgeon rather than a rapier, for the time being, then her only concern was that it should not be tarnished or injured in any way, and for all his vices, Louis was not a brutal man.

Satisfying the King was the smallest part of her duties, which were those of constant attendance. So that if he despatched her back to her quarters by four of the morning, it was necessary for Jules to have her back in the royal bedchamber, fully dressed in her dragoon uniform, by half past seven, standing stiffly to attention beside the enclosure which surrounded the bed, while Bertrand arranged for his cot – in which he slept at the foot of his master all night except when Geneviève was actually present – to be removed. And they listened to the whisper of sound as the antechamber without filled with anxious courtiers.

As the clock struck eight, Bertrand, who had spent the previous fifteen minutes outside collecting various petitions for the King, and arranging them in order of the bribes he received, opened the doors, entered the bedroom, and threw up the white and gold blinds. The drapes were then drawn, and His Majesty was gently awakened. Throughout this ceremony, and for the next hour, Geneviève was not permitted to move, but had to stand at the strictest attention, the King's personal bodyguard.

First into the room there came all the princes of the blood, this part of the morning's ceremony being known as the *entrée familière*. They invariably ignored her, even the Prince of Conti when he was present, while they gathered around the bed and gave the morning's greetings to their master. Once this was done there took place the *grande entrée*, the entrance of the great lords. By now the King was entirely awake, and he would sit on the edge of the bed while Bertrand hung his gown around his shoulders and placed his slippers on his feet. Once he was thus dressed the lesser nobles, all those who had secured a brief of admittance, were allowed into the room, and they were followed by the captain of the guard and the other officers. It was now at last Geneviève's turn to move, as she was required to fetch the King's shirt, which she handed to the senior person present, which was occasionally even the Prince of Conti, according to the state of affairs at the moment. The Prince in turn assisted the King into the garment, and this procedure was repeated with each of the King's clothes, until he was fully dressed. Geneviève then offered a tray on which were His Majesty's cravat pins, and from which he made a personal selection, as he did with his wig. It was then time for him to be shaved, and the barber surgeon was duly admitted, but Louis only indulged in this every other day.

Once the King's toilet was complete, Geneviève returned to attention, and the doors were thrown wide so that everyone else waiting in the antechamber could be admitted; the bedchamber now became very crowded indeed, with sometimes two hundred people present, lining the walls three and four deep. Now it was time for the royal watchmaker to wind the King's watch, and the royal chaplain to rehearse the day's prayers, while Louis knelt on his stool. Thence everyone trooped off to Mass, Geneviève amongst them, leaving the royal upholsterers to make the bed, which was guarded by one of the inferior valets until the evening.

Mass finished, the King breakfasted and then retired to his study with his chief ministers to carry out the day's business, reading the despatches and issuing the commands which would eventually affect the lives of everyone in the country, and Geneviève was at last released to have her own breakfast and sit down for a while, before it was time to attend the King at his dinner. Here, for the first time in the day, they made the acquaintance of the Queen. Indeed, on her first day as personal aide-de-camp, it was at this meal that Geneviève saw Her Majesty for the first time.

Maria Leszczynski was forty, seven years older than her husband. She was by no means an ugly woman, and as she had lived in Alsace since the age of six, when her father had lost the Polish crown, she was perfectly at home in both the French language and French customs. Therefore she knew her part as a wife, if not quite as a mother, was history, and in fact this meal was the only one at which she saw her husband. Not that Louis ever exchanged a word with her save for his initial greeting. Dinner seemed to bore him, as it bored Geneviève, who was at least not forced to eat any of the food, which was invariably cold by the time it arrived at the royal table, having been carried from the kitchen and across the roadway, up the great staircase, and through all the enormous reception rooms before finally being placed upon the table. The lengthy journey was extended because everyone who encountered the procession had to salute it. Even when it was placed before Louis, he could not immediately eat. Monsieur *le maître d'Hôtel*, who had marched in front of the waiters, first bowed to the King and ceremonially presented the scented napkin – which had to be renewed between each course – and then each dish, before serving, was tasted by its bearer for fear of poison. The King's wine was tasted *twice,* and while he drank, a saucer was held under the goblet.

The King and the Queen were the only people seated for dinner, or indeed eating at all. The remainder of the throng – and anyone who was at least reasonably dressed could attend the royal dinner – stood against the walls and looked on, save for Geneviève, who stood at the King's shoulder. She was introduced to the Queen at their first meeting, and Maria actually gave her a smile, but after that occasion there was no further conversation as the King did not care for it. But

Geneviève could not help but reflect that if all the time wasted in ceremony were to be applied to business, the kingdom must benefit. She ventured this opinion to the King, and to her surprise he agreed. 'But the ceremonial was decreed by the Great Louis,' he said. 'It would require a revolution to change it. And I am in no mood to start a revolution, my sweet child.'

Dinner completed, the King went stag hunting, as it was now autumn. Here was far more pleasure than standing rigidly to attention around draughty corridors. Geneviève was reminded less of a hunt than a royal pageant, for the ladies of the court insisted upon following the route, dressed in their best habits, every one accompanied by a party of gentlemen, while the whole was surrounded by a platoon of brilliantly clad guards, and all hallooing behind the hounds and the huntsmen, braying the morning with their horns. It was a madcap, tumultuous three hours, which ruined a great deal of splendid countryside as well as at least one splendid beast, while woe betide any unfortunate human who found himself or herself in front of the charge; things went hard enough with those of the hunt who happened to be dismounted; not a week went by without some unfortunate being forced to abandon court life for a while with a broken shoulder or worse.

The hunt completed, Louis generally allowed his son to pay him a visit. His daughter, Marie Louise, had already been married to the Duke of Parma and was seldom seen at court. The younger Louis, who was in fact a year younger than Geneviève herself, was a studious, thoughtful youth who appeared to disapprove of his father. He seldom accompanied the hunt, and always seemed more than glad to escape the daily audience.

The King too was happy enough to see it end, for it was now that he attended the Pompadour for the first time, although this was scarcely for amatory purposes. It was at these evening meetings that he discussed affairs of state with his inner cabinet, those ministers who had jointly raised the fishwife to her position of eminence, and who were the real rulers of France. Geneviève was of course not required on such occasions, although often enough the King discussed what had been said with her during one of their early morning romps. At eight o'clock it was time for the evening's entertainments to begin, and these were strictly divided between the available weekdays.

On Mondays, Wednesdays and Fridays, the King enjoyed a theatrical performance; on the other days he held what was known as an 'apartment', when he would play cards or billiards, and listen to music; it was on these occasions that foreign ambassadors were able to exchange a word or an idea with him. The Pompadour was of course always present, as was Geneviève, the one to play and smile and be witty, and the other as usual to stand rigidly to attention. Occasionally there was a ball, but the King was not very fond of them, nor indeed was anyone else, for by ten of the evening they were all usually so exhausted they could think only of their beds.

It was now that the King began to think of the Pompadour's charms, although even he did not attend his mistress every night. She invariably supped with him at ten o'clock, and then they both retired, whether separately or together. Geneviève also retired, by herself, immediately after supper and remained in bed until either summoned by Bertrand for his master, or by Jules for her daily round. It was the most exhausting and enervating timetable she could imagine, and by the evenings her legs were almost unable to support her any longer. Indeed, as time went on, she could not help but wonder exactly what she was at. No doubt she was an invaluable source of information to the Prince of Conti, who would often visit her after midnight, and would sit on the edge of her bed for all the world as if he was her lover, while she endeavoured to remember what the King had said to the Duke of Vendôme, and what the Duke of Vendôme had said to the King. But she was invariably so tired she doubted she was being quite as successful a spy as he had hoped. As for herself, she suddenly discovered her life entirely sterile, and her future more so. The King seemed pleased enough; he gave not the slightest indication of ever being bored with her, and she did not suppose he would, as long as she continued to debase herself in whichever direction his mood happened to take him. But neither did he ever give the slightest indication of being in love with her, except in a purely physical fashion. As she grew to know him better, of course, she understood that he was not really in love with anyone except himself.

One morning she stood stiffly to attention, as usual, beside the King's bed, and watched a tall, thin man, with hatchet features and piercing black eyes, enter the room close behind the royal princes, and make his way straight to the King, to be greeted almost with a shout of joy. 'Why, Richelieu, my dear, dear fellow. Versailles has not been the same without you.'

Geneviève realised that she was in the presence, at last, of Louis François Armand du Plessis, Duc de Richelieu, Marshal of France, and grand-nephew of the great cardinal. But this minister was a soldier rather than a priest, who had covered himself with glory at both Dettingen and Fontenoy, and had thereby earned himself the position of the King's most trusted confidante. As he was the Prince of Conti's most bitter enemy. As he was also, it was reputed, the most licentious man in all France, not excluding even the King.

And would he also be her enemy? He had kissed the King's hand, and now straightened. 'I have not lived, this past month, Sire, away from your side. But now I am returned, and I shall not go again, you may be certain of it.' He half turned his head, glanced at Geneviève, but it was a glance which took her in from head to foot, had her cursing the sudden heat in her cheeks as she supposed he could see through her jacket to the swell of her breasts. 'I am happy to understand that Your Majesty has prospered during my absence,' the Duke continued. 'Even to the extent of accumulating new toys.'

'New toys, Armand? New toys?' The King gave a nervous laugh. 'I have no time for toys. I have a new champion, if that is what you mean.'

'A boy?' Richelieu's tone was scathing.

'Who handles a sword like a master. Who is a master, indeed. You must take a turn with him, my Lord Duke.'

'I, Sire? I fight with men. I but find it strange that one of Conti's catamites should have pleased you.'

'Tut, tut, my Lord Duke. I must beg you to be more circumspect in your choice of words, especially where they concern my dear uncle. As for young d'Éon, I can assure you that *he* at the least is no catamite.'

'Then I withdraw my suggestion without reservation, Your Majesty,' the Duke said. Louis allowed Geneviève a quick glance of his own, and even a wink. He seemed to be enjoying the game that was being played, but she was terrified, suddenly aware of the Duke's piercing gaze whenever she turned her head.

She confessed as much to Conti, when next he visited her chamber. 'It is his eye, my lord. I swear it reveals a brain which will stop at nothing to attain its end.'

68

'Indeed you are right, my dear child,' the Prince agreed. He did not seem to be terribly concerned. 'We are approaching the crux of the matter.'

'My Lord?'

'If Richelieu supposes you to be a catamite, then in his opinion you will remain a catamite. You may depend upon it he will bring all his powers of persuasion to bear upon the King to send you away from court.'

'But my lord . . .'

'There is no saying he will succeed, Charles. Therefore I say we are approaching the climax of our endeavours. Oh, Louis is a weak and undecided man. But if anything will eventually decide him it will be the call of his loins. Do you not make him happy?'

'I believe so, my lord.'

'Well, then, we shall shortly find out whether or not you make him happier than the Pompadour.'

'But suppose I do not, my lord?'

He chucked her under the chin. 'One must never think of failure when undertaking a great enterprise. Just be sure that the next time you are summoned to the royal bed you excel yourself.

The opportunity was presented that very night, as at four in the morning Betrand presented himself at her door, and summoned her. 'His Majesty does not sleep,' he said.

Geneviève hastily splashed some water on her face, made sure her body was sufficiently perfumed, wrapped herself in her dressing gown over her nightshirt, and followed the valet along the secret passageways which connected her room with the King's apartments. Bertrand opened the innermost door to admit her, then closed it and sat himself on the chair outside.

A single candle burned by the bedside, but the drapes were drawn. Geneviève tiptoed across the room, slowly parted the brocade. Her heart thumped, but it was no longer with the uncontrolled pounding of the anxious maiden, only the concern of the experienced whore, she thought, that tonight she must surpass herself.

'Geneviève,' Louis said. 'Oh, my darling Geneviève. Come here.'

She slipped off her robe, lifted her nightshirt over her head, stepped out of her slippers and knelt beside him. He reached up to tickle her nipples, and sent shivers of distaste down her spine. As she assumed everything he wished to do to her was something the Pompadour had rejected, presumably *she* did not like

69

having her nipples tickled either. Indeed, Geneviève could not imagine a woman who would enjoy so feeble a pastime.

'You are anxious,' he said. For he held the theory that a woman's readiness for love could be judged by the tumescence of her breasts rather as a man's, more accurately, by the erection of his penis.

She allowed him a roguish smile. 'The nights grow cold, Sire.'

'And they would rob me of your warmth.' His hand slid up her arm to her shoulder, and he pulled her on to his chest. But his words had such a numbing effect on her brain she forgot to break her fall, and he gasped as she collapsed on to his belly.

'Sire?' She could not keep the alarm from her voice.

'Oh, they suspect nothing. You may be sure of that. Nothing of your sex.' He massaged her bottom, and this she liked. She nestled against him and felt him rise into her groin. The trouble with these early morning encounters was that she took some time to wake up. 'But they think the worst of me – that I am indulging a homosexual passion.' He nipped her ear. 'Is that not droll?'

'They, Sire?'

'Richelieu. He does not care for you.'

'Indeed, Sire, I find it difficult to care for him.'

The King smiled; she could feel his breath rushing against her ear. 'Who knows, you might well do so, given the chance. *His* amours are omnivorous, and you are a pretty lad, eh? His dislike stems entirely from the fact that you are Conti's creature. You would not consider switching your allegiance?'

Once again, a trap. How could she concentrate upon outdoing herself if he kept throwing questions like that at her? And what was she to reply?

'Would you value me the more, Sire, as a turncoat who constantly changed his allegiance?'

He rolled her off him, rose on his elbow to look down at her. 'You are a faithful child, Geneviève d'Éon. But faith is not always the wisest course.'

'I am faithful to you above all others, Sire. Tell me what you would have me do, and I will endeavour to please you.'

He gazed at her for some seconds, then lay down again. 'I shall have to consider the matter. I would not have you betray Uncle François. I am not sure it is best for me to be surrounded only by the members of a single party, and until your coming I did not know how to avoid such a state of affairs. But I will not be nagged.' His tone was suddenly petulant. 'Richelieu nags,

Vendôme nags. Pompadour nags. You never nag me, Geneviève.'

'I am here to please you, Sire.'

'Sweet girl.' He moved his hand up and down her stomach, sifting the soft hairs surrounding her pubes, sliding across her rib cage to her breasts . . . but he remained soft, and suddenly she realised that she was going to be given no opportunity for surpassing herself, at least this night.

Unless she took the initiative. With a king? But if she did not, Conti would be angry.

'Sire,' she said, reaching for him. But he caught her wrists.

'I have awakened you for nothing.'

'Oh, but Sire . . .'

'It is the nagging. And I am tired. So very tired. It is Richelieu. Where he gets his energy I cannot suppose. It is do this and do that every moment of the day. Sign this and decide that. Order this and punish that. I do believe the country prospered during his illness just because there was less government. My God, I am tired.'

'It is my duty to be here when you are tired, Sire, to lie with you and give you comfort. Why do you not just rest your head on my shoulder, and see if you can sleep?'

'I can sleep,' he said. 'I will now. The better for seeing you, my own little dove. I do adore you. Adore you, adore you, adore you.' He took her face between his hands and kissed her on the mouth. 'But I need my sleep. Be off with you, and be sure you are here at my awakening.'

'Of course, Your Majesty.' She rose to her knees, still uncertain whether he wanted her to obey him, or whether she should press the matter, but even as she looked at him his eyes flopped shut and he gave a gentle snore. If this was a failure, then she had most certainly failed. But he had said he adored her. Three times. And she dared not take the risk of angering *him*.

Very gently she slipped off the bed, drew the drapes once again, scooped up her nightshirt and dropped it over her shoulders, thrust her toes into her slippers, draped her undressing robe about her shoulders. She tiptoed to the door, brushed her knuckles against it, and gazed at Bertrand. His mouth opened in surprise, but she touched her lips with her forefinger and stepped outside. 'His Majesty is exhausted.'

He nodded. 'I had supposed so. I am sorry, mademoiselle, for awakening you.'

'I am at the King's call,' she said piously. 'I will bid you good night.'

He kissed her hand, and went into the room himself, to take his place as watchdog at the foot of the royal bed. Geneviève made her way along the darkened corridors, stifling a yawn, in her heart only too pleased at having avoided intercourse for this night at least. She rounded a corner, and then another, knew there was only one remaining before her own bedchamber, and came face to face with a man.

The surprise was so complete she stepped back in alarm, and bumped into another man, standing immediately behind her. This one scized her round the waist, while his other hand came up to hold her throat, squeezing it so hard she could utter not a sound. Desperately she kicked, her endeavour to scream causing a highpitched humming sound in her brain, but the man in front of her caught her legs easily enough and she was afraid to kick too hard in case the skirt of her nightshirt rode up. Whatever can they want, here in the palace, she wondered, her brain teeming? But she was the King's personal attendant. They'd not dare harm her fifty feet from his door. Yet they were carrying her, down a side corridor, and through an opened door into a small antechamber, lit by a single candle, in which there waited another man. She turned her head, from left to right, endeavouring to ascertain exactly where she was, and gazed at the Duc de Richelieu.

'Fetch the pear,' he said.

The man holding her legs released them, and they dropped to the floor with a thump. The other man still held her round the waist, and as she endeavoured to turn, he forced her into a chair and held her there, while she discovered his fellow standing immediately in front of her, in his hand what indeed looked like a ripe pear, but she realised it was made of wood and divided into two halves secured together with a spring.

The Duke drew his dagger, also stood before her. 'Keep still, wretch,' he said. 'Or it will be the worse for you.'

Geneviève gasped for breath, as the fingers slowly left her throat, 'You . . .'

'Quiet, boy,' the Duke said, so threateningly she hesitated, and had her chin seized again. This time the fingers ate into the base of her jaw with such force her mouth opened in spite of itself; the man with the wooden pear thrust it between her teeth.

She made a gigantic effort to expel it, but already the spring was released. Instantly the pear seemed to double in size, driving her tongue flat at the bottom of her mouth and itself pressing against the top, so that she all but choked as she was released.

'Secure him,' the Duke commanded, and the man who had been holding her head slipped his hands down her arms, jerked them behind the chair and looped round them a length of cord, which ate into her wrists even as it prevented movement. But her mouth was so uncomfortable as she strove for breath that she scarce felt it.

The Duke now bent his head close to her. 'Oh, you are a pretty boy,' Richelieu said. 'Had you truly been fortune's darling, you would have been found by myself, and you would have enjoyed a lifetime of sodomy. But I'll not have you, or that thing Conti, suborning the King. Bring the candle closer.'

The second man placed the candle on the table next to the Duke, and Geneviève remembered that her legs were free. She kicked at him, but he was wearing boots, and she only hurt her toes.

'They'll need securing as well,' Richelieu said, 'before we get down to business.'

Business, she thought wildly. What business? They meant to harm her, that was certain. But they'd not dare harm her. Not even Richelieu, surely. She discovered that despite the chill she was pouring sweat, and endeavoured to kick again, but the man knelt beside her, caught her right leg and tied it to the corresponding chair leg, before doing the same to her left, leaving her quite helpless as her arms were still secured behind the chair by the other man.

'Now, then,' Richelieu said. 'We are going to spoil your little game for you, sweet Monsieur d'Éon. Never more will you be permitted to abuse the royal backside. Have you the knife, Claude?'

'Mmmmm,' Geneviève shrilled, moving her head from side to side, straining her feet against the cords, feeling them begin to give, indeed, they had been tied so hastily, but still unable to move as the man behind her held her fast.

'Oh, aye, you shall scream, my pretty boy,' Richelieu promised her. 'But who shall hear your screams?' He frowned at her. 'There will be blood.' He stepped back, took off his sword belt and doublet, turned up his sleeves. 'I have never gelded a man before,' he said. 'It will be sport, but you will pardon me, monsieur, if I am a trifle clumsy.' He felt the edge of the knife blade with his thumb. 'And I do promise you that I will crop you short, dear boy. Not a sign will be left that you were ever a man at all. Press down there, or he will have the chair over.'

The man behind her released her wrists and instead held her shoulders and pressed her, and the chair, to the floor. Desperately she fumbled at the ill tied knots. Now she knew what they intended her fear had abated and she wished only to get free before they uncovered her secret. But she would not be in time. The Duke was kneeling before her, throwing aside her dressing robe and turning up the skirts of her nightshirt, and pausing in consternation at what he saw.

The man, Claude, holding the candle and peering over his shoulder, gave a shriek of the most utter terror, dropped the light, and ran for the door.

'Damnation,' Richelieu snapped. 'A woman, by God.' She heard him gasping for breath as he drove the knife forward, and counted herself dead. But the man grasping her shoulders had also released her in alarm, and as she had been pressing against the floor with her feet the chair shot over backwards; toes caught Richelieu on the arm and he gave another curse as he dropped the knife.

Geneviève's head hit the floor with a bump which made her see stars, but in the same instant her wrists came free. She rolled to one side, on top of the man behind her, who had also lost his footing, causing him to grunt as the chair accompanied her, landed on her hands and knees, and released her ankles. She could still hear Richelieu cursing as he searched the room for her, but the candle had by now gone out, and the darkness was Stygian. She pulled the pear from her mouth, cautiously attempted to straighten, and brushed the table. On which the Duke had laid his rapier. She slid her hand across the top, found the weapon and the haft at the same moment as the man on the floor recovered himself and caught her ankle. She stamped down with her other foot, and he gave a grunt and rolled away again. Then she had drawn the blade, the rasp sounding terribly loud in the confined space.

'My sword,' Richelieu snapped, close at hand. She lunged in his direction, and he gave a startled gasp and obviously threw himself to one side. 'The candle,' he called. 'For God's sake light the candle.'

Geneviève listened to the sound of a door close. She could not be sure whether someone had come in or one of her assailants had left the room, but with a sword in her hand she felt perfectly equal to them, even when she heard the rasp of another blade being drawn. Carefully she left the table, endeavouring to remember the room, bumping into a chair but not losing her balance as she moved behind it and found herself against a wall.

'Only a girl, lads,' Richelieu was saying. 'Claude, are you there? Light the candle, man. Only a girl.'

Geneviève remained still, slowly inhaling and expelling her breath, keeping her body in balance, the sword at her side, as she had no intention of alerting anyone as to her exact whereabouts until she had to. Her fear was entirely past, and in fact had been replaced by a mood of exultant fury, much as she remembered experiencing when facing Monsieur Lannes; she was quite looking forward to the coming brawl. Her very first, in earnest. She never doubted she would triumph.

Tinder scraped, and a spark flew; she inhaled the oil soaked cloth a moment before it flared, and then the candle in turn was lit, and the cloth was dropped to the floor. The room came into light and shadow as Claude, for it had indeed been he, half out of the room, who had returned at his master's summons, held it above his head. Geneviève took in the situation at a glance. The third man stood about six feet to her right, his sword in his hand. Richelieu had retired to the far side of the room to her left; he had no sword but still carried the sharp bladed knife, and would be deadly at close quarters. And as she watched, Claude now also drew his sword, moving to his side to place the candle on a table.

'Only a girl,' Richelieu said again. 'Who pretends to some knowledge of swordsplay. Who'll bring her down?'

Geneviève thought she could very probably get across the room and kill him before the other two could reach her, but now that her emotions were under control she doubted that would be to her advantage. The King might well take her side in the matter, but not if she had just despatched his chief minister, even if she could claim self defence.

'Come on lads,' Richelieu was saying. 'She'll not match your strength. Would you be humiliated by a chit of a girl?'

Geneviève took a long breath, gave a shout, and leapt across the room, throwing off her dressing gown to leave herself only in the nightshirt which scarce came to her ankles and allowed her total freedom of movement. Claude gave an equal bellow, raised his own sword, and had it swept from side to side as he attempted to parry a series of savage thrusts and cuts which left him gasping and in scarce more than a second found his defence wanting; he was turning away from her as he endeavoured to retreat, but his blade failed to find hers and she sank her sword into his stomach, thrusting with such violence that it penetrated almost to the haft. Blood spurted over her fingers, and she gazed at it, and the suddenly ashen face in front of her, for some seconds before recollecting herself and pulling with all her strength.

Claude gave a stricken wail, fell to his knees, dropping his sword and clutching the terrible wound in his belly. Then he slumped forward and struck the floor with the most dreadfully final of sounds. Geneviève had already turned, and backed to the door, in anticipation of an assault by the third man. But he seemed struck at once by the speed of her assault and its deadly culmination, and merely stared at her with lowered blade.

Richelieu had also seen enough. He gave his servant a startled glance, and then ran for the inner door. 'Take her, Jerome,' he shouted as he wrenched it open and made for safety.

But Jerome clearly had no intention of fighting, save in self defence, and Geneviève wished only to escape. She opened the door behind her, stepped into the corridor, and realised that her blade was still dripping blood. Her blade? It belonged to the Duke himself. Well, she thought, he will have to reclaim it.

She ran down the hall, and only then discovered that she was weeping. Tears rolled down her cheeks and the salty taste got into her mouth. It was the first real assault to which she had ever been submitted. That they had supposed her a man made no difference to the brutality of it, and the obscenity they had intended. But *she* had killed a man. She had not meant to do that, could still hear Claude's ghastly wail as he realised he had been slain echoing in her ears. She had killed a man. And everyone would now know her secret, and would know, too, that she was a bravo. She would be a marked woman, at once hated and feared. And besides, she realised with heart stopping horror, she had made an enemy of Richelieu, the most powerful man in the land, after the King himself. She was doomed. Oh, why had she not killed *him?*

She reached her own door in a long gasp of terror, leaned against it, felt it open before her; Jules gazed at her in amazement, for she had allowed the sword to brush against her nightshirt.

'Monsieur?' he cried. 'You are hurt.'

She shook her head, stumbled inside. 'Fetch the Prince.'

'Monsieur? It is not yet five in the morning.'

'Fetch the Prince,' she shouted. 'It is a matter of life and death. Tell him so. All of our lives and deaths.'

Jules scratched his head. 'My life, at the least, if he is displeased,' he muttered. But he left the room, and Geneviève discovered that she *still* held Richelieu's sword. Her fingers were so tightly clamped about the haft it seemed she would never let it go. She prised them loose, finished cleaning the weapon on her nightshirt – the garment was ruined anyway – threw it and the cambric on the floor, and washed herself at her basin; she felt so bloody she upturned the ewer over her head and shoulders, allowing the water to splash on to the parquet flooring and form a puddle. Then she towelled herself, lay on the bed, staring at the ceiling.

What would happen now? The end of all her dreams? Could the king take her side openly, against Richelieu?

The door opened, and she sat up. Conti wore a nightcap and looked ridiculous. And anxious. 'Geneviève? The King is unwell?'

'No, my lord.'

'And you have summoned me from my bed for anything less? You, have summoned me? I will have you whipped. By God ...'

'If you will but listen, my lord, for a very few seconds.'

He glared at her, but gestured Jules to close the door. 'A very few seconds.'

Geneviève told him, as quickly as she could, what had happened, watched his anger fade into concern, and then into something very like fright. Her heart sank.

'My God,' he said when she was finished. 'My God. I had not supposed Richelieu would go so far. You killed one of them, you say?'

'I did.'

'And put Richelieu himself to flight?'

'He ran like a frightened kitten.'

'My God, my God. We are undone.'

'Not if you act promptly, my lord.' She took his hands. 'He will be at the present distressed about what has happened. He will be uncertain as to what he must do next, what he *can* do next. Now *is* our time to act, my lord. To go to the King, and tell him the whole facts of the matter. You wished to bring things to a crisis my lord. Here is your crisis. And happening to our advantage, when our enemies are in disarray.'

6

'You think so?' Conti demanded. 'You suppose Richelieu will be distressed at what has happened? Richelieu has never been distressed in his life. You suppose he will be uncertain? He does not know the meaning of the word. And you have made him look a fool. That is one crime he will never forget. He will have your blood if it takes him the rest of his life. You must flee. Aye, flee. Get yourself dressed. Have Jules saddle you a horse. And ride and ride and ride. There is your only hope.'

He was on his feet, his face writhing with excited passion. While she could only sit and stare, and feel her world crumbling about her.

'Flee, my lord?' she cried. 'And where in all France could I possible flee without the Duke of Richelieu finding me?'

'Aye.' His face grew sombre. 'That is true enough. You must flee abroad.'

'Abroad. But, my lord, I have no languages, save French, and a smattering of English. I have no friends, save you. I have no money . . .'

'In the name of God, girl, what would you have me do? I shall have trouble enough maintaining my own position when Richelieu flaunts this tale.'

'*Will* he flaunt it, my lord? You spoke of him feeling a fool.'

'*Should* he, then the King will be involved in the amusement. Louis will never stand for that. He places his dignity above all others. And I am the author of this escapade. I will be sent to the Bastille. At the very least I will be exiled to my estates for the rest of my life.' He hesitated, looking at her. 'Should you escape Richelieu, you may well be sent to the Bastille, too. It is not a place for women. Oh, no, you would not like that'

'And you will do nothing to save me,' Geneviève said. 'And yourself? A single bold act now, and Richelieu, and Pompadour, might be displaced forever.'

Conti chewed his lip. 'I dare not,' he said. 'To tilt at Richelieu? He is a very devil. I dare not.'

Geneviève's belly seemed to fill with lead. She had never truly felt much more for the Prince than contempt. But she had never supposed he would so easily desert her, when she had done nothing more than play the role he had chosen. But she now realised, if he was so terrified of Richelieu, that she had been a sacrificial goat in any event; supposing she had so pleased the King he would himself have overturned the Pompadour, well and good. Supposing she did not, as she had not, then her

78

eventual fate was certain in any event, and at the very moment Richelieu returned to the Court.

Well, then, she wondered, was she merely going to submit, and be destroyed? Place her own neck on the block? Be what Conti undoubtedly supposed she was, a simple girl from the very lowest order of nobility, quite unable to make her way in the world of men? Would that not be a betrayal of herself, of all her hopes and ambitions, of her belief in herself? Would it not be better to *risk* the block to survive?

'Then it seems I must fend for myself, my lord,' she said, keeping her voice even. '*I* will go to the King, immediately.'

'The King?' He goggled at her. 'You cannot. You dare not.'

'I must,' she said. 'I will not lie down before Richelieu's assassins. I must risk all to gain all. His Majesty is fond of me. I know that. I will beg his protection. Richelieu will not tilt against that.'

'You are mad, mad, he cried, and caught her arm as she made to open the door. 'Do you really suppose His Majesty will risk a quarrel with Richelieu, supported as the Duke will be by the Pompadour? My dear girl, had he been going to do that he would have finished the matter already, while the Duke was ill.'

Geneviève hesitated, biting her lip.

'And besides, you will involve me in your ruin,' the Prince insisted. 'Our only hope is to melt away, out of sight as well as out of mind.'

But he had entirely restored *her* hope. If he was prepared to desert her, then she must be prepared to blackmail him. 'I have no hope, save from the King,' she pointed out. 'Therefore if I must involve you in my ruin, then I must. I will *not* die without at least trying to live.'

His turn to chew his lip. 'Wait,' he said. 'Wait. Let me think. You are a good girl. Oh, indeed, a good girl. You have served me faithfully and well. It would not be proper of me to abandon you.'

Geneviève shrugged her arm free, but she did not open the door. She could afford to wait.

Conti slapped his right fist into his left hand. 'There is an embassy leaving the day after tomorrow. That is the ticket. I will secrete you for the twenty-four hours, and you will depart with the Embassy. The Chevalier Douglas is the head. You will like the Chevalier. A Scot, to be sure, but a trifle more refined than most of that barbarous nation. There. Is not your every problem solved?'

Geneviève frowned at him. 'An embassy, my lord?'

'Indeed. Do you not see, Richelieu may be all powerful within France, but at a foreign capital, why, you will have little to fear. Especially ... yes ...' He began to stroke his chin. 'I have the very thing.'

'*Which* foreign capital, my lord, if I may be so bold?'

'Ah ...' He gave her a sidelong glance. 'To St Petersburg.'

'Saint ... ?'

'Russia,' he explained. 'You cannot possibly be farther away from France than in Russia.'

Slowly Geneviève sank on to her bed. 'Russia?' she whispered. 'St Petersburg? With winter coming on?'

'Well, what would you?' Believe me, Versailles is sufficiently cold in winter. The Russians order things somewhat better. And in St Petersburg you will be safe. But there are certain requirements. You will go in your proper station.'

'My lord?'

'As a woman.'

'My lord? Why?'

'Because it is time you abandoned this foolish subterfuge.'

'And I will be better protected as a woman?'

'In Russia, yes. I have your interests at heart, my dear. It came to me as a flash. I will send you as a present to the Empress.'

'A present?'

'Aye. A lady in waiting. Believe me, she will adore you. She is the Great Peter's daughter, you know, and a woman of character. She could hardly adopt a visiting man, but a young woman, especially one who is forced to absent herself from France ...'

'A present?' Geneviève repeated, her voice rising. 'Am I a slave, to be given away as you choose?'

Conti wagged his finger at her. 'You are a young woman in a highly dangerous position, whom I am attempting to save,' he pointed out. 'Once you obtain the protection of the Empress of all the Russias, no man in the world will dare lift a finger against you, at least in Russia.'

Geneviève thrust both her hands into her hair, and thought of it. 'But ... my hair ...'

'Will grow on the journey. One does not travel from Paris to St Petersburg in a matter of days.'

'But ... suppose the Empress does not like me?'

'She will adore you. Because you are adorable, and because you will travel with a letter from me.'

'You know her, my lord?'

'Of course. Now, haste. You will leave Versailles now, and be in Paris by dawn. Jules will accompany you.'

'Begging your pardon, my lord, but am *I* to go to Russia?' Jules inquired. 'With monsieur?'

'You may. But mademoiselle will have to have a maid.' He chewed his lip. 'I will give you an address. Mademoiselle...and as of now, Jules, you must remember to call her mademoiselle ... will go there, to a lady who is a dear friend of mine. I will give you a note. Madame Sophie will see to all of your requirements, my dear. Clothes. You must have clothes, and they must be ready by tomorrow morning. Sophie will see to it.' He sat himself at Geneviève's writing cabinet and began scribbling away.

'But...' Geneviève realised she was still holding on to her hair. 'I do not know how to act the woman. I have never done so.'

'That too you will learn on your journey,' the Prince said, without raising his head. 'Madame Sophie will also discover you a maid, and she will teach you everything you need to know. Besides, surely it is but a matter of acting naturally, for the first time in your life?'

Geneviève stared at herself in the wall mirror opposite her bed. Acting naturally. Going to Russia, to the snow and the ice, to a court but recently emerged from the depths of barbarism. Going into exile, for that was what it amounted to. And being forced to act the woman. Exiled, never to return. Because...

'The King will never forgive me for just disappearing,' she said.

'I will make your peace with the King,' Conti promised. 'Believe me. I give you my word.'

For what *that* was worth. But what alternative did she have? She had insisted that the Prince help her, and he was doing the very best he could think of. Certainly she needed the time to think, to take stock of her position, to decide what must be done with her life. She was only eighteen. There was time. Supposing she could keep alive.

She smiled at him. 'Then it seems I must prepare to be a woman.'

Madame Sophie turned out, as Geneviève had suspected, to be, the owner of a large and well-appointed Parisian brothel. She was small, slight and intense woman, clearly a beauty in her day, and still by no means unattractive, for her bone structure was very fine, and her eyes and voice were unimpaired, while there was not a wisp of grey in her black hair.

'From the Prince of Conti?' She inspected Geneviève, going round the back for a better look. 'You'll not seek employment, monsieur?' She gave a roguish smile. 'Which is not to say that I could not earn you a fortune.'

'And yourself, no doubt, madame,' Geneviève replied. 'If you would be so good as to receive me privately, I have a letter from the Prince which will explain my situation, and my requirements.'

'Your requirements, indeed,' Sophie remarked, and inspected Jules in turn. 'You'll stay here, fellow,' she commanded, and led Geneviève up the stairs and along a corridor, off which opened several doors, and out of which there peeped a variety of young women in various stages of déshabille, for it was still not yet eight of the clock. But all made some complimentary remarks concerning Geneviève masculine attractions. 'In here,' Sophie said, opening one of the doors, and Geneviève stepped into a delightful boudoir into which the autumnal sun was just starting to flood, illuminating the gentle greens and yellows of the upholstery.

'Well?' Sophie closed the door.

Geneviève took the letter from her pocket, making sure she selected the right one, for the Prince had also entrusted her with an epistle to the Russian Empress. And as she was destined for womanhood in any event, while Sophie perused the Prince's writing, she removed her sword belt and unbuttoned her jacket.

'Well,' Sophie said again, but in quite a different tone. She looked up, and Geneviève continued with her unbuttoning.

'Well,' Sophie said a third time, as Geneviève removed her coat altogether, and started on her shirt; this morning she had not bothered with her doublet.

'My dear girl,' said Sophie. 'What a singular situation.'

Geneviève took off her shirt, unbuckled her belt.

'You do realise,' Sophie said, 'that you would be as safe here as anywhere else? Russia. My God, my heart bleeds for you, Mademoiselle Geneviève. But here . . . and I would make your fortune.'

Geneviève removed her breeches. 'Sleeping with men?'

Sophie frowned. 'You object to sleeping with men?'

'Without some very good object in view, some very profitable object, madame, I do object. I have undressed that you may be sure there is no subterfuge involved, and that you may summon a dressmaker to measure me. I am in great haste.'

'As this letter says.' Sophie came closer. 'You are an absolute delight, my dear, dear girl. If only I could change your mind ...' She sighed. 'Ah, well. Young people have their way to make. I shall summon a seamstress. The very best. Oh, you will be equipped, at least partially.'

'Partially?'

'There are only twenty-four hours in a day, mademoiselle.'

'There is also the matter of my deportment.'

'I shall see to that personally. As you have been playing the gentleman for these eighteen years, I assume you are not unfamiliar with manners?'

'I have been educated, madame.'

Sophie smiled. 'You will do very well. Ah, etiquette, etiquette. It is the soul of civilised living. What a pity every young man is not as well brought up as you, mademoiselle. Now we must just be sure you can walk and talk like a lady as well as eat like one. To work.'

And to work she went; undoubtedly the Prince of Conti was one of her most important customers. The seamstress arrived within the hour, but by that time Geneviève, wrapped in an undressing robe belonging to Sophie herself, and which only came to her knees, had already paraded the room several times, a heavy book balanced on her head, while Sophie walked behind her and instructed her. 'Free your hips,' she said. 'You must make them move. Quite the reverse to a man. But you have beautiful hips, mademoiselle, and you must make all the men notice them.'

'I do not *wish* to be noticed by men,' Geneviève insisted.

'You do wish to be mistaken for a woman, no doubt,' Sophie replied tartly. 'And do not move your head,' she shouted, as the book clattered to the floor. 'Nothing is more disgusting than a young girl whose head is bobbing all the time. You'll have enough of that when you are old and crippled with rheumatism or the palsy.'

A horrible thought. But she had no time for considering even the immediate future as she was measured and twirled, as madame and the seamstresses plucked their lips and clicked their tongues; there was simply no time for a complete trousseau to be stitched, and therefore Sophie decided to take some of the clothes belonging to her taller girls and alter them where necessary.

'Whores' clothing,' Geneviève grumbled.

'All women are whores at heart, my dear mademoiselle,' Sophie reminded her gently. 'And these are good clothes. Feel that texture.'

And indeed Geneviève was already entranced, although she would never have admitted it, with the silks and satins with which she was suddenly surrounded, by the perfumes which were held beneath her nose, the petticoats which were draped about her waist, by the hoop suspended from her shoulders, by the patches which were placed on her face ... 'Not that you have need of them,' Sophie said. 'There is not a blemish in sight.'

But however much she regretted the way in which Geneviève was slipping through her fingers, Sophie was a professional. As there was little time, she delved into her own strong box to find a ruby ring, and a golden chain with a diamond set in a golden clasp.

'Madame,' Geneviève protested. 'I cannot possibly accept such gifts.'

'Silly child,' Sophie said. 'I am not *giving* them to you. I am selling them to you.'

'To me? I have no money, save the pittance the Prince has given me as an allowance.'

Sophie smiled, in a somewhat sinister fashion. 'The account will be sent to the Prince.'

'And do you suppose he will honour it, after I have left the country?'

Sophie's smile widened. 'The Prince will surely pay me anything I desire, my dear mademoiselle.' She tapped her bosom, in which the precious letter was residing. 'I do adore secrets.'

Geneviève supposed her new friend could look after herself, and indeed soon fell into a dreamless sleep, after quite the most terrifying and exhausting day of her life. Her last thought was that Sophie had not yet produced a maid for her, but she knew she need not have worried, and indeed, when she was called just before dawn the following morning, it was by a girl of sixteen, remarkably tall and large and rawboned so that it was possible to suppose that *she* might do very well disguised as a man. She curtsied, and said, in the most execrable of French accents, 'Good day, mademoiselle. I am Margaret.'

Geneviève sat up to scratch her head. 'You are not French,' she accused.

'By adoption, mademoiselle. I was borrrrn in Paisley.'

'And where might that be?'

'Scotland, mademoiselle. But me father was out in forty-five, and it was hard. Oh, it was hard.'

My God, Geneviève thought; they will not even give me a French maid.

'Now really, my dear mademoiselle,' Sophie protested. 'You'd not expect me to send one of my girls into the wilds of Russia? Besides, Margaret is all to the good. Your embassy is virtually a Scots affair, headed as it is by the Chevalier Douglas, who will be taking many of his countrymen with him. Outcast, they are, since the Butcher Cumberland got amongst them. Margaret will be a useful go between. Treat her kindly, pay her well, and she will be invaluable.'

Pay her well, Geneviève thought; there were Jules' wages as well, and the Prince had been uncommonly mean with the funds he had given her. But as usual her worries were immediately dissipated by the ceremony of dressing her for the role she was now to sustain. The role, she wondered? The role I was born to. I may as well enjoy it.

Madame Sophie began with a corset, which was strapped around Geneviève's middle and pulled tighter and tighter, while they kept looking at her and waiting for her to complain. But her exercise-hardened body and flattened belly found little to concern themselves with; indeed she could not help but wonder what all the fuss was about. Next she was draped in a linen shift, and over this, over her head as well, was dropped the hoop, a contraption of steel struts which weighed a ton, it seemed, and was suspended from her shoulders by stout cloth straps, very much as if she was again wearing braces to keep up her breeches. Over this in turn were draped six petticoats, the first three of linen, the top three of taffeta, which set up a most delightful rustle, but were only to be concealed beneath her pale blue taffeta gown. This was cut fashionably low, but now her breasts were to be concealed by a frilled white linen fichu ... 'You may remove this when in the company of ladies, or of men you wish to impress,' Sophie told her. 'But your bosom should never be exposed to the vulgar gaze.' To complete the ensemble, and to keep out the draughts, Sophie explained, her neck was enveloped in a vast blue velvet bow, which was intended to match her ermine trimmed blue velvet travelling jacket, to which was added a matching velvet hat, this to be worn over a white linen cap. Geneviève's immediate reaction was that she could hardly ever have looked so absurd, but when she gazed at herself in the mirror she had to admit that she made a most fetching sight.

'For travelling, of course, ladies usually leave their hair loose,' Sophie complained. 'However . . .' She burrowed into her chest and came up with a very small and light wig, not powdered in any way, but indeed made to look entirely like a normal head of hair, although the colour was dark brown instead of yellow. 'Left here by a lady of quality who had had the misfortune to go bald,' Sophie explained. 'I think it would do very well, and we do not wish to arouse any suspicions that you are not all you appear.'

'I will say Amen to that,' Geneviève agreed. 'Now there is just one thing remaining . . .' And she raised her leg to strap her poniard to the inside of her left calf.

'My dear child,' Sophie protested. 'Do you anticipate murder?'

'In my situation it is an extremely likely possibility, madame,' Geneviève said. Once again she stood in front of the mirror. 'Will I do?'

'Oh, very well, mademoiselle. Very well indeed. Should you ever return to Paris . . .'

'I *shall* return to Paris, madame, I promise you,' Geneviève said, and surveyed her two attendants. It was hard to decide which was the least prepossessing, Jules or Margaret. 'Well, then,' she said. 'Let us present ourselves to this Chevalier Douglas.'

Who turned out to be a large rawboned Scot who might have been a brother to Margaret, save that his clothes were considerably finer and his demeanour somewhat less rustic. 'Mademoiselle d'Éon,' he said. 'Ye'll no be a relative of the young man who squires His Majesty?'

'I am Charles' sister, monsieur.'

Douglas nodded. 'Aha. Well, I've had notice from the Prince of Conti that ye're to accompany the embassy, and as it is *his* embassy, so to speak . . .'

'I beg your pardon, monsieur?'

'No matter, no matter. Ye're welcome. The Prince has sent you these books to read.'

The five volumes turned out to be a history of Russia, down to only five years previously.

'How very thoughtful of him,' Geneviève said. 'Well, sir, I am at your service. Now tell me of this embassy. 'Tis the Prince's, you say?'

'It is no concern of yours, mademoiselle. Where I'm to put ye, that I scarce understand. But we'll find a way. Och, aye, we'll find a way.'

'It is of considerable concern to me, monsieur,' Geneviève said, catching his sleeve as he would have turned away. 'What do you mean, that the embassy belongs to the Prince of Conti? Is he accompanying us?'

'The Prince is not accompanying us, mademoiselle,' said the Chevalier, freeing himself. 'And it is not my place to inform you as to the exact purposes of my embassy. Ye'll understand that I will have discipline, mademoiselle. Och, aye. 'Tis a long journey on which we are embarked. Two months, at the very least, it will take us to make Petersburg. Longer if we do not reach our destination before winter truly sets in. In that time we must travel together, and sleep together, and eat together, and drink together, and experience our travails together, and hopefully, mademoiselle, also laugh together. I'll have no carping, no womanly jealousies and spites, or I will tell you this, niece to the Prince you may be, but I will stretch you across a barrel and redden your rump with my crop, that I will.'

She could only stare after him in impotent anger as he strode away. To be placed in the custody of such an uncouth rogue, who was not even a Frenchman, and to be surrounded by so many uncertainties ... at the least she had received one blessing in that the Chevalier clearly knew nothing of the scandal which must by now be rocking the court. And another, supposing that the Prince of Conti had given out she was his niece. But, *his* embassy? Whatever did it mean?

Not that she had much time for considering the matter, for the embassy was leaving that very morning, and all was hustle and bustle. Geneviève was found a berline, in which she was placed with Margaret, while Jules had to take his place upon the box beside the driver. Other carriages and horses were milling around them, dust was rising, the air was thick with orders and imprecations, even standing still the carriage was clearly a springless, uncomfortable vehicle – she wished she could be mounted, but obviously that was out of the question – and she was feeling thoroughly out of sorts when suddenly a face appeared at her window.

It was a horseman, bending from the saddle, and removing his hat as he did so. It was a plumed hat, and went well with his blue satin coat as much as his pigtail wig to suggest very much a young gentleman of fashion. Because he *was* young, and handsome in a rugged fashion, she supposed, with a square chin and a wide mouth set beneath a prominent nose and a high forehead, the whole brought to life by a pair of light blue eyes; and if he dressed like a court fop the hand holding her window sill was hard and muscular.

'Mademoiselle d'Éon?'

She knew at once he was not French, and that indeed he had to be one of the Scots.

'I am she.'

'Adam Menzies, mademoiselle. I but wished you to know that I command this part of the cavalcade, and will be ever at your service.'

She inspected him more closely. 'You are very young for such responsibility, monsieur.'

He smiled, the most winning thing about him, she decided, for it revealed genuine humour rather than a mere widening of the lips. 'I shall not fail you, mademoiselle. I was at Culloden.'

Another exile, she thought. 'And were defeated, monsieur.'

His smile faded, and in its place there came a look of quite startling determination. 'There will be another field, mademoiselle, Your servant.' The face disappeared.

'Ah, to be young and pretty,' Margaret sighed. 'When your hair grows, mademoiselle, you will have this cavalcade by the throat.'

'Why should my hair enter into it?'

Margaret blushed. 'You'd not let a man like Captain Menzies see you in déshabille with that crop you have there, mademoiselle?'

Let him see her in déshabille? Now why should she wish to do that? he was a personable, even a handsome young man, with no doubt, like all young men, an inflated opinion of himself. Based entirely upon the fact that he possessed an equally inflatable appendage between his legs, and that he had no doubt managed to reduce some gormless maiden to gasping ecstacy at some stage in his life.

As France was presently allied with Prussia, and with most of the north German states, as well as with Spain, it was only necessary for the cavalcade to avoid the possessions of the

Empress of Austria as it made its way towards the Rhine and thence the Elbe, its destination Lubeck, where it was hoped to take ship for St Petersburg before the ice closed the Baltic Sea. Never had Geneviève undertaken so lengthy a journey, indeed, she had hardly supposed it possible to travel for so long without entirely leaving Europe, nor had she ever known such discomfort. It was the Chevalier Douglas' preference to leave at dawn, which was generally shortly after seven of the morning, and following only the scantiest of breakfasts, unless one was awake well before that hour. The cavalcade then proceeded slowly on its way, along the most terrible rutted roads over which the berline jolted and shuddered, lurched and rolled; Geneviève had never been to sea, but she could hardly imagine that the worst of nautical storms could possibly equal the bone shaking discomfort she was forced to endure.

Where possible they avoided towns, but the Chevalier invariably sent riders ahead, and when they stopped for dinner, usually around two, they found the inn ready for them with the best meal available. But this, once they crossed the first of the rivers and were in Germany itself, could hardly be called appetising, consisting in the main as it did of cabbage soup and great lengths of distinctly tough sausage, the whole assisted only by black bread and a somewhat light beer.

'Think of it,' Adam Menzies said, sitting beside her at the long table down the centre of the tap room. 'These poor devils live like this the whole year round.'

'And do you better, in Scotland, monsieur?'

He winked. 'No. Unless one is wealthy. I was thinking of the effect it must be having on your own dear palate, mademoiselle.'

He could attempt to flirt all he wished. Even had she been in the mood their circumstances were quite damning to romance. Apart from the ache she had in every muscle and bone as well, she was hard put to it to find the least privacy. There were some hundred and fifty people in the embassy, and of these thirty-seven were of a rank at least equal to hers, including as they did the Chevalier's wife and two daughters, as well as the wives of several of his chief officers; there were never sufficient rooms to go round, and even the niece of the Prince of Conti could not be granted one to herself. Rather than share with five or six other ladies, or to bed down with the rest of the women and most of the men, she preferred to sleep the first few nights in her carriage. But there was insufficient room to stretch out properly, and besides, as they progressed into Germany the weather turned so bitterly cold, that at last she was happy to huddle beneath her blanket in a corner of the tap room, Margaret beside her.

The cold was accompanied by downpours of rain, which occasionally turned to sleet, and more than once the day was begun to the sound of cracking ice. It was impossible to get dry, as it was impossible to get truly warm. After the first week Geneviève never took off her boots, but once, to add an extra pair of stockings; the thought of undressing in order to bathe was terrifying, even supposing there had been water available for such a purpose, or a tub to put it in, or a place to sit in it without being overseen by the entire cavalcade. She prayed for a glimpse of the sea and the ships, where at the beginning she had been more afraid of this part of the journey than any other. And on the third of December they came to Lubeck.

And found that the Baltic was not yet frozen, and that their ships were awaiting them. Geneviève felt that she could shout with joy. But she very rapidly changed her mind, and came to the conclusion that her earlier judgement had been entirely justified.

At least on land it had been possible, when it had not actually been raining, to walk away from the carriages during the afternoon halt, to be alone; and at least the land had remained still. The ships were not very large, and all the passengers were herded into the great cabin, and there allotted places on the floor to spread their blankets. And if it was not quite cold enough to freeze an ocean, the wind, howling down from the Arctic Circle, was intent upon making it so as rapidly as possible, and in the meanwhile, was out to prove to the puny humans that they had no business to be at sea at all.

''Tis naught but a capfull of wind, mademoiselle,' Adam Menzies pointed out, holding a bowl for her vomit. 'Why, when I came down from the Orkneys, in a cockleshell, it blew a full gale for three days. We split a mast, and all but foundered. But that was the North Sea, in March. You'll have nothing like that in the Baltic, in December.'

I hate you, she thought. You are a despicable Highland lout. Would the Butcher had seized you and hanged you from the highest tree he could find. But she was discovering she hated them all. Firstly because they were there at all, and in such proximity; they lay shoulder to shoulder, most of them, like her, too sick to move, so that they groaned and snored and performed their necessaries without ever leaving the cabin, which became a place of nauseating misery. And secondly because for the first time in her life she was truly afraid. There was no opportunity here to seize a sword and shout defiance at the elements, to act the man. Even had she been a man that would not have been possible, with her stomach entirely disappeared into a seething cauldron. She could only pray for the voyage to end, and dream of her now happy seeming childhood, of the careless days spent fencing with Monsieur Lannes in the rose garden, or riding over the jumps in the paddock, days when she had had friends, when she had parents. Days when she had been able to love.

'Land,' said the irrepressible Captain Menzies. 'We are almost at the islands, mademoiselle. Sheltered water. Will you not come up and look?'

She realised that the howling of the wind had a trifle abated, the creaking of the timbers had ceased, and the ship was gliding rather than thumping through the water. And that her stomach had returned to its rightful place. She sat up, attempted to straighten her wig, and discovered it had come off in the turmoil; her own hair had been growing strenuously for the two months, and was again tumbling about her ears. But it was yellow, and straight, where her wig had been pale brown, and curly. And Menzies was most certainly interested.

'Then I shall come with you,' she said, and gave him her hand to be assisted to her feet. Between them they located her cap and her hooded pelisse, beneath her next door neighbour, and then went on deck. The air was so crisp and cold it took her breath away, and she gasped, but immediately was so absorbed by the sight before her she could forget her misery.

The houses, and there were several large enough to be described as palaces, appeared to be rising immediately out of the sea.

'This is because the islands on which the city is built are only a few feet above the water,' Menzies explained. 'Why, when the spring thaw sets in, they are invariably submerged altogether, and life is quite difficult. Dead of winter or dead of summer is the best time for St Petersburg.'

She did not agree, for she now realised that the ship had stopped moving, being held fast in the grip of a sudden sea of ice.

'It comes down from Lake Ladoga,' Menzies explained. 'We have gone as far as we can.'

'You mean we spend the winter here?' she cried in alarm.

'By no means. Indeed, we shall be put ashore with all possible speed, as you may be sure our captains will wish to get back to Germany before navigation is finished for the year. Look yonder.'

She followed the direction of his finger, and saw to her amazement that the ice was apparently thick enough to be used as a roadway, and indeed there were several open carriages, resting on sledges rather than wheels but none the less horsedrawn, if the strong little ponies could truly be described as horses, waiting at a distance of only two hundred yards, and far further than that from the shore itself. Not that the passengers were immediately allowed to disembark. Messengers had to be sent to and fro, shouted inquires and commands were hurled back and forth in unintelligible Russian, while remarkably, the day seemed to grow colder as noon was approached.

But at least the ship was still. Geneviève's spirits began to rise, and at last the necessary permission was forthcoming, and more particularly for her, as the Chevalier indicated she was to be first ashore.

Now all was bustle, as the boats were lowered, being placed side by side where they could not be moved, and she and Margaret were required to climb down ladders and then clamber from boat to boat, to the accompaniment of much rocking and shouting, all with the prospects of imminent immersion in the icy River Neva, until they could safely come to the ice. If the ice could be called safe, as it was not nearly so thick where they were landed as closer to the shore, and was constantly cracking and rumbling beneath their feet, while it was the devil itself to stand on, and they were slipping and sliding all over the place. Geneviève would certainly have fallen had Menzies not caught her arm, but Margaret had no such cavalier, and immediately measured her full length upon the frozen water.

She was recovered, however, and they were greeted by a handsome young man who was apparently waiting for them, ushered them into the nearest *troika,* as the carriages were called, and set off at great speed. 'Goodbye,' Adam Menzies called, waving his hat. 'We shall meet again soon.'

'But where are they taking me?' she bawled in sudden alarm.

His reply was lost in the hubbub, and a moment later they reached the shore, not that they had abandoned the ice, for the roads were also frozen over and their *troika* had no difficulty in continuing its breakneck speed.

'But what has become of Jules, mademoiselle?' Margaret gasped, each breath forming a small cloud before her face.

'What is to become of us, you mean?' Geneviève grumbled, realising that they had been separated from the entire embassy. She was so agitated it was difficult to take in much of her surroundings, although she was in fact rather disappointed as she discovered that most of the buildings, including several of the palaces, were merely made of wood, and in fact it was easy to see that the city, which after all had only been founded by Peter the Great a scant fifty years before, was still in the process of growing. The pall of smoke grew thicker as they rushed along the bank of the river to their left, to come to a screeching halt before the largest of the palaces, this one built of faced stone and quite attractive in a heavy way, placed so as to look over the harbour and the islands beyond, and outside of which there stood a cluster of white coated guardsmen.

The young man indicated that they should step down, gave a series of orders in Russian, and a moment later Geneviève found herself being hurried up a wide flight of steps and into a large salon, but with bare walls and paintless ceiling; the air of starkness was relieved only by the chandeliers, and was then increased again by the bitter cold; it was impossible to see how the guards who lined each wall managed to keep still, for they were wearing white uniforms without topcoats.

Geneviève followed her guide, along the length of the room, up another flight of wide steps, down an equally cold, guard lined hallway, and into a smaller chamber. Here there was a cluster of ladies, and before one of these the officer dropped on one knee. The woman bade him rise, and he obeyed, speaking rapidly in Russian, while Geneviève gathered that she had been hurried straightaway into the presence of the Empress of all the Russias. She had not entirely collected herself. managing to sink into a hasty curtsey, when the woman dismissed the officer with a wave of the hand, came forward, and in the most perfect French, remarked, 'What a pretty child.'

Chapter Four

Geneviève raised her head, and was pleasantly surprised. The Empress Elizabeth Petrovna was, as she had ascertained by her reading during the journey, in her late thirties, and retained a great deal of the beauty of her youth. She was, in fact, handsome rather than lovely, with magnificently strong features, high forehead, bold nose, thrusting chin, and a mouth which could either smile or resemble a steel trap according to her mood. Her eyes were brown, and sleepy, but this too Geneviève did not doubt was a matter of mood. In figure she was at once tall and well built, and obviously in the best of health. Her gown was made of crimson brocade, and sparkled with diamonds; she was bareheaded and curling dark brown hair lay on her shoulders. But the dominating aspect of her appearance was her aura of utter confidence, the contemptuous manner in which she moved, and looked, and spoke. Again from her reading Geneviève recalled how this daughter of Peter the Great had been kept in virtual imprisonment until quite recently, by those who would have ruled for her, and how, suddenly throwing off the mask of indifference, she had in a single night arrested the Regent and all her principal aides, and made herself mistress of the largest country in Europe.

Now the Empress extended her hand, and Geneviève allowed herself to be raised. 'I shall adore you,' the Empress remarked, still in the most perfect French. 'I am told you have a letter for me.'

'Indeed, Sire.' Geneviève opened her reticule, took out the somewhat crushed envelope.

The Empress glanced at the handwriting, then at Geneviève once again. 'I shall peruse it at my leisure. You have spent two long months upon your journey. You are tired and in need of a rest. And a change of clothing, I have no doubt.' None of her remarks were questions, which was understandable enough;

Geneviève supposed she could be smelt at a considerable distance. 'You have servants?'

'My . . . my maid is without, Sire, and I have a manservant also, but I have not seen him since landing.'

Elizabeth Petrovna smiled. 'He will be found. Maria Ivanova,' she said, without turning her head. 'You will show Mademoiselle d'Éon to her apartments, and grant her whatsoever she wishes.'

'Sire.' A somewhat plain young woman, but as richly dressed as anyone else present, gave a curtsey.

'I shall see you soon,' Elizabeth Petrovna said, and turned away through an inner doorway, the letter still clutched in her hand. Her attendants filed out behind her, leaving only the girl described as Maria Ivanova and the subaltern. This pair exchanged a few words in Russian, then the young man also left, and Maria Ivanova gave Geneviève a smile. 'If mademoiselle will accompany me?' She walked to the door, waited. Geneviève smiled in turn, went through the door, discovered Margaret slapping her hands together in an effort to keep warm.

'Lord above, mademoiselle,' she said. 'Do they not have firewood in this place?'

'Your rooms will be warm enough,' Maria Ivanova assured her, and led them up a succession of staircases and along a series of corridors, every corner guarded by an armed soldier in a white uniform – but the entire palace still suggested nothing better than an outsize barn.

'You speak very good French,' Geneviève ventured, determined to be polite.

'Of course. We are not barbarians. These are your apartments.' There were four rooms in all, a sitting room, richly if uncomfortably furnished, and an even more sumptuously furnished bedroom. The third room was much smaller, and was intended for sewing or reading, apparently; it possessed the only outside window, from which she could look down at a snow covered interior courtyard of the palace. The fourth room was the smallest of all, intended for her attendants to sleep, on the floor.

'In there, mademoiselle?' Margaret complained. 'And with these?'

For the other girls had obviously already taken up residence.

'It *is* rather small,' Geneviève ventured.

95

'It is for servants,' Maria Ivanova remarked contemputously. 'Should they complain, give them a dose of the knout.'

'The knout?'

'It is a special kind of whip. Very good for discipline.'

Geneviève smiled. 'I have no whip at all, and besides . . .'

'I will fetch one for you,' Maria Ivanova said.

'I was going to say, in France we seldom whip our domestics. Certainly not for complaining.'

'Serfs should be whipped, and often,' Maria Ivanova said seriously. 'Otherwise they grow impertinent. Is mademoiselle satisfied with her arrangements?'

'Indeed, with a single exception. I also have a manservant, as I told the Empress. But there does not appear to be a room for him.'

'He may sleep with the women,' Maria Ivanova said.

'Oh, really, I do not think . . .'

'Oh wherever else you choose, mademoiselle. It is not important.' She clapped her hands, and the four girls sprang to attention, to receive a stream of instructions in Russian. Maria Ivanova smiled. 'I have ordered a bath for you. Your trunks will be here in a little while.'

'Thank you,' Geneviève said, and hesitated, as the girl showed no intention of leaving. Perhaps she seeks a reward, she wondered.

'You will be happy here,' Marie Ivanova said.

'I am sure I shall,' Geneviève lied.

'The Empress is very good to her ladies,' Maria Ivanova said.

'I'm sure she is.'

'She but requires instant and complete obedience.'

'Empresss generally do,' Geneviève agreed, attempting to lighten the gloom. 'You will be telling me next *she* uses the knout, on you.'

'But of course, mademoiselle. Not the knout, to be sure, on her ladies. The knout destroys, and Her Majesty rarely wishes to destroy any of *us*. But the whip, certainly. It is her right, and our honour, to be whipped by the Empress.'

Geneviève felt her chin slipping, and hastily closed her mouth. 'I trust she will not seek any such course with me.'

'It is the Empress's right,' Maria Ivanova said piously, 'to whip anyone in Russia, should she choose. Your things are here.'

The door was opening, and her trunks were being brought in by half a dozen footmen, followed by a scandalised Jules.

'Kept in the snow, mademoiselle, and like to freeze. For over an hour, mademoiselle. By heaven, mademoiselle . . .'

'Hush, Jules,' Geneviève said. 'Or you will be whipped. It is the custom.' She smiled at his appalled expression. 'And I very much fear I will have to fall in with Russian custom, as we are here for an indefinite period.' She dared not admit to herself that it might be forever. 'Now place the trunks in the bedchamber, if you will. Madame . . .' She hesitated.

Maria Ivanova gave a little curtsey. 'Mademoiselle, if you please, mademoiselle.'

'You have been very kind. Now, if you will excuse me . . .'

'I am to see that everything is to your satisfaction,' Maria Ivanova said, firmly.

Geneviève glanced at Jules, then at Margaret, and shrugged. 'Unpack, will you, Margaret? Who is there?' For there had come another rap on the door.

The girls had returned, each carrying an enormous pitcher of boiling water, the steam from which promptly filled the room, and followed by another procession of footmen, bringing more and more ewers, while at the back two of them were armed with a tin tub. This they proceeded to place in the centre of the room, and fill with water, causing the atmosphere to become quite opaque.

'Margaret, send all those men away,' said Geneviève, 'and then assist me to undress.' How good that tub was going to feel, she thought. Two months. My God, I must smell like a sewer. She began removing her outer garments, and allowed Margaret to help her; her undergarments were so stiff she supposed they would stand by themselves, and glanced at Maria Ivanova to see her reaction; surprisingly the Russian girl did not seem to notice anything unusual at all. She was more taken with the body appearing before her.

'Why, mademoiselle,' she exclaimed. 'You are so . . . so . . . I do not know what to say.'

Geneviève sank into the tub; it was big enough for her even to get her legs inside, at least when drawn up. 'Am I not to your taste, mademoiselle?'

'Oh, you are lovely. Lovely.' Maria Ivanova herself knelt to scrub Geneviève's back. 'But so strong. You have muscles.'

'So have you, Maria,' Geneviève pointed out. 'I happen to have used mine, from time to time.' How good it felt, now that she was accustomed to it. She could feel the dirt, the unwashed smell, dissipating. And then, bed. To lie on a soft mattress, beneath proper sheets and a proper quilt, after so long ... she thought she could sleep forever.

There was another rattle on the door behind her.

'For Heaven's sake,' she shouted. 'Send them away, Margaret?'

But the girls were hurrying forward with a robe in which to envelope her, and Maria Ivanova was sinking into a curtsey. 'It is Dr Todorsky, mademoiselle,' she whispered. 'Come to instruct you in the Orthodox Faith.'

Slowly Geneviève rose to her feet; she was already shrouded in the voluminous bathrobe, but she could feel the water cooling as it ran down her legs. Standing before the door was a short, dark man, who wore spectacles and his own somewhat lank hair, and regarded her with a benevolent smile.

'Mademoiselle d'Éon,' he said. 'I am Simon Todorsky. Her Majesty said I was to waste no time in commencing your instruction.'

'In my own chamber, monsieur?'

Todorsky shrugged. 'It is the best place.'

'Well, monsieur, I do not receive gentlemen in my bedchamber,' Geneviève pointed out, and frowned at him. 'You *are* a gentleman?'

'Mademoiselle,' Maria Ivanova said in a scandalised whisper. 'Dr Todorsky is the Archimandrite.'

The doctor did not seem put out. 'Mademoiselle is modest,' he said. 'Which is an excellent beginning. If you will retire and dress yourself, mademoiselle, I shall wait for you here, and we may commence.'

'Commence what?' Geneviève demanded.

'Your instruction in the Holy Faith.'

'I am already instructed in the Holy Faith,' Geneviève pointed out.

'You are of the Orthodox Church?' Todorsky was surprised.

'I am of the Roman Church, Dr Todorsky.'

'My dear girl,' Todorsky said. 'My dear, dear girl. The Roman Church is heresy. In Russia.'

'I am French.'

'You are about to take up residence in Russia.'

Geneviève gave him her most withering stare. 'And thus I must change my religion?'

'Of course.'

'I will not.'

'The Archimandrite glanced at Maria Ivanova.

'Mademoiselle,' Maria begged. 'Dr Todorsky has been sent by Her Majesty. It is her express wish that you receive instruction. Her Majesty will have no attendants not of the true faith.'

'Then she had best send me back to Paris,' Geneviève said. She had not supposed it was going to be so simple to escape.

Simon Todorsky scratched his head. 'You would disobey the Empress?'

'Monsieur, I entirely respect your motives, and those of the Empress. But surely, so long as I believe in God the Father, God the Son, God the Holy Ghost, in the Holy Mother and the Angels, in all that is taught by our Holy Father the Pope in Rome, I am sufficiently proved to be a good Christian.'

'The Pope in Rome,' Todorsky muttered. 'The Pope in Rome.' He turned and left the room.

'Mademoiselle,' Maria Ivanova whispered. 'Her Majesty will be very angry.'

'Nothing was said about changing my religion,' Geneviève insisted. It was occurring to her that these girls were a little too afraid of their royal mistress. She could hardly be more of an autocrat than Louis XV, and he would never have dreamed of insisting a girl change her religion, providing of course she was not actually a Huguenot. And even there, did he not give shelter to renegade Scotsmen, Calvinists every one? Had he not, indeed, entrusted Mackenzie Douglas with this embassy? And sent with him that eager young man, Adam Menzies? She smiled as she wondered how *he* was finding Russian life.

'And now, bed,' she said. 'Oh, and dinner. I am quite famished.'

Maria Ivanova looked sceptical. 'I doubt there will be time...'

'Her Majesty said I was to be given whatever I wished,' Geneviève said. Definitely it was necessary to establish herself immediately, or she would be led a dog's life. 'And what I wish is something to eat, and a chance to lie down. You'd not deny me, mademoiselle.' 'By no means mademoiselle'. Maria Ivanova turned to the door, and checked at the knock. 'There.'

'Well, see who it is,' Geneviève said, her heart commencing to pound. And sure enough, it was one of the major-domos, who addressed Maria Ivanova in Russian, bowed, and left again.

'Her Majesty commands your presence, Mademoiselle d'Éon,' Maria Ivanova said. 'This very moment. What did I tell you? She will have you whipped.'

What nonsense, Geneviève thought. I am a subject of the King of France. That must never be forgotten. 'I am sure Her Majesty would scarce wish to whip me,' she remarked. 'Now help me dress.'

But she felt distinctly nervous as, escorted by Maria Ivanova, she was taken to the Empress's private apartments, and not by any secret ways here, as in Versailles; they marched down great wide and freezing corridors, guarded at ten pace intervals by white clad soldiers. Geneviève had never seen so many soldiers in one building in her life; she estimated there must be at least a thousand, more than double the company of Swiss Guards usually maintained inside the French palace. And all waiting to carry out their mistress's command. She would not wish to spoil me, she had said; but had she not, by those simple words, reduced herself to the level of a *thing,* to be played with or destroyed as the mood took the Empress? She could feel the anger gnawing at her mind, even as she told herself that she must preserve her independence and her identity, until she could find her way back from this frozen capital, until she could re-enter the civilised world.

She had dressed carefully in a rose coloured satin gown over a cream and blue damask underskirt, and had protected herself from the terrible cold by a woollen chemise which she wore beneath her corset, and by woollen stockings, while her fichu was white frilled linen; her only jewellery was the gold necklace given her by Madame Sophie. No, no, she kept reassuring herself; the Empress would not wish to destroy such a delightful creature. But what else would she wish to do with it?

The doors opened before her, held by two negro pages, and she stepped into the royal antechamber. But unlike that at Versailles, this was almost empty, containing only three men, heads close together in the far corner. They glanced at the two young women, and then resumed their conversation.

Maria Ivanova had meanwhile been instructing the major-domo, who stood before the inner doors, which were in turn opened for them. To Geneviève's surprise the private room was far more crowded than the antechamber; there were a good dozen people present, gathered around the Empress, as well as half a dozen spaniels playing at her feet. Geneviève identified Simon Todorsky immediately, but was more taken with the man standing immediately beside Elizabeth Petrovna, partly because he was so obviously taken with her.

He was quite young, certainly no older than the Empress herself, and was clad in a long coat, reaching to his ankles, trimmed with fur, to be sure, but also studded with diamonds, as were his buttons. He also wore a little black moustache, and no wig; his hair was concealed beneath a fur cap, but clearly it was black, in keeping with his black eyes and swarthy complexion, his aquiline features. He would indeed have been handsome but for a slackness of the lips, which hardly ever kept still, either smiling or twisting or sagging.

'There, Michael Ilarionvich,' the Empress said. 'Did I not tell you the exact truth?'

'Indeed, Sire, I never doubted it for a moment,' he said, also speaking French. 'She is quite delicious.'

'I have not made the gentleman's acquaintance, Sire.' Geneviève gave a brief curtsey. 'I am Geneviève d'Éon de Beaumont.'

'Michael .. Michael Ilarionvich Vorontsov, at your service, mademoiselle.' He kissed her fingers; his grip was pleasantly firm.

'Yes, yes,' said Elizabeth Petrovna, somewhat hastily. 'I am sure you and Mademoiselle d'Eon will get on famously, Michael. But she is here to tell me why she abused Dr Todorsky.'

'Abused, Sire?'

'You refused to accept instruction from him.'

'Sire . . .' Geneviève made herself hang her head. 'I was instructed in my own faith, from birth. What would you think of me were I to agree to change it?'

'Change it you must,' the Empress said. 'I will have no attendants, indeed, I will have no one about me, who is not of the true faith.'

'Sire . . .'

'I would have you meet my nephew. Peter Feodorovich.'

A young man left the other people and came over to stand before her. He was not altogether prepossessing, as he had popeyes and a long nose, and a habit of swallowing between almost every breath as if his prominent Adam's Apple was threatening to enter his throat. 'The Grand Duke Peter Feodorovich,' Elizabeth Petrovna said. 'He is the son of my dear sister Anna, unhappily gathered to her fathers, and as such is my appointed heir.'

Geneviève sank into a deep curtsey

'I am also Duke of Holstein-Gottorp, Sire,' Peter pointed out as if he considered this somewhat more important.

'Yes, yes,' said the Empress. 'The Grand Duke was a Lutheran before he came to live with us in Russia. Did you find the slight alteration necessary in your religion troublesome, Peter Feodorovich?'

'Of course not, Sire,' the Grand Duke said.

'Sire . . .' Geneviève began.

'And now I would have you meet the Grand Duchess, Catherine Alekseeyevna,' the Empress said, beckoning a young woman forward, and she was, very young, Geneviève realised, hardly older than herself, tall and willowy, with somewhat plain features but splendid eyes, not dominating like the Pompadour's, but deep and thoughtful. 'She too, after considerable thought, has fallen in with my wishes,' the Empress pointed out.

'I am sure Mademoiselle d'Éon will honour your desires, Sire,' the Grand Duchess said.

'Of course she will,' Elizabeth Petrovna said. 'Tea for Mademoiselle d'Éon.'

A serving maid hurried from the rear of the room, where Geneviève now observed an enormous samovar tended by a bearded footman; the girl carried a tray on which there was a glass mug, fitted into a silver container, and filled with boiling tea. The spaniels scattered before her, and recommenced sniffing Geneviève's dress.

'Drink,' the Empress commanded. 'It will warm you up. I have been reading Conti's letter. He wheedles and cajoles, as usual. There is no end to the man's ambitions.'

Very cautiously Geneviève sipped the scalding liquid, and withdrew her tongue as if burned, which indeed she had been. But she did not care for the taste very much either; it suggested medicine. And Conti's ambitions? Here in Russia?

'But at the least,' the Empress continued, 'he is prepared to pay. With you, my dear. He relates a tragic tale, of how you are banished by King Louis, and are in grave danger. Ah, Louis, Louis. It was proposed once, when I was but a child, that I should marry him. Would that not have been droll? Imagine it, Elizabeth Petrovna at Versailles. Do you not like tea, child?'

102

'It...it is very nice, Sire.' Geneviève hastily drank some more. It was certainly warming.

'But the Regent would have none of it,' Elizabeth Petrovna said, somewhat sadly. 'I speak of the French Regent, not ours. What, marry their prince to a barbarian? One can imagine the horror. Do you suppose I am a barbarian, mademoiselle?'

'By no means, Sire,' Geneviève lied. 'I think Russia is so...so elegant.'

'You dissemble well,' the Empress decided. 'But now you are banished from your sunny France. What tragedy. We shall endeavour to make you happy, my dear.'

'I shall be happy only to serve, Sire.'

'Do not overdo it,' the Empress commanded. 'Your eyes quite belie your words.' She frowned. 'Conti assures me you are a creature of great warmth, great passion. But you are cold. Cold. I can see it in your eyes. Or is it that you do not like me?'

Geneviève glanced from left to right to see what the Grand Duke and the Grand Duchess were thinking, or Vorontsov, for that matter; he smiled at her, but in a way she did not altogether like. Certainly there was no inkling as to whether or not the Empress's alarming changes of mood were to be taken seriously.

'I . . . I would like you very much, Sire. But . . . I am so very hungry. I have not eaten today.'

Elizabeth Petrovna frowned for another moment, and then smiled. 'I am a careless bitch,' she remarked. 'Food. Food for Mademoiselle d'Éon. You shall sit at my right hand, mademoiselle, and eat your fill.'

All was scurry. Geneviève found herself being led out of the room and into another, where a vast table was laid, at which Elizabeth Petrovna and her entourage seated themselves, Geneviève finding herself, as promised, next to the Empress herself.

'Tell me of Prince Conti,' she commanded.

Geneviève wondered exactly what she wanted to hear. She was, apparently, unmarried. Could Conti possibly be aspiring to her hand? Conti, of all men? 'He . . . he is a very fine gentleman,' she said. 'Of royal blood. He is uncle to the King of France.'

'I know that,' Elizabeth Petrovna said. 'And now he would be King himself.'

Geneviève's head came up.

'You did not know his plans?'

'No, Sire.'

'He seeks the crown of Poland. It was my father, Peter Alekseevich, who expelled Leczynski from Warsaw; the poor fool had made the mistake of supporting that madman Charles of Sweden, and against us. But would you believe the folly of men, while he remained on that tottering throne he persuaded the French to marry their king to his daughter. Instead of *me*. That is incredible.'

'Incredible, Sire,' Geneviève agreed. But her attention was wandering as by now the serving girls and footmen were hurrying into the room with steaming platters. The smell was not terribly appetising, but Geneviève was so hungry she thought she could have eaten a raw horse. An enormous bowl was thrust in front of her; to her disappointment she saw it contained a sort of soup, in which were floating odds and ends of fish. But this was no bouillabaisse; the mess also contained whole potatoes and turnips and carrots and pieces of black bread. It was at least hot, however, although this made eating it the more difficult. 'Food,' mumbled Elizabeth Petrovna, dribbling some of the soup down her gown. 'It is all that makes life palatable. Vodka, I must have vodka.'

Geneviève found herself tucking in with a similar lack of ceremony, wondering what the Prince of Conti would make of such table manners; at least the girls were now supplying linen napkins, while the head footman was pouring what appeared to be water from a large jug into crystal goblets, one of which he set before her. I must be mad, Geneviève thought, or dreaming. That is it, I am dreaming, still in my berline as we struggle across North Germany. I am having a nightmare, that I should be sitting at table with the most omnipotent ruler in the world – at least according to her books – as well as several other people of distinction, drinking soup with an iron spoon, and being served water instead of wine to drink.

Water. She was quite thirsty and gulped the goblet dry without drawing breath. The resulting shock, the explosion of heat as the vodka first of all burned the back of her throat and seemed to hurl itself at her stomach, caused her to drop the glass, which promptly shattered. She gave a scream, more of terror than of pain, and leapt to her feet, only to watch the Empress rocking with laughter, in which her companions duly joined.

'Vodka,' shouted Elizabeth Petrovna. 'It burns the throat and frees the mind. More vodka for mademoiselle'

Cautiously Geneviève sat down again. Maids were already wiping up the spilled soup. 'Sire,' she said. 'I am most terribly sorry.'

'Sorry?' demanded the Empress. 'What have you done?'

'Well . . . the soup . . . your tablecloth . . .'

'Bah,' Elizabeth declared, herself draining her goblet without turning a hair and holding it up for a refill. 'What is a tablecloth? We shall burn it. Burn it, do you hear, Michael Ilarionvich?'

'As you wish, Sire,' agreed the Prince. 'Now, or later?'

'Oh, when we have finished with it, to be sure. Mademoiselle, your glass is empty. Fill it up.'

A fresh goblet was thrust into Geneviève's hand. Cautiously she sipped it.

'No, no,' shouted the Empress. 'Vodka must not be sipped. It must be drunk. Like a Russian. Drink it.'

Geneviève had only had a few spoonfuls of soup, but suddenly she no longer felt the least hungry. She took a long breath, and downed her second drink; this time there was no burning sensation, and indeed she even regained her balance, could look around the table and smile.

'Bravo,' shouted the Empress, throwing an arm around her shoulders to hug her close. 'Vodka. More vodka for mademoiselle.'

'My God.' Geneviève opened her eyes, and hastily closed them again. She was back in the middle of the Baltic Sea, and the wind had increased in strength. The ship heaved and rolled, plunged and kicked, taking her stomach with it, sending her spinning through waves of pain; each movement seemed to open her skull and then close it again with a shudding crash.

'Mademoiselle? Mademoiselle? You must wake up.'

Geneviève rolled her head from side to side, moaned with pain, opened her eyes and closed them again, huddled beneath the bedclothes. The bedclothes? And the mattress was soft enough. On a ship at sea?

'Mademoiselle?'

'Margaret? Is that you?'

'I am here, mademoiselle. And I have prepared some supper for you. You must eat, mademoiselle.'

'Eat?' Her belly rolled at the thought of it. But the thought of food brought memory, seeping back at first, and then suddenly filling her mind with tumultuous anxiety. She sat up, pushing hair from her eyes, looked down at herself. She was fully dressed, her gown still stained with soup and vodka. 'Where am I?'

'In your bedchamber, mademoiselle. In your bed.'

'My bed?' She looked through the door at the parlour, where the fire roared in the stove, but she was still cold; Margaret had taken off her shoes. She tucked her feet beneath the coverlet. 'What time is it?'

'I do not know, in this country, mademoiselle. But it is several hours past dusk. The young women have prepared some food...'

Food. Once again her belly rolled, but she had to eat. Because she had had nothing all day, save a few cupfuls of soup, and some oysters, and some ghastly black fish eggs which had made her feel quite sick, before ... she rolled on her stomach, chin propped on her hands, gazing at the bedhead ... before the vodka, and the resulting rout. They had played, like children. The Grand Duke had suddenly taken command, had marshalled them all, maidservants and footmen, ladies in waiting and gentlemen, even Prince Vorontsov and his own bride, had made them form lines and march up and down while he gave orders, and the Empress had leaned back in her chair and laughed.

And they had drunk vodka.

Then they had sat on the floor and played at cards, the Empress with them. They had gambled with ... she frowned. Real money. But I don't have any real money. Not enough, anyway. My God, she thought. I am in debt.

And they had drunk vodka.

Then they had ... her frown deepened. Michael Vorontsov had put his arm round her shoulders, and squeezed her close, allowing his fingers to go right round and stroke the side of her breast ... and the Empress had been watching. My God, she thought. If he is her lover... but of course he was her lover. Then did she indeed risk disgrace.

And once again they had drunk vodka. She could remember nothing after that. She rolled over, sat up. Nothing at all. Then who had brought her in here and put her to bed? At least she was still fully dressed.

She watched the door open, pulled the sheet to her throat. But Maria Ivanova was as sombrely serious as when they had first met.

106

'Her Majesty sends you a syllabub,' Maria Ivanova said. 'To remove your headache.'

Geneviève gazed at her. No dream, she thought.

'Her Majesty also invites you to sup with her, mademoiselle,' Maria Ivanova said.

Geneviève's head came up.

'At ten o'clock,' Maria Ivanova said. 'It is now eight. So if mademoiselle would care to arise and change her dress, Dr Todorsky is waiting to commence your instruction.'

So much for my resistance, Geneviève thought, as she walked in the little walled garden below her apartments. In fact, there was not a great deal of difference between Orthodox and Catholic usage; it was the emphasis that she found most disturbing. But what choice did she have? And to tell the truth, she now supposed that without her daily conversation with the Archimandrite she would go mad with boredom.

She pulled her fur trimmed pelisse closer to keep out the unceasing wind which swept straight out of the Arctic, wriggled her toes inside their woollen stockings inside their furlined leather boots, just to make sure they had not frozen; she sank several inches into the snow at every step. The Russians already thought her mad, wishing to take exercise, out of doors, in March. But she was to be humoured. She was one of the Empress's toys.

Was it really March? Had she really spent four months in this prison? Because it was a prison, if lacking bars. It had its guards, and it had its barriers. St Petersburg was separated from the outside world as if surrounded by a massive, unscalable wall, as it was surrounded by a massive, impassable sea of ice. Those ships in the harbour had also been here for four months; those at sea had no chance of entering Neva for a similar period. Sleighs came and went from time to time, but the journey into the interior of the country, down to Moscow, for instance, was apparently a hazardous adventure, in which cold and blizzards and starvation and wolves vied for supremacy, it was not lightly to be undertaken, and the Empress had no intention of leaving her capital until the spring.

Instead she locked herself away in her winter palace and gave herself over to absurdity. Certainly there was little state business to be conducted. Elizabeth Petrovna consumed vast quantities of vodka, and she laughed or she wept as the mood took her, and she played cards or silly word games, and she spent long hours in devotion, praying in her private chapel or kneeling beside her bed, nor could Geneviève doubt that her piety was genuine. That she did more than this also seemed likely, as she was never to be found without the company of some handsome young man, either Vorontsov or the Shuvalov brothers, Alexander and Peter, or Alexis Razumovsky, who Geneviève suspected was her favourite of all.

But drinking apart, there was no great evidence of moral laxity in the Russian court. Rather was there a stifling, unutterable boredom, at least to anyone brought up in the world of theatre and conversation, to anyone with an active mind. The books, such as were available, were all history or religion, and all in Russian. Painstakingly Geneviève set to work to learn the language, but it was a slow business, with very little reward apparently to be obtained at the end of it.

If it were possible even to see an end. To contemplate remaining here, or spending her summers in Moscow, which even the Russian ladies told her was a tedious place, was unthinkable. But what alternative did she have? She was completely cut off from the other members of the embassy; her attendance on the Empress was only required during the afternoon, when no state business was conducted, and Elizabeth Petrovna could shut herself up with her intimates and amuse herself as she chose. Geneviève was not, apparently, to be allowed to fulfill the duties of a lady of the bechamber, until she was adopted into the Russian faith, at which time, she understood, her name would be changed and she would become Russian in fact as well as desire. Geneviève could imagine nothing more ghastly.

Especially as she did not know what else would be involved when she was truly acceptable. The Empress had an alarming habit of resting her chin on her forefinger and staring at her newest acquisition, her eyes sleepily opaque, obviously considering some very private thought, at the centre of which was most certainly Geneviève d'Éon. It could only be marriage. To a boyar? According to Maria Ivanova, who accepted it as entirely natural, Russian husbands beat their wives every night before going to bed, spent their time at least as drunk as ever the Empress, and withal indulged in the most disgusting habits.

And yet, she was so desperately lonely, she sometimes wondered if even to be beaten nightly and debauched the rest of the time might not be a relief. She was discovering that however alone she had always regarded herself, she had never been *lonely*. When she had been a girl there had been Monsieur Lannès and Madame Louvanne. At the Mazarin College her school companions, if certainly not her friends, had been there to quarrel with. How could she quarrel with Margaret, who was even more depressed than herself, or with the faithful Maria, who sought only to make her happy according to her own lights, but whose conversation never rose above the level of inanity? In her desperation she once attempted to leave her rooms and wander the palace by herself, to seek someone, anyone, with whom she could communicate. But always there were guards, staring at her impersonally, until she encountered a major-domo who gently but firmly indicated that she must return to her own apartments, and remain there until summoned by the Empress her mistress. Only in this frozen garden, with its patch of sky visible through the high walls surrounding it, could she even look at freedom.

Her emotions were hardly less troublesome, hardly less disturbing. Indeed, they were the most disturbing aspect of all, a sudden awareness that she *wanted*. What? A man? She hated the entire sex. But she had become used to them. There was a looming disaster. She refused to accept that her body could make certain demands, could leave her irritable and ill tempered because they were not to be granted. That would be to reduce herself to the level of other women, and she hated *them*, if anything, more than men, for their weakness and their eternal submission.

Once again, as in her schooldays, there remained Jules. But more than ever surrender to Jules was an impossible thought. Even supposing she was ever allowed any privacy, which she was not, save in the garden; if not Margaret one of the Russian girls was always present, so much so that she was forced to assume they were instructed to watch her. But she did not *want* a man. She wanted only the sensation which King Louis had so successfully induced on odd occasions. In the secrecy of her own bed, huddled beneath the heaped coverlets, with only the snores of her attendants to disturb her, it was possible to reproduce something of what she sought. Indeed she discovered she could induce a gasping ecstacy with very little trouble, even if she necessarily had to suppress her tumultuous excitement for fear of alerting one of the girls. Here was some relief. But

8

insufficient. She realised that love, of any sort, has to be shared to be truly enjoyed. It must exist in the mind as much as in the body, or it is like eating meat without salt or spices, a necessary affair when one is truly hungry, but scarcely a satisfying one. Love. I do not wish to love, she reminded herself. I wish only to hate. But I wish to *be* loved. There is my deadly, unutterable secret.

Where then was the girl who had determined to fight all of mankind, who had considered herself an outcast, who had been sure of eventual victory by her knowledge of human weaknesses and human capabilities? Were all of *her* talents going to be washed away in a sea of vodka?

But what could she do, while incarcerated in this snow prison? How could she resist the Empress where the Empress was all powerful? Where she *belonged* to the Empress. How could she dare even consider an independent stance?

It was all a dream, she thought sadly. All a miserable dream. I have never *been*. I am nothing more than a belonging, to my parents when I was first born, to Great Uncle Henri after that, to the Prince of Conti after that, then to the King, and now to the Empress. I have no more individual entity than a picture on the wall. I am a *nothing*.

'Mademoiselle.' Margaret, huddling beneath her pelisse, peering at her from the doorway. 'Mademoiselle.'

Geneviève went towards her, realised the tears were freezing on her cheeks. Hurriedly she wiped them dry. 'Yes?'

'There is a young gentleman to see you, mademoiselle. The young gentleman from the embassy.'

Geneviève frowned at her, went inside, climbed the stairs, past the eternal armed guards. Captain Menzies? She had seen or indeed heard nothing of the embassy for the entire four months. She had delivered *her* embassy to the Empress, and the Empress had been pleased. What could Captain Menzies wish now?

He was standing at the window in her parlour, looking out at the snow. He turned at her entrance, and bowed; he had put on his best satin jacket for this occasion, and rested his left hand on the pommel of his sword. One of the girls had already poured him a cup of tea.

'Mademoiselle. How charming you look. The air loses its bite when you enter the room.'

'Compliments hardly fit the Russian scene,' Genevieve said,

listening to Margaret close the door behind her. She took off her glove, gave him her hand to kiss.

'But we, mademoiselle, we are French,' he said. 'You by birth and myself by adoption. Russia can be nothing more than a setting in which we may disport ourselves.'

She presumed he had been rehearsing. She was far more interested in the glass of tea being offered her by the girl. She sipped, felt the warmth tracing its way through her body, through every vein. 'A cold setting, monsieur.' She gestured to the chairs. 'Will you not sit down?'

He perched himself on the edge. 'Indeed it is cold, mademoiselle. But we are informed that the first signs of spring are already in the air. That it will not long be delayed.'

Genevieve nodded. 'Indeed, monsieur, I have already noticed them.'

'And thus I have come to say goodbye.'

Her head turned, sharply. 'Goodbye?'

'The Chevalier Douglas' mission has been greeted most kindly by the Russians, and they have agreed to, or at least agreed to discuss, all the points His Majesty bade us raise. Indeed, our business has been completed these last two weeks, and we have been waiting only for an improvement in the weather. I had then assumed that you would be accompanying us back to Paris, but the Chevalier this morning informed me that you are remaining in Russia, having become so entranced with the country and its people that you cannot bear to tear yourself away . . ?'

He paused, perhaps both for confirmation of his suggestion and also because she was staring at him in consternation. Somehow, although she had seen none of the members of the embassy during the past four months, the realisation that they were departing, back to the sunshine and the unforced laughter that was Paris, the etiquette and the intrigue, the elegance and the energy, made her want to scream. They were going, and she was staying. Could summer in Moscow possibly be any different to winter in St Petersburg? Could the Empress possibly change her habits? Could *she* possibly hope for an improvement in her circumstances?

'Mademoiselle?' Menzies spoke gently.

'You are going,' she said. 'When?'

'As soon as the ice melts sufficiently for us to take ship, mademoiselle. Why, will you miss us?'

She glanced at him. 'Of course I shall, monsieur. I am not that much in love with Russia. I do not think I am in love with Russia at all.'

'As be assured that I shall miss you, mademoiselle,' he said with a gentle flush.

Geneviève frowned at him. He had not seen her for four months, and before that she had made her dislike, or at least her disinterest, plain enough, she would have thought.

'You'll forgive my boldness, mademoiselle,' he said. 'I am an uncouth Scot.'

My God, she thought. Of course, he is a Calvinist, being a Scot. The thought had not crossed her mind before. He is of those who renounce all pleasures. He wants *nothing* of me. And he is going, back across the sea to Lubeck and thence back to France.

Dare I return to France, unbidden? To add the Prince of Conti to Richelieu as my enemy, for undoubtedly the Empress would not be pleased were I to escape. But would not anything, a life of poverty in Cherbourg, be better than remaining here?

But then, dare I involve so young and innocent a man? For he will certainly be punished. Yet, she reflected, how can either Richelieu or Conti punish a Scot? Save by expelling him from France, and he must be prepared for such an eventuality. Besides, she realised, even if he is punished, even if he were to lose his head, he *is* a Calvinist, a creature of the devil, so Madame Louvanne and Prior de Maas had always insisted. I need have no concern with such as he.

'Mademoiselle?' He was now definitely anxious.

And again besides, she thought, shall I not make his last days on this earth happy? She smiled at him. 'You have not offended me, monsieur.' She snapped her fingers. 'Leave us.'

The girls glanced at the young man, broke into gentle giggles, and left the room.

'You too, Margaret,' Geneviève commanded.

Margaret obeyed, also with a sly smile.

'Mademoiselle,' Adam protested. 'It is not proper for me to be alone here with you.'

'Stuff and nonsense,' she said. 'We are not in France now, even less are we in Scotland.' She went into her bedchamber. 'Will you not come in?'

'Mademoiselle?' He hesitated in the doorway.

'I would speak with you, Monsieur Menzies,' she said. 'Privily. Nothing more than that.'

Cautiously he came into the room.

'And close the door,' Geneviève commanded.

'Mademoiselle . . .'

'Then I shall do it.' She walked past him, closed the door, turned the massive key. 'I do not think even the Empress's spies, and all my Russian servants are her spies, you may be sure of that, can overhear us in here.'

'Mademoiselle.' He licked his lips. 'I . . .'

'Listen to me,' she said. 'I would return to France. With you.'

'Return to France? But I understood . . .'

'I was sent here as a lady in waiting to the Empress. Yes. It was considered necessary to remove me from the reach of the Duke of Richelieu. But I can remain no longer. This place . . . it chills my bones. And Richelieu will have forgotten one such as I, by now. His quarrel was with my brother, after all. I must go, monsieur. I . . .' She searched her brain for a suitable lie. 'The Empress has decided to marry me off, to a boyar who lives in the very depths of Siberia. I should go mad. Besides, the man is four times my age.' She hesitated, wondering if her mathematics had been too exaggerated.

She doubted Adam had properly heard. 'Marriage? You? Sent to Siberia . . . oh, my dear mademoiselle . . .'

'Then you'll help me?'

He hesitated. 'It would be very dangerous . . .'

'I shall reward you,' she said. 'I swear it. You . . . you may ask anything of me, you may *have* anything of me, once we are on board your ship. I swear it.' She bit her lip. He did not seem particularly excited at her offer.

'Of course I can ask nothing of you, mademoiselle,' he said. 'I am a gentleman, and you are a lady. If I can possibly help you to escape such an unfortunate marriage, be sure that I will.'

My God, she thought; he is *innocent*. He knows *nothing*. My God, it is not possible. It could not be possible. She had never met a man in her life, beginning with Father, who had not wished to use her brain or her body for some purpose of his own. She had never met a woman either, save for Mama. But here was a young man offering her his help with no thought of reward? It had to be a subterfuge. Oh, indeed. Well, she was sufficiently used to subterfuge, to be sure. She did not doubt she could match *him*.

'Then I most gratefully accept your help, monsieur,' she said.

'And be sure that I *shall* reward you, whenever the opportunity arises. Now, let us make a plan.'

'It will be difficult and dangerous, as I have said, mademoiselle. Would it not be best for you boldly to apply to Her Majesty for permission to leave the country? She could hardly refuse you were you to say you wished to see your family for a last time before being married.'

Geneviève got up. 'She can and she will, monsieur. You do not know the Empress as I do. God forbid. No, no, it will be a simple matter. I will take my girl Margaret into my confidence, for she can be trusted; between us we will make for me a suit of men's clothing . . .'

'Men's clothing?' He frowned at her. 'You will dress as a man?'

'Why should I not?'

'Well . . . mademoiselle . . . you would have to walk like a man, and act like a man . . .'

'I assure you I am a very capable actor.'

'But in any event, mademoiselle, it is unseemly. Why, it is criminal. You would be burned as a witch.'

'Not if we succeed in getting away. I do promise you I shall change to my proper station as soon as we gain your ship. And what is the difference between being burned alive or frozen alive, when you come down to it?'

He hesitated, biting his lip. 'You are a very brave girl, mademoiselle.'

'I am a very desperate girl, monsieur. Besides, I shall have your courage to sustain me.' She waited, once again, to see if he would take advantage of their situation and her apparent admiration, but he merely flushed. Geneviève sighed. He was quite intriguing in his innocence; her always susceptible curiosity was wondering what he *would* be like, as a lover. 'Well, then, monsieur, you have but to find a means of letting me know when you intend to depart.'

'Be sure that I shall, mademoiselle. As soon as the snow begins to thaw.'

'I shall await your message with a beating heart, monsieur.' She extended her hand, and he seized it to kiss it, suddenly raising his head at the sound of a door being thrown back on its hinges in the next room. 'Mademoiselle?'

Geneviève frowned. 'You shall remain here while I see who so rudely enters my apartments,' she said, walked to the door, and was stopped by a most violent banging on the panels.

'Open up,' demanded the unmistakable voice of Elizabeth Petrovna.

'My God,' Geneviève gasped. 'The Empress.'

Adam's face paled, but his lips came firmly together. 'She will be angry at finding me in your bedchamber, and you bethrothed to one of her lords.'

'Angry. My God . . .'

Once again the crashing summons. 'Open up. I may break the door down.'

'Wait.' Geneviève twisted the key, gazed at Elizabeth Petrovna, with several men at her shoulder, and Margaret and Jules standing against the far wall in terror.

'Aha,' remarked the Empress. 'So the girl was right.'

When I discover which one of them it was, Geneviève thought . . . but now was time to think of herself. She sank into a curtsey. 'I am overwhelmed, Your Majesty.'

'You.' Elizabeth Petrovna pointed at Adam. 'You are one of the Chevalier Douglas' entourage.'

'I am, Your Majesty.'

'Lured in here by this . . . this siren,' the Empress said. 'Begone with you. You are innocent. I will not punish you, save to command you to leave Russia. Quickly, boy.'

Adam hesitated, glancing at Geneviève, whose belly was commencing to fill with lead. She had not seen the Empress angry before. Now it occurred to her that she was keeping herself under control only with a great effort.

No doubt her alarm showed in her face, for Adam suddenly squared his shoulders. 'I shall not leave, Your Majesty, unless Mademoiselle d'Éon. accompanies me.'

Elizabeth Petrovna stared at him in total amazement.

'Mademoiselle d'Éon,. if I may remind Your Majesty, is a subject of the King of France, and is not to be treated with contumely. She informs me that it is your decision that she should undertake a marriage to which she is opposed, and has asked me to assist her. This I have promised to do.' He paused, because the Empress had gone quite purple in the face. But now her colour faded, a little.

'You would defy me, Scotsman?' she asked in a low voice. 'In favour of that . . .' Her arm flung out, the finger pointing. 'But I had forgot. She is your paramour.'

Adam flushed. 'I do assure you, Your Majesty . . .'

'Leave, boy, or reckon with my anger.'

Adam glanced at Geneviève; she could think of nothing to say, or do. She had never dreamed he would attempt to defend her.

'Your Majesty, I . . .'

'Seize him,' Elizabeth Petrovna said, stepping to one side.

The guards moved forward, and Adam in turn leapt backwards, drawing his sword as he did so. Geneviève hastily scrambled across the bed, wishing that she too had a weapon. There was a clash of steel, a shout from Adam, and the first guardsman fell, while the others hastily retreated.

'One man?' the Empress demanded contemptuously. 'Fetch a pistol. Shoot him down.'

'One man?' the Empress demanded contemputously. 'Fetch a pistol. Shoot him down.'

'No,' Geneviève cried. 'I beg of you, Your Majesty, spare his life at the least. He has but acted out of love for me.'

Adam gave her a startled glance, and slowly lowered his sword point.

'You will be killed, if we do not surrender,' Geneviève said. 'You may kill several of them. I may kill several more.' She bit her lip; she had not meant to say that. 'But they must be too many for us in the end.'

'You have a cool head on those lovely shoulders, mademoiselle,' the Empress remarked. 'Do not suppose surrender will save you from my anger.'

'I ask for our lives,' Geneviève said.

Elizabeth Petrovna regarded her for some moments. Behind her there was a new hubbub.

'They have brought muskets, Sire,' said the captain of the guard.

'Tell them it will not be necessary,' the Empress said. 'I shall execute neither of you, Mademoiselle d'Éon. You have the word of a Romanoff.'

'I thank you, Sire. You had best put up your sword, Monsieur Menzies.'

Adam hesitated a last time, but he knew there was no alternative. He sighed, reversed his blade, extended the hilt towards the captain.

'Sensible fellow,' the Empress remarked. 'Your sentence is banishment to Siberia for the rest of your life.'

'Siberia?' he cried. 'You cannot.'

'I may do whatever I wish, in Russia,' the Empress said. 'And do not suppose King Louis will risk a diplomatic incident to save the life of a Scottish adventurer. Not one who was discovered in the bedchamber of one of my ladies.'

'Do not fret,' Geneviève said. 'It will be a new life, for us both.'

The Empress gave a brief laugh. 'Both? *You* are not going to Siberia, my pretty child. No, no. I wish to teach you your place. I wish to hear you scream.'

Geneviève stared at her, heart pounding. 'You gave your word . . .'

'And I shall keep my word, Mademoiselle d'Éon. I shall neither hang you nor shoot you nor sever your head from your body. But I shall certainly see to it that you are knouted into a proper frame of mind. Seize her.'

Chapter Five

Geneviève could only stare at the Empress in horror, too surprised even to move. Margaret gave a gasp and fell to her knees, no doubt afraid that she would suffer a similar fate. Adam Menzies gave a shout and leapt for the man to whom he had surrendered his sword.

'Remove that fellow,' commanded Elizabeth Petrovna. 'And bring the woman downstairs.'

At last Geneviève came to her senses. Far better to die with a sword in her hand than to have the skin slowly stripped from her bones. She ran forward in an attempt to help Adam and gain a weapon for herself, but was seized round the waist by one of the guards, while two others held her wrists, and pulled her back. She fought against them but lacked the strength to throw them off; Adam was already being dragged from the room, and as he continued to struggle, he received a blow on the head which sent him senseless to the floor, from whence he was picked up like a sack of flour.

'Sire,' Geneviève begged as she was dragged behind him. 'Spare that young man. He but came to bid me farewell. It was I kept him here.'

The Empress snapped her fingers, and Geneviève was thrust through the outer door and into the corridor. Clearly she was not going to escape them, and she had no desire to be dragged all the way to wherever she was going. Apart from the humiliation they were hurting her.

'Wait,' she gasped. 'I will come with you. I will surrender.'

But the men holding her were enjoying their work. They continued to grasp her wrists and arms, one even had hold of her hair, which he tugged from time to time, whenever indeed she would speak. They hurried her along the corridor, past the impassive guards, down stairs and along other corridors, and down more stairs, while the always chilly palace became colder, until finally they emerged through a doorway into a courtyard she had not previously visited. Here to her horror she saw there was a whipping stall – two posts connected by a crossbar some six feet above the ground – erected in the centre, jutting up from the snow, which was itself trampled and discoloured, with blood, she realised; as it had snowed during the previous nights this could only mean that some unfortunate had been flogged that very morning. Could such things be happening all the time, in this palace, without her knowledge?

At least she doubted she would properly understand her punishment; she had not been allowed to pull on her cloak, and the cold struck at her like a live thing, whipping the breath from her lungs even as she felt her cheeks and nose go numb.

She half fell, and was carried across the snow and placed between the uprights. Her arms were lifted above her head, and secured by lengths of rope to rings set in the crossbar; for a moment she hung from them, but as they immediately commenced to ache she thrust her feet downwards and found she could stand.

'The knout,' commanded the Empress, who had followed them down the stairs and now stood behind Geneviève. 'Show her the knout.'

Geneviève sucked air into her lungs, blinked tears from her eyes. Oh, why had she not seized a sword and died fighting beside Adam? Why, she might even have managed to kill the Empress herself. But she had played the coward. Why? She could not understand it. She had fought Richeliue's retainers without hesitation.

A man stood in front of her, smiling. In his gloved hands he held the whip. But what a whip. Geneviève blinked, and felt her chin sag in horror. The thick bone handle ended in four lashes, made of rope in which were twined lengths of wire. Her knees gave way and she hung for a moment before struggling back to her feet. It was the last time she would ever stand, she knew.

'Prepare her,' Elizabeth Petrovna commanded.

Fingers dug into Geneviève's bodice, pulled. The material ripped, and her shoulders commenced to freeze. But they were not merely going to bare her shoulders. Now they burst the straps by her petticoats, rolling them too down to her waist. The cold struck at her breasts and her nipples seemed to double in size. She felt fingers on her back and knew they were cutting the straps for her hoop; this took several minutes but her corset proved no obstacle; a moment later that too fell forward and she was naked from the hips upwards.

The man with the knout extended the whip, slowly, still smiling at her, shook it in front of her face so that she could smell it, through even the cold, a foetid smell, redolent of the hundreds of backs it had reduced to bloody pulp. Then he flicked it, and one of the lashes brushed her right nipple. He head jerked and she lost her breath.

The man walked behind her. Oh, God, she thought. What to do? Tense my muscles? Will that not be worse? Collapse and hope to die? I will die, undoubtedly, but not until they are ready. Oh, God . . . she realised she had closed her eyes, and opened them again. Nothing had happened as yet, save that the Empress had walked round in front of her, and was peering at her, and not merely her face or her collapsed hair, she realised. She watched the royal tongue come out and then go back in again. She had only ever seen such an expression on the face of a man, and she did not understand it at all.

The Empress spoke, in Russian. Geneviève understood enough of the language by now to realise she was about to be taken down. But why? For some even more refined torture? Her wrists were released and she would have fallen, but a man caught her round the waist.

'Carry her,' Elizabeth Petrovna commanded, her voice suddenly having lost its harshness. 'She cannot walk.'

Another man lifted her feet from the ground. The cold pain was so intense she wanted to scream, knew she had to scream, or she would go mad. She screamed, sending every last ounce of sound she could command out of her lungs and into the sky.

'Fetch a blanket,' the Empress commanded. 'She is in pain.'

The doors were opened and she was carried back inside the palace. How warm the palace, where she had supposed it the coldest place on earth. But the sudden rise in temperature made her scream again. She could scream all she wished, she realised. She could do anything she liked, allow her body total surrender to every urge. She was a dead woman, on her way to hell.

The men set her on her feet, had to catch her as she fell. A blanket was wrapped about her, and she was lifted again.

'To her own apartments,' the Empress commanded.

Geneviève was carried up the stairs, back along the corridors, while she shivered and shuddered, closed her eyes and opened them, moaned with the returning circulation which bit into her toes and breasts and fingers, seeped through her arms and wrists, had pins and needles even affecting her nose. The guards watched her return with their usual impassivity. She wondered if *anything* would cause one of these imperial puppets to blink an eyelid.

The doors of her apartment were opened. She saw the girls, one of whom had betrayed her, and then Margaret and Jules huddled together, and they had never really liked each other. She did not wish to see them, ever again, not after today, and shut her eyes. She was placed in her own bed, rolled beneath the coverlets, and released. Her knees came up and she attempted to hug herself into the smallest possible shape, to use heat from her knees to warm her breasts, from her heels to warm her bottom. But she doubted she would ever be warm again.

She heard the Empress's voice, giving orders, but she could not understand what was being said. Then her head was raised.

'Drink this.'

Elizabeth Petrovna, herself holding a mug of vodka to her lips. Whatever had caused the Empress to change her mind? Or had she never really intended to do more than frighten her? Geneviève could not believe that when she recalled that angry face, those flashing eyes, that harsh voice. But here she was, ministering like a nurse or a lover. And how good the vodka tasted; it filled Geneviève's throat with heat, and she could feel the liquid tracing its way down her chest and into her stomach.

'I will fetch some more vodka.' Gently her head was returned to the pillow, and this time she could leave it there instead of bobbing it down beneath the blanket. Now she found her breathing had returned to normal, and she could even think, her thoughts made pleasant by the alcohol rolling through her system.

'Drink.' Once again the Empress, kneeling on the bed. Geneviève obeyed, and lost awareness of the cold, although she knew she was still shivering. She turned her head, looked around the room. It was empty, save for the Empress, and the outer room was equally empty, the fire roaring in the stove, sending its warmth towards her.

She gazed at Elizabeth Petrovna, did not immediately recognize her. Gone was the aura of omnipotence, the arrogant confidence with which this most powerful of women habitually regarded the world. The daughter of Peter the Great looked like a little girl.

'I was angry with you.' she said. 'You made me angry with you. But how could I stay angry with you, Geneviève? My Geneviève.'

To Geneviève's consternation she pushed herself off the bed, began to undress. The Empress of all the Russias, undressing herself, in the bedchamber of one of her ladies.

'How do you feel?' Elizabeth Petrovna asked. 'Will you not speak to me, my Geneviève?'

Geneviève licked her lips. 'I . . . I am very cold, Sire.'

'I know. And I will warm you. But your clothes are even colder than your body, and ruined besides. Take them off, Geneviève. Take them off.' She smiled, and seemed to grow even younger. 'I would look upon you.'

If only it was possible to understand. But Geneviève only knew that to disobey might be to make the Empress angry again, and she was not prepared to risk that at this moment. For the first time in her life she had surrendered utterly. For the first time in her life she had faced the certainty of death, and however her survival was to be managed, she did not wish to look there again.

She sat up, pushed back the covers, got out of bed, and gave a moan of pain; her toes were still a mass of pins and needles.

'I will help you' Elizabeth Petrovna, already stripped to her shift, once again stood before her. Her hands were warm, but strangely, they rested first on Geneviève's shoulders, gently caressing the still icy flesh. 'You are so beautiful, my dear. I had not know how beautiful.' She gave a little laugh, and flushed. 'Or perhaps I did, because there is so much beauty in your face. But I rejected it. I should reject it now. It is wrong of me, sinful. Oh, it is sinful. I should have let them kill you, and then my temptation would have been behind me. But I am a poor, weak, sinful creature.' The hands slid down Geneviève's arms and then moved across to touch the still frozen nipples, while Geneviève could only stare at her in total amazement. 'You are so . . . so strong,' Elizabeth Petrovna said. 'I have never seen a woman with a body like yours, my darling, darling girl. These muscles . . .' The hands were at Geneviève's stomach, and she insensibly tensed her muscles at the suggestion. 'You could be a man, but for your beauty. Let me see the rest of you, my darling. Please. Let me see the rest of you.'

Geneviève released what was left of the ties for her gown, raised it over her head and threw it on the floor. Her petticoats followed and her destroyed hoop and corset fell of their own accord. Only the woollen shift remained, and this made the Empress smile.

'Wool,' she said, herself removing the garment. 'Next to the skin. You find our climate too cold for you, my sweet Geneviève. But you will not find me so, I promise you.' She fell to her knees. 'Oh, my sweet, let me kiss you.'

Geneviève decided she had to be dreaming, that the Empress of Russia was kneeling before her, and that handsome, haughty face was buried in her pubes, and that royal tongue was thrusting where only men or her own fingers had gone before. She sat down with the sheer surprise of it, and the joy of it too, because for how long had she wanted to be loved . . . but by a woman? By an Empress?

Her movement did not seem to disturb Elizabeth Petrovna, who continued to hug her close, but now released her with the suddenness of all her actions. 'You are cold,' she said. 'You are shivering. Beneath the blankets, quickly. I will warm you, my love.'

She held Geneviève's ankles, bundled her into the bed, stood up to take off her shift. Geneviève pulled the blankets to her neck, continuing to stare. Elizabeth Petrovna was as tall as herself, and more powerfully built, but all was voluptuous flesh. Huge breasts, surprisingly high – but then, she had never had children – and tipped with even larger nipples, made enormous by the chill. Wide thighs, enclosing a full, pouting belly, a massive thatch of curling dark hair, fleshy hips descending to long, strong legs. She was about the handsomest woman Geneviève had ever seen. Not, she realised, that she had seen very many women.

And she was getting into the bed beside her. Geneviève had no idea what would happen next, what she wanted to happen next.

122

Elizabeth rested on her elbow, looking down at her; her breast lay on Geneviève's arm. 'You are cold, my darling,' she said. 'You have not forgiven me.'

Geneviève licked her lips. 'I . . . I am cold, Sire. But *with* cold.'

'Then you *have* forgiven me?'

'I . . .' She only knew she had to keep the Empress in this mood, and for as long as possible. 'How can I dare to forgive an Empress, Sire?'

Elizabeth laughed. Her breath rushed against Geneviève's face. 'But I am not an Empress, now, my darling. I am a woman, surrendering to her passions, her criminal passions.' She drove her face forward, her mouth enveloping Geneviève's, her hand beginning at her breast but rapidly sliding down her belly to seek the slit, to introduce wave after wave of the most consummate passion Geneviève had ever felt. And suddenly she knew that this would not stop before she was sated, that she was going to enjoy the most magnificent moment of her life . . . with a woman? And an Empress?

The thrusting tongue left her own, the big, handsome face was inches away. 'You *are* cold,' Elizabeth accused.

Geneviève realised her muscles had tensed at the thought of what was happening. 'With cold, Sire,' she said. 'With cold. If . . . if I could have another glass of vodka . . .'

Elizabeth frowned at her for a moment. Then she nodded. 'One more. Too much vodka dulls the senses. Just enough, and one is in heaven. I will fetch it.'

She rolled out of bed, went to the table. Geneviève watched her. What to do? What to be? But offend her, and she might find herself back beneath that whipping post. Humour her, and all things were possible. It might even be possible to save that young Scotsman from his Siberian exile. Now why should I wish to do that, she wondered? Have I any reason to risk my life for his? Because he risked his life for me? Did he not only wish my body? Does not everybody only wish my body? Even the Empress? And I have no cause to love *her*.

But it was necessary to love her. For the glass of vodka was back at her lips. Elizabeth allowed her to drink half of it, took it away and drank the other half herself. Then she threw the goblet to the floor, where it shattered.

'Now, my darling,' she whispered, crawling beneath the blankets, and this time resting her entire body on top of Geneviève's, moving it to and fro, scraping breast against

123

breast, belly against belly, thigh against thigh, toe against toe, and then mouth against mouth. 'Now, I shall warm you up.'

Geneviève awoke to find herself alone. But she was as warm as toast, her only discomfort a slight headache. From the vodka. And against that there was the most magnificent feeling of lassitude, of well-being. Because she had . . . she sat up, the blanket clutched to her throat. The Empress's fingers, introduced so softly but so insistently between her legs, had sent her whirling through a long sensation of increasing passion, until she had thought she would scream, until, she remembered, she *had* screamed, as her body had writhed, as she had held Elizabeth tighter and tighter, and as Elizabeth had smiled her pleasure. Then she had wanted to lie still, and sleep, but then the Empress had wished her to reciprocate. And she had wanted to do it, to feel the Empress's own warmth, to kiss the royal nipple, to feel the imperial body begin to tremble against her, to know its explosion of passion, which had equalled her own, to hear the Autocrat of all the Russias whispering in her ear, 'Oh, Geneviève, my darling Geneviève, how can they know. How can they *know*.'

They apparently being the world of men. Or perhaps women also. The Empress possessed a very private world into which . . . Geneviève frowned. Was she the only one ever allowed in there? How could she be? Elizabeth Petrovna was nearly forty years old, and of those forty years the last six had been spent in a position of utter omnipotence, able to gratify her every whim. How long had she resisted the temptation? Or had she known the ecstacy of loving another woman even as a girl, shut up in her convent, unsure whether she would ever be able to scale the heights of autocracy?

She watched the door open, Margaret come in. The Scots girl hurried across the room.

'Oh, mademoiselle, mademoiselle. We were so worried.'

Geneviève gave her her hand to kiss, looked past her at Jules, standing in the doorway, shifting from foot to foot.

'We had counted you lost, mademoiselle.'

'Well, I have survived. Her Majesty appears to be a changeable woman. And I am hungry. You'll prepare food. And remove those clothes. I do not wish to look at them again.'

'Of course, mademoiselle. Of course.' Margaret hurried from the room, and Geneviève saw the four girls lined up against the wall.

'Nor do I wish to look at *them* again, Jules,' she said. She might as well take advantage of Elizabeth's sudden passion, she supposed, and one of those four had betrayed her. 'Send them away.'

'Of course, mademoiselle.' Jules turned away, stopped as the outer door opened to admit Maria Ivanova. Why, Geneviève thought, nothing might have happened at all. This might be a day just like any other, with yesterday nothing more than a dream.

'Good morning,' she said.

'Morning?' inquired Maria. 'It is past noon.'

'Good heavens. No wonder I am hungry.'

Maria came into the room, closed the door behind her, having seen Jules to the other side. 'The Empress commands your presence. You are to wear black.'

Geneviève gazed at her. Does she know, she wondered? My God, has *she* ever shared Elizabeth's bed? But she is not beautiful, not even attractive. Although she appears to have quite a good figure. Who could tell? How would she ever find out? Save by asking.

'Black?'

'The Empress wishes you to attend confession.'

'But . . . it will be a sin. I am not yet taken into the Church.'

'You will be adopted into the Holy Church today, Geneviève. It is the Empress's command. She will herself be your sponsor.'

Does she know, Geneviève wondered? Does she?

'The Empress is most kind,' she said. 'You will have heard that we had a difference of opinion yesterday.'

'I have heard,' Maria agreed. 'You were very foolish, Geneviève. Had Her Majesty not changed her mind, you could have lost your life. Certainly you would never have been the same. I have seen women knouted. There was a very noble lady incurred the displeasure of the Empress Anna, only twelve years ago. She was knouted in the public square, before thousands. Her back was cut to ribbons, and she lost the power of speech. Nor has she ever regained it, to my knowledge.'

Genevieve refused to shudder. 'But Her Majesty *did* change her mind,' she pointed out.

'She is given to moments of gentleness,' Maria said. 'For which, as I have said, you must be grateful. Now you must get dressed, Geneviève. Her Majesty will certainly not wish to be kept waiting.'

The Archimandrite had already just about completed her instruction, including the memorisation of the long confession of faith, which she now proceeded to recite before the assembly in the Empress's private chapel. In addition to Her Majesty, looking her normal regal self in a diamond studded gown, there were the Grand Duke and Duchess, Voronstov and both Shuvalovs, Maria and several other ladies in waiting. Do *they* know, Geneviève wondered wildly? Do they know of me, and her? But no one gave a sign, and she proceeded on her way, reciting the Nicene creed in its Orthodox form, declaring that the Holy Spirit proceeded from the Father only, and eventually receiving the sacrament and her new Russian name, which the Empress had decreed should match her own, Elizabeth. She could only pray to the Holy Mother to be forgiven for this apostasy, remind the Blessed Virgin that she had very little choice. So no doubt she should have been a martyr. But it would not have been a martyr to her religion, she reasoned. She would have been executed in the most horrible imaginable manner for angering the Empress.

Then it was time for her to confess. Elizabeth Petrovna herself accompanied her into the confessional, and they told the Archimandrite how they had loved illicitly, if not specifically with whom, and were bade to do penance, together, on six consecutive Fridays, dressed only in their shifts. Geneviève was inclined to be amused at this, but the Empress was very stern.

'Our sin is mortal,' she said. 'Terrible. Unforgivable. It must be fought against, Elizabeth Wilhelminova. Do not forget that. It must be fought against.' She sighed. 'But I am weak, weak, and you are too beautiful to be resisted.' And a moment later Geneviève was again in her arms.

So then, she thought, when she regained the privacy of her own chamber, I am debauched, and Conti will be highly amused, should he ever learn of it. But what do *I* think of it? Am I as shocked as I pretend? I have never wanted love, because I have known that I could never have love, not a creature who is half man and half woman. Love demands an intimacy, a sharing of the innermost thoughts, certainly a sharing of all the emotions, an understanding of everything that goes to make up a human being. But how could any other human being, man or woman, understand Charles Geneviève d'Éon? She did not understand herself. She never knew when her male upbringing would overtake her emotions, call upon her to resolve her problems by the sword rather than by her brain or her smile. She never knew which of her sexual passions would control her, especially when she was filled with vodka. For this was undoubtedly her main attraction to the Empress, who had many other pretty girls at her back and call. But none with muscles in arm and shoulder and belly and thigh, none who might suddenly take over the role of the dominant partner.

Because the Empress was not offering love. In that she was deluding herself. Geneviève supposed, in a minor way, King Louis had at least been fond of her, as he had confided in her, and as he had sent for her when he needed an intensely private service. Here in St Petersburg there was not even fondness. The Empress sought physical sensation. Nothing more sublime than that. Having been checked in nothing for several years, after a childhood of hovering on the brink of permanent incarceration in a convent, she had allowed her most bestial instincts to take control of her personality. Even Louis was restricted by form, by custom, by the rules laid down by his famous great grandfather. Elizabeth Petrovna recognised no rules. She slept when she was sleepy, she ate when she was hungry, she drank when she was thirsty, and she sought sexual passion when the mood took her, no doubt with one of her young men as a normal course, but with Geneviève when the secret forces of her mind became dominant.

And yet she was entirely at the mercy of her conscience, and her undoubted piety. Whenever she sought Geneviève's bed, the next day they wallowed in the confessional. If Geneviève had supposed their penance would be no more than an excuse for another romp, she found out on the very first occasion that she had been wrong. Elizabeth Petrovna had provided herself with a couple of stout birches, and she commanded Geneviève to stoop and hold her own ankles while her buttocks were fiercely assaulted, before allowing herself to be humiliated in turn. No doubt, Geneviève thought, the birching, the upturned bottom, was itself sexual, but it revealed a darker side to the Empress's nature than she had before realised to exist. She could never afford to forget that this woman was the daughter of Peter the Great, and by no lady of the court, but by a Lithuanian peasant who had been a whore before being plucked from the gutter by the Autocrat of all the Russias. With such a background it was impossible to suppose what might lurk in the recesses of the imperial mind.

But then, she wondered, what am I? Can I confess to being nothing more than an extension of that mind, a figment of her Majesty's imagination, possessing as much life as the dildoes with which she attacks me? If I have always hated having to surrender my body to a man, how much more do I hate having to surrender it to a woman, with not a man in sight? Can I exist in such an unnatural world?

But I am an unnatural creature, she realised, and there is the source of my misery. When sober, she hated her situation as much as she hated herself, could understand that she was in a prison, a prison from which there seemed no possible escape. But when she was filled with vodka, her own passionate nature took over. As she was doomed to be unnatural, she cared litle whether the organ which penetrated her was flesh or leather, save that the latter did not necessitate an immediate douching to prevent pregnancy. Nor could she truly convince herself that she was repelled by the Empress herself. Elizabeth Petrovna was in the very prime of life. To be held in her arms, to feel those magnificent breasts against her own, was to know immediate delight. To be kissed by those wet lips was far more arousing than ever to be kissed by the King of France, and she had known no other example. But far and away the most terrifying aspect of her situation was the understanding that with every day she was becoming more of a Russian and less of a Frenchwoman, or a Frenchman. With every day she looked forward more and more to her first glass of vodka, and with every day she needed one sip less to be ready for whatever her new mistress had in mind.

But fight she had to. To surrender completely would be unthinkable. In the first instance, the fate of the young Scotsman who had so gallantly offered to defend her, to rescue her, indeed, from this dragoness's lair, seemed her best objective. She broached the matter to the Empress the second time they shared a bed. She strained every nerve, every muscle, to be willing and excited and passionate and surrendering and dominating, all in turn, but kept her mind clear by only sipping the vodka she was offered, until Elizabeth Petrovna lay gasping and sweating in her arms.

'Sire,' she whispered. 'Oh, Sire, you make me so happy.'

'As you make me, my darling Elizabeth Wilhelminova.'

'I doubt that, Majesty,' Geneviève said. 'No woman could be happier than I. I am so ecstatic, I wish I could wave a magic wand

and make all the world, certainly all of Russia, as Happy as I.'

'And are they not?' The Empress breathed into her neck. 'Where a single person can find the warming arms of another, are they not happy?'

'Where such arms are available, Sire,' Geneviève said. 'But there must be hundreds, thousands of people cut off from such delicious activities.'

'To be sure,' the Empress agreed. 'Criminals and traitors. They deserve nothing less. I cannot help the old and the infirm.'

'Yet, Sire *I* would help all I could. I cannot but feel sorry for that poor young man, the Scot, Adam Menzies, whose only fault was to fall in love with me. Why, if that *were* a fault, then is Your Majesty equally guilty.'

Elizabeth Petrovna moved her head. 'Foul wretch,' she shouted.

'Sire?' Geneviève sat up in alarm.

'His crime was to attempt to make you fall in love with him, and to take you away from Russia. Do not attempt to deny it.'

'Sire, I have never loved any man. I swear it.'

'Liar. Will you pretend to be a virgin?'

'My maidenhead belongs to no one other than King Louis himself. Sire. This I swear, and the Prince of Conti will bear me out.'

'Ha,' remarked the Empress. 'The Prince stated as much in his letter. Louis, you say. There is a small world, as but for the short sightedness of his advisers, *my* maidenhead would also be in his keeping.'

'You may believe me, Sire, that it was not my desire, but what was a poor girl to do when summoned to His Majesty's bedchamber?'

'My heart bleeds for you,' Elizabeth agreed, once again taking her in her arms.

'As for seeking to escape Russia, Your Majesty,' Geneviève whispered against her ear. 'I cannot deny that desire. But what would you, Sire? Overcome as I was with love for you, but receiving no suggestion of such a passion in return, I was like to go mad with frustration, and thought it best to take myself away from the source of such temptation.'

'I know, you poor child,' Elizabeth said, holding her closer yet. 'But you are young, and not yet exposed to the questions, indeed the demands, of age. I speak of one's mind, one's conscience, as much as one's body. I was made to see the error of my ways some ten years ago, when I confessed my secret passion to my Almoner. His judgement was severe. A woman can never be a sodomite like a man, and can therefore never be exposed to quite the same quality of hellfire; nonetheless an unnatural passion such as I feel for you, such as I have felt in the past for other girls, can only be rewarded by eternal damnation.'

'We do no harm, Sire. We but make each other happy.'

'It is an illegal happiness we seek, and there is the end of it. And so I fought against it, although from my first sight of you I longed to hold you in my arms. I sought to wait until you became a member of the True Church, hoping that my passion might wane, and instead it grew, day by day.'

'And happy I am that it did so, Sire,' Geneviève said, stroking her back. 'I cannot believe that two people can ever be punished for loving each other. There were a negation of every Christian principle. No, no, Sire, I am happy that my escape was prevented, and my only grievance is that that poor young man should be forced to languish in captivity . . .'

'Wretch.' Elizabeth's head popped up again; Geneviève nearly bit her tongue. 'You love him still.'

'I never loved him, Sire. I swear it.'

'Well, he deserves to be punished. By God, he deserves to die. He should be hung from a tree and have his penis removed, slice by slice. Had I not sworn never to inflict the death penalty he would certainly be hanging by the neck ere now.'

Presumably, Geneviève reflected, she did not include a knouting as a death sentence.

Yet she would not give up. 'I have sworn, Sire, that you have no cause to hate him.'

'And I tell you that I have.' The Empress sat up, tossed her thick black hair back from her face. 'For he is the direct cause of *this*. Do you not understand? I had resisted all temptation. I might have continued to do so. When I was told that you sought to escape, I knew only anger, that you could so repay my kindness, that you could love a man, that you would seek to defy me. I would have punished you severely. Until I saw your body exposed before me. Then I knew I could fight against you no longer. Then I damned myself. And you.'

'To happiness, Sire. Only to happiness.' Geneviève put her arms round that plump body, caressed those enormous breasts. 'Are you not happy?'

'I am happy,' Elizabeth Petrovna sighed. 'And damned at the

same time. And it is the fault of that Scot. Do not ever mention his name to me, Elizabeth Wilhelminova, or I swear I will have his head. Remember that.'

When the summer arrived, the court moved down to Moscow, a huge army travelling slowly across the Russian plain, sending behind it a dustcloud which must have been visible for miles. And if the huge collection of wooden houses seemed no more attractive than St Petersburg, at least the Kremlin, the central fortress in which the royal palace was housed, was breathtaking, its huge walls rising sheer from the banks of the Moscow River, its enormous courtyards fronted by stone buildings of both size and elegance, while immediately before the entrance to the fortress there was a huge open area known as the Red Square – red in Russian being a synonym for bold – dominated by quite the most beautiful church Geneviève had ever seen, a mass of blue and gilt onion domes from which the sunlight sparkled.

But if she at last felt she was more truly close to the centre of Russian power, she was disturbed to discover that it meant no change in her own way of life, or basically in that of the Empress. As the roads and the seas were again passable, there was more news from abroad, and there were more embassies to be received, but this aspect of things did not concern Geneviève. Just as she thought she might well go mad at the prospect that this could be her existence for the rest of her life, a certain relief appeared, even if it was not one she would have chosen for herself. On a Sunday in July the Grand Duke Peter, whom she saw only at table and ignored as much as possible, but who was apparently as bored as everyone else – for the Empress allowed him no part in public affairs – suddenly burst out one day after dinner, 'Discipline. There is no discipline at this court. Sire, permit me.'

It was but a reproduction of the game they had played in St Petersburg, for Elizabeth was amused, and gave him permission to marshal her ladies and her gentlemen, his own wife once again included, and drill them in the dining room. But this time, almost without thinking, save that here at last was a change, Geneviève threw herself into the game. Where before she had slouched like the rest of them, now she remembered her training as a dragoon guard, and marched as if on parade before King Louis himself, with Colonel La Passe at her elbow. Peter was delighted. 'Look at her, Sire,' he shouted. 'She could have been trained as a soldier.'

Oh, my God, Geneviève thought, and gave her mistress a hurried glance. But Elizabeth seemed as pleased as her nephew.

'Halt. Halt,' shouted the Grand Duke. 'I do swear, my dear Mademoiselle d'Éon?, that you would not be a disgrace to my own Holsteiners, who are the finest soldiers in the world.'

Indeed, Geneviève thought, having never heard of them. I wonder what they would make of the De Beauffremont Dragoons?

'You will be decorated,' the Grand Duke continued, 'for a bearing beyond that to be expected of any woman.' He took one of the medals from his own breast, for he was fond of wearing several stars and ribbons presented to him by other German princelings, and pinned it to the bodice of her gown, needing to allow the fingers of one hand to steal inside while the other tenderly pressed her flesh. 'My congratulations, mademoiselle,' he said, and kissed her on each cheek.

Once again Geneviève stole a glance at the Empress, but Elizabeth still seemed to be more amused than annoyed.

'Sweet creature,' Peter whispered in her ear. 'I had never supposed to discover a woman who could stride out so like a man, who could understand the word of command so readily. You are a dream. You will sup with me.'

'My Lord Duke . . .' Geneviève licked her lips. 'I am in attendance upon Her Majesty.'

'Her Majesty has many ladies in waiting,' the Duke declared. 'She will scarce miss one of them.'

'My Lord Duke . . .'

'I will ask her permission.'

'My Lord Duke . . .' But he was already gone. Geneviève could only watch in horror, as he left the parade and hurried across the room.

'Sire,' he cried. 'Will you not grant Mademoiselle d'Éon? permission to sup with me? There can be no finer soldier in all the land.'

Geneviève felt the blood draining from her face; apart from the request his remark was not exactly a compliment to the Russian armies. But the Empress merely smiled.

'Of course my Amazon may sup with you, my dear Grand Duke. But first, she shall walk with me, and tell me where she learned such martial prowess.'

'Because, my sweet Geneviève,' Elizabeth said, as they strolled arm in arm through the rose garden behind the palace, 'it occurred to me, from the moment I first saw you naked, that you had at some time or other taken part in manly exercises. I am a fool not to have pursued the matter. Now come, confess to me this secret from your past.'

What to do? The temptation, as she seemed doomed to spend the rest of her life in Russia, was to tell the Empress everything. But her instincts commanded her to keep her secret. Clearly she would only ever escape Russia dressed as a man, and the chances of that would be reduced were Elizabeth ever to know she possessed the ability.

''Tis naught of importance, Sire,' she said with a smile. 'My father was a military man, and was disappointed of a son. Thus he drilled me as if I were a boy, well into my teens. It was not until I was well and truly a woman that he gave up.'

'And the habits instilled in childhood are not lightly put aside,' the Empress mused. 'How strange are the ways of Heaven, to be sure. I can almost feel that my sins have been forgiven.'

'Sire?'

'I meant, that you of all the young women in France should have been chosen by Conti as his gift to me. You are in a position, my darling Geneviève, to do me the greatest of services, and entirely thanks to your misguided father.'

'Sire?' Her mystification was growing.

'The Grand Duke is attracted to you.'

'So it seems, Sire. But . . .'

'He has never before shown the least attraction to any woman.'

'Well, Sire, married as he is to so lovely a princess . . .'

'The marriage has not yet been consummated.'

'Sire?' Geneviève's voice rose to a squeak.

'This is perfectly true. I chose the Anhalt princess for him myself. She is not beautiful, but she is handsome, and she possesses a deal of character. Perhaps too much. But necessary. You see an unhappy woman, my dear girl. I am husbandless and childless. The first is deliberate. Like my namesake of England, a hundred and fifty years ago, I have sensed that to share my throne with anyone would be to lose the love of the Russian people. The second has been accidental. You will know that I have had lovers, endlessly, less commanded by my heart than my mind, my sense of responsibility. A son, even a bastard son, would have made the succession secure. But it was not to be. No doubt God in His wisdom has ever punished me for my perverse desires.'

'An adoption, Sire?'

'Never. Peter the Great made this country great, and the blood of Peter must continue to flow in the veins of our Tsars. Thus this pale imitation. He is my sister's child. If only she had married a man instead of that puling Holsteiner. Still, as he is all we have, we must do the best we can. You will attend him as he desires, and you will grant him his every wish. You understand me?'

'I do, Sire. But . . .'

'Indeed it would be useful for you to encourage him to want things he may not previously have thought of.'

My God, Geneviève thought; will I ever in my life meet anyone who does not immediately seek to prostitute me? And as she has so rightly said, with such a puling youth?

'Well?' Elizabeth demanded. 'Why do you look so sad?'

'I but fear to share myself with anyone save Your Majesty,' Geneviève explained.

'I am asking you to share your body, silly girl, not your soul. That belongs to me, and will always belong to me. But I will love you even more if you can be the means of bringing my heir and his bride together. I shudder to suppose what might happen were I to die with their marriage still only a name. Do not fail me in this, my darling. It is an affair of state.'

About which there could be no argument. Geneviève dressed herself in a rose coloured satin gown with an echelle bodice, which she thought looked suitably military. Her underskirt was in cream and crimson damask and her frills at neck and sleeve were white lace. Russian ladies wore their hair far more simply than French, but she applied powder like any grenadier, and for jewellery wore her gold necklace.

'Aye, you will please the Duke mademoiselle,' Margaret agreed. 'But they do say he is a man of unusual tastes.'

'Is there such a thing as a man with usual tastes?' Geneviève demanded. Or a woman either, she thought.

Supper was a disturbingly private affair, for to Geneviève's consternation she discovered the Grand Duchess sitting at the end of the table. The other guests consisted of two gentlemen and one lady, all members of the considerable German colony in Moscow.

She was placed on Peter's right, which was even more disturbing, as she could feel Catherine's gaze throughout the meal, while the conversation, as might have been expected, was entirely upon military matters.

Geneviève had little to offer on this subject, and concentrated upon eating sparingly and digesting carefully in expectation of a vigorous drilling after the meal was finished. To her surprise, however, instead of summoning his guests to attention, Peter dropped to his hands and knees, while his footmen brought forward several boxes filled with leaden soldiers, painted in the colours of the various European armies. The guests, of both sexes, and not excepting the Grand Duchess, were required to join him on the bare floor, to arrange the toys in ranks and armies, to take command, and to issue orders, to fire little cannon detonated by real charges, which hurled leaden balls, each about the size of a thimble. The din was tremendous, for Peter and the other men insisted upon bellowing their commands as if on a real field, the room very rapidly filled with smoke and the smell of cordite, the ladies' coiffures collapsed and their faces and fingers became smudged with powder, while the cannon balls, if lacking the power to break the skin, could certainly inflict an unpleasant bruise where they missed their targets and struck one of the participants. Indeed Geneviève, having been hit on the thigh and the arm and the ankle, suddenly realised that from time to time the gentlemen were actually aiming at the ladies, for sport.

She happened to be kneeling beside the Grand Duchess when she was struck a fourth time, a particularly painful blow on the knee, as she had pulled up her skirts to protect them from the floor. 'Ow,' she grunted, and glanced at Catherine in embarrassment.

To her surprise, and for the first time that evening, the Grand Duchess smiled. 'Do you not suppose two can play at that game, mademoiselle?'

'You are right, Highness.' Geneviève hastily loaded her cannon. 'Who do you suppose fired that shot?'

'Why, it was the Grand Duke.'

Geneviève sat on her heels. 'Then perhaps . . .'

'Nonsense,' Catherine declared. 'It is all sport. Give me that cannon.' She took it from Geneviève's hands, aimed it, and pulled the lanyard. The ball struck the floor once, knocked over two members of the Prussian guard, and continued on its way to shoot up the inside of Peter's thigh.

'Oh,' he screamed. 'Oh.' He fell forward, hands between his legs. 'By God, I have been injured. Who fired that shot?'

'Why, my lord, it certainly came from Mademoiselle d'Éon's cannon,' Catherine said.

Geneviève opened her mouth, and then shut it again.

'Oh,' moaned the Duke. 'Oh.' He continued to writhe on the floor.

'Would you not like someone to rub it for you, my lord?' Catherine asked, her voice soothingly low. 'I could do it, or would you prefer Mademoiselle d'Éon? As she was responsible.'

Peter raised his head to look at his wife. His cheeks were flushed and there seemed a trace of tears. 'Out,' he said. 'Everybody. I have had enough sport for this night. Out.'

Catherine gazed at him for a moment, and then pushed herself to her feet. Geneviève followed her example, and the other guests did likewise.

'But you must stay,' Peter said, pointing at Geneviève. 'I claim you as a prisoner of war.'

Geneviève glanced at Catherine; the Grand Duchess's cheeks were pink, and her nostrils were dilated. Geneviève wondered if Peter had guessed who had actually fired the shot.

'Out,' he said again. 'I would interrogate my prisoner.'

The guests bowed, and took their leave. Catherine waited, and then she too curtsied. 'I shall bid you good night, my lord. Pray do not wake me when you come to bed.' She glanced at Geneviève, and Geneviève felt a chill run down her spine. My God, she thought; one day this girl will be Tsarina.

The door closed, and she was alone with the Grand Duke, save for the footmen, who were commencing to gather up the scattered toy soldiers.

'I . . . I am sorry, my lord,' she said. 'I did not mean to strike you.'

'Bah,' he said. 'It was Catherine's doing. She takes me for a fool. Do you take me for a fool, mademoiselle?'

'Of course not, my lord.'

'Ha.' He sat down, on a settee against the wall. 'But it hurts.'

Geneviève licked her lips. The Empress had commanded her to be forward. 'If I may assist you, my lord.'

'In what way could you assist me?'

'Well . . .' She found herself licking her lips again. 'I *could* rub it for you.'

His head came up. 'You would do that, mademoiselle?'

'If . . . if Your Highness wishes it.'

'Wishes it? My God . . .' A flush spread over his face. 'My God,' he said again, and clapped his hands. 'Out,' he bawled in Russian at the footmen. 'Leave those. Out.'

They hastily obeyed.

'Wine,' muttered the Grand Duke, clearly growing more uncertain of himself by the moment. 'Pour me a glass of wine. And take one yourself.'

'Of course, my lord.' Geneviève filled the two goblets, returned to the settee. 'Now, my lord, if you will just lie back as comfortably as you may, I will see what can be done.'

He hesitated, drank some wine, then swung his boots on to the settee and lowered his head. Geneviève also drank some wine, hastily. Now then, she thought, to what have you committed yourself? But she was agreeably excited. It was more than a year since she had known a man, and she had only ever known one man, the King of France, old enough to be her father. The Grand Duke Peter was hardly older than herself in years, and considerably younger, she estimated, in mental capacity. What of his body?

And as she had been commanded to it by the Empress, she reflected she might as well enjoy it. Besides, she thought, if his wife already loathes me, is not my only hope to make *him* fall in love with me?

Gently she slid her hand up the soft buckskin of his breeches, to find the bulge. But it was a shapeless bulge, although he seemed to enjoy her ministration. He gave a little wriggle, and a grunt of pleasure. Geneviève moved higher, unfastened his belt and his flies, gave a gentle tug on the cloth, and watched him move as his head came up.

'Whatever are you doing, mademoiselle?'

'Seeking to discover the source of your discomfort, my lord,' she explained.

'But mademoiselle . . .' He protested, too late. Another gentle tug exposed what she sought, and it was already half erected.

'Trust in me, my lord,' she promised him. For here was something quite different to King Louis, or Jules. For the first time in her life she beheld the penis of a boy, tumbling sideways out of the opening she had made.

137

'Mademoiselle,' Peter protested.

'You are beautiful, my lord,' she said, and she was not altogether lying. Where she had found her previous experiences distasteful, now she could only think that had she been truly born a boy she could have possessed something like this, as immediately responsive, as quickly filled with pulsing blood.

'By God,' Peter gasped. 'Mademoiselle . . .' He tried to move, but Geneviève had taken him into her hands. He gave another gasp, twisted his body, and then uttered a peculiar soft moan; the penis jerked against Geneviève's hands and she watched it spurt. She was at once dumbfounded and delighted; she had never seen a man come before, and her pleasure was redoubled because the Duke was, for the moment at least, utterly at her mercy, while she was unaffected. She had at last defeated a man.

He had immediately dwindled, and her hands were full. She stood up, looked down at him. His eyes were shut, his cheeks were flushed, and his breathing uneven.

But had he been pleased? He had not come inside her. He might very well be angry. But oh, if he was pleased, how simple life would be. He had come so quickly, so fully, at the mere touch of her hand. She could accomplish that with ease, whenever she wished. And if *he* was pleased, then surely every man would be so pleased. She conceived that she might hold the entire sex, literally, in the palm of her hand.

She went to the table in search of a napkin.

'Where are you going?'

'To dry my hands, my lord.' She turned, found that his eyes were open. 'My lord is angry?'

'Sweet mademoiselle,' he said. 'Oh, sweet, sweet, mademoiselle. You have made me the happiest man in the world.'

Geneviève crumpled the napkin, dropped it on the floor. 'It has been my pleasure, my lord.' She returned to the settee. He remained flaccid. 'Would you like it again, my lord?'

'Again? Oh, my sweet girl . . .' He held her hands, pulled her down to kneel beside him. 'Indeed. But not tonight. Oh, I am exhausted.'

Geneviève kissed him on the mouth, but his did not open. She came to the conclusion that his main problem was a total ignorance of anything save military matters.

'If I were to stay with my lord,' she said, 'perhaps sleep with him, then I am sure . . .'

'No, no.' He sat up. 'I cannot sleep with you, mademoiselle. I must sleep with my wife.'

'But . . .'

'Oh, she has no such art as you, to be sure. She is a confoundedly ignorant girl, I do assure you. But still, as we *are* married . . .'

Geneviève would not let go of his hands. 'I am sure she would be happy to honour my lord, were you to ask her.'

'Ask her? How could I possibly ask a woman to . . . to fondle me?'

'Well, my lord, perhaps it would not be necessary to ask. Only to take her in your arms . . .'

'No, no,' he said. 'She would laugh at me. She does, you know. Oh, yes. She laughs at me all the time. She thinks playing at soldiers is stupid. But what other occupation is there for a future king, a future emperor?'

'I still feel, my lord, as the Grand Duchess *is* your wife, bound to share your bed . . .'

'We'll talk no more of it,' Peter said with sudden decision, and freed himself to fasten his breeches. 'You have made me very happy, and I am grateful. I would have you sup with me again.'

'My lord, it will be my great pleasure. Supposing Her Majesty will grant me permission.'

'I shall ask her . . .' His face was suddenly anxious. 'You'll not tell her of what happened?'

'It shall be our secret, my lord,' Geneviève lied.

'Capital,' Elizabeth exclaimed. 'Oh, capital. Oh, Elizabeth Wilhelminova, you are a *treasure*.' She frowned. 'Have you done that sort of thing before?'

'Never, Sire. The King of France required servicing of a more normal nature.'

'Ha. Well, hopefully you will be able to steer the Grand Duke into similar paths. Certainly you must attend him whenever he desires.'

'Tonight again, Sire.'

'Then tonight it shall be.'

And in fact Geneviève found herself quite looking forward to another evening with the Duke. She could think of nothing she would rather do than again reduce him to gibbering exhaustion. And it was such a delightful plaything. She did not really wish him to enter her at all. Presumably this would be necessary at some stage, but she could see no need for haste. And she was at last doing something she really enjoyed. She conceived that life in Russia might even become acceptable, at least in the short term, while if she could become Peter's favourite, when he eventually succeeded to the throne, all things might be possible.

She dressed with great care once again, and this time was the life and soul of the party, which followed exactly similar lines as the previous night, save that the guests were different, apart from herself and the Grand Duchess, and that this time Peter *encouraged* her to bombard him with leaden balls. Catherine, however, was strangely silent; she smiled readily enough, and played the game with energy, but seemed to prefer not to speak unless spoken to, and not to speak to Geneviève at all. Definitely, Geneviève thought, I have made an enemy here. But she is only a woman.

The guests departed, the footmen were dismissed, and Peter retired to his settee. She was surprised to discover that he wanted exactly the same treatment as the previous night, and debated whether she should introduce him to the pleasures of kissing and mutual fondling. But she did not really wish him to kiss her or fondle her any more than she wished him inside her, and reflected that it was necessary in the first instance to make him her absolute slave. So she humoured him and amused herself once more, discovering to her pleasure that this night it was slightly more difficult to accomplish, and that therefore she had longer to play with her new toy. In the end he came, however, and she dried her hands and gently kissed him on the forehead.

'Tomorrow?' He clung to her hand.

'If Your Highness truly wishes it.'

'Truly, truly, truly. I wish it were possible to make you part of my household, my darling Geneviève, to have you always at my side, to see you there, all the time, to know you would always be there . . .'

'I will always be here, my lord,' Geneviève promised. 'So long as you desire it. Now I must leave you.'

'Yes,' he said. 'Yes. I must to bed. My wife must not become suspicious. Tomorrow, sweet Geneviève.'

Geneviève kissed his mouth, gently, and left his side. She straightened her skirts, opened the door, stepped into the corridor. A footman waited to take her place, and made a brief bow. She nodded in turn, walked round the corner, was surprised to discover no guards. She hesitated for a moment, frowning as she debated whether or not to return to the Grand Duke's apartments to inform him of this singular occurence, but then decided against it. After a couple of hours of rolling about on the floor she wanted only her bed.

She turned another corner, and a bag was dropped over her head. Desperately she kicked and wriggled, but the man, for it had to be a man, caught her round the waist, securing the bag as he did so, pinning her arms to her sides and preventing her making any attempt to reach the poniard, while another man held her ankles. Memory flooded back of the Duke of Richelieu's assault upon her, but he had supposed her to be a man; these fellows could be under no doubt that she was a woman.

Her brain spun and she attempted to fight them, but they were far too strong for her. What could they intend? She felt herself being carried a short distance, then she heard a door open. A moment later she was suddenly thrown away from her gaolers. For a long second she was in the air, at the same time as she realised that the bag had been whipped from her head. A kaleidoscope of lights flew before her eyes, and then she struck the floor with a jar which drove all the breath from her body. She was still gasping when a woman bent over her; Geneviève could only goggle at her in horror, for it was the Grand Duchess Catherine Alekseyevna.

•

Chapter Six

Geneviève sat up, pulled hair from her face. Her heart seemed to slow, and yet Catherine's face was remarkably composed.

'Leave us,' she commanded.

The men bowed, and closed the door behind them.

'I am informed you seldom go out without a poniard strapped to your leg, mademoiselle,' Catherine said. 'Would you use it on me?'

Geneviève licked her lips. 'I . . .'

10

'Because then, of course, you would really be forced to experience Russian justice. I think you would be broken on the wheel.'

Geneviève reached her knees. 'My dagger is for self defence, Highness.'

'And you would not suppose I have just attacked you?'

Geneviève stood up. 'I await only an explanation.' Remember, she said to herself: I am the Empress's favourite. This woman dare not harm me. Not until Elizabeth dies.

Catherine seemed able to read her mind. She smiled. 'An explanation,' she mused. 'And of course, I must give you one, mademoiselle, or you will hurry back to Her Majesty and tell your tales. But you should bear in mind that the Empress will not always be with us . . . Now I wish you to know,' Catherine continued, 'that I personally have nothing against you. I have lived at this court, in close proximity to our royal mistress, for several years, and it seems to me that she prefers you to most of her male friends. Therefore, as you are a shrewd wench, I presume that in humouring my husband you are obeying her orders, no doubt at considerable cost to yourself. Why, mademoiselle, my heart bleeds for you.'

Geneviève found she was having trouble keeping her breathing even; the Grand Duchess was a shade *too* calm.

'But I also wish you to know that whenever the Grand Duke is ready to fall in love with a woman,' the quiet voice said, 'that woman has necessarily to be me. I have no intention of being merely a royal consort, used as a child bearing machine and nothing else. I may say that my husband has never before shown the *slightest* interest in any woman, so much so that I had supposed him a victim to that curse which seems to affect so many of Europe's royal families. I am glad to be mistaken, but I will not have you suborning his affections.'

Was this really a girl of eighteen? Geneviève could only reflect that whenever she came to the Russian throne, even if only as a consort, Europe might well have something to think about.

'I do assure Your Highness,' she protested. 'Nothing could be further from my mind. I attend your husband, as you suppose, on the orders of our mistress, and with no more responsibility than to interest him in *you*, Highness, by awakening his carnal desires.'

Catherine rested her chin on her forefinger, gazed at her. 'Then you have done your task far too successfully, save that he is interested in you, not me.'

'Well, Highness, perhaps . . .'

'Perhaps nothing.' The arm was moved, the Grand Duchess sat straight. 'You have two choices; death or exile.'

The suddenness of the assault left Geneviève for a moment speechless.

'No doubt you suppose I dare not,' Catherine said, more quietly. 'Well, were I to have you executed, Her Majesty would undoubtedly be very displeased with me. But her displeasure would in time dissipate, whereas once you are dead, mademoiselle, you are most definitely dead, and nothing could possibly alter that. I may also point out that should I have you killed, I will see to it that you suffer as much as possible, that your death is delayed until you are on your knees begging to be put out of your misery. On the other hand, were you to consent to go into exile, while I should of course inform Her Majesty that you had run away, and you would thereby incur her lasting hatred so that were you ever to set foot in Russia again you would certainly suffer a fate equal to that which I have in mind for you, yet would you still be alive. Do you follow what I have been saying?'

Geneviève swallowed. She did not suppose she had a choice, especially as escaping Russia was her only aim in life. But the Grand Duchess must never suspect that.

'I do, Highness, and you may be sure of my decision. But suppose I attempt to leave Russia, and am arrested?'

Catherine smiled. 'An intriguing thought. But I cannot risk the possibility that Her Majesty might yet forgive you. You may trust in me, mademoiselle, to make sure that you are *not* arrested. I will guarantee your safety to the borders of Prussia.'

She was in too much of a hurry, Geneviève realised things were not as desperate as she had feared. 'I am a woman entirely without family or friends, Highness. You may guarantee my safety, but if I am going to die of starvation in any event, I may as well die here.'

Catherine continued to smile. 'I have a wallet containing two thousand roubles for you. Your coachman I shall pay myself.'

'I shall need passports.'

'I have already arranged them.'

'My servants?'

Catherine sighed. 'Are they really of interest to you?'

'My Russian ones, no. My maid and my butler, Highness, I could not possibly desert.'

143

Catherine tapped her chin. 'You make life very difficult. They are serfs.'

'They have served me faithfully enough, Highness.'

'Oh, very well. Fetch them hither. No. You will remain here. I will have them fetched.'

'We leave this night, Highness?' Geneviève's head commenced to spin.

'Indeed you do, mademoiselle. As I had always supposed you would choose life rather than death, the arrangements are all made. Just do not ever let me see your face again. And now, goodbye.'

The berline rumbled to a halt; for just a moment the dreadful lurching ceased, and Geneviève's throbbing temples came to a temporary rest.

'Whatever can the matter be now?' she complained. It had taken them three months, and in late summer, to make the journey from Moscow to Bavaria. In the beginning all had been haste, but the Grand Duchess had sent one of her own attachés with them, and he had smoothed the way past refractory officials and bad roads alike. He had abandoned them at the Prussian frontier, and with him had gone their fortune. Wheels had come adrift, they had taken wrong turnings, and generally she had supposed the journey would never end, while always she had been haunted by the fear that at any moment a patrol of Cossacks might come galloping after them to haul her back to face an enraged Empress.

Margaret pushed her head out of the window. 'There seems no reason, mademoiselle,' she said. 'The road is empty.'

Jules cantered beside the coach. 'Mademoiselle,' he said. 'At last. We are at the frontier.'

Geneviève frowned at him. 'Which frontier?'

'The French frontier, mademoiselle. It is merely a matter of preparing our papers.'

Geneviève sank back into her seat. She did not really believe it. She could not believe it. Three months ago she had been in Moscow, a thing, a creature of the Empress, a toy to be handed to whoever suited the Imperial purpose, subject always to an autocrat's temper, with the knout at the end of it. How had she survived? It did not seem possible for her to have done so. But she had, by the use of her wits and her charm and her body. And now she was free and Jules was free and Margaret was free. Only that poor boy Adam Menzies had suffered.

She frowned, and plucked at her chin. Did he still survive, in his Siberian forest? Or had he long frozen or been beaten to death? He had tried to save her. He had drawn his sword on an Empress in defence of her. No man could have done more. And he had sought nothing in return. At least, that was what he had said. But even supposing he had been lying, would it have been so terrible? He was a young man, only a few years older than the Grand Duke Peter Feodorovich. He could be no worse, and was in all likelihood much better, in every way. Would she not have enjoyed giving him his reward?

She sighed, as the berline began once again to move forward. Looking over her shoulder was a waste of time. As the Empress had promised, she had not heard from him again, and if he had lived, surely he would have found some means of reaching her with a letter or even a thought. Adam Menzies was dead, and perhaps that was all to the good. For the rest of her life she could preserve the memory of the one man, no, the one *person* in all her life not to want something of her, who wished, indeed, only to help her. That he had died so young was merely a reflection upon the way of the world, and a warning to her never to indulge in similar chivalrous heroics.

The berline had stopped again, and the Bavarian border guards were inspecting their papers, glancing into the coach to ascertain that there were only two women within, and then waving them onwards. The whip cracked, the carriage rumbled forward the few yards to the French post, and the whole rigmarole had to be gone through again. Geneviève settled back on her cushions. France. She had given not a thought to what she would do when she got here; all her mind had been directed merely to achieving that end. Well, then. She had been gone just over a year, and had in fact celebrated her twentieth birthday a week previously. A year, however it had dragged for her, was not really a very long time, and she presumed it would be dangerous for her to appear at court, at least until she discovered the lie of the land from the Prince of Conti. But she had ample funds remaining from the Grand Duchess's payment. There was no reason why she should not eventually continue to Cherbourg, and Mama. Dressed as a woman, she was sure of a welcome there. And from there it would be possible to write one or two letters, or perhaps send Jules upon a mission of investigation . . .

The Prince turned out to be waiting not in Paris, but in the town of Nancy, only just within the frontier, and Geneviève was there by dusk. She faced the steps to the house, a private house, tall gabled and overhanging the street. Why not an inn? But Conti shunned all publicity.

The door was already open, and a footman was waiting to see her into a narrow, dark panelled front hall. An equally narrow staircase mounted one wall, but the footman was indicating the door on the left, and Geneviève stepped into a neat little parlour, looking out on to a small lawn, and warmed by a huge fire. The Prince was the only other person in the room. He stood by the window, facing the door, his hands clasped behind his back. He did not seem to have changed a great deal during her absence, unless it was to become more wizened.

Geneviève filled two goblets of wine and handed him one. Her mind went back to their first meeting, in his Paris house. What a lot had happened since then.

The Prince pointed at her. 'You have failed in your mission.'

Geneviève stood before him. 'Perhaps, my lord, had you informed me of what my mission was, what it would entail, I might have succeeded.'

'You seek to defy me, slut? Oh, I know all about you. I know of you and the Empress. My God, that humanity can sink so low. I know all of your attempts to suborn the Heir. That is treason. I know all of your romance with some Scottish lout. My God, a heretic.'

'I had no romance with Captain Menzies,' Geneviève said, keeping her voice even. 'He has suffered most grievously for attempting to defend me from the Russian louts to whom you sacrificed me.'

'Ha. You do not deny any of my other charges?'

'I will never deny the truth, my lord. I would like to know how you have managed to discover so much.'

He smiled. 'Do you suppose I do not keep well informed? The Grand Duchess saw to that.'

'Ah.' Geneviève sat down without being invited. She was suddenly very tired. 'I should have known. My delays on the journey were paid for in advance. Well, then, my lord, you have the advantage of me. I can only acknowledge my failure, and beg your forgiveness. And promise you that I will trouble you no more.'

'Ha. Do not wheedle, Geneviève. It does not become you, and

146

I am not in the mood for it. I wish to know the truth, and I will have it if I must tear your flesh with red hot pincers.'

Geneviève drank some wine. 'I have told you the truth, my lord. I pleased the Empress and she took me to her bed. It was my misfortune that I also pleased the Grand Duke, and that the Empress saw this to her profit. It is all of our misfortunes that the Grand Duchess has proved herself to be a most formidable adversary. Certainly not one I could combat with the weapons available to me.'

'Oh, be quiet,' Conti shouted. 'I am not interested in what happened in Russia. I doubt I would ever have gained the Polish throne. And what would I have done with it? The Poles are a pack of squabbling dogs, who fight to the death over every single bone. I wish to know of your arrangement with Richelieu.'

Geneviève frowned at him. 'My lord?'

Once again the wagging finger. 'Do not attempt to deny it. You have turned your coat, you little she devil. You turned it before you ever left Paris. And in my embassy? I wish to know the purpose of it.'

Geneviève finished her drink. But dissembling was not a prospect at this stage; she was in any event too curious. 'My lord, I will swear to you that I have no idea of what you are speaking.'

Conti's turn to frown. 'Pour some more wine.'

Geneviève refilled his goblet, but left hers empty; she suspected she was going to need a very clear head.

'You deny that you had an interview with the Duke of Richelieu before leaving Paris?'

'My lord,' Geneviève said. 'How could I? You have but to fetch back Jules, and then question Madame Sophie, and then the Chevalier Douglas. Where could I possibly have found the time?'

'Hum.' Conti pulled his nose. 'Then explain to me why he did not denounce you.'

'My lord?'

'God curse you for a silly bitch,' he shouted. 'Can you not understand the King's French? You claim to have fought with Richelieu's people in a room at Versailles. You claim he was there, intent upon gelding you. You claim he fled after you had killed a man.' He paused for breath.

'That is the truth, my lord.'

'But nothing was ever heard of this.'

'Eh?'

'Not a word. Not even of a dead body. And when I encountered the Duke next day, he merely smiled at me and continued about his business.'

Geneviève sat down again, slowly. 'And the King?'

'Oh, you have forsaken *that* favour, my dear girl. He knows only that you deserted your post and fled, he knows not where.'

'Oh, my God.'

'Indeed. You are a deserter, and in time of war, I may add. Quite apart from being a deserter from the King's bed. Oh, he has a wheel waiting for your tender limbs, you may be sure of that.'

'Oh, Holy Mother,' Geneviève whispered. 'But you mean, my lord, that my journey to Russia was not necessary?'

'No doubt Richelieu had a reason.'

'My lord, if there is one person in all the world that the Duke of Richelieu hates, it is I.'

'You flatter yourself. And you are, as usual, lying. You prate to me about the truth? You do not know the meaning of the word. Well, I will have the truth, Geneviève. And do not suppose to draw your poinard on me. I am ready for you, and I have several stout fellows outside.'

'My lord . . .' Geneviève found her kerchief, patted sweat from her forehead and neck. She felt as if her feet had become caught in a bog, into which she sank, however hard she tried, deeper and deeper. 'Ask of me any oath, I will swear it. Torture me, and you will discover nothing more than I have told you. Because there *is* nothing more. My lord, I am the sufferer in this business. Russia was one long disaster for me. And what profit can the Duke have obtained by sending *me* to that frosty country?'

'I am waiting for you to tell me.'

'There was none,' she shouted. 'I swear it, I swear it, I swear it.'

He gazed at her for some seconds, sipped some wine. 'You dissemble very well, Geneviève. You are a girl of great talent.'

'I am *not* dissembling.'

'Then give me a reason. Any reason, for him not to condemn you.'

'My lord, who am I to consider the reasons behind the actions of a man like Richelieu?' But her stomach was beginning to settle; the immediate crisis was past.

'Hum.' The Prince got up, began to pace the floor. 'He is a devious fellow. Oh, yes. But what can he have had in mind? We shall have to see. Yes, we shall have to see.' He stopped, facing her. 'It will not be safe for you to come to Versailles. Not at the moment, anyway.'

'My lord, I have no desire to come to court. I have adventured sufficiently for one lifetime. My mother, as you know, has retired to Cherbourg. I wish only to be allowed to do the same.'

He plucked at his lower lip. 'Hum. So much talent. So much beauty. So much . . . wasted. Oh, I could have done great things with you, Geneviève.'

'Man proposes and God disposes,' Geneviève said, piously.

'Hum,' Conti said. 'Hum. Had you a little less independence of spirit, a little servility . . .'

'Then I would hardly be Geneviève d'Éon, my lord,' Geneviève pointed out.

'Hum. You'll to Cherbourg and disappear?'

'From court life, my lord, certainly.'

'For ever?'

Geneviève realised that she had won a complete victory. The Prince, for all his grandiose dreams, remained too timid for real intrigue. But as he had taken her life and fashioned it as he chose, at whatever risk to herself, he owed her more than a goodbye.

'Well, my lord,' she said. 'I would hope to do so, certainly. But who can foresee the future?' As long as my circumstances permit, of course I will remain in Cherbourg, but times are hard, and daily grow more so.'

'By God!' he said. 'You are a blackmailing little wanton. I wonder I do not call my people in and have you strangled before my eyes. There would be sport.' He glared at her for some seconds, and then went to a bureau in the corner, opened a drawer, and took out a suitably heavy bag. 'A thousand louis d'or,' he said. 'Let that suffice, woman, and do not let me ever see your face again.'

Geneviève gave a curtsey, picked up the money, and went to the door. 'Ah, what a romance we could have had, my lord,' she remarked, 'had you but been a man.'

A parting shot which gave her some satisfaction. But she was quite prepared to keep her side of the bargain. Jules and Margaret were overjoyed to learn that she really was going to retire to Cherbourg, and with a small fortune in her reticule. She could hardly believe it herself. Since Conti had come into her life, more than two years previously, she did not feel as if she had set foot on the earth, so rapidly had she been whirled through life. When she thought over her adventures, when she remembered being smothered beneath the body of the Empress or crawling about the Grand Duke's floor, she thought she must have been dreaming.

It took two weeks to cross the breadth of France, but at the end they found themselves rumbling through the apple orchards of Normandy, where the fruit was already tumbling down and the cider presses were squeezing away. She gained her first glimpse of the sea as they made their way up the Cotentin Peninsular by way of Granville and Cartaret. What memories that brought back; although the Channel was a different blue to the Baltic it appeared to be equally rough. Then it was into Cherbourg itself, a bustling seaport set in a bay at the very north end of the peninsular, and only sixty miles from the English coast. Geneviève gazed out to sea for some time; her history books had told her that whenever war broke out between England and France, and that was a ten yearly occurrence, Cherbourg was raided by the English fleet. Perhaps her retirement would not be so dull after all.

So what would she do, draw a sword and rush to the battlements, skirts flying? That is behind you, she kept telling herself. Now you are to settle down and play the wealthy young lady. And marry?

'That is what we must do,' Louise d'Éon said. 'Oh, indeed. My darling, darling Geneviève,' and she fell to crying all over again. 'To have you back. To see you dressed as a woman. To see you so beautiful. We must find you a husband. You shall have your pick of all the young men in Normandy. Will she not, Aimée?'

For Aunt Aimée, having visited Tonnerre several times in the past and patted her nephew Charles on the head, had to be admitted to the secret, as was her husband, Philippe Rameau, who was very interested in this sudden and beautiful addition to his household.

'You must tell us of your adventures,' he said, attempting to pinch Geneviève's bottom. 'I am sure they are exciting.'

'Not in the least, Uncle Philippe,' she said. 'I adopted male clothing in order to make my fortune, and now that I have made my fortune, why, I am content to be what I have always wished. But if I may whisper in your ear, dear uncle . . .' He obligingly lowered his head as Geneviève lowered her voice. 'If you pinch me again I shall break your finger.' She smiled at her mother. 'It really is too good to be home, Mama. But marriage . . . why, there is no need to hurry about that.'

'You are past twenty,' Louise d'Éon pointed out. 'Every young woman should be married by twenty. I was married at sixteen.'

'*I* was married at fifteen,' Aimée pointed out.

'Well, I shall marry when I discover someone I can love,' Geneviève said, with a glance at Uncle Philippe. 'For the time being, I would like to learn how to manage a household.'

But in common with all households in France, at least those with pretensions, the Rameaus were intent only upon apeing their betters, who were in their turn intent only upon apeing Versailles itself. Philippe Rameau could only rise to two servants, to whom Jules and Margaret were a welcome addition, but the system was as carefully, and absurdly, arranged. However small the house, the kitchen was at the furthest end away from the dining room; thus any callers could be impressed by the procession marching along the corridors – and the food always arrived at table in a mess of congealed fat. Another mark of belonging to an ancient, wealthy family was to have old silver. Uncle Philippe had only recently been able to afford any silver at all, and after every meal he would throw it all on the floor and walk on it, to give it a suitably battered look. All this while grumbling about the terrifying cost of living, because it was true that food and other necessaries seemed to grow in price every day, while the salt tax – the *gamelle* – was a major part of the family budget. As for actual household management, Aimée Rameau saw to this at dawn, the moment her husband had left the house for his office, from which he did not return until dinner, which was taken at two. Philippe did not work in the afternoons, but preferred to take a constitutional before settling down with a book until supper time. Louise d'Éon and Aunt Aimée spent their mornings sewing or embroidering, their afternoons walking, and their evenings gossiping; supper was immediately followed by bed.

In this carefully arranged mental and physical stagnation Geneviève was expected to join, and to her surprise she was happy to do so. She realised that she was truly content to be a woman, providing no one tried to make her do anything she did not wish. For there, she conceived, was the entire fault of womanhood. They served. However much some of them, like the Pompadour, might seem to manage others by the exercise of their beauty and their wits, at the end of it all they were still dependent upon the money of a man, the strength of a man, the goodwill of a man. Because they *needed* men, from the bed to the grave.

So then, did she not *need?* Would it not be a lie to pretend to herself that she did not miss walking the corridors of Versailles? That she did not miss the drunken revels in the Peterhof? That she did not miss the touch of another's hand? But whose hand? There was a problem she was not prepared to face. She had her own hands, and she had her memories, and her bag of gold, carefully put out to interest with a reliable goldsmith, to keep herself independent.

Yet she found it pleasantly titillating to be the centre of Cherbourg gossip and society. Louise put it about that her daughter had been to court, and betrothed to a great lord, who had alas died before the marriage could take place, but had left Geneviève an ample portion in his will. That she was wealthy could not be doubted, both from her style of living and the quality of her clothes, and besides, she could talk with perfect familiarity about all the great people in the land. Philippe Rameau's house became virtually a salon as the magistrates and merchants of Cherbourg gathered there at the slightest excuse to converse with Mademoiselle . What their ladies thought of her was easy to decide, but the men were like bees around a honey jar. And not all of them were old and unattractive. Geneviève realised that she could have her pick from some half a dozen very personable young men, either as a lover or a husband. Here was something to consider. Because it would be on her terms. There was the splendid prospect opening up before her. As the Grand Duke Peter had accepted her on her terms. Of all her memories she enjoyed that the most. If a woman must have a man, then there could be no finer way.

But did a woman *have* to have a man? This was something else to be pondered. Her initial consideration was that *she* certainly did not. The idea of surrendering her wealth and her freedom and her body to one single wretched male for the rest of her life was abhorrent. She kept reminding herself that *she* wanted no one. In her beauty and her strength and her hidden abilities, known to herself but to no other, she was surely free of all the inherent weaknesses which left women at a disadvantage in the world.

This point of view she maintained for over two years, but with increasing difficulty. Apart from the constant nagging of Mama and Aunt Aimée, there were the daily insinuations of Uncle Philippe, no longer bold enough to touch her, but constantly endeavouring to encounter her when she had thought herself alone, more than once opening the door of her bedchamber in apparent mistake, hoping to catch her in déshabille. While his conversation never left the same point. 'Girl or boy, Geneviève?' he would say. 'Which are you really? Why do you not prove it to me?'

These were irritations. Boredom soon became a more serious problem. Cherbourg was very much a provincial seaport. It was instructive to watch the great three-masted sailing ships coming home, laden with goods from the Spice Islands, from the Americas, and from closer at hand, Spain and Portugal and the Biscay ports. But she had no love for the sea, and could only remember her rolling stomach on the way to St Petersburg. For the rest there was very little to do, as the theatre was of a poor quality, and her uncle's books were few in number. Nor dared she practise any masculine sports, like fencing or riding astride, for fear of further arousing his curiosity. There were no towns close at hand. It was possible to travel east for some twenty miles and arrive at the historic little port of Barfleur, from whence, it was said, William of Normandy had set out on his conquest of Britain – but Barfleur was only a village. To go west was even more desolate, for there the road ended in the cliffs of Joburg, from whence she could look down on the rushing waters of the Race of Alderney, and beyond at this tiny island itself, an outpost of England set almost against the French shore. On a clear day, and further to the south, she could even make out the other Channel Islands of Guernsey and Sark, but for her purposes they might have been the sun and the moon, even supposing she had some inclination to visit them. In her desperation she almost wished the English *would* declare war and mount a raid, and as most people in Cherbourg spoke the language, she settled down to learn it herself. But it came too easily to her quick brain; soon becoming fluent, she found herself bored all over again.

She suddenly realised, on her third summer since her return from Russia, that she was as much in a prison in Cherbourg as ever in a snowbound St Petersburg. Without even the titillation of sexual encounter to relieve her. She was twenty-three years of age, and in her absolute prime, she supposed. She would spend long hours seated before her mirror and peering at her face in search of wrinkles, fortunately unsuccessfully. The clear blue eyes, the milky white skin, the straight yellow hair which shrouded those crisp, arrogant features – she would strip herself naked to complete the parade, to admire the gentle curve of her breasts, the pout of her belly, the rambling thatch covering her groin, and best of all the long, muscular legs which rippled with concealed power as she moved. Power which must remain concealed forevermore, just as her beauty must be admired only by her in the loneliness of her room . . . unless she accepted her true place.

She lay in bed gazing at the tester above her, and realised that her decision had been made without any conscious will on her part. The decision to wed, certainly. But to whom? She was back to terms. He would wish children. She was determined never to become a mother. He would wish domination. She was determined never to be dominated. And he must be prepared to leave Cherbourg, to take up residence in some more exciting city, somewhere closer to Paris.

But he must also, she reasoned, be socially superior to herself. She could see no point in sliding down the scale, as her thousand louis d'or would not last forever. A man to be carefully chosen.

She sat up, plucking at her lip. And did love, passion, attraction, not come into it at all? Attraction, certainly. She would marry no monster. As for passion, that was a physical business, surely, like the headache or the monthly bleeding which cursed her femininity. If he caressed her breasts, kissed her tenderly, got his hand or his lips or his penis between her legs, she would know passion, just as if she had a glass too many of wine she would feel drunk. And he ... why, he would feel passion just by looking at her, just by knowing that all that beauty was his. But no love. Why should there be? She would be offering a fair barter. Her body for his protection and his wealth. Because he would have to have wealth. But she had no desire to love him. She had no desire to love anyone. She had never in her life met a loveable man, beginning with Father and going right down to Uncle Philippe. Well, perhaps that was being a little unfair to poor Adam Menzies. But had he been loveable? Gallant, certainly, and attractive certainly, and brave certainly. But these were exteriors, which proved nothing of what lay beneath. Beneath, he had been as loathsomely self-centred and grasping as everyone else. But even had he not, love was a debasing, puerile, weakening emotion; it would reduce her to the level she most feared, that of a mere woman. Let the man love *her*.

The man. Having made the decision, she set about selecting him with the greatest of care. Where her interest in her gentlemen-callers had been waning for some time, she now sat with them and allowed herself to sparkle, to the gratification of Mama. And where she had answered a smile or a word with a frown, when out on her promenades, now she returned smile for smile. Thus encouraged, the young men of Cherbourg clustered even closer. But none of them came up to her requirements. Another summer crept by, and she realised where she was making her mistake. The Normandy nobility were of course not interested in any woman who did not carry with her entrée to Versailles. However lovely Mademoiselle d'Éon might be, she was to all intents and purposes a country girl, who offered nothing more than a handsome body and a thousand louis d'or.

Versailles. She had promised never to return, and it would be highly dangerous. She no longer possessed a single friend at court, and she did possess a host of enemies starting, if Conti was to be believed, with the King. And yet . . . she was young and they, Conti and Richelieu and the like, were old. And Pompadour had now reigned for some eight years. The King might well be ready for a change. Back to the surely remembered girl-boy with whom he had romped so merrily for one autumn? Supposing he could be persuaded to forgive her for her desertion? But supposing she told him the truth? Surely it could be proved?

Versailles. It dawned on her how much she missed the excitement of court life. How much she yearned for it. But how? It would certainly be safest to mount a reconnaissance before risking an assault. And how was that to be done? Why, by the way all the other ladies had accomplished it. She must marry, the level did not matter, and then have her husband presented at court, where he would be noticed. This surely could be accomplished by the usual methods of bribery and some suitable fawning. She had forgotten that her body was a weapon, and weapons were not intended to be kept concealed, and lovingly admired in private. Weapons were meant to be used, for defence and for advancement and for profit. It did not matter if her husband was not high born. It only mattered that he would be prepared to advance.

That necessitated a professional man, and at last she made her choice, one Jean Artry, another lawyer. He was in his middle thirties, tall and somewhat foppish in appearance, for he waved his hands more than usual when he spoke, and when he finished a sentence was inclined to let them hang from the wrists as if exhausted. He appeared to be well-to-do, dressed carefully if modestly, and certainly seemed to be clean in his person. His face was unexciting, with rather sharp features, and she could not tell about his hair because he never took off his wig, but she certainly intended to achieve that objective before actually attending the altar. And that he was infatuated with her was undoubted. He had been one of the first callers when she had arrived and had been struck dumb when she had entered the room. Since then he had attended the Rameau household at least once a week, and would sit and stare at her and sigh, for all the world like a young boy rather than a full grown man. Of all the men she had met in Cherbourg he was the most obvious choice, which only made her the more angry that she should have wasted four years in indecision instead of acting immediately. But now was time for haste. He had long since ceased importuning her, so it was necessary to take the initiative.

'My dear Monsieur Artry,' she said, sitting beside him. 'I feel a new woman with the arrival of spring. Does it not make your blood tingle?'

'Oh, indeed it does, my dear, dear mademoiselle.'

'I am glad to hear it, monsieur. Once you would have invited me to walk with you on the promenade.'

He goggled at her for several seconds, while his face alternately flushed and went pale again. 'My dear mademoiselle,' he managed at last, 'you have given me to understand that you preferred to promenade alone.'

'It is a woman's privilege to change her mind, Monsieur Artry. But if you are too busy to escort me . . .'

'Too busy? Too busy? My dear, dear mademoiselle, I am entirely at your service.'

'Then, my dear monsieur, shall we say three o'clock tomorrow afternoon?'

'My dear, dear mademoiselle . . .' He seized her hand to kiss it. 'You have made me the happiest of men.'

By agreeing to walk with him? She smiled. 'I shall look forward to it, monsieur.'

Mama was delighted, as was Aunt Aimée. 'My dear

Geneviève,' they said. 'We are so happy that you have at last decided to be sensible. And you could not have made a finer choice. Monsieur Artry, why, there is solid worth there. Oh, indeed. There is no finer advocate in all Cherbourg.'

'And you will be continuing the family tradition of service in the law,' Mama added. 'I am so proud of you.'

'Even if I take him away?'

'Geneviève?' Mama frowned at her. 'What do you mean?'

'Simply that I am sure you are right, and Monsieur Artry is the finest lawyer in Normandy. In which case he is surely wasting his talents here. I think he should to Paris. As soon as we are married, of course.'

Mama's frown deepened. 'Geneviève. You are not seeking to re-renter that dismal, profligate life?'

'I am seeking the best for my future husband, Mama,' Geneviève said. 'And I shall find it, too. Now let us decide what I must wear.'

She selected a pale blue silk walking-out gown, with cream satin bows securing her bodice, and her sleeves. Her frills and her fichu were of white lace, but she tucked the fichu as far down as possible so that the tops of her breasts could be seen; few Cherbourg ladies ever revealed so much, and she had no doubt Monsieur Artry would be suitably impressed. A plain straw hat with a blue ribbon round the crown, and a cane completed her ensemble.

She was in fact quite excited at the prospect before her, especially as she realised she would be doing most of the wooing, and was dressed long before dinner; not that she supposed she would feel like eating a great deal – for the first time in more than three years there were butterflies in her stomach.

'Ah, you look delightful, my dear girl,' Uncle Philippe remarked. 'By God, but that Artry is a fortunate fellow. Still, once you are wed, eh, who knows? Many a woman casts aside her silly modesty once a ring is on her finger.'

'Be sure there is no woman would take off her ring for *you*, Uncle Philippe,' Geneviève said with a sweet smile.

'Foul-tempered bitch,' he growled. 'I've a mind not to give you your letter.'

'Letter?'

'The post came in from Paris this morning. There is a letter for you.'

'From Paris?' she cried. 'Where is it?'

'Here.' He patted his pocket.

'Then give it to me.'

'All in good time, my dear. Are you not going to purchase it?'

'I am going to kick you on the ankle,' she promised. 'You've not read it?'

'Eh, not I.'

'Then give it to me.'

He hesitated, slowly drew it from his pocket. 'But I can tell you who it's from. The Prince of Conti, no less.'

Geneviève's heart seemed to skip a beat. A letter from the Prince, after all these years? And after he had sworn never to look on her face again? Could it be that news of her return had reached the King, and he had forgiven her? She snatched the packet, glanced at her uncle, got up and crossed the room to the other chair by the window. She tore open the outer envelope, discovered there were two more inside; the smaller one bore the Conti crest; the larger was plain, and very dog-eared as if it had been crushed more than once before reaching her.

Slowly she slit the smaller envelope, took out a sheet of crested paper:

'My Dear Geneviève,' the Prince had written. 'The enclosed arrived for you a few days hence, in our diplomatic mailbag from St Petersburg. It is, as you can see, addressed in care of myself, and so I took the liberty of opening it, in the hope that, after all this time, your mission may have proved less abortive. In the event, it contains nothing of interest to me, or, I doubt, to you any longer. So enjoy your memories.

'I trust you are well, and appreciating the sea breezes. Would you believe that I think of you from time to time, villainess that you are? Had you but continued to obey me implicitly, what a future you might have had.

C.'

Wretched catamite, Geneviève thought. But her heart continued to pound. From Russia? Who could it possibly be? Her hands trembled as she slit the second envelope, took out a sheet of crumpled paper; the writing was in pencil and in some places had faded so completely she could hardly make it out — the date was more than a year old.

'Dear Mademoiselle d'Éon.' The hand was upright and bold; she had never seen it before. 'You will observe that I have survived my three years of *hard* labour. That is to say, while I

158

remain very much of an exile, I am no longer a prisoner. I am allowed to find my own lodgings and, in what time I have to spare from building this interminable roadway through an equally interminable forest, I am allowed to farm an acre of land. It is not mine, but the produce is. Indeed, mademoiselle, I survive, and even prosper, as there can be no doubt that the frontier life is conducive to excellent health.

'My object in writing is to inform you of these facts, as I fear that you may be concerned at my fate. On the other hand, I have learned nothing of *you*, save that I know, from another exile who has recently made the journey from Moscow, that you must either have survived your knouting or were reprieved from it, for he remembers seeing you in the Kremlin, but some time ago. My dear, dear mademoiselle, should you be able to spare the time to reply to this letter, at the address above, it will surely find its way to me, and a line from you would make me the happiest man in the world.

I should not presume upon our brief acquaintance, and I know that, as you are alive and well – for so my acquaintance assured me, when last he saw you – that you will have prospered, for never was woman more certain of prosperity than your own sweet self; but if, at a distance of a thousand miles, and in the sure certainty that I shall never see you again, I venture to indicate the depths of my regard for you, I pray, mademoiselle, that you will excuse such boldness. I can only say that having held your hand, and been privileged to draw my sword in your defence, I regret not a moment that has passed since, as my memory remains sufficient for me to endure any ills. Were the occasion to arise again, and were I certain of one more touch of those beautiful fingers, be sure, mademoiselle, that I should play the same role, and with enthusiasm.

Your obedient servant,
Adam Menzies.'

Geneviève raised her head, and to her horror found that her eyes were full of tears. He was alive. Adam Menzies. How memory flooded back, of his first appearance at the window of her carriage, of him holding the bowl for her to puke into, of him escorting her on deck for her first glimpse of St Petersburg. And of him facing a dozen armed men, in defence of her. And now he was alive, and apparently as optimistic as ever, for all that he was buried alive in Siberia.

She peered at the address. Somewhere called Ekaterinburg –

Catherine's town. The very name made her shiver. But was she not buried alive in Cherbourg?

Save that she was taking steps to escape. Oh, if only it could be with Adam Menzies. They could ride together across the steppes, for ever and ever and ever. What a pair they would make, because he could be as gentle as a woman, and she could be as violent as a man.

My God, she thought. You are falling in love with the memory of someone you have not seen for four years and will never see again. But then, she smiled, was that not the safest way to fall in love?

'Letters from Paris,' Uncle Philippe said portentously over dinner. 'The Prince of Conti no less. Our Geneviève has some great friends.'

'The Prince?' Mama asked, face paling.

'He inquires after my health, Mama, and yours, to be sure,' Geneviève lied. 'Nothing more than that.'

But she ate even less than she had expected. On a sudden her body and her mind had become a raging torrent of ... she did not know. Restlessness. She had wasted four years, idling in Cherbourg, while Adam had laboured in the ice or the abominable heat of Siberia. She had lifted not a finger to help him. How could she? And she had not even supposed him alive. But now ... he wanted a letter from her. That she would most certainly do. They would exchange letters, vow their love, at a distance of several thousand miles. Now there was romance.

'My dear, dear mademoiselle. You have made me the happiest of men.' Artry was dressed in his very best, and allowed his hand to brush against hers. But he had said those very words yesterday. What a *fool* he was.

Then what a fool she was being, in considering him as a husband.

They walked along the waterfront, past the row of ships waiting to be loaded, past the smells and the scents of other countries, of the sea itself, of all the wide world that waited beyond the prison that was Cherbourg.

'I am, of course, desirous only of attending to your wishes,' Artry explained. 'But I cannot help but feel a certain elation, that after all these years ... well, a certain boldness, too, mademoiselle. A certain optimism. A certain feeling ...

The man was a driveller. She wondered how he ever performed in court.

'A feeling that perhaps you are considering me in a light more sublime than merely that of escort. Am I being too bold, mademoiselle?'

You, she wondered? Bold? 'I am but a girl, monsieur,' she explained, 'and know little of sophisticated practices.'

'A very sweet girl,' he insisted. 'Oh, indeed. Mademoiselle . . .'

'Whatever is going on over there?' she inquired. As they approached the fourth vessel in a row she saw what appeared to be a fight at the foot of the gangplank.

'A brawl,' Artry explained. 'Seamen are ever brawling.'

'But it is six against one,' Geneviève cried. For indeed, the six seamen appeared to be engaged in beating one unfortunate fellow, a black man, who had fallen to the ground and was endeavouring to shelter his head from the kicks aimed at it.

'Aye, well, no doubt the fellow deserves it. He is naught but a blackamoor, in any event.'

'And what has the colour of his skin to do with it?' Geneviève freed her hand, and hurried forward, holding her skirts to her ankles. 'Wretched men,' she shouted, striking one across the back with her cane. 'Stop that.'

The men abandoned their victim for a moment as they turned to stare at their assailant, while the man she had struck rubbed his shoulder.

'Be off, mademoiselle,' one of them said. 'This is no concern of yours.'

'I shall be off when that poor fellow gets up and walks away,' Geneviève informed them.

The sailors exchanged glances. 'Now look here, mademoiselle . . .' began the spokesman.

Geneviève discovered Artry tugging at her arm. 'My dear mademoiselle,' he said. 'Geneviève, my sweet, do come away. It would not be seemly for either of us to become involved in a brawl.'

'She's yours, is she?' demanded the sailor. 'Well, you'd best take her off, monsieur. We were just considering tanning her backside for her.'

'Why, you . . .' Geneviève pulled on her arm.

'You are offensive, monsieur,' Artry said, dropping his hand to the hilt of his sword.

'And you draw that toothpick and I'll break it over your head,' the sailor said.

'Why, sir . . .' But Artry's face was paling and he was stepping backwards.

'You'll not be so insulted, monsieur,' Geneviève cried. 'Nor permit me to be.'

'I'll not fight with low fellows,' Artry said, and lowered his voice. 'Besides, there are six of them and only one of me.'

'Then let me,' Geneviève shouted, all the angry frustration she had been experiencing throughout the day suddenly bubbling to the surface. She freed her arm, and as he attempted to catch hold of her again, pushed him on the chest while seizing the hilt of his sword and drawing it as he staggered back. .

'Mademoiselle,' he protested. 'Geneviève.'

But Geneviève had already turned to face the seamen. 'Well, now,' she said, raising the rapier in a salute. 'Who was it meant to tan my backside?' She could hear a growing noise behind her as a crowd gathered, excited comment rising into the spring air along with the rustling of clothes and the stamping of feet. But for herself she knew only the exultation of feeling the hilt of a sword once again in her hand, the desire to resolve her doubts in physical action, the masculine curse which had haunted her since her childhood.

The seamen were not easily to be put to flight. They exchanged glances, and even grins as they moved forward. Geneviève saw the danger of being encircled, uttered a shout, and charged, her blade whipping left and right, sending them tumbling to and fro, one fellow clutching the sudden wound in his arm. At the end she nearly fell over the man she was intending to rescue, and brought herself up short, inhaling to get her breathing under control, turning once again to face them.

'Geneviève,' Artry wailed, backing into the crowd.

'Throw me that hangar,' growled the sailor who had first spoken to her.

'She's naught but a girl,' objected another.

'She's a virago,' said the first man. 'I'll teach her a lesson, that I will. The hangar man.'

Geneviève waited, allowing her breathing to settle, using her left hand now to scoop her skirts entirely from the ground and bring them almost to her knees.

'Now then, missee,' said the sailor, advancing, his cutlass held in front of him. 'You'd best put down that pigsticker before I take off your ears. Or maybe you'd sooner lose a tit?'

Geneviève's heart seemed to swell until her very chest was expanding. This was what she had missed more than anything. Not necessarily the swordplay. The excitement of danger, of facing a man with naught between them but their skills and their courage. 'May God forgive me,' she breathed, 'for taking a life.'

Because there was no help for it. The crowd gave a great gasp of horror as she moved forward, skirts flailing in the afternoon breeze, rapier point flickering to and from with dazzling speed. The sailor was no tyro. He managed to meet her first and second and even third thrusts, and the steel rang into the afternoon. But the fourth was too much for him; their blades slithered together for a moment and then she was free, hurtling forward with such force that she cannoned into his chest. He gave a terrible gasp, and the flat of his blade struck her across the shoulder, while the heated liquid which was spilling over her hand told her that he was dead; her sword had passed right through his body and protruded on the other side. His eyes glazed, and she released the hilt and stepped backwards, the front of her gown already stained with blood. The sailor's knees struck the cobbles, and then his body in turn flopped forward like a sack of grain. His head was the last to hit, with a terrifying thud.

Geneviève gazed at his companions. She had left her sword deep in her first opponent's belly, and there was no hope of withdrawing it immediately. But the other sailors had no intention of fighting her. They huddled together like several frightened sheep, the wounded man still clutching his arm, while the negro regained his feet, and then bowed to her.

'I am in your debt, mademoiselle. If I can ever repay you ...'

His French was almost perfect. Geneviève gave a little curtsey. 'Be sure I shall think of something, monsieur. For the moment, if you could but take my arm ...'

Because as ever following a bout, certainly where she had killed a man, she suddenly felt faint. But the negro gave her a strong arm to lean on, and she could regain her breath, and take a last look at the man at her feet, the blood on her gown, blink back the sudden tears, and wonder what overtook her so suddenly and so devastatingly, to make her such ... such a virago, as the poor fellow had called her, moments before he had died.

She could also look at the crowd, who were staring at her as if she were a freak or a wild animal, at Monsieur Artry, face paler than ever, long chin slipped down almost to the middle of his chest, hand busy with a kerchief to wipe the sweat from his brow. And at four soldiers of the guard, commanded by a sergeant, pushing their way through the throng. She licked her lips. Here was far more serious opposition than any she had ever encountered. And she was unarmed.

'My God,' said one of the musketeers. 'Blariot is dead.'

'The rascal deserved it,' said another.

'None the less, he is murdered,' said a third. 'And by a woman.'

'He is not murdered,' Geneviève said angrily. 'He died with a weapon in his hand. It is still in his hand. Look for yourselves.'

They had surrounded her, leaving their sergeant to face her. 'Duelling is against the laws of France, Mademoiselle d'Éon.' Oh the scoundrel! His name was Roumille, and he had been an early caller at Uncle Philippe's house; but he had also been quickly discouraged by her lack of interest, and no doubt now hated her.

'A duel?' she asked scornfully. 'This was no duel. I interceded for this man's life.'

'A man is dead, mademoiselle,' he said seriously. 'Therefore it is my duty to arrest you. I am but giving you the choice of charges, murder, or duelling?'

Geneviève bit her lip. She had not expected to be faced with such a question, before so many people. 'Well, then, monsieur,' she said, 'I presume it was a duel, as you supposed.'

He smiled; she did not like it at all. 'Then I arrest you for duelling, mademoiselle. Where one of the participants dies, the end is the same. It is called murder by the court.'

Geneviève glared at him. Foul wretch, she thought. Had I my sword ... but two of the soldiers were already behind her, and another was pulling a pair of manacles from his belt.

'Monsieur,' she protested, keeping her voice soft. 'There is no need for such measures. I will accompany you. I am sure any magistrate will be able to appreciate my point.'

'Secure her,' the sergeant growled.

Geneviève looked for Artry. 'Will you suffer me to be so treated, monsieur?' she shouted.

'My God,' Artry said. 'My God ...' He came closer, still mopping his brow. 'There have been rumours ...'

Geneviève felt sick. Rumours? In Cherbourg? They could only have been spread by Uncle Philippe. My God, she thought, when I get home ...

But it was a case of if she got home, for the fetters were being clapped on her wrists.

'You may accompany Mademoiselle d'Éon to gaol, if you

wish, Monsieur Artry,' said Roumille.

The lawyer started as if stung. 'Me? No, no, I'd best be away. To ... to inform her family of this catastrophe.'

'They will learn of it soon enough, monsieur,' Geneviève said coldly. 'Pray do not concern yourself. I am sure you would rather not.'

One of the soldiers held her arm and propelled her forward, and the crowd was opening to let her through. She kept her head high and met their stares, their sly smiles and surreptitious whispers with haughty contempt, while inside her stomach was rolling over and over. God in Heaven, she thought; what devil runs at my heels, constantly endeavouring to trip me up? Endeavouring? He has succeeded. My God, what is to become of me?

Her existence was intolerable. Confined in a cell barely eight feet square, she was allowed no books to read, allowed no privacy, and her gaolers were men, not women. She had but half an hour's exercise, a walk up and down the prison yard every day, the most meagre ration of food, and above all, cleanliness was impossible for she was not even allowed a change of linen. In the beginning, Geneviève did her best, combing her hair with her fingers, taking off her gown and outer petticoats in order to prevent them being crushed. But as day succeeded day she began to despair. Conti had indeed abandoned her – a letter to him had produced no result. Then why did they not bring her to trial and cut off her head? What could they be waiting for?

Mama was no help. As her daughter dissolved from the groomed, sophisticated creature she had always pretended to hate and fear, her visits grew shorter and shorter. She would converse only about the most meaningless gossip, gave Geneviève no inkling of what might really be happening. 'I do not know,' she would protest. 'Justice moves slowly. We must hope, and pray.'

Pray. How can I, with the brain of a man imprisoned in the body of a woman, pray, Geneviève wondered? What God have I? And what God would waste His time to look upon me, . apostate that I am? That I was forced to be. But worse even than that thought, was a sudden realisation that Mama would probably shed very few tears *were* she to be executed. There was that thousand louis d'or waiting to be inherited.

And once she had supposed herself lonely.

After four weeks she thought she would welcome the axe, jerked her head almost hopefully whenever the door of her cell was opened, whenever even one of the gaolers slid back the cover for the peephole, and they did this regularly enough, as they delighted to watch her. Well let them, she thought, and stripped to her shift as the weather grew warmer, one day, indeed, removing even that to stretch on her bed. That afternoon the peephole remained open for over an hour. There is my only hope of immortality, she thought; not even my dirt can conceal the beauty of my figure, and they will remember me.

It was two days after that, as she lay beneath her grimy blanket enjoying the blessing of sleep, that she was awakened by the sound of her bolt being drawn. Her head raised immediately, heart pounding; it was barely dawn, and in June. It could be no more than three of the morning.

A man stood in the doorway. Geneviève sat up, holding her blanket to her throat. Her heart pounded, and she felt sick. There could be no other reason for her to be awakened at this hour. She peered into the gloom. He was taller than her gaolers, and far more richly dressed but she could not immediately make out his face. The magistrate, perhaps, come to interrogate her.

'Bring a light,' he said.

Geneviève frowned, and felt her back against the wall, as she had insensibly retreated to the head of the bed. The voice was familiar. But it could not be. She could not accept it.

The torch was held by her gaoler, above his head as the Duke of Richelieu came further into the cell. He was frowning at her. 'A month, you say. My God, but she smells like it. Up girl.'

Geneviève licked her lips, slowly moved the blanket, pushed her feet to the floor.

'Dress yourself,' the Duke said. 'Haste, now.'

Geneviève got out of bed, reached for her petticoats.

'This place stinks like a sewer,' the Duke said. 'I shall wait in my carriage. You'll stay with her.'

'Yes, my lord,' the gaoler agreed.

The Duke disappeared. Geneviève could hear his heels on the stone floor, slowly receding. Out of my life, she thought. It could only have been a dream. Then why am I getting dressed, dragging on my clothes in such haste. And why is this fellow standing still rather than insulting me as is his usual custom?

. She dropped her gown over her shoulders, settled it, fastened her buttons. The gaoler jerked his head, and she stepped through the door. No dream. Unless she was about to wake up.

'What business has the Duke with me?' she asked, as they walked along the corridor.

He shrugged. 'The Duke has business with everything, has he not, mademoiselle? For you, he is fortune. Eh?'

Geneviève wondered. She had not seen Richelieu since he had stood in front of her with a knife in his hand. Fortune?

The door was swinging open and she was stepping into the courtyard. It was broad daylight now, and the berline was waiting for her, its door also open.

'I have a château not far from here,' the Duke said, 'where you may be bathed. But for the moment, mademoiselle, would you mind sitting in that far corner?'

Geneviève slowly lowered herself into the seat. The door was closed and the carriage was moving forward. Geneviève licked her lips. 'My lord . . .'

'You are even more lovely as a woman than handsome as a boy,' the Duke mused. 'And you are surely looking at your very worst. I can confess that I am impatient. Tell me, is your puss still as delightful as the last time I beheld it?'

Geneviève gazed at him. She did not suppose he really wished an answer.

'And of course you have recently proved that your right arm remains as deadly. You must tell me of your adventures these last five years, Geneviève. That is your real name, is it not?'

She nodded, glanced out of the window. The berline had gathered speed as it reached the open road, and was careering along, with the sea distant to her left.

'And now you are mystified,' the Duke remarked.

'I had hopes of the Prince of Conti, my lord.'

'Forget him,' the Duke advised. 'He is presently disgraced.'

'Then, my lord, I do not see . . .'

Richelieu smiled, 'Do you play chess, Geneviève?'

'I know the moves, my lord.'

'I play it very well. The object of the game, as you will know, is to checkmate the opponent's King. But this is not always immediately possible, and certainly not until one has developed all of one's pieces. Even then a decisive plan may not be apparent, so what does your chess player do? He continues to develop his pieces, and his pawns. He places them on the best squares, not knowing when or how he may need them, but sure that they *will* be needed, at the end. You are such a pawn, my dear Geneviève. I do not know how you became what you are, although I look forward to hearing your tale, but I do know that you are unique. As a pretty boy with some knowledge of swordplay, you were nothing more than commonplace. As a pretty girl you were hardly even commonplace. But as a lovely woman who has the ability to play the man so successfully none can tell her from the real thing, and who in addition is a master swordswoman, why, you are a piece, not a pawn. A very valuable piece. It so happens that when I first beheld you, you were on the opposing side. But now circumstances have changed. At the moment you belong to no side at all, and your future hardly seems to exist, unless you choose mine. And believe me, Geneviève d'Éon, I am much more powerful than the Prince of Conti, even now. Serve me, and you will prosper. Oppose me, and you will die.'

Chapter Seven

How good it felt, to sit in a warm tub. Geneviève realised that bathing was just about her greatest pleasure; she indulged in one at least every fortnight, however much Mama and Aunt Aimée might frown and shake their heads and mutter about the dangers to health and the lack of hygiene involved in sitting in water which steadily became more dirty – the correct way to bathe was in a river, when the weather was warm, and not at all, when the weather was cold. But, she realised, Mama and Aunt Aimée, and Uncle Philippe, no longer mattered. Once again she had been caught up by the hurricane wind which was her life, its source her father's ambition.

For the door was opening, and the Duke of Richelieu was entering the room, to snap his fingers and have the two maids who had been attending her scurrying out and closing the door behind themselves. Geneviève drew up her legs, and waited, aware that her heart was pounding most painfully. She supposed this was the only man on earth she feared. She did not suppose she truly feared any woman, unless it be the Grand Duchess Catherine Alekseyevna.

'Are you pleased with your new quarters, Geneviève?'

Geneviève glanced around the room, glad to escape his eyes if only for a moment. The furnishings were sumptuous, the upholstery all in cloth of gold, as was the coverlet on the bed, the mirror an enormous cascade of glittering glass, the panels in oak decorated with an acanthus design. 'It is a considerable improvement upon the Cherbourg gaol, my lord.'

Richelieu smiled. 'And is but a fraction of what may be yours, if you are a good girl, Geneviève. Now come, get up and let me look at you.'

Cautiously Geneviève rose to her feet. Water dripped from her wet hair on to her shoulders and then rolled down her back and her breasts to join the stream down her legs.

'Remarkable,' the Duke said. 'Quite remarkable. How old are you?'

'I am twenty-four, my lord.'

'And how many men have had your keeping?'

'But one, my lord. His Majesty.'

Richelieu frowned. 'You'll not lie to me, girl.'

'I would not, my lord.'

'Well, well.' He sat on the bed. 'Come here.'

Geneviève stepped out of the bath, stooped to pick up the towel left by the girls.

'No, no,' he said. 'I would have you as you are.'

She straightened again. 'My lord?'

'I would sample your charms, Geneviève,' he said patiently. 'Would you refuse me?'

Obviously there could be no question of that, however distasteful the idea might be; he was some years older than the King. On the other hand she had learned a great deal since she had lost her virginity in an antechamber at Versailles. She did not suppose a withered old stick like Richelieu would be able to defeat her, but there was every chance that she might gain a victory over him.

She moved closer to the bed. 'I was but considering, my lord, that the covers will be ruined.'

'They can be changed,' he said. 'Closer.'

He remained fully dressed. She stood six inches from his nose, and waited; she could feel his breath and feel her nipples hardening. She closed her eyes, and waited, and suddenly felt his hands, no, his finger tips, because he was not grabbing and massaging, as the King had done, but rather was sliding his fingers very gently over her flesh, beginning, strangely, at her hips, and moving round behind to trickle a forefinger down the cleft of her buttocks, yet without any indication of wishing to go between. The sensation tickled and titillated at the same time; she suppressed a shiver with an effort, and felt his breath rush against her as he smiled.

'Undress me.'

The fingers were gone. Geneviève opened her eyes, discovered the Duke stretched out on the bed. And now she was cold; her flesh was a mass of goose pimples, but this increased tumescence seemed to please him. Trembling with a mixture of anticipation and the chill, she removed his shoes and rolled down his stockings, freed his doublet, untied his cravat. He sat up to allow her to free these and his shirt. 'Why do you leave my breeches?'

'The best until last, my lord,' she said, a sense of triumph starting to relax the tightness of her mind. He was intrigued, and he was excited; she could tell this even without removing the garment. Suppose she could make the Duke fall for her as the King had done? Gently she removed the last of his clothes. His body was as thin in the flesh as it had appeared when dressed, but his penis was enormous, jutting away from the shallow belly. She could not prevent a small gasp, and his smile widened.

'You find me formidable?'

'Indeed I do, my lord.'

'Then lie on me. Cover me.'

Cautiously she climbed on to the bed and lowered her body on to his; if she touched his toes with hers, her mouth still came to his chin.

'Cold,' he said. 'You are like ice. There is nothing sweeter than the feel of a cold female body. One day I must try lying beneath a corpse. It is one of the few pleasures I have never experienced.'

Geneviève's head jerked, but he continued to smile.

'Imprison me.'

Geneviève opened her legs, allowed him between, he did not enter, but stood like a pole against her.

'Now move,' he said. 'Slowly, up and down.'

She obeyed, and felt his fingers return, gently stroking her slit and therefore, she realised, gently stroking himself as well.

'Slowly,' he whispered, his breathing starting to labour. 'Slowly.'

Her mouth had flopped open, because she felt her own mind leaping into a garden of passion. It could not be. She would not be seduced by this treacherous rogue. She did not want him to be able to see her, and lowered her head, to suck and kiss at his chin. But she continued to move, up and down; she did not suppose she could have stopped now even if commanded. Then everything happened at once. His fingers ceased caressing and were instead parting her legs again, his penis had slipped inside, and he had come with a tremendous gush at the same time as she climaxed herself. For a moment longer she continued moving, then her breath and her muscles also seemed to lose their strength together, and she collapsed on his chest, her mind dead, and yet prickling with anger and with apprehension. She had supposed a victory was hers for the taking, and once again she had been defeated. God curse the eager lubricity of my body, she thought. God curse the evil day that had me born a woman. I can never win. Never, never, never.

Because, she realised, she could not have been more defeated than today; he had never even kissed her.

But something had happened to him. His fingers were back, and not stroking, but digging into her flesh. 'Quickly,' he gasped. 'Help me.'

Geneviève raised her head. 'My lord?'

'I have lost a ball. Help me.'

She pushed herself off him, gazed at him in alarm. Certainly he seemed to possess only one testicle.

'My lord?' To her annoyance her voice had risen into a squeak. 'It has receded,' he said. ''Tis a hernia. Help me, for God's sake, Geneviève. Bring it down.'

Geneviève bit her lip in uncertainty. She had no idea what to do. She ran her fingers over his groin and next to the remaining testicle, and found that indeed she could feel the missing one, inside his pelvic cavity. Gently she pressed into his groin, and to her relief the ball moved, and a moment later slid back to is proper place. proper place.

'My lord?'

'Oh, Geneviève, Geneviève,' he muttered. 'Christ, but it is a nuisance.'

'Every time, my lord?' Here was an unsuspected advantage, which would leave him far more at her mercy than ever if she had not climaxed.

'Only when I am on my back. But what would you, 'tis my favourite position. Now wash me clean, girl, and then dress yourself. I would wager you could stand some good food after prison fare.'

Geneviève obeyed, dried him with the towel, and then used it on herself.

Her brain was tumbling. In the space of a few minutes she seemed to have known this man all of her life, as he had given her the best orgasm of her life. But he was her sworn enemy, who regarded her only as a weapon. As she regarded herself, surely. But oh, my lord, she thought, were you to ask me...what? What do you want of him, she wondered? It was difficult to think, both from a combination of the events of the last hour and from her hunger, because the mention of food had her realising just how famished she was.

She had been found an undressing robe which belonged to the Duke himself; it encased her from the neck to the floor and then extended another few inches after that. In this garment she was allowed to sit at table, on the Duke's right hand, and tuck into an enormous repast, four plates of various kinds of soup, a whole pheasant, a partridge, a large plate of salad, two slices of ham, mutton with gravy and garlic. The Duke ate in silence and she was glad to humour him, pausing only to drink some very pleasant claret wine. Not until she was consuming pastry together with several hard boiled eggs, and eyeing the fruit bowl to decide whether pears or apples would make a perfect finish to the best meal of her life, did he address her.

'You are a hearty trencherwoman, Geneviève.'

'My lord, if you knew what it is like to exist on black bread and water for nearly a month...'

'I have campaigned,' the Duke pointed out. 'But you...you are a treasure. I could sit here forever, just watching you.' He smiled at her. 'And occasionally touching you.'

'My lord is a flatterer.' Geneviève swallowed her last egg, and selected a pear.

'I have never been so accused before. You see, my dear, your attraction lies not in your beauty, which is considerable, or your passion, which is delectable, it is in your...what shall I say? Your ambiguity. I see you there, every inch the lovely young woman, yet your every movement is made like a man, and I do believe you think like one as well. And then, suppose I were to dress you in male clothing, I would see you, definitely a young

172

man, and yet I would know that you possessed the sweetest hole on this earth. As I may have said before, you are unique. I could almost fall in love with you.'

Geneviève bit, and felt the juice squirt out of the side of her mouth. 'Almost, my lord?'

'Who knows, perhaps I shall. In time. But for the moment... the Duchess knows of your existence.'

Geneviève raised her eyebrows. 'The Duchess?'

'Pompadour. You did not know she has been made a Duchess? Why, my dear, you provincials. My dear Jeanne is now all powerful. Since you left Paris, why, the King has become a doter.'

Geneviève finished her pear, placed the stalk on her plate, washed her fingers in the bowl. 'I see.'

'Indeed I think you do. Women are an ungrateful, ambitious sex. How much of a woman *are* you, Geneviève?'

Geneviève drank some wine. Conti had once asked her if she would ever grow greater than her protector, had advised her against it. But was it possible to grow greater than a king? The point at issue at this moment was whether it was possible to grow greater than the Duke of Richelieu. Whether it was possible to *dare*.

'You do not reply,' the Duke remarked. 'At the least you have the brain of a man, my dear girl. But as I said, our female tyrant learned the news of the strange goings on in Cherbourg, where a woman assailed and defeated six sailors, handling a sword like a master at arms, the same moment that I did. I would estimate her assassins are at this moment knocking open the gates of your cell.'

'But you acted with more despatch, my lord.'

'There is where women will always be defeated, Geneviève. They lack that little spark of decision.'

Geneviève wondered what he would make of the Grand Duchess Catherine, or would he merely say that she should have assaulted her rival after the first night instead of waiting for the second. 'And I am grateful for your decision, my lord.'

'As you should be,' the Duke agreed. 'As I am grateful for your reappearance. The question which taxes me is how best to use you.'

Geneviève allowed herself a delicate belch. She did not suppose it was possible to feel a greater sense of well-being. Her entire system was so sated she was not even prepared to be angry. Because underlying the contentment there was the excitement she had missed so much over the past four years, the sense of being at the centre of great events. And this time she was no inexperienced girl. Let them decide to use her; this time she was determined that *she* would choose where her feet would finally fall.

'Because, you see,' Richelieu continued, 'His Majesty appears well content with the present state of affairs. And the Pompadour is a shrewd hussy, to be sure. She studied what very nearly happened five years ago, what would have happened, had I not so foolishly interfered . . .' He allowed himself a smile. 'And thus she knows that as she alone cannot keep the King's passions occupied, she must at the least control those who do. He exists in the centre of a veritable harem, every member of which is a creature of the Duchess. Displacing her now will be an immeasurably more difficult task than it might have been once. Of course there is always the chance that His Majesty, were you to be reintroduced to court, might once again fall desperately in love with you. But this is exposing our prospects to chance, which is basically unsound. And at the best, did it take him only twenty-four hours to make up his mind, in those twenty-four hours the Pompadour would have had you seized and strangled. As you have revealed to the world your prowess, you may be certain *she* would not attempt to waylay you with but two men. She would send Shirér himself against you.'

How that name, and that face, drifted through her memory. And that skill. The world was more full of men to be feared than she had thought. But she was not going to let Richelieu see that he could frighten her. Geneviève decided to eat another pear.

'So what I want of you, my dear Geneviève,' Richelieu said, 'is to be available, a weapon to be used the very moment the opportunity arises. Because arise it must, by the course of human nature. Either the King will be taken ill, and have a change of heart, or the Duchess will be taken ill, and forced to absent herself from court, or some other event may occur which will give us the opportunity we seek. Patience, that is the game we must play, while at the same time advancing our cause to the best of our ability. Do you not agree?'

'I am at my lord's command,' Geneviève said humbly.

'So what I am primarily seeking is a place and an occupation where you may be safe from the Pompadour's seeking fingers, for be sure as she will know you have been taken from Cherbourg

174

by me, she will hunt you down.'

'My lord?' He did, after all, have the power to terrify; Geneviève reached for another pear and swallowed a large piece.

'Be certain of it. Fortunately, I have just the place for you, and just the task for you. A post where you will be doing me, and France, a great service, and where you will be absolutely safe, until I have need of you.'

'Then, my lord,' Geneviève said, 'you have but to indicate the direction in which you would have me travel.'

Richelieu smiled at her. 'It is a way you know well, Geneviève. I wish you to return to St Petersburg.'

Geneviève swallowed the entire remaining portion of pear, and choked. The Duke waved away the footman and himself patted her back.

'You must be careful, mademoiselle,' he said. 'Have you never been told that if you swallow fruit pips the tree will grow out of your mouth?'

Geneviève glared at him. Slowly she got her breath back. 'My lord is fond of his little joke.'

'I never joke, Geneviève.'

Geneviève drank some wine, and felt better. 'Then you are unacquainted with sufficient of my history.'

'On the contrary, Geneviève. My correspondent in Russia is the Empress herself.'

Geneviève gazed at him.

'She has not been well. Did you know that?'

Whatever game he was playing, he had, as ever, to be humoured, at least in her present circumstances. 'No, my lord. But the Empress has ever been given to bouts of illness.'

'Inherited from her father,' Richelieu agreed. 'But perhaps brought on by aggravation at losing her favourite handmaiden. Do you not suppose she would welcome you back with open arms?'

Geneviève licked her lips. 'My lord, believe me, I should be going to my death. It scarce seems sensible to come all this way to save me from the headsman merely to hand me over to the knout.'

'You exaggerate.'

'Believe me, my lord,' Geneviève cried. 'God knows, I fear the Empress, however fond of me she may be. But I fear the Grand Duchess more.'

Richelieu frowned. 'A mere girl?'

Geneviève inhaled. 'She is my age, my lord. Now consider, me with the power of being future Tsarina.'

'An intriguing thought. Well, well. What a treasure you are, Geneviève. I will tell you frankly that I had never considered the Grand Duchess to be of the slightest importance. What was she before she went to Russia? Sophie of Anholt-Zerbst? Could there possibly be a less important principality in the entire world?'

'My lord, I do assure you . . .'

'Oh, I believe you, Geneviève. I would never have supposed to see *you* frightened. But you looked frightened then. Yet go to Russia you must.'

'My lord . . .'

'Be quiet, and listen to me. That peace we patched up four years ago was nothing more than a truce. Things are moving once again in the direction of hostilities. For Heaven's sake, our colonists and the English are already at each other's throats, in India, in the West Indies, and in North America. Soon it will come to full scale operations here in Europe. Now the sides are already taken, by the main protagonists. It will be England and Prussia against France. Heavy odds. The King, which means the Pompadour, has hopes of Austria, but to be frank Maria Theresa did not prove a very serious antagonist in the last set-to and I have my doubts as to whether she will prove a very useful *ally* in the next, even if she agrees. But I must discover an offset to Prussia. That has to be Russia. I happen to know, from my correspondence, that Elizabeth Petrovna loathes Frederick the Great. He has referred to her as an apostolic hag, and she is not a woman to forgive a slight.'

'My lord . . .'

'Think of the gain to my reputation should I manage to bring the Russians in. Pompadour has no use for them. She remembers that they did not exactly cover themselves with glory five years ago. But that was because the army commanders had not yet learned loyalty to their new empress. Now it will be different. Don't you understand, Geneviève? If Pompadour is proved wrong, and I am proved right, I shall go a long way to regaining my proper place at court. And when I achieve that, I do assure you that you will be the first to benefit.'

do assure you that you will be the first to benefit.'

'Supposing I am still alive, my lord. You have just reminded us both that Her Majesty does not readily forgive a slight.'

'She adores you.'

'I still ran away from her.'

'Nonsense. She knows the truth of that matter.'

'And does she also know that the Grand Duchess has sworn to kill me the moment I set foot back in Russia, however great the imperial displeasure she incurs?'

Richelieu rested his elbow on the table, and his chin on his forefinger, and stared at her for some seconds. 'You have naught to fear from the Grand Duchess, Geneviève. My agents inform me that she is with child.'

'My lord? That is impossible.'

'Yet I do assure you it is true. Thus you could not choose a better moment for a return visit. And the Empress has made her terms quite clear to me, Geneviève. We in France have nothing to offer her, save you.'

'I cannot believe she would go to war to possess my body.'

'I suspect she means to go to war in any event, Geneviève. But why should she, as our ally? And as she points out, it is such a little thing she asks . . .'

'My lord!'

'In the context of the issues at stake. And I do promise you complete safety.'

'My lord, you have never been to Russia.'

'And neither have you, as Ambassador.'

Geneviève sat up straight.

'Well, not as Ambassador,' Richelieu corrected himself. 'La Chétardie is already in residence. But you will go as the special envoy of the Prime Minister of France. What is more I shall give you the rank commensurate with your responsibilities. Chevalier. How about that? The Chevalier d'Éon.'

'My lord, my head is spinning.'

'Don't you see? Conti sent a young woman as a gift to the Empress of Russia. That young woman has since disappeared. What could be more natural than for Geneviève d'Éon's brother, Charles, to go seeking his sister as well as carrying out a diplomatic mission for his country? I do promise you, my dear girl, that no one will dare to molest a special envoy from Versailles.'

Geneviève chewed her lip. 'But . . . the Empress . . .'

'You will reveal your true identity to her, and to no one else.' He chuckled. 'Who knows, she may prefer you as a man.'

'She will very soon find out the difference, my lord. The Empress is a woman of demanding tastes.'

177

'So long as no one else finds out the difference, Geneviève, there is nothing to fear.'

'And the future, my lord? I had hoped I was going to be of some use to you, here in France.'

'You will be. I will fetch you back, my dear girl. Be sure of that. Once an offensive alliance is signed you will be sent for. Oh, it may be necessary to pull some wool over the imperial eyes, say that you are returning only to confer. I swear I will never ask you to go back to Russia. And think of it. The Chevalier d'Éon will suddenly re-emerge from obscurity, and be the hero of the hour. The King will welcome you with open arms, quite literally I imagine, as he will know your secret. Can you imagine a brighter future?'

'And the Duchess of Pompadour?'

'Will gnash her teeth in impotent fury as she slips from power.'

Geneviève found herself chewing her lip again. She would have been a fool ever to suppose that Richelieu's employment, in whichever direction, was not going to be dangerous. And she *had* successfully played the man for the better part of her life. Besides, as a man, with a sword at her side, the Grand Duchess would not find her so easy a victim. And if Catherine *was* pregnant, then surely it meant that she and Peter Feodorovich were reconciled and she need fear nothing from any woman.

Then what of Russia? The gloom and the cold and the stifling boredom. But only for a short while, if Richelieu could be trusted. And if he could not, she might as well cut her own throat straight away. Then what of the Empress? Could she really pretend that she did not miss the utter sensuality of that imperial embrace?

And all for the good of France. There was an easy sop to conscience.

'Well, now,' the Duke said. 'I see an understanding of your true advancement entering your face.'

Geneviève glanced at him. A tool, she thought. A weapon. That is all I am, save to the Empress. And to her I am but a body. Have I no being, no existence in myself, save as a frustrated young woman in some provincial town? Do I not live, in myself, as a woman, to anyone?

She frowned. They had taken away the letter when they had searched her, but she could remember every word of it, stilted, anxious, uncertain, like its writer, but expressing the only true feelings for her she had ever known. And she was returning to Russia.

178

'Well?' Richelieu demanded.

'You will not deny that the mission you intend is dangerous, my lord?'

'Marginally.'

'Yet the danger is there, my lord. Am I not entitled to some physical reward, just in case things go astray?'

'And you shall have it, the moment you return. Ten thousand louis d'or.'

'I am not interested in money, my lord, and I would rather have it in advance.'

'Now *you* are confusing *me*.'

Geneviève licked her lips. 'There was a young man, my lord, who once did me a very great favour, or perhaps I should say, he attempted to do me a very great favour . . .'

'Ha ha,' Richelieu shouted. 'And here was I supposing you to be the coldest little fish that ever swam in this sea of ours. Attempted? Oh come now, my dear girl, were you that difficult to breach?'

Geneviève cursed the heat in her cheeks. 'You mistake the situation, my lord. His purpose was to aid me to escape from Russia. He failed, was detected, and sentenced to eternal exile in Siberia. A Frenchman, my lord. Well, a Scot living in France.'

'Your taste in admirers does you no credit, Geneviève. I know of this fellow. Menzies. The Chevalier Douglas reported the event. He was found in the bedchamber of one of the Empress's ladies.' He stared at her. 'My God. *Your* bedchamber.'

'While we were making our plans, my lord. Nothing more than that.'

'Aye, well, if you will have it so. In any event, as he was exiled to Siberia some four years ago, he is most certainly dead by now.'

'On the contrary, my lord. I received a letter from him not a month ago.'

'A letter?' Richelieu frowned. 'And what would you have?'

'His freedom, my lord. If I must go to St Petersburg, he must be freed in exchange.'

'Must? Are you seeking to defy me?'

'By no means, my lord. I am but assuming that you would wish me to give you my best efforts, my enthusiasm, in the task you have set me.'

He continued to gaze at her from some moments. Then his face broke into a smile. 'You are very much your own woman,

Geneviève. But then, I would not have you any other way. You shall regain possession of your rude Scotsman, I promise you. And now let us return to bed. Just looking at you makes me hard as a rod. And we are to be separated, are we not, if only for a brief while?'

So once again, St Petersburg. But what a difference to make the journey in summer! If the roads of North Germany had not improved since the last time she had bounced over them, the Baltic was like a lake, and this time they were enabled to enter the estuary of the Neva, and bring up alongside the docks themselves, surrounded by the palaces of the city, overlooking the grim fortress of St Peter and St Paul, built on one of the islands facing the waterfront.

For landing Geneviève wore a red velvet coat, waistcoat and breeches, with gold buttons and braid embroidery – all provided by the Duke. Her shirt was white cambric with lace ruffles, her stockings were white silk, and her shoes black leather with jewelled buckles. Her hair had once again been cropped and was concealed beneath a white pigtail wig over which she wore a black tricorne, while in addition to the sword at her side she carried a sword cane with a diamond studded hilt. On the forefinger of her right hand she wore an emerald ring presented to her by the Duke; 'Emeralds are my lucky stone and will be yours too,' he had said. She thought she had never looked better, or indeed more confident; she did not suppose there was anyone who would recognise in this splendid young man the hapless girl of five years before, and she had to admit to herself that she felt far more in command of herself when dressed as a man. Even the presence of Jules was a reassurance, although he was less pleased than herself to be informed that he was being returned to Russia.

'I doubt we shall escape with our heads this time, mademoiselle,' he had grumbled.

'Monsieur,' she had insisted. 'Monsieur. That is why we are leaving Margaret behind. For God's sake remember.'

As it happened, the Empress was in the Kremlin, and it was necessary to make the long journey across the Russian plain. But even this was a pleasure in summer, and certainly every possible assistance was given to the French envoy, a platoon of Cossacks being detailed to ride with his carriage and make sure that he was not interrupted or troubled in any way. Yet the butterflies started to flutter in Geneviève's belly as the smoke pall that marked the Holy City came in sight, and as she watched the sun reflecting from the onion domes on St Basil's. That had been her last glimpse of the city when she had stolen away four years before. Now . . . but she dared not let herself suppose anything miscarrying. Only boldness and determination would succeed here.

The doors were opening, the major-domo was thumping the floor three times with his staff, and bellowing in Russian, 'His Excellency the French envoy, the Chevalier d'Éon.'

Jules had, as usual, been left outside. She was on her own. She blinked, gazed into the familiar room, at the familiar faces, and felt all the strength leave her knees. Elizabeth Petrovna sat in a high-backed chair, facing the doors; her spaniels played at her feet. Alexis Razumovsky stood on her right, Michael Vorontsov on her left. The Grand Duke Peter was a little distance to their right. Behind them were several other ladies and gentlemen Geneviève knew very well, but at the moment she could spare the time to identify none of them; she was only grateful that the Grand Duchess Catherine was not present – no doubt her condition could be thanked for that.

'My dear Chevalier.' Elizabeth Petrovna spoke French, as usual. But she did not rise, merely extended her hand. 'Welcome to Russia.'

Geneviève took the long fingers, was dismayed to discover that they seemed to have lost a great deal of their strength; indeed, as she stooped to kiss the knuckles she saw that the Empress's face had also lost some of its purpose, and was beginning to sag.

'It is my pleasure to be here, Your Majesty.'

She straightened, looked into Elizabeth Petrovna's eyes. But she could not decide on the expression. Interested, certainly, but . . .

'As you will know, Chevalier, we had the pleasure of entertaining your sister here, oh, several years ago,' Elizabeth said. 'And you are most definitely her brother; the resemblance is striking. Have you news of the dear girl?'

'She is well, Your Majesty, and sends Your Majesty her felicitations. You will know that she did not leave Russia of her own accord.'

Elizabeth Petrovna gazed at her for some moments, and then nodded. 'It was an unfortunate business, by all accounts. You have letters for me, from the Duke of Richelieu?'

'Indeed, Your Majesty.' Geneviève held out the wallet.

Elizabeth Petrovna waved her hand, and Vorontsov stepped forward to take it. For the first time Geneviève met *his* eyes; they gleamed with an instant dislike. Can he possibly recognise me, she wondered?

'I will study them at my leisure,' the Empress said. 'In the meanwhile, Chevalier, you will join me for dinner. There are matters we must discuss.'

Geneviève bowed, and was taken to her quarters, where Jules was already installed. 'Indeed, monsieur,' he said, 'I feel that I have entered a prison, all over again. And what are we to do about these?'

For as usual there were several attendants waiting; three young men and an elderly woman.

'Certainly we cannot risk arousing their suspicions by dismissing them,' she decided. 'But it must be made perfectly plain that I wish to be undressed by you alone, and that I will take my baths in the privacy of my bedchamber, again with you alone. I am an eccentric Frenchman. You will see to it, Jules.'

'Of course, monsieur,' Jules said. He was happy enough to be restored to his old position of intimacy with her. But problems with her attendants were the least of Geneviève's concern at the moment. She knew that the crisis was rushing upon her; it wanted only an hour to dinner. And sure enough, she was seated on the Empress's right hand, and had barely taken her first sip of vodka when Elizabeth Petrovna leaned across, and said, 'I have studied my lord of Richelieu's despatches, Chevalier, and I must confess I do not understand them at all.'

'The Duke fears that Europe may soon be engulfed in a general conflagration, and seeks to discover his friends and his enemies. Nor has he any doubt that in Russia he has a friend.'

Elizabeth Petrovna turned her head, slowly. 'I am not discussing politics, Chevalier. Your master well knows that if my conditions are met I will happily march against that upstart Prussian. It is those conditions I wish to discuss. The Duke blandly informs me that they *have* been met, and leaves it at that. Do you know anything of the matter?'

Geneviève took refuge in some more vodka. 'I am entirely in the Duke's confidence, Your Majesty.'

'Then where is your sister? Tell me that. I find the whole thing very confusing. Why, when she lived with us, she told me she *had* no brother. Yet there you are, as large as life. I really do not know what to make of it all.'

Geneviève chose her words with great care. Geneviève is given to strange fancies, Your Majesty. But she is close. If you would...'

'Close? In your entourage?'

'No, no, Sire. But she is waiting to rejoin Your Majesty. If I could have the privilege of a private audience.'

Elizabeth Petrovna glared at her. 'You seek to hoodwink me. Geneviève cannot be in Russia. I would know.'

'A private audience, Your Majesty. My master desires me to convey some secret information to you before he completes his part of the bargain.'

Elizabeth Petrovna remained gazing at her for some seconds. Then she turned back to face the table. 'Out,' she commanded. 'Everybody out.'

Her guests gaped at her.

'Out,' she repeated, raising her voice. 'Out!'

Chairs scraped as the ladies and the gentlemen rose. Razumovsky remained seated.

'You also, my dear Alexis,' Elizabeth said.

'But Sire . . .'

'You also,' Elizabeth repeated, allowing some iron to enter her voice. 'I will explain later, but this young man and I have some most private matters to discuss.'

'Private from me, Sire?'

'Even from you.'

Razumovsky allowed his gaze to drift from the Empress's face to Geneviève's, then he got up. 'As you command, Your Majesty.' He left the room.

'He is angry,' Elizabeth said. 'He cannot reconcile the position of husband with that of subject.'

'*Husband?*'

Elizabeth shrugged. 'Well, what would you. A woman grows lonely as she grows older. Now, had I the knowing of a handsome young man like yourself, Chevalier . . . but it is too late. Tell me of your sister.'

My God, Geneviève thought, she is married. What does that mean to my Embassy? But she still asks after me. And besides, there was no other way for her to play the game. 'She is well, Sire, and most desirous of again making your acquaintance. She fears, however, that your anger may transcend your affection.'

'And I have told you that I know she did not desert my service of her own accord. Perhaps I would have preferred had she boldly opposed the Grand Duchess's wishes, but in the circumstances I cannot blame her. No, no, Chevalier, you may be sure that I shall welcome her with open arms. Although we shall have to be discreet, oh, discreet.'

'Geneviève is ever discreet, Your Majesty.'

'I was thinking of her safety, Chevalier. The Grand Duchess is a strange child. Sometimes I wonder if I do not fear her myself. Certainly I fear for Russia, once I am gone. Those eyes, the way she looks at you, the depths . . .'

'But Sire,' Geneviève protested. 'We have heard that the Grand Duchess is with child.'

'Indeed she is.'

'Then does that not mean that she and the Grand Duke are reconciled, that their marriage is consummated?'

The Empress gave a brief laugh. 'Would that it were so. I very much fear that marriage will never be consummated. She regards Peter Feodorovich as a child. Well, who is to say she is not correct? He is certainly retarded.'

'Then the father . . .'

'I do not propose to tell you his name, Chevalier. That is a secret between the Grand Duchess, the man, and myself. Suffice that I gave my permission when I was informed of the situation.'

Geneviève found that her goblet was empty, got up and went to the sideboard to pour some more for herself. Russian morals were just a shade too extreme even for her. As an afterthought she filled the Empress's as well.

'I can see that you are shocked, Chevalier,' Elizabeth Petrovna remarked. 'But what would you? I must have very serious doubts about the suitability of Peter Feodorovich to rule. Russia must be *ruled*. The Dynasty must be preserved.'

Geneviève pulled her ear. She remembered this woman saying that it was the blood of Peter the Great that must be preserved. But she decided against commenting about that. In any event, she did not see how it could possibly work. 'But Sire, if I may be so bold, when the child is born, will not the Grand Duke . . ?'

Another bark of laughter. 'Peter Feodorovich? You will not grant this, Chevalier, but he does not yet understand how babies are procured. He sleeps in the same bed as his wife, as a rule, and eventually a child is born. To his mind there will be an end to the matter. Now will anyone enlighten him? I would have the guilty blabber skinned alive. Even you, Chevalier. Remember that.'

Geneviève sat down, drank some vodka. 'And with all this happening, the Grand Duchess still wishes vengeance upon my sister?'

'What would you? She is a woman. She may not want her husband, but she is determined no one else shall have him. Men are very easily ruled by women, my dear Chevalier, and Peter will be Tsar, in name if not in fact. But enough of my domestic problems. I shall guarantee Geneviève my protection, you may be certain of that. And my love. You may be certain of that too. Now tell me where she is and how soon she can be brought to Moscow.'

Geneviève licked her lips. 'There is one other small matter, Sire.'

'What is it now?'

'I think the Duke my master mentioned a certain Scot, one Adam Menzies, who incurred Your Majesty's displeasure, and was exiled to Siberia.'

'Menzies,' Elizabeth growled. 'He was mentioned. But your master clearly does not know the truth of it. This fellow attempted to seduce your sister.'

'The devil,' Geneviève agreed. 'Yet is he an officer of great importance to France, Sire. My master instructed me not to inform you of my sister's whereabouts until his release and return to Paris had been assured.'

'Bargains, bargains,' Elizabeth growled. 'Your Duke is like an Arab trader in a marketplace.'

'I do assure you, Sire, that my sister has always sworn to me that there was nothing between her and the young man. She but attempted to enlist his aid in escaping Russia, for reasons I am sure she has outlined to Your Majesty. Why let a little petty spite stand in the way of your true happiness?'

Elizabeth glared at her for several seconds, then she shrugged. 'You are right, of course. I will send instructions for him to be released. But not until your sister stands before me.'

'Have I your word, Sire, as Empress and as a Romanoff and as a daughter of the True Church, that Captain Menzies will be escorted in safety to the borders of your country?'

Her head came up. 'Is he *that* important?'

'He is, Sire.'

Elizabeth sighed. 'Very well, you have my most sacred word, Chevalier. But now my patience is entirely worn out. Here am I, granting you all of these things, and you have not yet even told me where Geneviève is. She might be a thousand miles away, for all I know, and months may have to elapse before she can arrive. I am the victim of trickery, Chevalier. I can see it.'

Her anxiety was quite distressing. Geneviève realised that to bargain any further might be to lose everything, and she was perfectly satisfied with the oath she had obtained. Elizabeth Petrovna of all women would never break such a vow.

'Your patience does you great credit, Sire,' she said, and removed her hat and wig.

Elizabeth stared at her in utter amazement. 'Chevalier? Have you taken leave of your senses?'

Geneviève got up, removed her sword belt, took off her coat. 'On the contrary, Sire. I am merely taking leave of my sex.' She unbuttoned her vest.

The Empress crossed herself. 'What devilment is this?'

Geneviève took off her vest, and unbuttoned her shirt. The Empress stared at her for a moment, then uttered a shriek, and fell back in a dead faint.

Instantly the doors burst open. Geneviève dragged her shirt shut, turned her back on the people hurrying into the room, headed by Razumovsky. Oh, my God, she thought, what have I done? What will happen now?

'Away,' she shouted over her shoulder. 'Her Majesty will not be disturbed.' She lowered her voice, patted the Empress's cheeks. 'For Heaven's sake, Sire, wake up.'

'You have injured her,' Razumovsky stood at her shoulder.

'I have not,' Geneviève insisted, afraid to raise her head, and at that moment Elizabeth Petrovna opened her eyes.

'Wretched . . .'

'Boy, Sire. I am a wretched boy,' Geneviève said urgently. 'I had not meant to cause Your Majesty any distress.'

'Sire,' Razumovsky said. 'Has this Frenchman insulted you? If so, let me . . .'

'What are you doing here?' Elizabeth Petrovna demanded.

'You cried out, Sire, and . . .'

'I said I was not to be disturbed.'

'But Majesty, you cried out . . .'

'And I may well do so again,' the Empress declared. 'But the next person who comes through that door unbidden will farm in Siberia this winter.'

There was a moment's silence. Geneviève did not dare look over her shoulder at the expression on Razumovsky's face; after all, he was the imperial consort.

'As you will, Your Majesty,' he said at last. Geneviève listened to the feet slowly withdrawing across the floor, and to the door closing. She allowed herself to breathe. 'I had thought we were undone.'

'Undone?' Elizabeth Petrovna pushed herself up. 'You had best give me some vodka. You deserve to be undone, you wicked girl. For practicing such a dreadful subterfuge.'

'I but obeyed my Lord of Richelieu, Sire.' Geneviève hastily held a goblet to the imperial lips.

Elizabeth Petrovna drank deeply. 'I do not mean the clothes, Geneviève. They become you. When I was a girl I also used to delight in wearing breeches from time to time. I meant this play-acting about the Scotsman. You love him.'

'I do not, Sire. But I cannot bear the thought of him suffering on account of me, when had it not been for him I would never have known the warmth of your arms. Oh, Sire . . .' She sat on Elizabeth's lap, hugged her close; her shirt had once again fallen open and she could feel the Empress's lips searching her flesh. 'I do not know how I have survived.'

'Oh, Geneviève, Geneviève. If only you had remained here. Oh, Geneviève . . .'

'I am here now, Sire. So let the poor boy go. Besides, you gave your word.'

She had pressed too hard, and received a sharp nip on her left nipple.

'Ow!' She leapt to her feet.

'Wretched girl. How I hate you. I hate you, for running away, I hate you for coming back. And all for that boy. I hate you!'

Geneviève stood before her, trying to control the thumping of her heart. 'Sire . . .'

'But I love you too. Oh, how I love you. Come here.'

Geneviève obeyed; she had attempted all she dared. She sat on Elizabeth's lap and was *loved,* with utter desperation.

'We shall to my chamber together,' the Empress whispered. 'Oh, how I long to sleep with you in my arms, my darling girl. And let us hear no more talk about treaties and Scotsmen.'

'Alas, Sire,' Geneviève said, raising herself on her elbow. 'I am constrained.'

Elizabeth Petrovna's eyes were closed, and she breathed slowly and evenly. She at the least was utterly content. Then what of me, Geneviève wondered? This was not the woman who had seduced her four years earlier. Gone were the firm contours, the thrusting breasts, the powerful legs; even the bold, handsome profile had dissipated into drooping fat and despairing age. Now, she thought, have I truly prostituted myself for the first time, and all for Richelieu and Adam Menzies.

'Constrained, my darling? How can you be constrained?'

'To obey my Lord of Richelieu's commands, Sire.'

'Richelieu has no power here in Russia.'

'Over me he does, Sire. He . . . he holds my family, my poor widowed mother, my dear sweet aunt and uncle, and is sworn to have them executed should I not return with both the treaty signed and with Captain Menzies.'

Elizabeth Petrovna opened her eyes. 'Return?'

'The Duke's very words, Sire.'

'And he would destroy an entire family to gain his ends? My God, what barbarity. We cannot let that happen, my darling Geneviève.'

'I thank Your Majesty from the bottom of my heart.'

'You have the word of a Romanoff. I shall send tomorrow the order for the release of this Scotsman. He will be conveyed straightaway to the borders of my territories, and be commanded never to return, upon pain of death.'

'Sire, I shall forever be in your debt.'

'And tomorrow, I will sign an offensive treaty with France against Prussian designs. This Frederick has done too much, with his mouth as well as his soldiers, to the insult of Russia. Oh, I shall sign.'

'Your Majesty has made me the happiest woman in all Europe.'

'And will those things satisfy the Duke, and keep your family safe?'

'Oh, indeed, Your Majesty.'

Elizabeth Petrovna smiled. 'Why, then I think we may deny Richelieu his final requirement. You shall not return, my darling girl. I have found you again, and I shall never let you go.

About that, Geneviève thought, we shall have to see. The Empress's revelations had already given her an idea as to how she could extricate herself; it would be dangerous, but hardly more dangerous than her situation as it was. As for blackmailing the Grand Duchess, she supposed that was rather like playing hide and seek with a poisonous snake, but if it could be done . . . how she would love to get her own back on that arrogant girl. But it was necessary to be patient; she was not prepared to risk Adam's life another time. After all, she had only exposed herself to this ordeal for his sake, and any other course would be foolish. So she dissembled, and took her place once again at the Russian court.

But as the Chevalier d'Éon. Not only did the Empress suppose that it might well be dangerous for her to reveal her true sex, but as with Louis, she seemed to be fascinated by possessing a handsome young man who could at any moment become a beautiful young woman, and having a tremendous sense of humour, Elizabeth Petrovna also enjoyed the extremely private joke she was playing upon her own courtiers, and more particularly upon her husband.

For the rest, Geneviève studied the Grand Duke. The Duchess she did not immediately see at all, as Catherine was big with child, and had spent the summer in St Petersburg. Peter was there quite often, apparently, as the Empress had said, quite convinced the coming babe was his, and in a great state of contentment, confessing openly that he had never supposed fatherhood could be such a simple affair. Geneviève could not help but wonder why no one amongst his attendants possessed the courage to risk the Tsarina's wrath and tell him the truth, just as she wondered which of the boyars *was* the actual father of the future Tsar of Russia.

Or had that happy man already been done away with? For all the Empress's pious professions of humanity, Geneviève did not doubt for a moment that she was capable of murder.

And Adam. She could hardly remember what he looked like. Would he truly remember her? And supposing he did, would he ever know who had secured his release? Would they ever meet again? It was really quite absurd, she told herself. He was a man, a member of the sex she was determined to oppose, and eventually conquer, if it took her all of her life. And he was a Calvinist, who if he could know the truth of her, or even suspect the truth of her, would hate her as an undoubted agent of the devil. And yet, in some unfathomable manner, he had touched a chord in her, and she had risked much to save him. She realised it was the first time she had ever gone out of her way to help *anyone*. Perhaps it was her conscience, some last twitch of middle class sobriety and piety surging in her heart; once Adam

Menzies was freed from his exile, then let the Heavens rip. It would be Geneviève d'Éon against all humanity, and she was looking forward to the battle.

In the autumn, as was usual, the court removed itself from Moscow to St Petersburg, arriving there as the first snow fell. The child was not due to be born for another couple of months, and Catherine remained strictly in her own apartments. But towards the end of November, when the ice was already thick and the Neva was blocked to navigation, Elizabeth Petrovna one evening announced that she trusted Geneviève was sufficiently happy, as Captain Menzies had that day been escorted across the border into Poland. 'No doubt suffering from frostbite,' Elizabeth remarked with a malicious gleam in her eye. 'But you were in a hurry to have him released, were you not, my darling?'

'I but seek to carry out my instructions, Sire,' Geneviève said. But her heart gave a great leap. There was no necessity after all to spend an entire winter in this horrendous place, subjected to the caresses of a decadent monster. All that was necessary was to secure an interview with the Grand Duchess. And this was no difficult matter once it was decided. She got Jules to contact one of Catherine's ladies, and to inform her that the Chevalier d'Éon had information of great importance, for the ears of the Grand Duchess alone. 'As the Chevalier is the brother of the woman Geneviève d'Éon, who was resident in St Petersburg four years ago,' Jules was instructed to say, 'the Grand Duchess will be able to judge for herself the possible importance of the communication.'

'Are you sure you know what you do, monsieur?' Jules asked. 'The Grand Duchess is your bitterest enemy.'

'She is my sister's bitterest enemy,' Geneviève pointed out.

'And do you not mean to reveal yourself to her?'

'I do. Sometimes one must risk all to gain all, unless you actually intend to spend the rest of your life here. I have considered the odds, Jules, and they are in our favour. So do as I wish, and leave the worrying to me.'

After that it was simply a matter of waiting, and not for very long. Soon a message was conveyed back to the effect that the Grand Duchess would be pleased to receive the Chevalier, but privately, and at eleven of the clock the following night.

Geneviève told the Empress she was suffering from a headache, and made her way down the secret corridors. At the appointed place a maid was waiting for her, all suppressed giggles and sidelong glances, for the Chevalier d'Éon was a most handsome fellow. And what, Geneviève wondered, does she suppose her mistress, all swollen belly and in the most unfortunate condition in which any woman may find herself, will wish with such a man?

But soon enough they were at the doors to the royal apartments, and Geneviève was being ushered into a small antechamber which contained but a single table and a settee, with two straight chairs. There were no pictures and no ornaments, and the whole rather resembled a cell. A moment for doubt. Geneviève remembered that occasionally in the past she had pressed too hard, not always with happy results. But the door was opening, and she bowed as Catherine entered. The Grand Duchess had clearly not borne pregnancy with equanimity; her face was as swollen as her belly, and there were lines of ill temper formed in her face. Therefore will she be the more anxious, Geneviève reminded herself. One of the ladies accompanied her, and saw her seated on the settee.

'Well, monsieur?' she demanded. 'I am by no means sure why I should receive you at all. I doubt your sister, or news of her, can mean a great deal to me.'

'My sister recalls, Highness, that you were the means of her escaping Russia, and is forever grateful,' Geneviève said.

Catherine smiled. 'A mutual service, I do assure you, Chevalier.'

'One which Mademoiselle Geneviève hopes may be repeated, 'Highness.'

The Grand Duchess commenced to frown. 'I doubt either of us have much to offer the other at this stage, Chevalier.'

'On the contrary, Highness. If we could be left alone . . . ?'

Catherine considered her for a moment, then nodded. 'Leave us, Natasha.'

'But Highness . . .'

'Oh, come now. The Chevalier is a gentleman, and an envoy from France. Even if he were neither, he would scarce find me sufficiently attractive to risk losing his head. Be off with you. I shall call you when I am ready.'

The girl Natasha hesitated, then curtseyed, and left the room, closing the door behind her.

'Well, Chevalier? Be sure it would go hard with you were my husband to discover you secreted with me. Nor would your friend the Empress be pleased, I suspect.'

Geneviève kept her voice even, endeavoured to disguise the thumping of her heart. 'As for the Empress, I cannot say, Highness, but I do believe that His Highness would be overjoyed at discovering me here. It is to prevent this catastrophe, for us both, that I now approach you.'

Catherine's frown was back. 'I do not understand you, sir. Speak plain.'

But by now Geneviève was an artist in the business of revealing her true sex. A flutter of her fingers, and she had opened coat and doublet and shirt. Catherine gazed at her, the frown slowly deepening. 'My God,' she said at last.

Geneviève waited.

'Does the Empress know of this subterfuge?' Catherine asked. And then answered herself. 'But of course she does. That would explain a great deal that has been setting the court by its ears this last summer. What mean you here, mademoiselle?'

'Her Majesty herself sent for me, Highness,' Geneviève explained. 'When she discovered that I had returned to France, she demanded my restoration, on pain of forfeiting the alliance proposed between France and Russia. So I was plucked from my Norman retreat. But it was deemed best for me to don male clothing, and by Her Majesty. She supposes I need protection from you, Highness. And who is to say she is not correct?'

Catherine continued to gaze at her. 'You play a deep game here, mademoiselle. I doubt it is one you can sustain. So why do you come to me? I have no cause to love you.'

'You have every wish to see me removed from Russia.'

'You could say I have every wish to see you dead, mademoiselle. Indeed, as I recall, I promised you that fate did I ever set eyes on you again.'

Geneviève permitted herself a smile. 'A favourite of the Empress?' Catherine's turn to smile. 'As before, mademoiselle, you put too much store by that relationship. I bear the Romanoff heir in this belly.'

'The *Romanoff* heir, Highness?'

The frown was back. 'You'll explain.'

'Her Majesty loves me,' Geneviève said. 'We have no secrets from each other.'

'By God,' Catherine breathed. 'That stupid, wicked old woman. And to such a creature. Would you threaten me with blackmail?'

'I had not supposed it necessary,' Geneviève said, perfectly truthfully. 'I but fear the attentions of the Grand Duke. Should he discover his favourite woman is returned to him . . .'

Catherine snorted.

'Can you take that risk, Highness? More, can you take the risk of his discovering that the child in your belly is not his, cannot be his, is the result of an intimacy between man and woman he does not suppose to be possible?'

'Ah,' Catherine said. 'Then you *do* intend blackmail.'

'I hope I do not, Highness. I do not wish to remain in Russia. Once before you were kind enough to risk the Imperial wrath and send me away. I would have you do the same. Be sure that this time I shall never trouble you again. There is no need for it. And as you say, Highness, so far as the world knows, it is indeed the Romanoff heir you carry. There can be no censure for yourself. Indeed, if you explain to Her Majesty that you had thoughts only for your relationship with the Grand Duke, for fear that I might suborn his affections . . .' She paused. Catherine was regarding her in a most speculative manner.

'That would mean confessing that you had revealed yourself to me, mademoiselle.'

Geneviève inclined her head. 'But only after I was beyond the reach of Her Majesty's wrath, Highness.'

Catherine's turn to nod. 'You have as usual considered the matter very fully, mademoiselle. You are the most cunning, the most conniving little whore I have ever encountered.'

'You may call me whatever you wish, Highness,' Geneviève said. 'I wish only to leave Russia.'

'To leave Russia,' Catherine remarked. 'Ha. And suppose I call my people in to have you strangled?'

Geneviève allowed her left hand to drop on to the hilt of her sword. 'Be sure I shall not be so easy a victim this time, Highness.'

Once again the long, appraising stare. 'You seek to bluff me, mademoiselle,' the Grand Duchess said at last. 'I doubt you know one end of that thing from the other.'

'Then summon your guards,' Geneviève said, beginning to grow angry, and just a little desperate. Things were not going according to plan.

'And how would you explain to Her Majesty that you were discovered brawling in my apartments, supposing you escaped with your life?'

Geneviève allowed herself a confident smile. 'I may explain

whatever I wish to Her Majesty. She is in love with me.'

Once again the rather incongruous snort. 'I doubt it is safe to put one's trust in the love of princes. Or princesses. More heads have been lost from such misguided confidence than from any other source. Well, my dear mademoiselle, I suggest you apply to your lover for leave to depart these shores. You have not done your homework. Peter is already lost to me, it seems. You have not heard of Elizabeth Vorontsova? For that alone I should have your head. You taught him several disgusting habits, and on your departure he quickly found another able and willing to satisfy his requirements. As for telling him my child is that of another man, why, I doubt he will believe you; he still does not suppose having his penis pulled bears any relationship to procreation. Besides, he hates your sister as well, Chevalier, for deserting him. I told him, you see, that you had run off with some uncouth rogue who made better use of your body than he had ever done. Some Englishman once said that hell hath no fury like a woman scorned, but I do assure you that he was wrong. There is *no* fury like a man who believes himself abandoned by a woman he has aspired to love. It is the more dangerous because it does not bubble out in violence, at the moment of knowledge. It lurks, deep in the breast, like a canker, seeking only some means of avenging itself upon the object of its loathing. Indeed, I am surprised that the Grand Duke has not chosen to avenge himself upon you, as a man, so much does he hate the very sound of your name. So be off with you, silly girl playing at boy. Enjoy the embrace of the Empress while you may, and make her happy, while you may. She has not long for this earth, and then, my dear, dear Chevalier, you will be left to the disposal of my husband and I. I wonder who will have the greater pleasure from it?'

Chapter Eight

Geneviève felt exactly as if she had been kicked in the stomach. But she was not going to allow the Grand Duchess to know that. She bowed. 'Your Highness will certainly know more of her domestic problems than I can possibly hope to discover. I stand abashed, and filled with pity that so promising a marriage should be so blighted. I shall withdraw, with your Highness's permission.'

'You,' remarked Catherine, 'seek to pity me?'

'I would pity any woman whose husband did not love her, Highness.'

Catherine glared at her. 'And what will you do now, Chevalier? What dark scheme is already seething in your twisted little mind? Or shall I put an end to them all by seeking an audience with Her Majesty?'

Still Geneviève refused to show the very real fear that was biting at her nerves. 'That is your privilege, Highness. I would but beg you to remember that there are two sides to every coin. Her Majesty, I know, is concerned with but one thing regarding you and the Grand Duke; that the Romanoff Dynasty be continued. In her desperation she will even accept the bastard in your belly. But consider your situation should your husband manage to impregnate Mademoiselle Vorontsova.'

'And you can affect that issue?'

Geneviève gave another bow. 'Who knows, Highness? I have the honour to be in Her Majesty's innermost council. You would, I do promise you, find me more useful as an ally than as an enemy. I will bid you good night.'

She let herself out, smiled at the curious attendants huddled in the outer room, and gained the passageway. And could give way to her despair. Her bluff was not likely to last very long. The moment Catherine Alekseeyevna had a chance to think, and she was undoubtedly thinking this very minute, she would realise that it *was* a bluff. No one could deny that it was the Chevalier who had asked for the interview. Therefore it was going to be impossible for the Chevalier to deny that she sought once again to escape from Russia. It was necessary to concoct some very good story to tell the Empress, when the moment came.

And for the time being, to present her usual imperturbable front to the world. She squared her shoulders, rested her hand on the pommel of her sword, and walked boldly past the guards and along the corridors. The hour was late, and she was intent on gaining the security of her own bedchamber. But she kept her mind alert; never again was she going to be assaulted while in a brown study. Thus the moment she saw the man waiting for her, while only a single staircase away from her own apartment, she halted, checked behind her to make sure that the corridor was empty, and then faced him, still at a distance of some twenty feet.

'Has monsieur business with the Chevalier d'Éon?'

He took a step forward, and she held up her hand.

'You'll state your intention before you approach me, monsieur, or I shall take offence.' She peered into the gloom, trying to identify him, but without success as he kept his hat well pulled down over his eyes.

'Why, simply, Chevalier, to invite you to a gathering of gentlemen, who are making merry not far from here.'

He was no one she knew, a big, powerful fellow with a scarred face. 'At this hour?' she inquired.

He shrugged. 'Does the hour matter, monsieur?'

'To me it does,' Geneviève assured him. 'I am for my bed.'

'But I insist,' he said, and showed her the pistol he had been keeping concealed beneath his cloak.

'You are mad,' Geneviève pointed out. 'You'd seek to shoot me, here in the palace? You'd be broken on the wheel. Supposing you succeeded before I brought you down.'

'I mean you no harm, Chevalier,' he insisted. 'But my friends are most anxious to talk with you.'

Geneviève frowned at him. A conspiracy? And directed against whom?

'I give you my word, Chevalier,' he said, as he saw her considering his proposal, 'as a gentleman and as an officer in the Preobraschenski Guards, that I and my companion will deal with you only in the most honourable fashion, as a Chevalier of France.'

Certainly he wore the olive green coat over the red vest and skirted breeches of the guards, as his hat was a mass of white feathers.

'Then you will prove it by handing over to me your pistol,' Geneviève said, her curiosity getting the better of her caution. But she reminded herself that if there *was* a conspiracy in the Peterhof, here was a speedy way to be sure of the Empress's favour, no matter what the Grand Duchess might tell her.

'Willingly, if you will promise to accompany me.'

'Just give me the pistol, and lead,' Geneviève said.

He came closer, carefully reversing the weapon to hand it to her. Geneviève wrapped her fingers around the butt and the trigger. 'Now remember,' she said, 'that should I feel you are betraying your oath, I shall kill you before anyone else.'

He nodded, and she followed him along another succession of corridors, her interest growing as she realised they were approaching the Imperial apartments. But they were going down instead of up, and soon arrived at a door where her guide gave a gentle tap. The door swung inwards and Geneviève, hesitating, saw that there were six men inside, sitting around a table, the remains of their supper before them. And what men. To her surprise she saw that one was the Grand Duke Peter Feodorovich, and another was Alexis Razumovsky, the Empress's husband. Also present were Michael Vorontsov and both the Shuvalovs. The sixth man she did not know, but he was clearly her guide's brother, equally large if not quite so rugged in appearance.

'You'll stop, monsieur,' Geneviève commanded, thrusting the muzzle of her pistol into the guide's back.

'Do you not trust us, Chevalier?' Razumovsky asked, getting up.

'I fear I am outnumbered,' Geneviève said. 'It might be wiser for me to conduct our conversation from here.'

'Did not Orlov give you a safe conduct, Chevalier?'

'*He* did.'

'It extends to all of us, I promise you. It will be broken only should *you* wish to fight *us*.'

Geneviève considered the situation. No one here had much cause to like her; nor did she care for the way Razumovsky had framed his last sentence. But they were all most definitely gentlemen who would regard their words as more sacred than their lives. And her curiosity was bubbling.

'Then I am content to be your guest. Monsieur Orlov?'

The giant seemed to have been holding his breath; now he released it in a gentle sigh, and walked into the room. Geneviève followed him, and closed the door behind her.

'You'll take a glass of wine, Chevalier,' Vorontsov invited.

'Thank you, but no.' Geneviève decided a clear head was best on an occasion like this. 'And as I am somewhat weary, I should appreciate it if you would state your business and allow me to retire.'

The men exchanged glances. Thus far the Grand Duke had not uttered a word, although he had not taken his gaze from her face.

'Will you not sit down, Chevalier?'

'I prefer to stand.'

Razumovsky shrugged. 'Very well then, monsieur. We gentlemen, as you are no doubt aware, are friends of Her Majesty, and the Grand Duke Peter Feodorovich is, in addition the husband of the lady whose private apartments you have just left. Now, monsieur, we will tell you frankly; we deplore the intimacy which seems to have sprung up between Her Majesty and yourself, but we recognise that Her Majesty is a lady of strong passions and should you please her, on however temporary a basis, then we her friends must accept her decision and await better times. What we cannot do, monsieur, is watch you at the same time pay court to Her Highness the Grand Duchess, especially in her present delicate condition. Such a course of action is scarce that of a gentleman, monsieur, at least of a Russian gentleman. I do not know what is the practice in France. Now, monsieur, how do you answer these charges?'

They had promised her safe conduct, saving only she attacked them. Therefore she could see quite clearly what was going to happen next. And as it was going to happen, boldness was her safest course.

'I see no reason to answer you at all, Count,' she said. 'How I pass my time is my affair, and that I should be admitted to intimacy with two such charming ladies is my advantage. As for your connubial concern, why, messieurs, you should take more interest in your wives.'

They certainly had not expected such a retort. For a moment there was absolute silence; then the other Orlov put down his goblet, with such force that the stem shattered.

Razumovsky got up. 'Monsieur, you are a scoundrel and a charlatan.'

Geneviève bowed. 'As I am your guest, my lord, I shall refrain from offering my opinion of you.'

'Then, monsieur, you are also a puling coward, as I have long suspected, and with it, a fop and a macaroni. What say you to that monsieur?'

'You are attempting to make me fight you, my lord,' Geneviève pointed out. 'Now why should I do that? I assure you I would . . .'

'Coward,' Razumovsky shouted, slapping her face with such force her head twisted sideways and she tasted blood.

'Oh, let him go,' the Grand Duke said, speaking for the first time. 'We are all witnesses to his cowardice. What do you suppose Her Majesty's reaction will be to such news? She prefers *men.*'

'. . . hate to kill the husband of the Empress of Russia,' Geneviève continued, controlling her breathing with an effort.

'But if you insist, my lord . . .' Because despite her resolution, she was becoming angry.

'Well, well,' Razumovsky said, stepping back. 'There is manhood present after all. You'll move the table, gentlemen.'

'And you'll only take off an ear, Alexis,' the Grand Duke said. 'I wish my turn.'

Geneviève drew her rapier, discarded her sword belt, removed her coat; but going back to her childhood, she had always retained her doublet. But she took off her wig, gave her hair, which was again commencing to grow, a shake. 'You gentlemen may each take your turn,' she said. 'As long as you assault me one at a time.'

'The puppy pretends to some skill,' said the Orlov who had guided her. 'Show him how a Russian fights, Alexis Cyrilovich.'

Razumovsky was unfastening his own coat, while the Orlov brothers moved the table, and the others arranged their chairs against the wall. This promises to be interesting, Geneviève thought, but already her heart was pounding and the adrenalin was hurrying through her veins. I should be a professional swordsman, she thought. It affects me more than making love. It is my greatest passion. I am, at the end of it all, an assassin. But of the Tsarina's husband?

'First blood, my lord?' she asked, as she kissed the hilt of her sword.

'Ha ha,' Razumovsky laughed. 'So that is your game, my little French cockerell. In Russia we fight to the death.'

'Hum,' Geneviève said. 'Do you suppose, my lord, that Her Majesty would really like either of us to be killed?'

'It is I wish to kill you, monsieur,' Razumovsky shouted, and charged. He was really so clumsy as to be almost laughable. Geneviève avoided his thrust with the greatest of ease, not even having to parry, and she faced his back long before he could turn. But she had still not made up her mind how to deal with the situation, and when he did turn, he assaulted her with a series of swinging cuts which took her breath away; as they were using rapiers he would hardly kill her should he connect, but he would certainly tumble her to the floor.

She gained the other side of the room, almost falling over Vorontsov's boots, which had been carelessly thrust in her path. Razumovsky was resting on his sword, gasping for breath. 'Stand and fight, damn you,' he shouted.

There was only one thing for it, no matter how Elizabeth

Petrovna hated her afterwards.

'As you will, my lord,' Geneviève said, and charged in turn. But hers was no senseless gallop. She crossed her feet in a perfect passado, flicked her point against his, clashed with his steel-lower down as he brought the weapon up in a quite inadequate attempt at a parry, and had his entire chest exposed to her thrust. But with icy cool decision she turned her sword point and drove it deep into his right shoulder. He gave a mingled groan and howl of pain, and the sword clattered from his fingers to the floor.

Geneviève withdrew her weapon, retreated against the wall; blood dripped from her blade and Razumovsky slowly sank to his knees, clutching his arm, his face the picture of dismay and despair.

'Next,' Geneviève said.

But the other men merely stared at her, no less astounded by what had happened, and she realised that Razumovsky had been their best swordsman. There would, after all, be no necessity to kill any of them. Yet she was in no mood to let them off lightly.

'Well, messieurs?' she asked. 'My Lord Duke, will you not take up the sword?'

Peter licked his lips.

'Do not, my lord,' Razumovsky groaned. 'This man is a devil.'

'Bah,' Peter said. 'I would not consider fighting with anyone not of royal blood.' He smiled. 'And have we not achieved our objective, my friends? This bravo has grievously wounded Her Majesty's husband. His days are certainly numbered.'

Slowly Geneviève lowered her sword. 'Then, my lord, perhaps you will permit me to depart while I may.'

Peter waved his hand. 'Get you gone. And say your prayers.'

'I shall, my lord,' she agreed. To the one god who can now save me, she thought, as she closed the door behind her, and discovered herself to be trembling. But there was no time for womanly weakness. She sheathed her still bloody sword, ran along the corridor and up the stairs, burst into the imperial antechamber. Instantly she was surrounded, by four guardsmen, two major-domos, and three ladies in waiting.

'I must see Her Majesty,' Geneviève said.

'Her Majesty is asleep, and is not to be disturbed,' the first major-domo said. 'Not even by you, Chevalier.'

'She will be disturbed,' Geneviève insisted. 'Believe me, it will go hard with you if you do not admit me.'

He hesitated, glancing at his companion. Geneviève seized

the opportunity to step past them and reach the inner door.

'Stop there,' they shouted, but she had already entered the Empress's sitting room, where two more maids sprang up from their pallet beds. Geneviève closed the door behind her, waved them aside.

'I will see you mistress.'

'But Chevalier,' they protested. 'She is sleeping.'

'Alone?'

'Yes, I am alone, Chevalier.'

Geneviève's head jerked; Elizabeth Petrovna stood in the inner doorway, her dressing robe loosely hung from her shoulders. 'What means this loud intrusion?'

Geneviève fell to her knees. 'A matter of life and death, Sire.'

'Indeed?' The Express came farther into the room. 'You'll explain, monsieur.'

'If we could be alone . . .'

Elizabeth Petrovna waved her hand. 'Away with you.'

'But Sire . . .' The two girls exchanged glances. They were quite used to the Chevalier d'Éon visiting their mistress at night, but never wearing a sword.

'Out!' Elizabeth shouted.

They curtsied, and obeyed. Outside the hubbub was growing, and Geneviève did not suppose she had more than a few moments before Razumovsky made his appearance. Hastily she closed the door again, turned the key.

'You grow too bold, my darling,' Elizabeth said. 'What has happened to your headache? But I am not feeling well, either. More and more I am not feeling well. God, I wish I could regain some of the energy of my youth. How I wish that, my Geneviève. And do stop kneeling there . . .' For Geneviève had resumed her supplicatory posture. 'As you are here . . .'

'Sire, I must beg your forgiveness,' Geneviève said.

'My forgiveness? You have not fallen in love with some other Scottish lout, I hope?' But her tone was bantering.

'Far worse, Sire. I can only pray you to understand that it was self defence.'

'Self defence?' Elizabeth Petrovna's head came up as loud voices sounded even through the wall, while immediately after there came a banging on the door.

'Sire?'

'It is Alexis Cyrilovich,' the Empress declared. 'You'll admit him, Geneviève. He sounds most upset.'

'He is the reason I am here, Highness,' Geneviève said. 'Hear me. I beg of you.'

Elizabeth Petrovna commenced to frown. 'You, and Alexis?'

'No, no, Sire. He has assaulted me, but as a man. He and the Grand Duke, and Vorontsov, and the Shuvalovs and the Orlovs, they waylaid me, Sire, and challenged me to fight them, for entering your apartments in the dead of night.'

'My God.' The Empress looked genuinely shaken. Slowly she sat on a chair, gazing not at Geneviève but at the door, where the banging continued. 'And what did you do?'

'What choice did I have, Sire, save that of revealing my true identity. This I dared not.'

Elizabeth's frown deepened. 'I wish to God he'd stop that banging. You fought them?'

'I fought Count Razumovsky, Sire.'

'But . . . he is the best swordsman in Russia. And you are alive? Or did you flee?'

Geneviève sighed. 'I am one of the best swordsmen in France, Sire.'

The Empress stared at her in total consternation. '*You* defeated *him*? You . . .'

'He is banging on the door, Sire. But grievously wounded.'

'My God. My God. And the others?'

'They preferred not to assail me, Sire.'

'My God.' Elizabeth got up, took a few steps towards the door, hesitated. 'Stop that infernal row,' she bellowed, and the banging ceased. 'What's to be done, Geneviève? What's to be done? Alexis Cyrilovich is a man of strong passions. He will never forgive you. What's to be done?'

Geneviève drew a very long breath. 'If he were to wish to meet me again, when he has recovered . . . but Sire, I fear a stab in the back, or poison.'

'My God.' Elizabeth Petrovna marched to and fro, wringing her hands. 'You are right. He will stop at nothing to avenge himself. Especially now you are here. My God, what possessed him to do such a foolish thing. I am very angry. Very angry.' She ceased her perambulation, glared at Geneviève. 'How badly is he hurt?'

'A thrust in the right arm, Sire. He will recover, I promise you.'

'*Could* you have killed him?'

'Indeed I could, Sire.'

The Autocrat of all the Russias chewed her lip. 'He will

certainly know that. He will *hate* you. But he is wounded. My husband. I *must* let him in Geneviève. Gather yourself.'

'And what of me?' Geneviève demanded, and she did not have to pretend to the desperation in her voice.

'What to do? What to do?' Elizabeth Petrovna looked ready to tear her hair. 'He is my husband.'

'And I am your lover,' Geneviève cried. 'You made me so, Sire.'

Elizabeth stared at her for some moments. 'You must leave court,' she said. 'Yes, there it is. I must send you away. Just for a while my darling. A little while, to let tempers cool.'

Geneviève got up. 'I could not bear it, Sire.' Her heart was commencing to pound; she felt like a bird the door of whose cage was slowly, but surely, swinging open.

'Neither could I, my darling. But it must be done. I could bear even less the thought of you dead.'

'But where could I go, Sire, and escape the vengeance of the Count?'

'My God, but you are right. As my husband he can stretch his hand over all Russia.'

Geneviève licked her lips. 'I could leave Russia, Sire. For a little while.'

The banging was commencing again. 'Let me in, Sire,' Razumovsky was shouting. 'Listen to nothing that wretch has to say to you.'

Slowly Elizabeth's head came up. 'Leave Russia?'

'I could . . . I could return to France, Sire. For just a visit. For a *last* visit.' She made herself smile. 'I could say goodbye to my mother. She is very old, and very ill. She had no idea there was any possibility of my not returning from this journey. And it has been much on my mind, that she should die without my taking leave of her.'

'France,' the Empress muttered. 'I must go to my husband. He is wounded. France. It is too far.'

'For only a visit, Sire.'

'France.' Elizabeth went to the door, hesitated. 'There is another stairway. Use it. Quickly.'

'And France, Sire?'

Once again the lower lip was sucked between the teeth. Elizabeth Petrovna looked like a little girl, as she had done when she had first seduced her, Geneviève remembered. Then she nodded. 'Passports will be delivered to you tomorrow morning. I will keep Alexis Cyrilovich occupied until then. Oh, Geneviève . . .'

Geneviève ran to her, was folded in those arms for the last time. Oh, indeed, the last time, she told herself. She'd rather die than ever return to this desolate hell.

The Empress kissed her on the lips. 'Now go,' she said. 'I shall dream of you every night.'

She wanted to dance and sing and shout, with joy. But she had wanted to dance and sing and shout all the way across Europe, once the borders of Russia had fallen behind her berline. Twice she had found herself in the clutch of the bear, and twice she had escaped. She had been so happy, so excited, she had even kissed Jules when she had regained her apartments. Now he shared her pleasure, as she handed their passports to the border guards; they were back in France, and there was nothing ahead of her but triumph. She had succeeded in everything she had set out to do. France and Russia were allied, Adam Menzies was free . . . wherever was he now, she wondered? . . . and she was back in France, with the congratulations of Richelieu and ten thousand louis d'or waiting for her. She was twenty-six years of age, and she had all of her life in front of her. She could even forgive Papa, at last. For had he not allowed his ambition to outgrow his common sense, why, she would even now be living in desperate boredom in Cherbourg, married to someone like Monsieur Artry, as helpless a creature as poor Mama.

Whereas now . . .

'Where shall we drive, monsieur?' Jules pushed his head in the window.

'Drive? Why, we shall drive to Versailles, Jules. To Versailles. I seek the Duke of Richelieu.'

Jules frowned at her. 'But monsieur . . . would it not be safer to return to Cherbourg, and perhaps send the Duke a message?'

Geneviève blew him a kiss. 'I am safe enough, Jules, old friend. Do you not realise that as he has secured the alliance with Russia, Richelieu is again all powerful at court? And how may I return to Cherbourg? I have no doubt there is still a warrant out for my arrest. But at Versailles I will be under Richelieu's protection. Versailles. I scarce wish to stop. Versailles.'

Yet it was necessary to proceed with some caution, to be sure of reaching the Duke at all. She opted to remain as a man, both because it was simpler to travel and to go her own way, and because she was happier in doublet and breeches and with a sword at her side than ever as a lady hampered with hoop and corset and half a dozen petticoats. But it would be far too risky to attempt to reenter the palace dressed as a subaltern in the De Beauffremont Dragoons; she supposed technically she remained a deserter from that regiment. So she chose her red velvet suit, which was still the finest thing she had ever owned, and which she thought showed her up to the very best advantage, had Jules once again crop her hair, and polish her boots and sword belt, and prepared herself for her triumph.

Versailles. Had she really supposed it would still be there, had not only been a dream? But Versailles was only somewhere to be when one had friends in high places, or money in one's pockets. Now she was going to have both.

'Halt there.' The officer on the gate inspected her from head to foot. 'What's a handsome lad like you trying to get in here for?'

There was the usual crowd of onlookers hanging about the fence, hoping to catch a glimpse of royalty or one of the great dukes, and the usual squad of guardsmen immediately within; beyond the lakes and walks were emptily beautiful, and she could just see the towers of the château itself. So near, and yet so far. But this lout could be nothing more than a delay.

'I seek an audience with the Duke of Richelieu,' she said.

'The Duke of Richelieu, now.' He smiled at her. 'And what might a pretty lad like yourself be wanting with the Duke, or shouldn't I ask?'

'It is an affair of state,' Geneviève said. 'And very important. Look, you'll convey this ring to him, and he'll send for me.'

The captain took the ring, held it to the light, turned it this way and that. 'Valuable,' he remarked. 'You'd not really want to give it away, monsieur.'

'I am not giving it away,' Geneviève pointed out. 'It belongs to the Duke. You had best see that he gets it.'

'You had best see that yourself, monsieur,' the captain said, once again holding it through the bars. 'I think Normandy.'

'The Duke is in Normandy?'

'And like to remain there, monsieur. He has been banished from court.'

Geneviève decided she must have misheard. 'Banished? From court? But why? How?'

The captain laid his finger alongside his nose. 'A quarrel with the Pompadour. Now that is the quickest way to disgrace. Even for Richelieu. And more so for those who are his men. So if I

14

were you, monsieur, I should stop claiming patronage from such a source. Just advice, mind.'

'But . . .' There was so much she wanted to ask. He had succeeded in his aim, through her, of achieving the Russian alliance. What could have gone wrong? And now . . . banished, to Normandy? No doubt she could find him there, and no doubt he might even be happy to have her resume her place as his mistress. But there would be no advancement. And the Duke, being the man he was, would immediately seek to use her again, might even wish to send her back to St Petersburg to enlist the Tsarina on his side. To go to Normandy would be putting a ball and chain around her ankle.

But where else *could* she go? In addition to being a deserter from the army she was also an escaped felon; either charge carried the death penalty. And nowhere else in France did she have a single friend. Save perhaps Monsieur Lannes, in Tonnerre. She thought she had enough money left to reach him. But what then? He might employ her as a fencing teacher. And that would be that. She was so angry she wanted to weep, and indeed tears sprang to her eyes before she could stop them. To have dared so much, undergone so much, to end up where she had set out from twelve years before with nothing to show for it but a suit of handsome clothes, a sword, and a few jewels.

But as the guard captain had said, to remain standing here was foolish and risky. She turned away, shouldered her way through the crowd, reached the roadway beyond; she had left the berline and Jules at lodgings in Sèvres, had hired a nag to bring her here, and he waited patiently, held by one of the grooms always in attendance outside the gates. Someone to be paid. She was suddenly aware of how poor she was.

'Monsieur? If I may be so bold?'

She turned, her heavy stomach suddenly losing its weight as she recognised the voice. Something of the voice. But surely it was the slight brogue she remembered.

The young man raised his tricorne. 'It is unforgivable of me, I know, monsieur, to address you in this fashion. But your face . . . you would not by any chance have a sister?'

Geneviève realised her mouth was open, and closed it again. But she could not stop herself. 'Adam,' she said. 'Adam Menzies.'

Because it was. A somewhat heavier, harder Adam Menzies, with eyes which had looked into the darkness of despair, with for all that much of his natural humour left in the lilt of his mouth, and if anything an increase of confidence in the squareness of his shoulders.

'Adam,' she said again, and seized both his hands.

'Monsieur?' He looked bewildered and a little suspicious.

Geneviève bit her lip. She could not explain here. She did not know if she dared explain at all. But having found him, so strangely, after all these years, she dared not let him go, either.

'My sister has spoken of you.'

Adam's frown deepened, and he freed his hands. 'Truly I know Mademoiselle d'Éon for a most remarkable as well as beautiful lady,' he said. 'But I had no idea she was also able to paint.'

'She described you,' Geneviève explained. 'She spoke of you, often. No, continuously. Monsieur Menzies, she will be overjoyed to know that you are returned from Siberia. You'll sup with me.'

'Well, monsieur...' Adam hesitated. 'I should remain here, in the hopes of an audience...'

'With whom?'

'Well... I hardly know. I have sent my credentials to the Chevalier Douglas. But this was two weeks ago, and he has not yet deigned to receive me.'

'Then surely you are in need of a good meal?'

'I'll accept no charity, monsieur.'

'And I have none to give,' Geneviève answered. He had not really changed at all, the Calvinist oaf. 'I but prefer to eat in company than alone. As you will have seen, I am also disappointed in my hopes of patronage. Would it not be sensible of us to put our heads together and consider what is best?'

Still he hesitated. 'I doubt we have that much in common, monsieur.'

Geneviève smiled. 'We have Geneviève in common, monsieur. She would never forgive me did I not entertain you, and learn of your recent fortunes.'

Adam's face cleared. 'And to say the truth, monsieur, I would never forgive myself did I not learn more of her.'

They mounted, rode together to Sèvres. For a mile or two Adam remained silent, apparently not wishing to appear over eager, and Geneviève was willing to let him make up his own mind, as she already knew the answers to all the questions he might expect *her* to ask. But at last he could contain himself no longer.

'Mademoiselle Geneviève is well?'

'Never better.'

'May I ask . . .' He flushed. 'If she ever received a communication from me?'

'Why, I believe she did,' Geneviève said. 'Did she not reply?'

'I am sure she did,' Adam said. 'But my life has suddenly changed, these last few months, and I doubt that any mail would have found me. You'll know I was for a time a prisoner in Siberia?'

'So my sister told me. My heart bled for you.'

'I survived, monsieur. Indeed, it was scarce worse than campaigning, although the most abominable climate I have ever endured. My misery . . .' He hesitated, bit his lip. 'The fact is, monsieur, I feel emboldened to open my heart to you, as Geneviève has actually spoken of me to you, and therefore she cannot but feel some softness towards me. Monsieur, my misery was caused entirely by my uncertainty as to her fate, and then when I knew that she had survived the dread sentence pronounced upon her by the Empress, that I should be separated from the one woman I have ever known with the ability to command my entire person, heart and soul and body. There monsieur you have it, my confession of love, which drew me to address you. Now monsieur, you have it in your power to make me the happiest or the most miserable of men.'

My God, Geneviève thought; he loves me. Or he says he does. He loves a memory, a dream which has sustained him these six years. Besides, he loves a vision, which has no substance save in his imagination. No doubt he remembers me curled by the fireside in a German inn, or vomiting into his bowl, and supposes he is as intimate with me as with his mother. What would he say to the truth, supposing he could ever learn it?

And what am I to say to him? Love. He would inflict love upon me. The Chevalier d'Éon can never love. But oh, how the Chevalier d'Éon longs to be loved. And he is tall and strong and handsome and unutterably healthy. He will be all men rolled into one, with the body of a demigod. But to love. To surrender. To *confess*. Because love for her, she knew without even considering the matter, could be no business of mutual fondling, mutual sensation. Having existed for all of her life without love, should she ever admit it to her heart she would surrender utterly, completely, without reservation, without ambition, without thought, save to please the man. Therefore it must never be, could never be, should never be. The Chevalier d'Éon could never love.

But she could be loved. And who better than a young man with whom she had already shared so much?

'Monsieur is silent,' Adam remarked. 'He thinks a penniless Scottish adventurer unworthy of his sister. Or is she already betrothed to another?'

'She is not betrothed,' Geneviève said. 'As for being a penniless adventurer, am I any the more fortunate?' She pointed. 'Yonder is Sèvres.'

Adam gave the houses a brief glance. 'Well, then, monsieur . . .'

'We shall decide what shall best be done,' Geneviève said. 'After we have eaten.'

Jules was awaiting her return with some anxiety, frowned when he saw Adam; clearly he did not immediately recognise him. 'What news, monsieur?'

'Nothing good. Richelieu is disgraced.' Geneviève kicked mud from her boots. 'You'll remember Captain Menzies, Jules?'

'Captain Menzies? But . . .'

'Captain Menzies will dine with me,' Geneviève said. 'But it shall be in private. Upstairs. You'll see to it, Jules.' She led Adam up the stairs and into her chamber; it was small, and dark, lit by a solitary candle and with nothing more than a gable window looking down at the street. The furniture consisted of a single bed, a table and two chairs. ''Tis all I can afford,' she explained.

'You should see mine.'

. 'Well, then, make yourself comfortable.' She took off her hat and sword belt and coat and wig, realised that he was watching her.

'Your resemblance to Geneviève is quite uncanny,' he said. 'Can you be twins?'

'Not twins.' Geneviève chewed her lip, for the first time in her life uncertain how to go about revealing herself.

'Well, you could pass for it.' Adam also divested himself of his outer clothing, just as Jules arrived with a bottle of wine, some fresh baked bread, cheese and some saucisson. These he placed on the table, face as black as thunder; he could tell what Geneviève had in mind; he had known her for too long.

'Monsieur,' he said. 'If I might have a word in private . . .'

'You may not, Jules. Have your supper in the taproom, and

find yourself a bed for the night. Captain Menzies and I have a great deal to discuss, and are not to be disturbed.'

Jules gave Adam a perfectly poisonous glance, and then left the room.

'It is the strangest thing,' Adam remarked, sitting down and commencing to eat without invitation – he was clearly very hungry. 'But I could swear I have seen that fellow before. Almost, my memory tells me, in attendance upon your sister, when last I saw her in Russia. But of course that is impossible.'

Geneviève sat opposite him. 'Do you count many things impossible, Adam?'

His head jerked at the use of his Christian name. 'Is it to be a philosophical discussion? I would rather discuss Geneviève.'

'We *are* discussing Geneviève, believe me. I merely wish to know if you are a doubter of nature's marvels.'

'I prefer to believe in things I can see, and touch, and smell.'

She smiled. 'Then we shall have no point of difference between us. But you spoke just now of loving my sister. How can one see, or touch, or smell love?'

'One cannot.

'Therefore how can one believe in it? How could my sister, for example, believe in *your* love?'

Adam poured wine for each of them. 'There are certain things that transcend the physical. I love. I know I love. As you, apparently do not, it would be futile for me to attempt to tell you of my emotions.'

'You have not seen her for several years,' Geneviève pointed out. 'And before then you were never close, as I understand it. Can you be sure, should you see her again, that you will love *her*, or are you infatuated with some memory?'

'I do see her again,' Adam declared. 'Now. Because you are as alike as twins, as I have suggested. It is as if Geneviève is seated opposite to me, save for your hair and your clothes, and even your hair is the same colour. Believe me, monsieur . . . pardon me, but I do not know your name . . . I could love *you*, if you will forgive the liberty, just for looking like her, for talking like her, for reminding me of her.'

'You are a romantic,' Geneviève said, and got up to stroll the room, her back mostly to him while she unfastened her doublet. Her heart kept up a most pleasant timpani. There was no lust here, only love. Perhaps he would not even wish her body. Perhaps, when he touched her, she would not want *him*. But he

210

loved her. Surely nothing else mattered. 'You asked for my name.'

He was cutting into some more cheese. 'You do have the advantage of me, in that while your sister appears to have discussed me with you often enough, she never mentioned you to me at all.'

'She had nothing to mention me for,' Geneviève pointed out, throwing her doublet on the chair and turning to face him. 'My name is Geneviève d'Éon.'

Adam's hand was on its way to his lips with a piece of bread. Now he put it down, slowly, swallowed what was in his mouth.

'Do you not believe me, Adam?' She moved closer, stood above him. But she had no desire to unbutton her shirt. He could see what lay beneath, and she did not wish to play the coquette here.

'Geneviève?' His voice was nothing more than a whisper. 'Geneviève? Oh, my darling Geneviève . . .' He took her hands, pulling so very gently, and she went to him, sat on his lap. 'Geneviève . . .'

She held his cheeks and kissed his mouth. As he had been speaking it was open, and she found his tongue. But it remained a shy, almost a chaste kiss. And now he pulled away.

'Geneviève . . . if I could understand . . .'

'Does love demand understanding?'

He frowned at her for a moment, and then smiled. It was his smile she most clearly remembered. 'Love demands nothing, my own dear Geneviève. But as you are here, in my arms, as you invited me here . . .'

'Love does demand reciprocation,' she said thoughtfully. She hated to lie to him. Yet she could not hurt him. 'I journeyed back to Russia,' she said, 'yielded myself once again into the power of the Empress, to rescue you from Siberia. Would you not call that at least a form of love?'

'You did that? Oh, Geneviève, my Geneviève.' He hugged her close, buried his face in her breast.

'So will you not love me?' she whispered, stroking his hair.

'Love you,' he said. 'Here?'

'Here and now,' she insisted, and freed herself, to get up and remove the rest of her clothing. He remained seated, gazing at her as she emerged before him.

Geneviève,' he said. 'Oh, my Geneviève. You are the most beautiful thing I have ever seen.'

He will comment on my muscles, next, she thought. But he did not, took off his own clothes. She sat on the bed to watch him in turn, and to be pleased. Five years in Siberia had turned the strongly built boy into one of the most powerful men she had ever seen, from his big chest, pleasantly coated with curly brown hair, through the flatness of his belly to the power in his thighs and calves. And between, only half erect as yet, but with all the surging energy she had hoped for. He looked at her, and she held out her arms. Then he was against her, and she could feel the penis rubbing against her belly as his lips found hers and they were lying on the bed, and rolling, over and over, locked together. Already he was inside, bottom working to slide to and fro, each surge seeming to travel the length of her slit and up her vagina to her womb, to send a perfect spasm of the most utter pleasure cascading through her body. Here was perfection, such as fingers could never possibly induce. But as he was hard and so eager, he would surely come too soon. She did not want it ever to end, allowed him only a few more thrusts and then rolled away from him..

'Geneviève?'

'I do not want you to come, my darling.'

'Nor shall I, until I am ready.'

'You can control it?'

'Up to a point, certainly.' And he was inside again, sending the blood pounding through her temples as she enjoyed first one and then a second orgasm, as he could tell from the fine sweat which suddenly shrouded her skin. 'Now we can rest awhile,' he said, propping himself on his elbow beside her.

'That was good,' she said. 'So good.' But she wanted so much more. If this was truly love, something she had never dared experience, if she could truly think of pleasing herself rather than of pleasing her companion, then she wanted everything that had ever been done to her to be done again, and by this one man. 'Kiss me,' she said. 'Oh, kiss me.'

He slid down the bed, spread her legs, touched her very gently with his tongue. She wanted to close on his head, but he held her thighs open with his hands; the straining against him made her even more excited, and she came again and again as his tongue entered her.

He raised his head. 'You will be exhausted.'

'I want to be exhausted. I want . . . I want to kiss you.'   He lay on his back, fingers gently stroking her back and occasionally sliding up into her hair before drifting down to her bottom, while she took him into her mouth, carefully, teeth safely concealed beneath her lips, tongue flicking and stroking, sucking and sucking until he touched the back of her throat.

He tapped her on the shoulder. 'Do you wish me to come in there?'

'No.' She released him. 'Not this time. I wish you inside me.'

'Then it had best be now.'

She lay on her back in turn, and knew once again the ecstasy of those raking surges, soon to be followed by the explosion of heat as he came, the supreme pleasure of feeling him slowly dwindle, his movements cease, his head rest beside her, his breath on her ear.

Geneviève d'Éon, she thought; you are *loved*.

They ate, sitting up together in bed, while outside the day dwindled into night. Jules came up for the tray, glared at her, left. 'Now listen,' Geneviève said.

'You do not have to tell me anything.'

'I want to. Listen.' She recounted the entire story of her life, omitting not a detail that she could remember. By the time she was finished it was nearly midnight. 'So you see,' she said. 'In addition to being an entirely unnatural creature, I am a profligate wretch, a religious apostate, and a murderer. I would not have you suppose anything different of me.'

He nuzzled the warmth of her side. 'You are unique. And I am the most fortunate fellow in all the world. And your past is your past. You will never wear men's clothing again.'

'Never?'

'Never. Swear it.'

How serious he was. But she suddenly realised how important it was to him. And why should she ever wear men's clothing again? As her life of intrigue was apparently ended. 'If you will swear to remain ever at my side.'

'I do so, willingly.'

'Then I also swear, never to wear men's clothing. But I doubt I am doing either of us a service. At the end of it all,' she brooded, 'I am also penniless.'

'No woman with talents such as yours can ever be penniless, my sweet Geneviève.'

It was time to love again, not quite as passionately as before, but with perhaps an even greater appreciation. Then they slept, but Geneviève's slumber was fitful. She was happy. She had found Adam again, and she had found in him everything she wanted in a man. She did not want it ever to end.

'Marriage,' he said as they breakfasted.

'Marriage?'

'Well . . .' He flushed. 'I am a Scot, not a Frenchman, no matter how hard I try. We approach things in a different fashion, in Scotland. It is more important to have a loving wife than a loving mistress. I would like to marry you, Geneviève.'

Marriage, she thought. My God. It was not a condition she had ever considered, except as a means to an end. Marriage would mean, what? A certain continuation of that magnificent tumbling. But would they not grow bored even with that? It would also mean a surrendering of self and body which she could never permit. It would involve children, and she would never permit that either. It would involve love, and there was the greatest imponderable of all. She loved him against her. She loved everything about him. But did she love *him?* She had no means of knowing the answer.

Besides, marriage, in mutual poverty, mutual deprivation? Was that to be her final reward for all these years of struggle?

'But you do not wish to marry me,' he said.

She gave a guilty smile. 'I am a Frenchwoman, Adam. And so I find it difficult to believe that love and marriage go well together. Besides,' she hurried on as he would have spoken, 'we cannot get married. We have no money and no prospects.'

'We will find prospects, my darling.'

'Where?'

'Well . . . the Chevalier Douglas will eventually see me, I do promise you.'

'And then what? What can he offer you? A position in some regiment of foot, perhaps.'

'Soldiering is all the profession I know.'

'And where is the benefit to either of us in that? You will be away campaigning . . .'

'In time of peace?'

'There is very soon going to be a war,' Geneviève said. 'I have it on the best authority. So some cannon ball will blow off your head, and I will be left a widow who has not even enjoyed her husband's love as often as she should.'

'Well, then, I will seek employment elsewhere.'

'As what? Will you labour on the roads?'

He sighed. 'I am a confoundedly ill-equipped fellow for anything save fighting,' he explained. 'I have done nothing else since I was sixteen.'

'It is an honourable profession,' she pointed out. 'It is a fact of life that the less honourable professions are the more lucrative. I think it is essential that before we contemplate setting up a domestic establishment we set up our finances, and it appears to me that it should be left in my care.'

'You?'

She kissed him on the nose. 'I have my talents. Disreputable ones, to be sure, but none the less I think they can be made rewarding.'

He frowned at her. 'You'll not do it.'

Her turn to frown, then she laughed as she understood his meaning. 'I'll not whore, if that's what you mean. No, no. But I have another talent, which I have used insufficiently. I was considering it last night.'

'Well?'

'Swordsmanship.'

'You?'

'Would you care to try me, Captain Menzies?'

He looked completely mystified. 'I'd not call you a liar, Geneviève. But I still fail to see . . . you'll maintain men's clothing, and set up as a teacher?'

'I am no teacher, Adam. I lack the patience. No, no. I shall wear women's clothing, and set up as a duellist.'

'Duelling is illegal.'

'Not if undertaken as an exhibition, with no real bloodshed involved.'

'But . . . who shall you fight? And think of the danger. Even the best of swordsmen eventually gets hit. It is unthinkable. If anyone is going to fight for a living, it should be me. Fight for a living? I do not understand . . .'

She laid her finger on his lips. 'Listen to me, my darling. I am sure you could fight and kill every tyro in the land. But as you have just pointed out, why should they fight *you,* for money. But can you imagine a young man of perhaps a local reputation refusing to fight a woman, for say, a wager of a thousand livres?'

'My God. But . . .'

'Leave it to me,' she said. 'We have but to discover a suitable site to begin. Our reputation will soon spread.'

'Your reputation. But Geneviève, the danger of it . . .'

'There is none, I promise you, Adam.'

He sighed, and then brightened. 'It is all a dream. Where is our thousand livres?'

'We shall have it soon enough. I promise you that too. For a start, we need only to practice a little subterfuge, and next to swordsmanship, I am best at subterfuge.'

She discovered herself to be enormously excited at the prospect of doing something for herself, at last. And besides, she reminded herself, it is but a temporary measure; such are the ups and downs of French court life that soon enough Richelieu must be returned to favour, and when that happens I shall very soon knock on his door. But until that day, why, I shall enjoy myself by being myself and no one else, by loving the man I prefer above all others – she still could not bring herself to consider loving him as he loved her – and by practicing the art I enjoy above all others.

She set her plan into motion the very next day, while Adam and Jules trailed behind her, Adam half amused and certain that nothing would come of it. Jules, who knew his mistress much better, gloomily forecasting nothing but disaster. But then, Jules was a pessimist.

They went into Paris, and she led them to Madame Sophie's establishment. 'This place?' Adam exclaimed.

'Why, have you visited it before?' Geneviève asked, mischievously.

'It is beyond my purse. What I mean is . . .' He flushed. 'I have heard of it. An absolute den of iniquity. I had no idea *you* were acquainted with it.'

She had forgotten about it when recounting the events of her life. 'I did tell you that I am no misplaced saint,' she pointed out. 'And have you now entirely stopped loving me?'

'I could never do that.'

'Well then, let us consult with Sophie.'

She was overjoyed to see her. 'My dear Geneviève,' she cried. 'I did here that you had returned to France. But that was several years ago. What has became of you since?'

'Times have been hard,' Geneviève agreed.

'Of course. You were arrested for murder.'

'A trumped up charge. It was a perfectly fair fight.'

'Of course,' Sophie agreed. 'As I see you still have your head in

216

the right place. And now you have at last realised where your true future lies.' Now how, Geneviève wondered, could the old hag possibly know I am not here as a customer?

'My dear,' Sophie said, throwing her arm around Geneviève's shoulders. 'I will make you the most famous courtesan in all Paris. In all France. In all Europe. But I must tell you one rule,' she said, with a contemptuous glance at Adam. 'I'll have no pimps in my establishment. When a girl comes to me, she comes alone.'

'You mistake the situation entirely, my dear Sophie,' Geneviève said, disengaging herself. 'I am not here to whore.'

Sophie frowned at her, and then snapped her fingers, and a negro page boy hurried forward. 'Wine for my guests,' Sophie said, and sat down. 'Then I apologise, my dear girl, although I do so with tears in my heart. The profit you are throwing away. You wish a girl, or a boy?'

Geneviève sat beside her on the settee; Adam remained standing. 'Nor am I here as a customer. I wish to borrow a thousand livres.'

Sophie removed a goblet from the tray, drained it, and took another. 'I had never suspected you of humour.'

'Nor am I attempting it. The money will be repaid, in very short order, and with whatever interest you command.'

'A business venture? A gold mine to be dug? A new colony to be founded? Risky business.'

'Absolutely safe business.'

'You will have to tell me.'

'Of course.' Geneviève outlined her plan, and Sophie stared at her with her mouth open.

'You are mad.'

'Would you care to summon anyone you know, to oppose me?'

Sophie gazed at Adam, her mouth still open. 'But why should anyone fight you? Certainly after the first time?'

'Because no one will believe it. Because no one will be able to resist the temptation. I will offer one thousand livres against fifty. A woman. Twenty to one odds. That is why I need your help. I must be able to display the coin, to prove that there is no fraud intended. Why, every young man in the country will discover a quick way to place himself in possession of a fortune.'

'Indeed? And suppose the first man who comes at you is Monsieur Shirér, and you are killed?'

'Every business has *some* risks attached to it,' Geneviève pointed out. 'Surely we would have to be dreadfully unlucky to encounter someone like Shirér before you are repaid, at the least.'

'Hum,' Sophie said. 'Hum.' She drank some more wine. 'I do not see the reason for risking anything at all. You want a fortune? It is easiest made on your back.'

'I prefer to earn it on my feet,' Geneviève said. 'And besides, you are not doing your arithmetic. What do you charge for your best girl?'

'We are expensive,' Sophie said. 'A livre for half an hour.'

'Therefore,' Geneviève pointed out, 'should I fight one man a day, I will be earning as much as any one of your girls, supposing she has a man with her from midnight to midnight. And should I fight two a day . . .'

'You will not get the custom,' Sophie said. 'Your prices are too high. But the idea is not without merit. Will your permit me to be your manager?'

'Happily.'

'Then you will wager one hundred livres against ten. There is a more readily accessible sum, and I do promise you that you will earn just as much in the long run.'

'And you will lose less should Mademoiselle d'Éon make a mistake,' Adam pointed out.

'Of course, monsieur. I did not get where I am today by taking unnecessary risks.'

'First of all,' Sophie decided, 'you need clothes. Your gowns must be light, to enable you to move, and yet entirely feminine.' She ruffled through the enormous collection in her wardrobes. 'This one.'

It was a cream satin sack, pleated at the back and open in front to the navel; this was intended to show the white under-bodice, modesty being preserved by an echelle of blue velvet bows, but these could be worn very loose to allow the maximum freedom of movement. White sleeve frills were added, as a possible distraction, and Sophie also decided on a white lace cap to be worn beneath the tricorne that Geneviève would remove for the actual fighting. 'That is deliciously feminine,' she explained. 'Our only problem is the hoop. The skirt will have to be taken in.'

'But I intend to wear a hoop,' Geneviève insisted.

'My dear girl, you cannot move quickly in a hoop.'

'Do you not understand, if anyone suspects the slightest trickery on our part we shall lose all. I shall fight in a hoop.'

Sophie threw up her hands in despair, and turned to Adam for support. But he was by now learning about the woman with whom he had fallen in love.

'At the least, madame,' he said, 'all of those skirts may save Geneviève from the worst effects of a low thrust. Now, my sweet, as you are intent upon making sure no one can possibly suppose you are *not* a woman, I would like to see your bodice stuffed with leather, just in case.'

'What nonsense,' Geneviève said. 'My bodice has never needed stuffing with anything. My problem has been how to flatten it.' She allowed herself a gentle twirl in front of the full length glass. 'I think we had best commence.'

Because she was more nervous than she would have been prepared to admit. On two counts, firstly, that her challenge might not be taken up at all, and secondly, that they might just be that unlucky, and have her encounter a master at arms on her first day. She was not afraid for her life, as she was planning exhibition, not murder, but she was afraid of Sophie's constancy should she lose a couple of hundred livres in rapid succession.

Their pitch had already been selected, the spring fair in the Bois de Boulogne, where everyone in Paris visited at least once. Sophie did the arranging, and made the necessary payments, they were given a tent to themselves, outside of which Jules took up his position with the aid of a large placard, and two pretty girls borrowed from the brothel for the afternoon.

'The greatest challenge on earth,' Jules bellowed. 'Who will dare to oppose his blade to Mademoiselle Geneviève, the finest swordswoman in all the world? Mademoiselle Geneviève will fight any man, to the first blood, wagering one hundred livres against ten that it is she who draws it. Come now, my friends, will no man try his skill against Mademoiselle Geneviève?' At which point, carefully coached, he would lower his voice. 'She is but a woman with a certain skill, messieurs. Nothing more than that. Why, promise me ten livres of your winnings, and I will tell you her weaknesses, for I watch her practise.'

Jules was obviously born to the circus. Within the tent, Geneviève waited with Adam; Sophie had decided not to attend, except as an onlooker, for she was too well known and she was afraid some of her customers might be amongst the challengers. Adam was armed with broadsword and pistol, and was there to prevent any treachery or horseplay. And Geneviève was sweating. It had been Sophie's decision that she should remain out of sight until a challenge was made, for effect. But suppose a challenge was never made?

'A glass of wine,' she decided. 'I must have a glass of wine. I am as nervous as a kitten.'

'No wine,' Adam said. 'If you are determined to go through with it, you must be sober.' But he no longer feared for her, as he had experienced her skill and her power too often during their practice to suppose her in any danger; she was far superior to himself, at least with a rapier.

'But no one will come,' she moaned. 'I may as well get drunk and forget about it.'

'They'll come,' he promised. 'Listen.'

She raised her head.

'Fight a woman?' someone was demanding of Jules. ''Tis no sport for gentlemen.'

'But this is no lady,' Jules pointed out.

'The wretch,' Geneviève muttered.

'She is a freak of nature, messieurs. Oh, she will lead you a pretty dance. But at the end of it, why, will you not chance your skill against her blade, for a hundred livres?'

'By God, I'd like to see the bitch,' remarked another voice.

'One of us will have to fight her,' said a third.

'Oh, indeed, messieurs,' Jules said. 'Mademoiselle Geneviève will not emerge until the stake money has been produced.'

'And *her* stake money?'

'Will be displayed.'

The voices descended to a vague muttering. Geneviève found herself about to bite her nails. Then the first man spoke again.

'Their, monsieur. There is ten livres. Now produce this dragon of yours.'

'Indeed I shall,' Jules agreed. 'Mademoiselle?'

Geneviève was already on her feet, drying her hands on her kerchief. Adam waited with two rapiers in his hand. He blew her a kiss, and she opened the tent flap and stepped through, filling her lungs to their utmost as she did so. For a moment the bright afternoon light dazzled her, and she blinked. When she could see, she was horrified at the crowd which had gathered, at least a hundred people. While in the foreground were the three bloods who had been conversing with Jules, every one younger than herself, she reckoned, and now staring at her in consternation.

'Gad, mademoiselle,' said the first, removing his hat and sinking into a courtly bow. 'This rascal has been suggesting you are all of a hermaphrodite. My most humble apologies. My friends and I are abashed, and would withdraw.'

Geneviève stepped forward. Her knees touched once, and then she made herself relax. 'You have made a wager, monsieur,' she said, 'which I have accepted. Your money is forfeit if you do not draw.'

'But . . .' He glanced from left to right. 'Mademoiselle, be reasonable. You are young and beautiful, and I . . . I am the premier swordsman of the Sorbonne. How could I draw upon one such as you?'

Geneviève smiled at him, as contemptuously as she could manage. 'How can you not, and be branded a coward, monsieur?'

He shook his head. 'No, no, I cannot.'

'Oh, teach the wench a lesson,' said one of his companions. ''Tis my money you have wagered. Scratch her pretty skin for her, or allow me to do so.'

'As you wish,' Geneviève said. 'It is immaterial to me.'

'Then have at you, mademoiselle,' said the second man, drawing his rapier.

'You'll pardon me, monsieur,' Geneviève said to the first man, and turned towards Adam, who held out her two swords, hilt first. 'This one, I think, today,' she said, taking the weapon and making a little pass with it. 'Are you ready, monsieur?'

'Ready,' he said.

'Mind you leave her titties,' said the third man. 'When you have beaten her, we'll all have a squeeze.'

'When,' Geneviève agreed. 'On guard.'

It was absurdly easy. The young man was really nothing more than a novice, and his scanty training had not in any way prepared him to meet so skilful and vehement an assault. Geneviève whipped forward, knees banging into her hoops, but she was used to this by now, sword flickering in front of her like a beam of light. The blades met but once, his was brushed aside, and she had pinked him in the shoulder. She stepped back; she was not even breathing hard.

'Thank you, monsieur.'

The young man glanced at the blood dribbling down his

shoulder – he was obviously very little hurt – then gave a roar and rushed at her. But they had suspected that something like this might happen, and instantly Adam had stepped in front of him, the other sword held across his chest.

'Hold, monsieur. The terms of the wager were first blood. You have lost.'

'It was an accident,' he shouted. 'A lucky stroke. I demand another bout.'

'Of course you may have another bout,' Geneviève said, carefully cleaning the point of her sword with a white kerchief. 'All you require is another ten livres.'

'You . . . you trickster,' the boy shouted.

'Trickster?' Adam inquired. 'I appeal to you all,' he called to the crowd. 'Did not Mademoiselle Geneviève win, fair and square?'

'Fair and square,' they shouted. 'Fair and square.'

'None the less,' said the man who had at first refused to fight, 'it smells of trickery. Mademoiselle was quick, very quick. I wonder how she would do when expected, and against a more worthy blade?'

'I await your pleasure, monsieur,' Geneviève said. 'And your ten livres.'

'Always ten livres,' he said.

She smiled, and shrugged. 'I am but a young woman, monsieur, with a living to earn.'

'Then I must destroy that living for you,' he said, and produced the additional coin from his own pocket.

''Tis all you have,' muttered the third man.

'Would you have us disgraced? This tale will get about. And besides, we shall soon be a hundred the richer.' He drew his sword. 'Mademoiselle, look to yourself, I beg of you.'

He seemed a very decent fellow. Geneviève hoped she would not have seriously to hurt him. She raised her hilt to her lips, took her stance. The crowd had grown even larger, and their heat as well as their excited comments were clouding the air. And this would be no quick affair, Geneviève knew – if only because he would be expecting her assault. So she preferred to hold her ground, and wait for him to make his move. Which he did, very rapidly, crossing his legs in perfect balance as he came towards her. But the thrust was easily parried, and as she skipped aside her hoop swung to catch him a blow on the shin, so that he slipped to one knee.

'Now's your chance, mademoiselle,' someone in the crowd shouted.

But Geneviève waited for him to regain his feet. 'I apologise, monsieur,' she said. 'The hazards of fighting a woman.'

He gazed at her for a moment, regaining his breath, then advanced again. Their blades clashed and sang in the afternoon, and she allowed herself to be forced back, slowly circling round the ring, keeping her breathing under control while he thrust and cut and lunged, and she parried each movement with perfect timing, with deft flicks and easy sweeps. His face reddened and his breath began to come in pants, and at last he stopped when she skipped out of range for a seventh time while the crowd roared its applause.

But it was time finish the matter, for he was beginning to grow angry.

'And now, monsieur,' she said, and moved forward. His sword came up, but his breathing was too laboured for speed, and her point, easily evading his swishing blade, whipped into his coat and swept upwards, splitting the material and the waistcoat and shirt, bringing a start of blood from the scratch beneath. Geneviève stepped back and lowered her sword. 'I thank you, monsieur,' she said, and gave him a curtsey.

'One thousand five hundred, ten, twenty...' Madame Sophie concentrated as she counted the coins, arranging them in little piles in front of her on the table. 'One thousand, six hundred, ten, twenty...'

Geneviève and Adam held hands and sipped wine. It had been a splendid summer. The most spendid summer of her life. Of both of their lives, she hoped.

'One thousand seven hundred, ten, twenty, thirty... there we are, Geneviève. One thousand, seven hundred and thirty livres. Now let me see, that is three hundred and forty-six for me, and one thousand three hundred and eight-four for you.' Lovingly she brushed the money into a bag. 'Would you like me to invest it for you?'

Geneviève shook her head. 'I think Adam and I will take a holiday. We will go... to Italy. To Florence, and Venice, and Ravenna, and Rome and Naples. I have always wanted to visit Italy. Would you like to do that, Adam?'

'It sounds entrancing. But my darling, it is your money, and you are spending it all on me.'

'What nonsense, it is *our* money. We are partners. Do you suppose I could manager without you at my back? How many times this summer have my opponents refused to accept a scratch as their defeat? And every time it has been your strong arm has prevented them taking advantage of me.'

'It is still you who take all the risks.'

She kissed him on the cheek. 'Purely because of our circumstances. Believe me, were it possible for you to dress up as a woman I would willingly share your winnings. Italy it shall be. I shall book our places on the next coach.'

'The next coach after tomorrow,' Sophie pointed out. 'If you have finished billing and cooing. Your summer is not yet over. There is the fair of St Giles; had you forgotten tomorrow is the seventh of October? It is the very last fair of the summer, and will be well attended. Oh, yes. We should pick up another thirty livres, I swear.'

She had thrown herself into the scheme with the enthusiasm peculiar to her, once she was sure it was going to pay. She had escorted Adam and Jules and her two girls and Geneviève into the countryside, as far as Orléans and Tours, to reveal Mademoiselle Geneviève's uncanny skill with a sword. Geneviève had fought in so many market places she had forgotten most of them. And it had all been amazingly easy.

Every man who counted himself a gentleman in France might wear a sword and be anxious to draw it at the slightest excuse, but she had been forced to the conclusion that very few of them had ever taken their lessons seriously. Her most dangerous opponents had only been the odd professional soldiers who had accepted her challenge, but not even these had been able to match her skill. While whenever the local authorities wished to close them down, they were helpless before the fact that Geneviève was doing nothing more than exhibiting her talent; no one was ever seriously hurt.

And as she had fought several times in each day, besides practising with Adam, her skill had even grown. She doubted that even if she *were* opposed by a master at arms she would lose, now; and in any event it had never happened.

It had become a way of life, and she looked forward to the morrow without the least qualm. She now had an assortment of gowns, as her confidence had increased she even occasionally presented herself in heavy velvet or brocade. This day at St Giles her dress was a glowing crimson, her hair, which had regained its normal length, was piled on the top of her head, and she even sported a black patch on her left cheek to add to the impression that she was a lady of fashion. Her opponents fell into the usual mould, two young men and a gentleman farmer, every one convinced that he could take home the bag of jingling coins paraded by Jules. And every one doomed to a sore arm or a scratched chest, while the crowd roared their pleasure, and Adam collected their winnings.

But at last even the farmer had retired disconsolately, and they were able to regain the privacy of their tent, where Geneviève could wipe her brow and dry her neck, and release her hair, and look forward to her bath.

'There,' she said. 'The last. Now for Italy. I have booked us on tomorrow's coach. We shall be in Florence in a week, I am assured. And then Venice. Will you swim with me in the Grand Canal?'

'I didn't know you could swim.'

'I can't. You will have to teach me, or support me. You will have to support me while you teach me. Nothing could be finer. Well, Jules?'

He stood in the entrance. Not even a successful summer had entirely removed his gloom, and now he looked even less happy than usual.

'Mademoiselle, there is someone to see you.'

'I am taking no more challenges.'

'Hardly a challenge, mademoiselle.' The man pushed past Jules and stood just inside the tent, inspecting her from head to foot. He was an elegant fellow, certainly no country gentleman, with a satin coat and a jewelled rapier. 'You are every bit as attractive close to as from a distance.'

Geneviève gave him a curtsey. 'My lord is a flatterer.'

'And discerning too.' He held out his hand. 'I am the Seigneur de Guerchy.'

Geneviève allowed him to take her hand and raise her; he kissed her knuckles.

'I am honoured, my lord. But is this then a social call?'

He smiled at her. 'Your fame has spread far and wide, mademoiselle. Who in all France has not heard of the skill, the charm, the beauty, of Mademoiselle Geneviève? Your reputation has even penetrated the hallowed halls of Versailles, mademoiselle. I am here on a mission for His Majesty himself. You are to appear before him, and tomorrow evening.'

Chapter Nine

'My God, my God.' Madame Sophie wrung her hands. 'What a catastrophe.'

'Not necessarily,' Adam objected. 'We do not have to go.'

'Not obey the King's summons?' She was aghast.

'Geneviève and I, most fortunately, have our seats booked on tomorrow morning's stage for Savoy. We shall be south of Lyons by the time the King sends after us, supposing he does so at all.'

'He will,' Sophie declared. 'He knows, I tell you. He knows.'

'He will still not catch us,' Adam declared. 'But if you are afraid for yourself, Sophie, why, you have but to insist we left without informing you, or failing that, come with us.'

'Leave Paris? I shall be ruined. Ruined. But I shall be ruined in any event. My God, my God.'

'You will not be ruined,' Geneviève said. She had been enjoying her bath while they had argued, had now finished drying herself, drew her robe round her shoulders. 'I have no intention of running off to Savoy.'

'But Geneviève,' Adam protested.

'Isn't this what we both wish?' she demanded. 'We met, each trying to get inside the gate at Versailles. Now we have been invited there.'

'At what risk?'

'Very little. I agree with Sophie; I think the King does suppose – and even *hope* – it may be me. Think of the possibilities.'

'You would prostitute yourself,' he said bitterly.

'Oh, come now, how can I prostitute myself to a king? It is our future I am thinking of.'

'Our future lies in that bag.'

'A few hundred livres? Or would you have me carry on this farce for the rest of my life? Eventually I will get hurt. Do you not care?'

'Geneviève.' He took her hands. 'Of course I do not wish you to spend the rest of your life fighting. It is not necessary. There is enough money in that bag to set us up.'

'As what?'

'Well, a country inn . . .'

'An inn?' she shouted. 'You suppose I will spend the rest of my life waddling about with a tray of glasses?'

'We will have each other. We will be happy.'

'Of course we are going to be happy. But as wealthy people, not innkeepers. Once I regain the favour of the King . . .'

'And the Pompadour?'

'Will be helpless. Do not suppose I am still the young girl she managed to terrify. I will meet her on her own ground, this time.'

Adam shook his head. 'It is too dangerous. I cannot permit it.'

She glared at him, hands on hips. 'You cannot permit it? Are you my husband?'

'Now, Geneviève . . .'

'I am sure Adam has only your safety in mind,' Sophie protested.

'Permit me to be responsible for my own safety,' Geneviève said. She was being unreasonable, she knew, and she knew too that in all probability they were right. But the fact was she was not just attracted by the possibility that she might regain the King's favour, that she might still achieve the position she had sought for so long; even more was it the thought of returning to court, to the glitter and the glamour, the grandeur and the intrigue. It was like the breath of life to her, she realised, and she had never wanted anything else.

'I had supposed we were partners,' Adam said quietly, 'if not yet husband and wife, although I had anticipated that as well in due course.'

'And you also suppose that such a prospect makes me subservient to your wishes,' Geneviève said.

'It is not an unreasonable point of view.'

'To me it is,' Geneviève declared. 'You forget that I am not just a woman. I have the brain of a man. I think like a man. I am just as used to weighing possibilities and making decisions as any man.'

'Well, then,' he agreed, 'will you not at the least accept my advice, and my recommendation as one half of a partnership?'

'I am going to Versailles tomorrow night.'

His head came up. 'Then you'll go alone.'

She glared at him. But her anger was growing all the time, the more so as she knew how unjust it was. 'Then I *shall* go alone. Do you suppose I need you, Captain Menzies? I have managed often enough without you at my side. I shall go alone, and you shall take the coach to Lyons. Bring that bag. We shall split the money down the middle.'

He gave her a brief bow. 'The money is yours, mademoiselle. You earned it. I shall bid you goodbye.'

He left the room, and Geneviève gazed at Sophie.

'You had best run after him and make your peace,' Sophie said.

'Why should *he* not run after *me*?'

'Because he is a man, and proud.'

'And I have not the right to feel pride?'

'If you would be a woman, Geneviève, you must suppress it, at least in your relationship with a good man. And you will not find a better man than Adam Menzies.'

'And if I would be a man?'

Sophie shrugged. 'Then go to Versailles, my dear. I shall look forward to having you back when they tire of you. But just remember that in five years time your value as a whore will be halved.'

My value as a whore, Geneviève thought. We shall see about that. But she felt more lonely than for a very long time as her hired carriage arrived at the gates of Versailles the following afternoon. She had dressed with great care in a dark blue velvet gown, edged with ermine, and secured with jewelled brooches on the bodice; her underskirt was white satin, with an embroidery pattern in gold up the front; there was lace at her neck and her sleeves, and pearls at her throat and in her hair, which she wore loose and lying on her shoulders. She aimed for a perfect blend of elegance and simplicity, and had Jules with her to carry her swords. If this evening's work did not immediately launch her upon the career she had sought five years ago, then she supposed she might as well go trailing behind Adam and seek her inn.

Adam! She had refused ever to consider loving him, and now she knew how right her judgement had been; the fault was entirely hers, that they had quarrelled, but she was what she was – what Papa had made her, she reminded herself – and as she had always known, love was not for Charles Geneviève d'Éon. But he had loved her.

And now she had sent him away. Or at least allowed him to go. Adam Menzies. They had been separated once before, through no fault of their own, and yet managed to come back together. This time the fault *was* their own. Would they meet again?

She squared her shoulders as she watched the Seigneur de Guerchy walking towards her.

'Mademoiselle Geneviève.'

She sank into a curtsey.

'And where are your other accomplices?'

'Accomplices, Seigneur? We practice no crime.'

His smile was cold. 'Not even a fraud, mademoiselle?'

'Not even that.'

He nodded. 'We shall see. You'll accompany me, mademoiselle. But not your man.'

'And who will carry my weapons, Seigneur?'

'Why, that shall be my honour, mademoiselle. You have no other need of this fellow, do you?'

'Indeed not,' Geneviève agreed, and nodded to indicate to Jules that he could hand over the rapiers. So let the court suppose there was some fraud involved. She would soon show them different. The Seigneur was waiting, and she walked beside him, through the halls she knew so well, past groups of courtiers who stared at her and whispered comments; certainly she remembered some of *their* faces, so it was reasonable to suppose that some of them remembered her. But they were nothing to her at this moment. Only the King mattered, and there he was, at the end of the Salon de Diane, standing in the midst of a group of gentlemen and ladies, waiting to be entertained.

She drew a long breath, wriggled her fingers inside her gloves in an attempt to dry the perspiration. Once again the Seigneur, swords tucked under his arm, was politely waiting for her. She gave him a brief nod, accompanied him up an aisle formed by parting courtiers and their ladies, her heart starting to skip about as she recognised the Duke of Vendôme, and Marshal Saxe, and then, standing beside the King, and giving her a most appraising stare, the Duchess of Pompadour herself. The fishwife had changed, and Geneviève decided for the worse. Her features had coarsened, and her arrogance had grown, while she had certainly put on some weight. But these tendencies easily discernible after a separation of several years, remained muted beneath the power of those splendid eyes, the utter confidence of that unforgettable bearing. And that she retained her influence over the King was impossible to doubt, for he remained in conversation with her as Geneviève approached, although the entire salon was a buzz of comment.

But then, she thought, what was she to make of Louis himself? Louis the Well Beloved. Could any woman love such a gross sensualist? Good living showed in his heavy jowls, his flaming nose, his protruding belly; utter surrender to his passions showed in the drooping lips, the heavy eyes, the caked powder which hid the swelling of his cheek veins. Can it only have been five years, she thought, since I was happy to lie with this monster?

But she *must* be happy to lie with him again. My God, she thought. And she had asked Adam, how can one prostitute oneself to a King.

Now his head was turning, slowly.

'The woman, Mademoiselle Geneviève, Sire,' the Seigneur de Guerchy was saying.

Louis' gaze played over her, and she sank into a deep curtsey. For a moment the salon was absolutely hushed, and then she smelt his perfume and knew his hand was extended. She kissed it, and was raised, allowing her own eyes to come up and meet his gaze, and to feel relief pounding through her stomach like a laxative.

'Geneviève,' he said. 'Geneviève.'

'Well, well,' remarked the Pompadour. 'I was right, after all, Sire. It is a fraud.'

'A fraud?' Geneviève demanded.

'Hold your tongue, miserable wretch,' the Pompadour shouted.

'A fraud?' Louis inquired. 'How can it be a fraud, madame?'

The Pompadour was pointing. 'Does that ... fellow, deny that he is Charles d'Éon de Beaumont, a deserter from the De Beauffremont Guards, now masquerading as a woman?'

'Bless my soul,' the King remarked.

Geneviève licked her lips, uncertain how he wanted her to reply.

'Well?' the Pompadour demanded.

'I ...' Geneviève gazed at the King, seeking some instruction.

'I am sure you are mistaken, madame,' Louis suggested. 'Unless my ageing eyes are entirely deceiving me. Eh? Ha, ha, ha, ha.' He looked around himself for support, and the courtiers obligingly tittered.

'Stuffing,' the Duchess declared.

'I do assure you, madame,' Geneviève began.

'*Stuffing*?' the King cried.

''Tis a simple matter, Sire.' The Pompadour stepped forward, tucked her fingers into Geneviève's bodice, and tugged. The emeralds in the brooches scattered across the floor as the bodice fell open. Geneviève never moved, merely gazed at her rival, allowing herself a slight smile at the discomfort in the Duchess's face.

'By God,' the King said. 'By God. Well, madame, satisfied? By God, *I* am satisfied. Never have I seen a prettier pair of tits.'

One of the courtiers hurried forward to pick up the scattered stones and hand them to her, but Geneviève was determined not to let her advantage slip. 'Never, Sire?'

'Ha ha,' shouted the King. 'Ha ha. But you are right, mademoiselle.' He gave the Pompadour an angry glance. 'Never.'

The Duchess had flushed scarlet, now her colour slowly began to fade. 'I . . .'

'Satisfied?' the King said. 'By God, you must be satisfied. Say so, madame. Say so.'

But a man Geneviève did not know had been whispering in the Pompadour's ear. And she had recovered a good deal of her confidence. 'Mademoiselle Geneviève is certainly well endowed from the waist up, Sire,' she agreed. 'But is it not possible that she is equally well endowed, in a different fashion, from the waist down?'

'Eh? Eh? You'll explain, madame.'

'Your Majesty is aware that there are some unfortunate creatures who are born with the exterior evidences of belonging to each sex.'

'Eh?'

'The Duchess means an hermaphrodite, Sire,' the man who had first suggested it remarked.

'A hermaphrodite?' the King repeated. 'Mademoiselle? Are you such a creature?'

'Of course I am not, Sire,' Geneviève said. As you well know, she thought.

'Well, there you are,' the King said.

'You'd accept the creature's word, Sire?' inquired the Duchess. 'When all is required is for her to hoist her skirts.'

'Madame, your vulgarity amazes me.'

The Pompadour refused to be abashed. 'I but seek to save Your Majesty from embarrassment.'

'By causing it? There'll be no hoisting of skirts in my salon. No indeed. Mademoiselle Geneviève is a woman and there's an end to it.'

The Pompadour sank into a curtsey. 'As Your Majesty wishes. Well then, Sire, shall we not proceed with the entertainment?'

'Entertainment? What entertainment?'

'The display of swordsmanship.'

Geneviève, engaged in refastening her last brooch, raised her head.

'I doubt I am in the mood for it,' the King said, gazing at her. 'I would prefer to receive Mademoiselle Geneviève in a private audience, that she may explain to me the secret of her marvellous powers.'

Geneviève's turn to curtsey. 'I shall be happy to please Your Majesty,' she said.

'No doubt,' the Pompadour agreed. 'All in good time, mademoiselle. Sire, these good people have been assembled here in the hopes of enjoying some sport. Would you rob them of their pleasure?'

'I doubt there is anyone here up to matching his blade against Mademoiselle Geneviève's,' the King suggested.

'On the contrary, Sire. I have one who is anxious to do so.' The Pompadour raised her hand, and a man came from the back of the hall. Geneviève felt her stomach constrict; she had not seen him for several years and then only for a moment, but she recognised him immediately – Shirér. And he was even more disturbing close to; the very picture of strength and health, tall and powerfully built, with wide shoulders tapering to narrow hips, while his face retained the bitter arrogance she remembered so well.

The King was frowning. 'Shirér? madame, this is some humour of yours.'

'By no means, Sire. This young lady; if that is what she is, has earned herself a great reputation this last summer. But against whom? Shall we not put her to the test, and against a real swordsman?'

'An assassin, you mean,' someone muttered, loud enough to be overheard. Shirér paused, and glanced around him, his hand falling to his sword hilt.

'Shirér is a professional,' Louis objected.

'And does not Mademoiselle Geneviève fight for money?' The Pompadour paused for a moment, to smile at Geneviève. 'And besides, Your Majesty, the terms are only to first blood.' She raised her voice. 'How now, my friends, will it not be sport to see how Mademoiselle Geneviève fairs against Monsieur Shirér?'

There was a chorus of assent, whether genuine or inspired by a desire to please the favourite Geneviève could not be sure; she was suddenly aware that she was sweating – this was the one situation she had always feared, and to have it happen here ...

'Hum,' said the King. 'Hum. First blood, you said. Nothing more than that, madame.'

'Of course, Sire. Just the merest touch of steel on flesh, I do assure you. Clear a space.'

Geneviève gazed at the King, who raised his shoulders in a helpless gesture. 'First blood,' he said.

'Your sword, mademoiselle,' said the Seigneur de Guerchy. He was smiling. Pompadour's creature. She had been trapped, as Adam had feared, as Sophie might even have known. Oh, what a fool she was. An overambitious fool.

She watched Shirér being divested of his coat and vest. And he noticed her interest. 'Would mademoiselle care to disrobe?' he inquired.

She would need every possible advantage here. 'Yes,' she said. 'If His Majesty will permit me?'

'Disrobe?' he demanded.

'My outer garments only, Sire.'

'Do you usually disrobe when engaged in your duels, mademoiselle?' inquired the Pompadour.

'I do not, madame. But normally I fight in the open air, and on grass or cobble. Here it is close, and the floor is polished. You would not wish your champion an unfair advantage?'

'By God, no,' the King shouted. 'You may, mademoiselle, disrobe.'

'I thank you, Sire.' Geneviève laid down the sword, and unfastened her gown. She moved very slowly, while the murmurings in the salon died. By the time she reached her underskirt the room was still, and the only sound as she sat down to hitch up her petticoats and roll down her stockings was the rustle of her own taffeta. Her boots joined her stockings on the floor, and she stood up in her bare feet and wearing only her petticoats. Her shoulders and arms were exposed, and the whispered comments began again as men noticed the muscles at her bicep, the power in her shoulders, and also as they admired her calves as she gave a gentle twirl and whisked her sword to and fro.

Well, she thought. Here I go. First blood. But the Duchess did not mean her to escape unharmed, that was certain.

'On guard,' said Guerchy, who had taken upon himself the duties of umpire.

Geneviève kissed the hilt of her sword, watched Shirér do the same. She crooked her left arm, curled her toes to gain some additional purchase on the polished floor. The courtiers and their ladies formed a large circle around the two combatants, their whispered comments as they inspected Geneviève and made wagers on the result proving very distracting.

'Ha.' Shirér moved towards her, quickly. But this was no more than a trial. Their blades brushed against each other, and she moved to her right as they disengaged.

'Bravo,' called the King.

'Ha,' Shirér said again, and performed exactly the same manoeuvre, again with little effect as Geneviève parried, disengaged, and continued her slow circling of the room. But she was uneasy. So far he had revealed no trace of the professional.

'Ha.'

Perhaps he means to tire me, she thought. If so he will find it difficult. And this warning he transmits before beginning his advance is absurd. Yet there it was again.

'Ha.'

The blades touched and she decided it was time to consider some offensive work of her own. She needed nothing more than a scratch to gain the victory. Now, she thought, and was taken completely by surprise as Shirér also moved forward, and without his customary grunt. Their blades clashed and this time he pressed home. Desperately she parried and endeavoured to disengage, but stumbled into one of the spectators, who promptly pushed her away, resting his hands on her buttocks and squeezing as he did so. She flushed with anger and with a realisation of looming disaster, for Shirér was with her as she turned, his blade flickering forward to drive her to one side and leave her breast for a second exposed. My God, I am hit, she thought, jerking her head backwards, just in time to evade the point of his sword, which instead of tearing at her chest had flicked upwards and now passed less than an inch from her cheek in a cut, which, if successful, would have laid her face open from chin to forehead and left her scarred for life.

She scuttled across the room, endeavouring to regain her breath and her tumbling thoughts. So *that* was his game, undoubtedly dictated by the Pompadour. She could not be killed, or the King might be angry. But were she scarred, he would lose interest.

Shirér was turning, his face eager. He knew she had escaped him that time by accident, just as he knew he was the better swordsman. But was he necessarily the better *duellist* she wondered, as her heart settled down? If he intended to handicap himself with so limited an area of contact ... as ever when there was a technical problem to be solved, her fear vanished and she became absorbed in the task at hand. She even ceased listening to the whispers of the crowd, but instead advanced slowly into the centre of the ring. Shirér also came forward, until he was at his preferred distance. But, she was realising, he also fights to a pattern. And there it was.

'Ha.'

On he came, but she knew now that his announced charges were merely preparations for the decisive move. She stood her ground, allowed their swords to clash and then run together so that their bodies thudded against each other, and their faces were so close their breaths mingled.

'Mademoiselle is a clever little girl,' Shirér said.

'And monsieur is not,' she agreed, jumping backwards, landing on the balls of her feet, and immediately thrusting again. Shirér was taken off guard by the suddenness of her movement, and failed to do more than instinctively parry a blow aimed at his body. But his descending blade only just caught Geneviève's, saving his life, certainly, but still sending her sword point deep into his thigh.

Geneviève whipped the blade back and retreated, watched the sword slowly lower as blood spurted from the wound and trickled down his leg.

'Aaagh.' Madame de Pompadour gave a shriek and appeared to faint.

The King was on his feet. 'By God,' he shouted. 'That was well done. Well done, Mademoiselle Geneviève.'

The onlookers took their cue from their King rather than

their mistress, and clapped, surrounding Geneviève to shake her hand and pat her shoulders and squeeze every portion of her body they could reach. She was at once bruised and breathless when they suddenly left her again, and she found Louis standing in front of her.

'Geneviève,' he said. 'My Geneviève. I would talk privily with you, that I may learn the secret of your skill.'

'Geneviève, my Geneviève,' he whispered, against her ear. He was exhausted. At times she had supposed he might well do himself an injury, so eager had he been, and he no longer had either the figure or the stamina for it. Well, so was she exhausted. He had taken her straight from the duel, her flesh coated with sweat and her brain still seething with endeavour, had demanded instant satisfaction. But she had given that satisfaction, and she had even managed to obtain some for herself. She was back where she belonged, she supposed, lying on the King's belly, having him whisper in her ear.

'You are a wretched girl,' he said. 'I should have you whipped. I should have you hanged. I should have you broken on the wheel.'

She raised her head. 'Me, Sire?'

'Are you not a deserter? From the army as well as from my bed?'

'Do you suppose I left your side of my own will, Sire?'

'Geneviève . . .' His hands drove into her buttocks, pulling them apart, pushing them back together again. Apart from having lost his figure he was no longer the gentle lover she remembered. But he was still the King.

'Tell me of it.'

Geneviève rolled off him, got up, poured some water and drank. 'Sire?'

'Yes,' he said. 'Yes. The same cup. After all of these years, I wish us to be as one, my Geneviève.'

She refilled the goblet, held it for him, told him something of her adventures. She omitted all reference to Adam, or to her affair with the Empress. She doubted he would approve of either, made up for it by embroidering her brief liaison with the Grand Duke. She wanted to take her time, because she wanted him to harden again, and enter her again. She wanted him to count this evening as the finest of his life. She did not wish him ever to let her go again.

'What a tale,' he said. 'What a tale. You have been cruelly treated, my sweet girl, and I have been cruelly misled. Oh, I shall see to the miscreants, you may be sure.'

'I am happy, Sire, just to have regained your bed,' Geneviève said, and began to stimulate him with her fingers.

He watched her for some seconds, and then sighed. 'You will not succeed. I am an old man, Geneviève.'

'You, Sire? You will never grow old.'

'Even kings grow old, my dear, dear girl. And I more than most. Do you know that is the first spurt I have known this month.'

'Sire?' She was so surprised she let him go.

'True. I am a spent reed.'

'But Your Majesty, surrounded as you are by willing beauty, by Her Grace of Pompadour . . .'

'They can do nothing for me. I had supposed myself doomed to a lifetime of at best masturbation, and you came along. Oh, my darling, darling Geneviève . . .' His hands slid over her stomach, cupped her breasts, drifted down to play between her legs.

While Geneviève's heart pounded with a growing sense of triumph. She had won. She had dared all, and she had won. What would Adam say now? Where *was* he now? But as the King's favourite she could bring him back.

Or would that be dangerous?

'And to hear that you negotiated the Russian alliance as well,' he said. 'Oh, I love you, Geneviève. I will raise you to heights of which you have never dreamed. I shall reward you. I shall exhalt you . . .'

'You have but to give me a bedchamber in the palace,' she said.

'Sweet child. Do you know how many women would immediately have asked for a title?'

She smiled at him. 'I have a title, Sire. I am Chevalier d'Éon. It was given me by the Duke of Richelieu.'

'The Chevalier d'Éon.' He smiled. 'It suits you. But do you desire nothing higher than that?'

'I desire your love, Sire.'

'Oh, you have that.' He sighed. 'Now, you must leave me. Are you lodged nearby?'

'Yes, Sire, but . . .'

'I will make the necessary arrangements for you to have

accommodation here. But for tonight you had best be away.'

'May I not spend the night with you, Sire? After all these years?'

He chucked her under the chin, sat up. 'I wish you could. But I must attend the Pompadour. And she will be in an ill humour at the defeat of her champion.'

'Then why go, Sire?'

'Eh? Because if I do not she will scold me.'

'She, will scold you, Sire?'

'Oh, you do not know her temper. It can be terrible. No, no, you must sleep in your own bed this night, and leave me to make arrangements.'

Geneviève got up, picked up her shift. 'And will your arrangements suffice, do you suppose, Sire? If Madame de Pompadour wields such power that she can command your movements, will she not very rapidly have me disposed of?' She bit her lip, wondering if she had been a shade too bold.

But the King seemed entirely absorbed by the problem. 'Indeed she may try. Oh, dear me. I shall have to prevent it. But how?'

'Sire . . .' Geneviève began. She found it hard to believe she was speaking with a king. Or could he secretly have married the fishwife? There would be catastrophe. Certainly he seemed mortally afraid of her.

'Some mark of favour,' Louis mused. 'Oh, indeed. Let me see . . .'

'The greatest mark of favour, Your Majesty, would be to allow me to remain here with you.'

He shook his head. 'No, no. She would never forgive me for that. Never. But if your services were made clear, how you secured the Russian alliance . . .' He snapped his fingers. 'I have it. I shall give you an award. Oh, indeed. The highest we possess. The Cross of St Louis. Will that not be fine? It carries a pension.'

'A medal?' Geneviève cried in disgust.

'I knew you'd be pleased. Oh, indeed. Not even Jeanne could carp about that, in view of your services.'

'A medal,' Geneviève said sadly, and began to pull on her stockings.

'Oh, damnation,' Louis said. 'What catastrophe.'

'Sire?'

'Medals may only be given to men. Oh, curse this protocol with which I am surrounded.'

'Well, then, Sire,' Geneviève said bitterly, 'you will have to think of some other mark of favour.'

'Ha ha,' shouted the King. 'Ha, ha. What sport. We shall make a ring around protocol, my darling girl. The medal shall be given not to Mademoiselle Geneviève d'Éon, but to her brother, the Chevalier Charles d'Éon. Is that not sport?'

'Yes, Sire,' Geneviève said sadly. 'That is sport.'

She stood rigidly to attention, dressed once again in the uniform of the De Beauffremont Dragoons. Louis had done her proud, she thought contemptuously. Not only had the charge of desertion been quashed, as had the charge of murder down in Cherbourg, but she had been promoted to the rank of Captain, and now was to receive the highest order in the land. After seven years she was back to where she had started. Had she remained in the palace she would surely have risen to captain, and had she merely been a good soldier she might well have accumulated a medal.

She gazed at the King as he took his place upon the throne, for such an award must be made in the Salon d'Apollon itself. And found her eyes drifting to the Duchess, standing beside her lord. What do you *have,* she wondered? That I do not? You have only possession. But possession, in the case of such a spineless imbecile as this Louis is ten tenths of the game. Possession. And because I lack it I must resume this dismal life as a man, just so the King may please himself with me and not anger you. How I hate you, she thought. But then, there could be no doubt that the Pompadour also hated her; above the smiling mouth the eyes glittered like emeralds.

The Duke of Broglie was reading the citation, recalling the splendid achievements of the Chevalier d'Éon in the fields of diplomacy with the Russians. It would be posted in every provincial town. Adam would read of it. He would be pleased for her. He was a man, and for any man there could be no higher award than the Cross of St Louis.

Well, then, she thought, why are you not also pleased? Are you not happier as a man? And are you not at the least assured of the King's favour? You have ever prospered, as a man. Only when you have acted the woman have you come close to disaster. And you are younger than *she.* A fact she well knows. She raised her head, once again met the glittering eyes, tilted her chin and allowed herself a smile.

The King was on his feet, and it was time to kneel, to permit the ribbon to be placed around her neck and over her shoulder, to allow the cross to be settled on her breast. Then he raised her, held her close, kissed her on each cheek, and held her close again. 'Geneviève,' he said. 'Now you have joined the ranks of the immortals.'

The salon rang with applause, and men were hurrying forward to congratulate her. Their names and their smiles swirled about her, and she turned back to face the Pompadour.

'My congratulations,' she said. 'Now come, Chevalier, will you not tell *me* the truth? You have no sister, despite His Majesty's claim. I have investigated the matter. So answer me straight, are you man, or woman?'

'Why, madame,' Geneviève said, as coolly as she could, 'I am a dragoon in His Majesty's army. What would that suggest?'

'That you *are* a fraud and a charlatan,' Pompadour remarked, without losing her smile.

'And a royal whore, madame,' Geneviève pointed out. 'I would not wish to be considered your inferior.'

Now the smile did fade, and the Duchess's brows drew together. 'You overestimate your power, mademoiselle,' she said, her voice a breath of Arctic chill. 'Be sure you will learn your proper station, soon enough.'

Geneviève discovered the King standing beside them, and gave a hasty bow.

'Quarrelling?' he inquired.

'What have we to quarrel over, Sire?' the Duchess inquired. 'We were but comparing how much we have in common, for all that we are of opposite sexes. Why, Sire,' she added with a roguish grin, 'as the Chevalier is so handsome, and so winning, I feel his powers may even assault my own heart. What would you say to that?'

'Ha ha,' Louis said. 'Ha ha ha ha. Is Her Grace not droll, my dear Chevalier? But come. You will sup with me, as you are my most honoured courtier, this day. Madame? You'll accompany us? Why, take the Chevalier's arm, as you have just revealed your weakness.'

He strode away from them, and Geneviève gave the Duchess a bow, making an arm at the same time. 'Your Grace?'

The Pompadour glared at her.

'His Majesty has commanded us,' Geneviève reminded her.

The Duchess extended her own arm, and Geneviève immediately imprisoned it, walking beside her towards the dining room. Behind them the other courtiers and their ladies fell into place, the room filled with whispered comment.

'And should we not be friends, Your Grace?' Geneviève asked. 'As we *have* so much in common. Why, madame, it might well suit His Majesty to share his bed with us both, and at the same time. Would that not be droll?'

'Be careful, trollop,' the Pompadour breathed. 'You aim too high. Remember Icarus.'

'Ah, but madame, my wings have been burned so often, having been exposed to so many suns, that they are now impervious to heat.' She was enjoying herself with the passion of desperation. Louis wanted her, needed her, even loved her ... but only as his unnatural companion, a girl who could be a boy or a boy who could be a girl. She lacked something, some spark, which enabled the Pompadour to retain her hold over him. And for the life of her she could not decide what it was. She was better looking, better smelling, younger, certainly more intelligent and better educated, and obviously far less inhibited. What could be her rivals secret? Because so long as the Duchess preserved that secret she was indestructible.

They entered the dining room, and took their places; the King had Madame de Pompadour on his right, and the Duchess of Broglie on his left. Geneviève found himself next to the Duchess with the Duke himself on her left. Pompadour's creatures. On the Duchess's right was the Seigneur de Guerchy and then another lady. Broglie; De Guerchy, as once it had been Richelieu. It came to her in a sudden flash of insight. The King could not oppose his mistress because that would mean opposing his entire ministry. She could do what she liked, providing as she got rid of one minister, such as Richelieu, she had another, such as Broglie, waiting to take his place; but the King, lazy and dissolute as he was, could never face the task of replacing an entire government.

So then, she wondered as she sipped her soup, how does one accumulate a body of men fit to become a government? Why, they accumulate you. Conti had tried that, without success. No doubt such intrigue was a continual part of court life. She had failed that time, and so was to be forgotten. But the King had been happy enough to have her back. Could she not find another group of lords, opposed to the Pompadour, who would surround her with their power and their possibilities? There had to *be* such a group.

'Well now, ladies and gentlemen,' the King was saying, 'you have all seen how gratified I am to have my faithful Chevalier returned, from the snows of Russia, where as you will know, he has done so well. I give a toast, to the Chevalier d'Éon, France's most faithful servant.'

They all rose, even the Pompadour, holding their glasses high, and Geneviève found herself blushing with embarrassment. She had not expected such adulation. Her fingers stroked the cross on her breast. Perhaps her star was in the ascendant after all.

'Believe me, mesdames and messieurs,' the King continued, sitting down again, 'finding suitable employment for my Chevalier's undoubted talents is a conundrum, but one which I have laboured to solve. France cannot neglect such abilities, and at such a critical time in her history. We hear of nothing but wars and rumours of wars, and there can be no doubt that soon enough a European conflagration will encompass us. Now, thanks to the Chevalier, we have little to fear from Frederick. The great bear is lurking on Prussia's Eastern frontier, ready to enter the contest upon our side the moment the first shot is fired. It is our other antagonist concerns me. England is too strong, and daily grows more so. She is grasping and arrogant. She glares at our colonies, in the Americas, in the West Indies, and in India with bloodshot eyes. England, my friends, there is our main enemy, there is the force we must, if possible neutralise.' He turned his head, to smile at Geneviève. 'There, my Chevalier, is where duty next takes you.'

'Sire,' Geneviève begged. 'Your Majesty. This is a betrayal.'

'A betrayal?' Louis sat on the edge of his bed in a nightshirt, and scratched his chest. 'I have given you the Cross of St Louis, the highest award I can. That is a betrayal? I am sending you to London as First Secretary of the Embassy with special powers. You are how old? Twenty-seven? And you are a First Secretary. And you talk to me of betrayal?'

Geneviève sighed, removed the last of her clothes, sat beside him. 'I had supposed, after our long separation, that you would wish to keep me at your side.'

He shook his head. 'It cannot be. In giving you the Cross I announced to the world that you are a man.'

'I served you once before, as a man.'

'Then you were a girl. I mean a boy. Now you are a woman. I mean, a man. God above, it confuses even me.'

'And do you not love me, Sire?'

'Oh, Geneviève.' He hugged her against him. 'I do, I do. I love you dearly.'

'But you would prefer to do so at a distance of several hundred miles.'

'Oh, Geneviève...' He disengaged himself. 'You are too much for me. You consume, like a fire. I can think of nothing save you, when I know you are near. And my doctors tell me you are bad for me. My heart is not what it was. I am worn down with care, and ... with care.'

She wondered if he had almost being going to admit, dissipation.

'I love you, Geneviève,' he continued. 'I wish you to prosper, but here ... I fear for you, too.'

'Under your protection, Majesty?'

He sighed, and sat down again. 'It will be best. For you. For me. For us both.'

Her turn to get up. 'Sire, would it not be best to speak the truth? Is this not Madame de Pompadour's doing?' She wondered if she was as angry as she pretended. Would it not be a relief to escape his overweight boorishness? And as First Secretary? Save that she had no idea how to go about her duties, what would be required of her. And in fact doubted anything would be required of her. It was all a trick to get her away from court. What *could* she do in England?

'Now, Geneviève,' he said.

'No, Sire, I must speak my mind. Sire, it is ... it is disgusting, to see how that woman, that fishwife, rules the King of France. Even people in the streets are amazed and dismayed by the power she wields. And by what virtue?' She panted, with emotion and with fear at her own temerity. 'Is it the warmth of her thighs? Are mine cold? Are her fingers better instructed than mine? Does she make you laugh and I make you weep? Am I not sufficiently well born for you? I assure Your Majesty that Éon is a better name than Poisson. What must I *do*, Your Majesty, to prove that I am as good as she? Better than she.'

She stopped, her breath coming in short gasps, her heart pounding.

Louis held out his hands. 'Come here.'

Slowly she crossed the room. He held her thighs, sat her on his lap. 'You are acting the woman,' he said. 'Do not ever act the woman with me, Geneviève. It is the man in you I love.'

She bit her lip. 'It is love for you makes me so, Sire.'

'Aÿe. It is good to be loved. But your love is too much for any one man. You will go to England. Great things await you there. Richelieu will speak of them. He understands it all. He will see you tomorrow. It is a mighty task I give you, Geneviève. Do not fail me.'

'Richelieu?' she cried.

'Well . . .' The King of France actually looked embarrassed. 'He is the best Minister I have ever had.'

'Richelieu?' she shrieked.

Louis put his hands over his ears.

'Richelieu,' she whispered. Richelieu, back in power. He must have patched up his differences with the Pompadour. And now he would send her away again. 'But *why*?' she cried. 'Just tell me that. Why?'

'You are a servant of France, Chevalier.'

'And Madame de Pompadour?'

'Is also a servant of France, in her own way. I'll discuss it no more, Geneviève.'

'Your Majesty . . .'

He stood up so suddenly she slipped off his lap and hit the floor. 'Ow.'

'Leave me,' he said.

'Sire?' She scrambled to her feet, forgetting to rub her bottom.

'I am tired. You have wearied me, Geneviève. You are acting the woman. I have too many women. Leave me.'

She hesitated, biting her lip. Oh, damnation, she thought. I have pressed too hard. But what did I have to lose? This man does not love me any more than I love him. So once again I have tilted at the sun, and had my wings burned. Will there be another opportunity?

She stooped, and gathered her clothes.

'Chevalier, my dear, dear Chevalier.' There was a secretary in the room, and Richelieu contented himself with a kiss on each cheek, although he allowed his hand to come between them and gently squeeze the front of her tunic. 'You do not change, save to grow more handsome.'

Geneviève extricated herself from his embrace. She had spent the night in an ecstasy of despair, had cried herself to sleep. But had awoken in a far more sensible frame of mind. Because after all, was she not prospering? She had aimed too high too soon. Why, the Pompadour had been her age before she had first attracted the King, and it had been a few years more before she had ousted Richelieu and assumed control of the state. So what was she losing? Merely the trauma of trying to bring to orgasm with some regularity, the constant fear of an assassin looking over her shoulder. What had she wanted when she had left Tonnerre? Why, wealth and fame, and did she not now have both of those, to which could be added a pleasant aura of mystery caused by the general uncertainty as to her true sex.

And in addition to those very concrete advantages, was she not once more in the employ of the Duke of Richelieu? If only she could trust him. If only she could discover what he was really about. 'Neither do you change, my lord, save in situations.'

He smiled at her. 'France, it seems, cannot do without me.'

'You have resolved your differences with the Pompadour?'

He laid his finger on his nose. 'We have achieved a certain equilibrium, to be sure.'

'And my reward, for having served you faithfully and well, is to be packed off to England.'

'Faithfully and well? Do you know how we have been besieged by letters, by demands, from St Petersburg? It seems Razumovsky is prepared to forgive you his wound. You are fortunate you are not being packed off back to Russia.'

'It was necessary to see to my own safety, my lord, as there was no one else going to.' She refused to be browbeaten. 'And why *am* I not going back to Russia?'

'I do not consider it necessary. The Tsarina may be a besotted old lecher, but she is no fool. She knows as well as I that Frederick is the man we must pull down, before he pulls us. I have assured her that the Chevalier d'Éon will eventually be returned to her ...'

'Never, my lord. I would rather die.'

'... as soon as he has carried out a small mission for us, a mission for which you are peculiarly suited, with your remarkable combination of looks and courage and ability, your delightful habit of wriggling out of the most desperate situations, always with advantage, and your other ... ah ... assets. Besides, you will like England. As for the Tsarina, my information is that she grows more infirm every day. I do not think you have to worry about her, providing you do your duty to France. No, no, England is where your destiny, all of our destinies, lie. Because make no mistake,' he said, walking the length of the room, 'there is our bitterest enemy. There can be no accommodation with England. No indeed. Eventually we must destroy her. Utterly. But one thing at a time. We wish her to keep the peace while we settle with Frederick, while we achieve the hegemony we need, here in Europe. Then we shall see, about England.' He turned, arm outstretched, finger pointing. 'This is your task. Your first and most important task. Because Nivernais is an utter fool. I do believe he has spent too many years in London. He has become almost an Englishman himself. Well, the arrival of a new First Secretary, in the person of yourself, my dear Chevalier, should shake him up. Because, who knows, should your mission be crowned with success, it might be an appropriate moment to replace him, eh?'

Then he does mean to reward me; ambassador to England, she thought, dreamily. There is achievement, at twenty-seven. Even without the Pompadour, then will my feet be set firmly on the road to eventual power.

She sat up straight. As a man. My God, she thought, am I as confused as everyone else? But there it was, inevitable and certain. She might be the subject of much gossip and sly comment, but Louis had decreed that she should be a man in giving her the Cross of St Louis, and now Richelieu was further decreeing that she be a man by giving her this appointment. How could she ever reveal her true sex again, after that?

But did she want to? When had she ever enjoyed being a woman? When she had been with Adam, this last year. There would be other times, with Adam. But where *was* he? And supposing he could be found, would he agree to live with her, as a man?

'Are you listening to me, Chevalier? I do assure you it is important for you to understand and remember what I am saying.'

'Forgive me, my lord. My attention did wander.'

'Hum. Well, as I was saying, you will have letters of introduction, and Nivernais will also have letters seeking to place you in the very best society. It is there you must do your work, and you must aim at the very highest. His Majesty assures me you are ... hum ... accomplished in this direction.'

'I shall do my best, my lord,' she said, trying to concentrate.

'Of course. Now, the situation there is rather confusing at the moment, owing to the fact that the heir to the throne has recently died. He received an injury, playing at cricket, of all things. Do you know cricket?'

'It is an insect.'

'Oh dear me, no. Not in England. In England it is a pastime where the gentry mingle with the commons, and they throw little balls at each other, attempting to protect themselves with sticks. These balls are uncommonly hard, and what would you? The Prince of Wales received one of these objects in his hum… the seat of his manhood, an abscess developed, and there it was. Can you imagine anything more puerile? But useful for our cause. The King, George the Second, is very old and really cannot be considered as permanent. And the new heir is a young man of seventeen, very much, so I have heard, tied to his mother's apron strings while she, good lady, is tied to a Scottish nobleman. She is a German, of course. Oh, England is a hotbed of backstairs government.'

'More so than France, my lord?' Geneviève asked innocently.

He gave her a quick glance, decided to take her seriously. 'Much more so. Now, the men you must seek to… hum… get to know, and humour, are Pelham, who is the Duke of Newcastle – he is the Prime Minister since the death of his brother – and a Mr Henry Fox.'

'Mr?' Geneviève inquired.

Richelieu shrugged. 'What would you, Chevalier? England is a very strange country where one does not necessarily have to be a count or a duke to hold a position of importance. Mr Fox is the Secretary of State, which means that he handles most of the business in the Commons. Because this is another strange thing about England, not only do they keep summoning their States General – they call them parliaments – but the Upper House, the Lords, can do nothing without the agreement of the Lower House, the Third Estate. We may thank God that here in France we have avoided such excesses.'

'Thank God,' Geneviève agreed reverently. But God in Heaven, she thought, at the end of it they wish me to prostitute myself to a commoner.

'As I was saying,' Richelieu continued, 'these two may be your main objectives, in the beginning. But I wish you to keep in mind a greater. Opportunities will arise, and I wish you to seize them.'

'My lord?'

'The Princess of Wales, dolt,' he snapped. 'Can she possibly prevent her heart going out to one so young, and so gay . . . you will be gay?'

'Presumably.'

'And one so brilliant, and one so experienced, and one so . . . delectable, eh?'

'You'll forgive me, my lord,' Geneviève said, 'but am I undertaking this embassy as a man or a woman?'

'Ha ha,' he shouted. 'Ha ha. My dear Chevalier, what a thing to say.' He lowered his voice. 'Why else do you suppose I chose you, my dear girl?'

'And how do I seduce a woman? Who is not of unnatural tendencies?'

'I am not suggesting you sleep with her, Chevalier. I merely wish you to suggest that you *will* sleep with her. My information is that she is a bewildered romantic rather than a royal whore. She will be content with sweet nothings. Of course, should she reveal any other inclinations . . .'

'And the Marquis of Bute?'

'Oh, he is nothing. The Princess leans upon him as she would lean on a staff, desperate for support since the death of her husband. Father and son never got on, you know. And daughter and father-in-law are no more friendly. No, no, properly approached, the Princess will seize any help that may be to hand. Deal with her as you dealt with the Empress of Russia, and all England will fall into your lap. And then, my dear Chevalier, then . . .' He tapped his nose. 'Who knows?'

Who indeed, Geneviève wondered. And what of me, at the end of it? Must I share my bed once again with a woman? Or with a man I detest? Must I hate and loathe and feel disgust, for the rest of my life? What will happen to me when I start to age, when my beauty dissolves into wrinkles? What employment can they find for me then, as my only asset seems to be my ability to seduce those of either sex with whom I come into contact? It seemed to her, on a sudden, that all her life had turned into so many dead ends.

So then, what did she want from life? Would wealth alone suffice? Once she had thought that, because wealth would enable her to purchase the things that made life acceptable. Even love, as she had then thought. If she knew better now, what was she going to do about it?

'Well, Chevalier? Do you understand your mission?'

She sighed. 'Yes.'

'Good.' Richelieu snapped his fingers. 'Is my carriage waiting?'

The secretary bowed. 'Yes, my lord.'

Richelieu got up. 'We are to take a journey.'

'My lord?' Geneviève asked. 'I am somewhat weary.' She really was in no mood to endure one of his peculiar advances, however skilled a lover she remembered him to be.

'Affairs of state,' he said, and led her down a private flight of stairs and into a courtyard where a small berline was waiting. Geneviève was ushered in, and the Duke sat beside her. The secretary did not accompany them and Geneviève braced herself for the coming tumble as the coach rolled out of the Park and on to an empty road. But to her surprise the Duke leaned away from her and regarded her with a smile.

'Now,' he said, 'for the nub of the matter.'

'My lord?'

'These English are a stiff necked lot,' he pointed out. 'And as I have said, an insatiably greedy lot. It is possible that they might ... hum ... enjoy your charms, and still, at the end of the day, opt for war.'

'It is possible, my lord. I can charm, but I cannot work miracles.'

'In this instance you must, of one sort or another.'

'You will have to explain that.'

'You are being given plenary authority. Do you understand the meaning of the word?'

'Well ... it means that I have all embracing powers. Powers to act on behalf of the King of France without reference back to him.'

'I can see that your education was not neglected, Chevalier. Now, supposing that your mission fails, what must be your next move, bearing in mind that you are acting on behalf of the King of France?'

'I ask for my passports and return here.'

'You think that will aid the cause of France?'

'I can at least serve my country, my lord, which I could not continue to do in England once we are at war.'

Richelieu leaned back, rested his chin on his forefinger. 'You think not?'

Geneviève's head came up. 'You had best speak plain, my

lord. Is my mission really one of spying? I cannot see any point to it. I have attracted a certain reputation. My face is not readily forgotten. Once war is declared I do not see *how* I may remain in England.'

'Once war is declared, no. But you above all people, Chevalier, will know before anyone else, at least in France, whether or not war *is* to be declared. Precious moments, perhaps no more than hours, in which you may act, in which you may indeed do much to ensure our eventual victory.'

'I am afraid I have lost your drift, my lord. What would you have me do, attempt to seduce the entire English fleet? Not even I could do that in a few hours.'

'Ha ha,' he shouted. 'Yet have you shown your understanding of the situation. Oh, you are a clever fellow, Chevalier. The English fleet. There is the secret of victory or defeat. *You will destroy it.*'

Geneviève only half concentrating as she glanced out of the window, found herself sitting up very straight. There was no great pounding of blood through her veins. Nothing more than a gradual slowing of her heartbeat together with a sudden exhaustion, as if she had drunk too much without getting tipsy.

'My lord?' Her voice was nothing more than a whisper.

'We are now in the autumn,' Richelieu said. 'It is the English custom to withdraw its West Indian fleet, and its European fleet, with the onset of winter. All these great ships, and they amount to very nearly a hundred, I do assure you, will soon be moored in Spithead, which is a roadstead within the Solent, an area of water enclosed by the Isle of Wight and situated very close to Portsmouth.'

'A hundred ships,' Geneviève said, trying to envisage such a number and failing.

'The greatest fleet in the world. And that does not take into account the Mediterranean fleet, which winters in Minorca. But one cannot have everything.'

'I suppose not,' Geneviève said absently. 'My lord . . .'

'Hush. We have arrived.'

The berline had come to a halt before a small country house, set back from the road in perhaps half a dozen acres of land. The place looked somewhat decrepit, and was clearly the home of an impoverished noble. But so close to Versailles?

There were footmen waiting to open the door and roll down

the steps, and there were others waiting to open the front door. Which but compounded the mystery, for the house inside was equally decrepit, damp smelling and with rotting wainscoting, and a complete absence of decoration, while there was not a single pane of glass left in any window.

'It is falling down,' Richelieu admitted. 'But it serves our purpose, eh? *Voila.*'

A footman had opened an inner door, and Geneviève paused in surprise. She stood at the top of a shallow flight of steps, having passed right through the entry hall. Here she surveyed what must once have been quite an attractive garden. Now the lawn was rutted and the flowerbeds were overgrown, but the ornamental lake remained, some fifty feet square, she estimated. And in the centre of it, floating gently upon the water, was a fleet of model ships, each about eighteen inches long.

'One hundred, to be precise,' Richelieu explained. 'I would have you meet Monsieur Beaucamp.'

Somewhat reluctantly, Geneviève allowed the man to kiss her hand. He was big, but a caricature of what a man should be. His hair was long and straggly, for he wore no wig; his shoulders were humped, and his legs too short for his body which appeared the more ill proportioned because he was very fat. His clothes were clearly soiled and did not fit him very well, while the buttons of his vest were unfastened so that the garment hung like a sack and revealed a very dirty shirt underneath. His face suggested several potatoes stuck together somewhat carelessly, and his large nose was adorned by a pair of horn rimmed spectacles.

'I would have you meet the Chevalier d'Éon,' Richelieu explained. 'Now, monsieur, we have come for a demonstration.'

'Of course, my lord.' Beaucamp waved his hand, and the door behind them closed. The three of them were alone in the garden.

'Those fellows can be trusted?' Richelieu demanded.

'They are my own people, my lord. Now, Chevalier, if you would come to the edge of the water . . .'

Geneviève glanced at Richelieu, and received a nod. She walked beside the scientist, for undoubtedly that was his profession, and stood at the side of the lake.

'Here, Chevalier,' Beaucamp said, 'you have a fleet at anchor. A very large fleet. The largest fleet in all the world. I wonder who it could belong to? But let us suppose there *is* such a fleet, monsieur. There it is at anchor. And all very carefully proportioned, I do assure you. Why, it has taken me two years to fashion this fleet.'

'It is very pretty,' Geneviève agreed.

'Now, monsieur, how would you go about destroying such a fleet, at anchor?'

'It is not possible,' Geneviève said.

'What of fireships? You will see that the vessels are anchored within a cable's length of each other. Set fire to half a dozen, and might it not be possible to ignite a great conflagration?'

'I doubt that, monsieur,' Geneviève said. 'Let us consider when last fireships were used in earnest, at Calais, when the English sent them about the Armada. Did not the Spaniards merely cut their cables and put to sea? You might destroy half a dozen vessels, but what is that in a hundred?'

'You will understand that the Chevalier is no fool, Monsieur Beaucamp,' Richelieu remarked.

'I could tell that at a glance, my lord. And he is absolutely right in his estimate. What is required is a fireship introduced into the very centre of the fleet, so that there is no one way the ships can flee.'

'One fireship, monsieur?'

'Ah, there you have it, Chevalier. And how would you introduce enough to begin a conflagration sufficient to destroy the main part of the ships?'

'You could not,' Geneviève said. 'You could not even get *one* in there without a challenge.'

'A ship, no, Chevalier. But what about a raft?'

'A fire raft?' It would burn away in seconds, and be easily detected by its guns and barrels of explosive.'

'Suppose it had no guns? And when I say a raft, I am thinking more of a large rowing boat, which could perhaps drift amongst the centre vessels without causing much comment. There are always hundreds of bum-boats about a fleet at anchor.'

'And this rowboat would destroy the British fleet?'

'I have such a rowboat here,' Beaucamp said, taking one from the edge of the lake, where, with a twin, it had been resting on the grass. 'You will observe that it is no bigger than my hand. Now here also I have six barrels of gunpowder, which is all that it can carry without sinking. Now watch, Chevalier.' He carefully placed the barrels, each about the size of Geneviève's thumb, into the boat, and then removed his shoes and stockings, rolled up his breeches, and waded amongst the anchored ships, the boat in his hand. He got to the very centre, placed the boat in the water, planted a short length of fuse amidst the gunpowder, and waded back again, but only a short distance before turning to watch. The fuse fizzled, and then the six barrels exploded as one. There was a flash of fire, a gush of smoke, and Geneviève was for the moment blinded. When she had blinked her eyes clear, she saw that the two ships nearest the explosion were burning, their masts gone and their sails sizzling as they struck the water. The rowboat was sinking.

Geneviève glanced at Richelieu; the Duke seemed unperturbed. 'Fifty rowboats, my lord,' she remarked.

'Monsieur Beaucamp?'

'A failure, you will agree, Chevalier.' Beaucamp waded towards them. 'Ah, well, we shall have to try again. Here we have another boat.' He lifted it from the grass. 'And here we have another barrel of . . . explosive. A large barrel, to be sure, but we possess only two of them. I fit them into the boat like this, together with my length of fuse, like this, and I return into the middle of the fleet . . .' He waded amidst the ships, stretching out to place the rowboat as near the centre as he could without allowing it too close to the two ships which were still burning away merrily. 'Then I light my fuse, and I run,' he shouted, splashing through the water, scattering indeed the vessels nearest to him. Geneviève drew a long breath and had it swept away by the vehemence of the explosion, a shattering bang which knocked the tricorne from her head and had her staggering into the arms of the Duke, who had himself lost his hat. Poor Beaucamp was on his knees, sent there by the blast, only his head visible above the water. While the fleet . . . Geneviève stared in horror. Seven ships had been destroyed; two more were on their beam ends and would clearly sink, and six more were on fire, and not just masts and spars, these; the entire wooden hulls were blazing. The rowboat had disappeared.

'In the name of God,' Geneviève said.

'A very impressive demonstration,' the Duke agreed.

'You have never seen it before, my lord?'

'Oh, I have. But never put to a practical purpose. Monsieur Beaucamp, I congratulate you.'

The big man splashed towards the bank, attempting to dry his spectacles on his shirt, which had come out of his trousers. 'I thank you, my lord. Is that sufficient?'

'Fifteen ships at one blow? His Majesty's fleet has never gained such a victory in history. Chevalier?'

'What was it?'

'A secret. A new form of explosive upon which Monsieur Beaucamp has been working for some years. Oh, its basic ingredient is gunpowder. As to what he adds, why, that is the secret. Even from you, my dear Chevalier.'

'But . . . applied to artillery . . .'

'Ah, there lies a problem. We have no cannon strong enough to take the charge. But as an infernal device, why, it is unequalled in the history of explosives. Now, then, Chevalier, do you still think the project unworkable?'

Geneviève studied the burning ships. Monsieur Beaucamp had been several feet away from the explosion, say half a mile, she reckoned, pursuing the scale upwards. 'No, my lord, it is perfectly workable, but it is a certain form of suicide for whoever lights the train.'

'Not certain.'

'Odds of ninety to one.'

'Perhaps. Men have survived longer odds than these.'

'And this is the task you would set me,' she said. Oh, indeed, Pompadour was a clever wench. She dared not harm, or even oppose, the Chevalier at Versailles. But she could send her to certain death, all in the name of France. 'I doubt the King would approve of thus using my talents, my lord.'

'The matter has already been discussed with the King,' the Duke said, and smiled at the expression on Geneviève's face. 'Not that he proposes to send you to your death, Chevalier. No, no. We have our agents in England, and these have been instructed to make contact with you as soon as you arrive. The purpose of that contact is known to no one save you. You will give them whatever instructions you see fit. They will supply the boat, and make all the necessary preparations. You have but to say when.'

'Then would I be sending half a dozen good men to their certain deaths.'

Richelieu shrugged. 'You are a soldier, Chevalier. Do you not hope to rise to field rank? Then you might well find yourself sending several *thousand* men to their deaths. In war the individual has a sorry lot.'

Geneviève gazed at him. She had never thought of that. And she could not think of it now. She was not a soldier. She was not even a man. At the end she had, after all, been betrayed by her sex.

'I am sorry, my lord. Your plenipotentiary I shall be, if you require it. Your assassin, of thousands of men, I shall not be.'

Richelieu's brows drew together. 'You refuse the King's command?'

'Has His Majesty seen a demonstration of this explosive?'

'He has a very good idea of what it can do.'

'He has not seen it. Let the command come from the King himself.'

'Well, well,' Richelieu remarked. 'It was suggested to me that you might not have the stomach for such a task, and I laughed at the idea. The Chevalier d'Éon? The French government is not accustomed to have its orders refused, Chevalier.'

'None the less, my lord, what you are proposing is bloody murder, not war. I cannot believe the King has been truly informed as to the possible outcome of this venture.'

'Then you had best have a look at these,' Richelieu suggested, and from the pocket of his coat took four envelopes. 'One will do. This one.'

Geneviève frowned, took the envelope; it was not sealed. Inside there was a brief piece of parchment. It was the first time she had ever actually see a *lettre de cachet*.

'You think to frighten me, my lord?'

'I do indeed, Chevalier. I look at you, young, handsome, talented, your future is the brightest in all France. I see you as Ambassador to England, should you manage to keep the peace. Or I see you as Minister of War should you fail, but succeed in destroying the English fleet. And instead I see you, sitting in your solitary cell in the Bastille, growing old and grey, with no company but your gaoler and the rats. I see you going mad with miserable boredom, wracked by the cold in winter, by the feverish heats in summer. And I say to myself, what a terrible waste. Alternatively, of course, I could send you back to Russia. The Empress would be overjoyed. So, I think, would be the Grand Duke and the Grand Duchess, to think that when the Tsarina is no more you will belong entirely to them.'

'The King . . .'

'Study the signature, Chevalier.'

Geneviève's stomach seemed to fill with lead. Because there it was, Louis, Roi. He cared nothing for her, after all. As he was the greatest lecher who had ever lived, he was content to use her body whenever it became available, always providing the use of it did not trouble the Pompadour. For the rest, to him as to

Conti and Richelieu and all the others, she was something to be used. A nothing. A creature.

'And should you be disposed to foolish martyrdom,' Richelieu said gently, 'there are three other letters here, as you will see. One for your uncle, one for your aunt, and one for your mother.'

Geneviève's head came up. Mama, in a prison for the rest of her life? Simply because she had had the misfortune to bear a daughter when she should have borne a son? How happy would they all have been, she thought, had I but been born a boy.

'Well, Chevalier?'

Geneviève sighed. 'I shall be in England, my lord. And the explosive will be here.'

He smiled, and slapped her on the shoulder. 'Spoken like a man. It shall be delivered. Do not fear about that. It shall be delivered. Now let us return to Paris.'

Chapter Ten

'Well, Chevalier?' The Duke of Richelieu tapped his knee in time to the rhythm of the coach. 'Any questions? Anthing you require?'

Geneviève realised she felt sick. It could be the excitement, as it could be the motion of the coach. Or it could be sheer horror at what she was expected to do. Commanded by the King. Who she had thought in love with her. Commanded by Richelieu, who she had thought would wish to keep her by his side. Whereas all the while they were regarding her as nothing more than a weapon. Oh, why had she not fled with Adam, to the obscure safety of some Savoyard inn?

'Well, then, let me give you some information,' Richelieu said, leaning back. 'No one is in the secret of your mission, save for His Majesty and myself.'

'His Majesty, my lord? Must that not mean Madame de Pompadour as well?'

'No,' Richelieu snapped. 'That would be a disaster. Oh, she supposes she has engineered your removal from Versailles. But she does not truly understand your mission. That must be our secret, and our triumph.'

'Your triumph,' Geneviève muttered. 'I shall doubtless be dead.'

'Oh, come, Chevalier. You have extricated yourself from more difficult situations. I assure you that no Englishman is as dangerous as a Russian.'

Geneviève sighed, and looked out of her window.

'Which of your party you acquaint with your intentions must be up to you, of course,' the Duke continued. 'But if I may offer a word of advice, keep your plans for the ultimate to yourself until you are ready to strike. That way you will best avoid betrayal. And under no circumstances is de Nivernais to be let into the secret. He would not understand our methods at all.'

Then he is a man of honour, she thought, and they are apparently rare.

'Now, as to the matter of the explosive, this is to my mind the most difficult aspect of the entire situation, as you will need a considerable quantity. However, plans have been made. The barrels are being assembled at a secret cove on the Cotentin Peninsular, and we are arranging for them to be transported to a similar privy place on the south coast of England.'

'You mean they are to be smuggled into England?'

'Well, we could hardly ship them through Portsmouth.'

'My lord, this affair smacks more and more of the fantastic. What happens when they get there?'

'I have agents making the necessary arrangements.'

'And you said the project was a secret between three of us?'

'It is. The purpose for which the explosive is to be used is the secret. Indeed no one knows the quality of the explosive at all, and it will be assumed that it is ordinary gunpowder. There is naught for you to worry about. You have but to give the necessary command.'

'To whom?'

'One of my agents in England will contact you soon after your arrival. He will not approach you until you require him. This you will do by walking in Covent Garden, which is a large open market-place, with a single white feather in your hat.'

'And he will identify me through that?' Geneviève demanded, well aware how popular white feathers were amongst the young gentlemen of Paris.

'Indeed he will.' Richelieu tapped his nose. 'No one in London will be wearing such a distinguishing mark, as the white cockade is the mark of a Jacobite, and would certainly land its wearer in gaol on a charge of treason. But you are an accredited French diplomat, and any unpleasantness will soon be smoothed over.'

He certainly knows how to inspire confidence, Geneviève thought.

'As I say, my agent will wait for your signal that you require him to set the ball rolling, so to speak, but of course you will not leave it too late. The explosive will certainly be in England by the end of the month, so you may make your move at any time after that. You will need funds for all this, of course. Nivernais is instructed to make available whatever you may require.'

'Suppose my other negotiations are still hanging fire?'

Another tap on the nose. 'I rely entirely upon your judgement, Chevalier.'

But he means me to use it, she thought. Oh, there could be no doubt about that.

He was smiling at her. 'You really will find it much more simple than you suppose, Cheavlier. There is no need at all to look so confounded. Perhaps you are concerned with your escape from England, should it come to that. It will be arranged, Chevalier. But in any event, should you handle the affair with your well known skill, no one will be able to connect you with an explosion in Portsmouth. I look forward to seeing you back in France, the triumph of an age.'

'This man of whom you speak, this agent who will be seeking to contact me, will he head the force which will plant the explosive?'

'He will do whatever you command him to, Chevalier.'

I am to send a man to his death, she thought, and not even be there to see him die. Murder, by proxy.

'But if there is anything else you require, Chevalier, you have but to mention it. His Majesty has given me *carte blanche* to meet your requirements.'

She sighed. 'My establishment?'

'I was coming to that. You will need trustworthy servants, to be sure.'

'My man, Jules.'

'Of course. I have here a list of other people you will find realiable.'

She shrugged. 'Jules will be sufficient.' Poor Jules. He had followed her from one end of Europe to the other, grumbling, and hoping. Poor Jules. Now he might well be following her to his death.

'It has also been decided that you should have a personal equerry.'

Richelieu's smile was sly.

'I do not think that will be necessary, my lord,' Geneviève said. 'It is difficult for me to keep my . . . secrets in any event, from those near me. The fewer they are the better.'

'But in this case we insist. And this young man knows your secrets already. He is a Scot, named Adam Menzies.'

Geneviève's head jerked. 'Adam? But . . .'.

'My dear Chevalier, it is my business to know everything that happens in France. Certainly everything that may affect an agent of mine.'

'Sophie,' she said. 'By God . . .'

'Tut, Chevalier. Madame Sophie merely told us where he could be found.'

'But . . . he cannot accompany me to England.'

'Why not?'

'He was out in the forty-five. He will be hanged.'

'Not if he goes as an accredited French representative, which he will.'

'I will not permit it. I shall refuse. He has suffered enough on my behalf as it is.'

Richelieu smiled at her; she did not like the expression at all. 'I have just explained that he will be immune from English law. But should you persist in acting the fool, Chevalier, he will certainly suffer perpetual imprisonment, under French law.'

'On what charge, my lord?'

Richelieu's smile widened into a grin. 'Sodomy, my dear Chevalier.'

'Sodomy? Why . . .'

'Will you deny that you have shared a room with this young man throughout this summer? Ever since your return from Russia, indeed. Oh, there are witnesses enough.'

'And that is proof of sodomy?'

'It could be. It is certainly proof of a remarkable, an unnatural fondness. And this is attested by those who have seen you together. Oh, nothing was thought of it at the time, because you dressed as a woman. But now that the truth is known . . .'

She refused to lose her temper. 'Anyway,' she said, 'we

quarrelled. He will never return. And to serve under me? That is impossible.'

'Bah,' Richelieu said. 'A lovers' tiff. It is already over. I think Captain Menzies was overjoyed to return to Versailles.'

The berline was at that moment entering the gate.

'He is here?' Geneviève cursed the way her heart went pit-a-pat; she knew the colour was revealing itself in her cheeks.

'He awaits your pleasure, Chevalier. Oh, we wish you to have every comfort on your mission. Of course, should you at any time feel unable to complete your task, Captain Menzies' diplomatic immunity could be withdrawn, and in addition, the true facts of your relationship would be made known to the British Government. In England, my dear Chevalier, they do not imprison a man for buggery; they hang him. And his accomplice.'

She glared at him. 'My lord,' she said. 'You are not an honourable man.'

'One can seldom afford to be, in politics. But Chevalier, are *you* an honourable man? Incidentally, this Scotsman of yours knows nothing of your mission. Whether you tell him or not is up to you. But remember this, Chevalier; succeed, or you both die, and your relatives spend the rest of their lives in gaol. Remember that.' The carriage was stopping. 'Now go to your Scotsman.'

Her heart pounded and the sickness had returned. Adam. But it was also partly anger at the contempt with which Richelieu had treated her.

But am I anything different to their supposition of me, she wondered? Am I not as confused as they? Do I know what I want, what I prefer? The thrust of a man's penis or the warm understanding of a woman's love? Am I not damned beyond recall, no matter how I twist and turn and wriggle and fight? I am at once a freak and a monster and an apostate – strange how that betrayal of her birth and upbringing lingered to the distress of her conscience.

And Adam. What absurdity. He will never accept me as a man. How will I convince him? Adam? It will be impossible. And my oath. Of all men, Adam would be most bound by oaths.

But how I want to see him again. To hold him in my arms again. To sleep with him again. And more than ever on such a mission. How can I live, without some *meaning*? Then, you silly bitch, you have fallen in love, after all your vows, all your determination. No, I shall never fall in love, because I *can* never fall in love. But to remain human I must have around me someone who loves me. That is as essential as food and drink. Someone who loves me. And if he loves me, he will understand me. Then what will he ask in return? Why should he ask anything in return? If he loves me.

She stood straight, listening to the sound of heels outside her door. She was exhausted.

Knuckles played on the panels.

'Enter,' she said, and felt the blood rushing to her cheeks.

The door opened, and he stood there, left hand resting on the hilt of his sword, face registering a mixture of disbelief and pleasure.

'Gene . . .'

'The Chevalier d'Éon welcomes you, Captain Menzies,' she said.

He frowned, glanced at the two men who stood behind him.

'You may enter, Captain Menzies,' Geneviève said. 'And you may leave him here, fellows.'

'His Grace of Richelieu instructed . . .'

'I am instructing you,' Geneviève snapped. 'The Chevalier d'Éon. Do as I command.'

They saluted, and withdrew.

'Do come in,' Geneviève suggested. 'And close the door.'

Adam stepped inside, shut the doors behind him. 'You make a very fine soldier, Chevalier.' His tone had grown cold.

'You at least know the truth of the matter,' she said.

'Do I, monsieur? I know not what secrets you possess, what powers you exercise. I know that I was seized in my bed, by half a dozen armed rascals, and despatched here to Versailles without so much as a by your leave. Your doing?'

'No. But I am glad to see you. Adam!' She held out her arms. 'Without you I am nothing.'

'With me you are less. You swore an oath, Chevalier, that such things were behind you forever.'

'And circumstance have forced me to break my word,' she said. 'I would have supposed you would understand. You of all people.'

'I understand,' he agreed. 'Oh, I understand, Chevalier. You are an hermaphrodite, at least in your brain. Your gods are money and power. You will sacrifice anything to attain those ends. You are not human, Chevalier. You are a monster. A thing of evil. And you may draw on me if you wish.'

'Draw on you, Adam?' She sat down. Her shoulders rose and fell. 'I made a mistake. You were right. Better by far to have run away with you, and become the innkeeper you wished to be. I aimed at the sun, and I have been burned. But Adam, the sun warms as well as burns. I am to be First Secretary at the London Embassy, with plenary powers. More powerful than the Ambassador, when you come down to it. Look, I am invested with the Cross of St Louis.'

'And with manhood,' he pointed out.

'Well,' she said. 'Surely that is a small price to pay.' Oh, say yes, she thought. It is a small price. Convince me, Adam. Convince me.

But his face remained cold. 'You and I pursue happiness in different ways Chevalier.'

'Happiness? Is that the only goal in life?'

'Can you offer me another, of equal value, Chevalier?'

'For God's sake stop calling me Chevalier,' she shouted. 'I am Geneviève. To you I am Geneviève. That is our secret, and no one can gainsay it.'

'You are not Geneviève' he said. 'While you stand before me dressed as a man you are the Chevalier d'Éon.'

'Oh, very well. Then love me as the Chevalier d'Éon.'

'I doubt that is possible.'

She raised her head. His face was set and angry. But was he not being the fool? What did he have to offer her? Nothing but a life of drudgery. What did she offer him? Wealth and power for the rest of his life, would he only accept her as what she was.

'So if you will permit me to withdraw, Chevalier, I shall return to Savoy. Unless you have a cell arranged for me in the Bastille.'

She glared at him. I need *you,* she thought. I cannot play the role to which I am forced without you.

'There is a cell,' she said, 'waiting for you. So you had best swallow your foolish pride and accompany me.'

He frowned at her. 'You'll explain?'

'I am appointed to a post of some importance. I need an equerry, someone with whom I can share my . . . my innermost thoughts. That has to be someone I can trust. I have chosen you, because I know of no one else. You will accompany me to England.'

'And if I refuse?'

'Then indeed it shall be the Bastille, and for the rest of your life.' She risked a smile. 'Oh, Adam, Adam, cannot we cease this fighting, and be friends? Lovers? If you know how my body aches for you.' She got up, reached for his hands. 'My bedchamber is through there, and I am panting for you. Adam, Adam . . .'

He freed himself. 'Chevalier, you would make me into a catamite. I loved a girl, called Geneviève. Your sister, Chevalier. You may command me to your service, but you cannot command me to your bed. I shall bid you adieu, until the Embassy sails.'

She told herself he was merely being ridiculously stiff-necked. And she was glad to have him back, for they were forced to see each other most of every day as they were outfitted and equipped for the task that lay ahead. Not that it took very long; it was already approaching the end of October, and Richelieu was in a hurry to have them in London, apparently the international situation, exacerbated between England and France by the rivalry of their colonists in various parts of the world, was deteriorating every moment.

She saw nothing of the King during this time, nor did she wish to. He had shown his true regard for her, and she had been left with no alternative but to make her way in the society of men as a man; well then, she determined that she would do just that, even if it meant turning herself into a mass murderess. Her resolution was hardened by Richelieu himself, who kept their relationship upon a severely master/servant basis. But she was glad of this. Her role, she reminded herself, had been forced upon her throughout her life; as she had endured all the hardships it had involved for twenty-seven years, it would make a nonsense of everything did she collapse beneath its weight now. She had known from the very beginning that it was Geneviève d'Éon against the world, and she would either conquer or die in the attempt. People like Adam were bonuses thrown in to make her journey palatable, not seriously to be considered as an end in themselves. Her decision made *their* relationship much easier, as she was able to treat him with an equal coolness. As for the loneliness of her bed, she was content that this should be so, for the time being. She was working for both of their futures, and in time he would understand.

But to her surprise, the night before they were due to sail, she was summoned to the Pompadour's apartments at seven of the clock, a time, as she well remembered, when the King would be there.

'I am to be bid a formal farewell,' she said to Jules as he helped her to dress. 'Wretched woman, she wishes to gloat at my departure. But we will be back, will we not?'

'If monsieur says so,' Jules agreed lugubriously.

Yet it was difficult not to control her anger as she waited for the doors to be opened. That a fishwife should command her presence, and that she should have tamely to obey . . . the doors were swinging open, and the major-domo was facing the room.

'The Chevalier d'Éon.'

'My dear Chevalier.' Madame de Pompadour had never looked more dazzling, and she was on her feet to greet her guest. 'You grow more handsome every day. Or is it more beautiful? I really am not sure.'

'As you more and more suggest some aquatic goddess, madame,' Geneviève said, bowing.

She straightened, and for a moment they glared at each other, then the Pompadour smiled. 'And now you are setting forth on a diplomatic mission of vital importance. We could not let you go without wishing you success. Your Majesty?'

'Chevalier.' Louis took her hand and for a moment she thought he had forgotten and was about to kiss it. 'I am sure the English will adore you. I look to great things from this Embassy. Oh, great things. And do not stay away too long, eh? Versailles will not seem the same without you.'

'I shall be back by the Spring, Sire,' Geneviève said. 'You have my word.'

'Oh, splendid. Splendid, eh Jeanne?'

'I can hardly wait, Your Majesty,' the Pompadour agreed. 'Now, Chevalier, I would have you meet my other guests. The Duke of Richelieu you already know.'

Geneviève bowed. The Duke's face was expressionless.

'And the Chevalier Patourelle.'

Geneviève bowed.

'And of course, the Seigneur de Guerchy.'

Geneviève bowed.

'I look forward to sharing your burden, Chevalier.'

'Monsieur?' But she glanced at the Pompadour.

Who was smiling. 'I have a surprise for you, Chevalier. His Majesty has been representing to me the dangers of your mission, alone amongst the barbarous English. Why, Chevalier, I understand they stop at nothing to achieve their ends.'

'Your concern is touching, madame. But I am well protected. I have as personal aide-de-camp an experienced soldier.'

'So I understand,' the Pompadour agreed. 'Yet will he not always be present, will he? She smiled. 'So I have decided to see to your safety by making you a present of the Seigneur de Guerchy, as your personal bodyguard.'

'De Guerchy?' Geneviève cried.

'I shall study only to serve you, Chevalier,' Guerchy said with a bow.

Geneviève turned to the King. 'Your Majesty . . .'

'Oh, do not thank me, Chevalier. It was all Madame's idea.'

'But . . .' She bit her lip. 'May I have a word in private, Your Majesty?'

'I doubt that will be possible,' the Pompadour said. 'There is a play to be watched, and His Majesty is very tired. While you depart for Calais at dawn, do you not? You will need a good night's rest.'

'I would sleep better without the attention of your creature, Madame,' Geneviève said in a low voice.

The Pompadour continued to smile. 'My creature, Chevalier? The Seigneur is sworn to serve you, is he not? Oh, you will prosper with him at your side. I am sure of it.'

Geneviève looked at the King again, but there was nothing to be gained there. Richelieu? He did not seem to know what it was all about. She was plunged back deep into a conspiracy, but to what end? The ruination of her mission? That scarce made sense. It was something to be considered. But not here. And at least she knew from whence the Seigneur was coming. She bowed. 'Then I shall take my leave, with Madame's permission. As you say, I leave at dawn.' She bowed to the King, straightened, and looked at Guerchy. 'Be sure you are ready, monsieur.'

The white cliffs shimmered in the afternoon sunlight, and Geneviève heaved a sigh of relief. They were only three hours out of Calais, but the wind was fresh and her stomach was rolling. She had refused to go below; memory was too clouded with the stench of the great cabin as she had crossed the Baltic.

And now the breakwaters of Dover Harbour were opening before her.

'England,' Jules remarked. 'We shall have out throats cut, Chevalier.'

Geneviève glanced at Guerchy, apparently unconcerned at the approach of land. Indeed, throughout the journey from Versailles which had now lasted for two days, he had been the perfect companion, ever attentive, ever polite, ever anxious to carry out her every wish. But that he was here for a purpose, and that that purpose was not to her advantage, she never doubted.

Beyond the Seigneur Adam also waited, but he was peering at the distant shore. Here were his enemies, rushing towards him. But he made no remark. She had debated endlessly, during the week of their preparation, whether to confide in him the true purpose of their mission, and decided against it. He would never betray her, but she did not yet know herself what she would have to do at the end, and she knew *him* well enough to guess that he would vehemently oppose any suggestion that she might seduce one or more of the British ministers, while on the other hand he would be all in favour of dealing the British navy a crippling blow, and without further consideration. Time enough to share that secret at the right moment. Just now, even if he would not visit her bed, it was sufficient to have him where she could see him, every day.

Time enough too, to remember that she was the Chevalier d'Éon, and that in contrast to all her previous adventures, she was travelling with almost unlimited powers. And she had seen to it that she also dressed the part, wore a blue-grey velvet coat, with enormous silk embroidered cuffs, her pocket flaps in pastel shades of blue and green and yellow; her breeches were grey as were her stockings, and there were jewelled buckles on her black leather shoes. Her wig was a white tie, secured with a blue bow, her shirt white cambric. Not only did she enjoy the display, but she reckoned the more foppish and effeminate the English thought her the better chance she had of ultimate success. Certainly the Dover harbour officials stared as they came aboard.

'The Chevalier d'Éon?'

'I am he.' Geneviève presented her passports.

'Captain Adam Menzies.' The customs officer glanced down a list held by his side. 'A Jacobite, monsieur. Wanted for treason.'

Adam's hand dropped to the hilt of his sword.

'My aide-de-camp, sir,' Geneviève said. 'And protected by a diplomatic passport. What, would you risk war?'

The officer made a growling sound in his throat, then returned the passports. 'You may land, monsieur.'

'I thank you.' Geneviève walked across the gangplank, glanced to her left, and saw a sloop of war, flying an enormous white ensign, alongside the quay but a few yards distant. Her heart seemed to skip a beat as she watched the jack tars carrying barrels of food and water on board. They were the men she had come to destroy, and with them, their splendid ship. She prayed it would not be necessary.

'Chevalier?'

She turned, found herself facing an elderly man, dressed very quietly, with not a jewel in sight, and not even wearing a sword. His wig managed to be untidy, and there were food stains on his shirt.

'Yes?'

The man inspected her, slowly, from shoes to head. '*You* are the Chevalier d'Éon?'

'I am, sir.'

He sighed, held out his hand. 'I am the Duke of Nivernais, His Majesty's Ambassador to the Court of St James.'

'My lord.' Geneviève removed her hat in a deep bow. 'I am flattered that you should have chosen to meet me.'

'Curiosity, Chevalier. Curiosity. Your reputation has travelled before you. We'll ride in my carriage.'

'My people . . .'

Nivernais waved his hand. 'There are other equipages. They will be cared for, Chevalier. But I would have a word with you in private.'

Geneviève glanced at Adam, then got into the Ambassador's berline. He sat beside her, the door was closed.

'I have received a despatch,' Nivernais remarked. 'Informing me of your imminent arrival, and indicating that you would be possessed of plenary powers.'

Geneviève nodded. She was too interested in the town through which she was passing, such a contrast to France, in that there were no palaces to be seen – although there was a massive fortress overlooking the harbour – and instead nearly all the dwellings were of a similar state of repair. The same could be said about the people, she realised, in that while there was a total absence of elegance in the dress of either men or women, there did not appear to be any great poverty, either.

'My God,' Nivernais remarked, half to himself. 'No doubt you have letters confirming your rank and powers, Chevalier?'

'Eh? Oh, yes. In here.' She handed him her wallet.

'May I open it?'

'Of course, Your Excellency.' Now the houses were fading, the water was being left behind, and they were travelling up a straight and remarkably well surfaced turnpike, cutting like a river between rolling fields, and dominated, every so often, by strange looking buildings, like enormous chimneys rising straight out of the ground.

'Hum,' Nivernais remarked, having found what he wanted. 'It would appear that I am yours to command, Chevalier. May I say that you are somewhat young for such an important responsibility?'

'I am twenty-seven years of age, Your Excellency,' Geneviève pointed out. 'And I have been in the forefront of the diplomatic service since I was eighteen. You'll have heard I have been special envoy to St Petersburg?'

'I have heard a great many things about you, Chevalier.'

She allowed him a smile. 'And no doubt you will discover that they are all true, Your Excellency. Now perhaps you can tell me something about England. Those remarkable dwellings.'

'They are not dwellings, Chevalier. The crop grown in these fields is hops, and those furnaces are where the beer is prepared. The English are a nation of beer drinkers. You will have to get used to it.'

'Is wine unobtainable?'

'At a price, Chevalier.' He smiled in return. 'Most of it is smuggled from France. Duties, you understand. The English impose a most prohibitive duty on any wine save it comes from Portugal.'

'Ah.' The countryside commenced to grow boring, and she leaned back in her seat. 'How far is it to London?'

'Ninety odd miles. We shall break our journey for the night. An inn is arranged. But perhaps you would outline to me what your mission entails, whom you wish to meet.'

'Why, Your Excellency, my mission is a simple one. It is to secure the neutrality, if not the friendship of England in whatever trials may lie ahead of us.'

'The neutrality of England? The friendship? That can never be.'

'And yet, Your Excellency, the effort is to be made.'

'I have been trying to secure English friendship for five years. Do you really suppose you will succeed where I have failed?'

Geneviève smiled at him. 'Perhaps I may be able to bring a different approach to the matter, my lord. Now, first of all, I wish an interview with the Prime Minister. Then I wish to meet Mr Fox.'

Nivernais nodded. 'I suppose that is reasonable enough. You will find them both utterly stiff-necked.'

'So long as not only their necks are stiff, Your Excellency, I shall be well satisfied.'

He gave her a quick glance, allowed his gaze to drift down her body. 'I have been away from Versailles for too long,' he said. 'Very well, Chevalier. I will also arrange for your credentials to be presented at court.'

Geneviève nodded. 'And I would also like to meet the Princess of Wales. I mean the Dowager Princess of Wales.'

Nivernais raised his eyebrows. 'Why, Chevalier, you appear to be omniverous.'

'Will you arrange it for me, Your Excellency?'

'I will see what can be done, certainly. You are aware that there is considerable enmity between the King and his daughter-in-law?'

'Just arrange the meeting, Your Excellency,' Geneviève said.

'His Excellency, Minister Plenipotentiary of His Majesty the King of France, the Chevalier d'Éon.' The major-domo paused for breath, and the huge room fell silent. Geneviève gave Adam, rigid at her shoulder, a quick glance, and then slowly began the march up the carpet which stretched before her all the way to the throne. To either side the huge room was crowded, with men and women; despite all their efforts to keep still there was a gigantic rustling of taffeta and crepe de chine, a shuffling of feet, which was slowly overtaken by a murmur of gossip as Geneviève went forward.

'Gad, sir, a mere boy,' someone muttered.

'But handsome,' said a woman.

'Rare,' said another.

'They do say . . .' whispered a third.

'Best swordsman in France.'

'Strange fellow . . .'

'A damned macaroni . . .'

'Worse than that . . .'

'I'd heard he's really a woman.'

'What nonsense.'

'Aye, but . . .'

Geneviève thanked the self control she had gained over the previous years in that no colour entered her cheeks, nor did she glance from side to side. Let them think what they wished, say what they wished. I am here to destroy *you,* she thought. Enjoy your sport while you may.

'Chevalier.' The voice was guttural, the face almost disappeared beneath a mass of wrinkles, the head itself lost between the massive, overweight shoulders. She reminded herself that this king, this George the Second of Great Britain and Ireland, was seventy-two years old, and he looked every day of it. His eyes belonged to a man who knew he was at the end of his span.

She bent into a deep bow. 'Sire.'

'Stand straight, sir,' the King commanded, and she obeyed. 'Your reputation has preceded you, Chevalier. I apologise for de rudeness of my court.' Even after nearly thirty years on the English throne, he had not lost his German accent.

'I have learned to live with my reputation, Your Majesty,' Geneviève said. 'But should any of your English gentlemen care to investigate me further, be sure that I shall be happy to accommodate them.'

'My dear Chevalier, you are here as my guest,' The King said. 'I would have no man forget that. Eh, my lord?'

'I had presumed the Chevalier came on a mission of peace,' said the man standing beside the throne.

'Allow me to present my prime Minister, de Duke of Newcastle,' the King said.

Geneviève bowed, but her heart sank. The Duke was over seventy himself. My God, she thought, are these the people the Duke of Richelieu is afraid to fight? Every one practically senile? Certainly she could see no advantage to be gained here. For all his age the Duke was handsome enough, but he was showing very little interest in the good looking young man presented to him, and even if he was so inclined, would she not be utterly wasting her time in attempting to seduce him? Within a year he would be replaced by someone else. Her immediate task was to discover who that someone might be.

But in the circumstances there was nothing for it but to prepare for the worst. That afternoon she announced that she would take a walk through the city.

'Well, of course, Chevalier, your time is yours to be used as you see fit,' Nivernais agreed reluctantly. 'But to walk in London, it is scarce an occupation for gentlemen. These people are not French.'

'I had observed that, my lord.'

The Ambassador flushed. 'What I mean is that they are subject to less disciplines. The London mob, why it is feared even by kings. I would but beg you to be careful.'

'I certainly mean to offend nobody,' Geneviève said, keeping her face straight. 'I merely wish to get amongst the people. You'll accompany me, Captain Menzies?'

Adam bowed. 'If you wish it, Chevalier.'

'I do wish it.'

'And I also shall accompany you, Chevalier,' Guerchy announced.

'As you wish.' She reflected that if there was going to be a brawl he might very well get his head broken, which would be no bad thing. 'I think I shall change my hat. Jules, the velvet tricorne.'

'Of course, Chevalier.' Jules hurried off, returned a moment later with her new hat, its white feather bobbing gently.

'My God,' Nivernais cried. 'You'll not go out in that?'

'I permit no man to criticise my dress, my lord,' Geneviève said.

'But ... Chevalier, have you not been told? That is the emblem of the Pretender, Charles Edward. You will cause a riot.'

'Nonsense.'

'I'm afraid His Excellency is correct,' Adam said. 'You will be risking a great deal, Chevalier.'

'I do not believe a word of it,' Geneviève declared. 'But I have no desire to cause a disturbance.'

'Well said,' Nivernais agreed. 'You'll wear another?'

'I will not, Your Excellency. But I will do my sightseeing from a carriage. Will that not satisfy everyone?'

The men exchanged glances, and shrugs. Clearly they regarded the Chevalier as mad. And Adam? He made no comment. Perhaps he too thought she had lost her senses. But he took his place opposite her in the Ambassador's coach, sitting beside Guerchy. The two men seemed to have become quite friendly, as Adam knew nothing of Guerchy's past, and Geneviève had not yet informed him. She was playing a very lone hand, entirely because she could not decide Adam's reactions. Time enough to confide in him when she had made contact with Richelieu's agent. But my God, she thought, as she peered out of the window, her hat for the moment resting on the seat beside her, what a labyrinth I have got myself into.

They proceeded down a wide thoroughfare, with the river Thames flowing to their right, and some very stately houses to their left. London was far more elegant than she had at first supposed, at least as regards architecture, and that there were even better things to come she could tell by looking towards the city, where the great dome of the new cathedral of St Paul's dominated the skyline, only to be itself overshadowed by the high battlements of the Tower of London further along. Contrasting with these great buildings were the little wooden hovels which crowded the waterfront on both sides of the river, but even here the greater equality of English life was evident, for there did not appear to be any Thieves' Kitchen such as existed in the very heart of Paris, where even the King's Officers dare not set foot unless invited. Yet there was great poverty; she saw some children wearing ragged gowns, and nothing else, not even wooden shoes, and it was a damp and chill November morning, with the mist clinging to the river and sending a chill even into her well covered bones. There was as much slush to be found in these streets as ever in Paris, and the wheels of her carriage sent it scattering across their bare legs and had them hopping up and down and screaming curses at her, a pastime in which they were joined by their equally ragged elders as they recognised the crest on the coach.

'Away with you,' Guerchy shouted out of the window.

Which merely earned another stream of curses.

'Covent Garden,' Geneviève said. 'I wish to look at Covent Garden.'

'You will scarce find it an improvement,' Adam remarked, but he raised the hatch and gave the necessary instructions. And in fact the moment they turned away from the Strand they abandoned some of the mud and the worst of the people; now they drove slowly through narrow streets, insalubrious enough as windows were constantly opening to allow the contents of slop buckets and chamber pots to be thrown on to the cobbles without the slightest concern for those beneath. The noise was deafening, for in addition to the endless stream of curses and repartee between the housewives and their victims, there were carriages rumbling to and fro, and a variety of persons, varying from old men to young girls, each with a barrow and an apron, proceeding slowly along the sidewalks and offering their wares, which might be anything from fresh shellfish to an ability to sharpen knives, at the tops of their voices. Yet the whole had an energy, an aliveness, which was absent in Paris, and certainly in St Petersburg or Moscow. Geneviève realised for the very first time that perhaps Richelieu had not been as mistaken as she had supposed in fearing these people, once they had girded themselves for war.

The coach was stopping before an absolute mass of people, congregating about a large open space. Here the noise was even louder, for instead of barrows there was a perfect forest of stalls, every one selling some kind of fruit or vegetable, and every one besieged by a crowd of equally loud customers seeking some especial bargain.

'Covent Garden,' Adam explained. 'You wished to come here, Chevalier. I doubt we shall make much progress.'

Geneviève peered out of the windows, at the houses which surrounded the square. It seemed impossible that anyone would be able to see her white feather from that distance. But she could only do as she had been instructed.

'Why, then,' she said. 'We shall walk amongst them.' She put on her hat.

'Wearing that?' Adam demanded.

'Why, gentlemen, are you afraid of a few English louts? The white cockade may be the mark of a Jacobite, but it is also a badge of the Bourbons. This hat was given me by His Majesty himself, and I for one will never be ashamed to wear it.'

'Well said, Chevalier.' Guerchy himself opened the door and jumped down. 'You'll wait for us,' he told the driver.

Adam descended, rolled down the steps, waited for Geneviève to join them. She took a long breath, ducked her head, and emerged on to the step, remained for a moment, looking around her, for she was more conspicuous there than she would be in the mob.

Immediately there were some remarks, mainly of curiosity, she decided. She reached the ground, and made her way into the crowd, pushing people to left and right, while Adam and

Guerchy followed, one to each shoulder to guard her back. People turned to look at them, for they were by far the best dressed men in the crowd, and the remarks commenced to grow.

'Chevalier,' Adam said, 'as you value your skin, I beg of you to return to your coach. You of all people do not wish to be pulled about by a mob.'

He had spoken a moment too late, for before she could reply someone had attempted to knock her hat off, only to be checked by Guerchy.

'Hold there, villain,' the Seigneur shouted, attempting to secure her assailant.

'Jacobites,' someone shouted.

'Frogs,' bellowed another.

'Staves,' yelled a third, and immediately there was a great hubbub.

'They mean to assault us,' Guerchy snapped, drawing his sword.

'Put it up,' Geneviève ordered. 'Bloodshed would be worst of all. Why, good people,' she smiled at them, 'as you do not like our company, we shall withdraw.'

'You'll stamp on your hat first, monsewer,' said the man who had tried to knock it off.

'By God,' Guerchy growled.

'Hush, monsieur,' Geneviève said. 'It seems the Ambassador was right, and I have been too bold. I will willingly take off my hat and stamp on it, if it will please these sturdy fellows.'

For they were entirely surrounded by large young men behind whom were a crowd of angry women.

'You will stamp on your hat to please a mob?' Adam demanded.

'It is preferable to having us torn limb from limb, is it not?' Geneviève took off her hat, threw it into the mud. 'Here we are, good people.' She stepped on the crown.

'Three cheers for the monsewer,' shouted her assailant.

'Hip hip hooray,' bawled the mob, scattering pigeons.

Geneviève discovered she was in as much danger from their good humour as from their anger, as she was slapped on the back and her hands were seized to be shaken. But at the least she reckoned she could hardly have attracted as much attention if she *had* been torn to pieces.

Extraordinary,' Nivernais remarked that night at supper.

'The Chevalier is a law unto himself,' Guerchy commented. But he was no less angry than Adam.

'Nevertheless, Chevalier, deliberately to set out to antagonise a mob, and then to surrender entirely to their demands without the least resistance, I find that odd.'

'You must permit me to conduct my own affairs in my own way, Your Excellency,' she pointed out. 'Having met the King and his Prime Minister, I but wished to discover who are the true rulers of England.'

'Newcastle was never the ruler of England,' Nivernais said. 'He was given the post entirely because his brother, Pelham, held it before him. The men who rule England are Fox, and Pitt.'

'Pitt?'

'He does not at the moment have a ministry. But he is even more of a power in Opposition.'

'Still, he is Opposition. It is Mr Fox I shall concentrate on. Do you not agree, Captain Menzies?'

For Adam sat in stony silence at the end of the table.

'Your approach to your problem must be your own, Chevalier,' he said. 'I do not even know what the problem is.'

'Why, to secure England as a French ally.'

'Then, Chevalier,' he said, 'you will have to do without my advice, as I am entirely against your purpose.'

She sighed. 'Well, then, Your Excellency, tell me of this Mr Fox.'

'Ah, now there is a scoundrel. I tell no tales. He is quite unprincipled.'

'How old is he?'

'About fifty, I should say.'

'Married?'

'Indeed. And the father of three boys. There was a fourth, but he died.'

'What of his tastes?'

'He has but one taste, Chevalier. Money.'

'Hum.' She drank some wine. 'I should like to meet him, none the less.' She pushed back her chair and got up. 'And you will not forget my wish to meet the Princess of Wales.'

'I have not forgotten, Chevalier. Although I am bound to say that if anything is likely to prejudice the success of your mission it would be to let the court suspect you are paying homage to Richmond Lodge.'

'Can it not be arranged privily?'

'My dear Chevalier, keeping secrets of that nature are difficult at the best of times. And your disfavour with the court would be compounded were it discovered.'

· 'That is a risk I must take. I must insist upon meeting the Princess. And the young Prince as well, if that is possible. Now I will retire. Captain Menzies, I should like a private word.'

· Adam rose and bowed. 'You'll excuse me, Chevalier, but I have a prior engagement. I have said I have no advice to offer, as I have no opinion on this mission other than to wish its failure.'

She glared at him, stamped her foot in anger. 'None the less, Captain, I insist . . .' A sudden agonising pain rose from her stomach into her throat. She found herself on her knees, gasping for breath, while darts of the purest agony surged into every part of her body. She tried to speak, found she could not, tried to raise her head to look at them, found them staring at her, Nivernais completely bemused, the footmen patently terrified, and Guerchy . . . her brain flickered. Guerchy. Now he looked concerned. But for just a moment . . .

Adam was kneeling beside her, pushing her head back. 'Poison,' he snapped. 'It must be poison. Bring me mustard and water.' He squeezed her jaw, and she fought against him. The pain was so intense she wanted to grit her teeth tighter and tighter. But his fingers were too strong for her and a moment later they were inside, forcing their way down her throat. She tried to scream and instead vomited, her head jerking forward, her body sliding off his knee to strike the floor.

'My God, my God,' Nivernais was saying. 'Poison? In my house?'

'That is impossible, Your Excellency,' Guerchy was insisting. 'The Chevalier is having a fit. I have seen such things before, in the East. You will remember that he has been to Russia? It is some disease he has picked up out there.'

Geneviève wanted to shout his name, to denounce him to the world, but the room was now spinning around her head as she vomited again, and hit the floor again, and felt herself being dragged up again, while the pain tore at her belly like a living enemy.

'A surgeon,' Nivernais decided. 'We must have him to a surgeon. He must be bled.'

No, she wanted to scream. My God, no.

'No,' Adam said. 'It will not be necessary. Here, Chevalier, you must drink this.'

She inhaled the potion and retched again. Mustard. Once again he held her jaws apart while he poured the nauseous mixture down her throat. She gagged and retched and rolled across his knee to vomit again and again.

'What a to do, eh, what a to do,' Nivernais was saying, walking round and round her. Guerchy was silent. The wretch, she thought. My God, when I recover the use of my limbs . . . but it was a case of if. The pain was fading, but she found to her horror that she could not move.

'A stretcher,' Nivernais was saying. 'He is paralysed.'

'I will see to it,' Guerchy said.

No, she screamed, insider her head. Do not let him touch me. Pompadour's creature.

'*I* will see to the Chevalier,' Adam said. 'It is my duty.' He turned her over, very gently. She could feel vomit trickling away from the corner of her mouth and down her cheek. But she *could* feel. And she could feel Adam's arms going under her knees and her shoulders, and raising her from the ground.

'I will come with you,' Guerchy said.

No, Geneviève begged with her eyes. For God's sake, no.

'That will not be necessary, monsieur,' Adam said.

'But I insist. If you are her equerry, I am her deputy. This is a serious matter.'

'One to which I shall attend,' Adam said, still holding Geneviève in his arms.

'Would you deny me, Scotsman?'

'If I must.'

'Why, monsieur, you'll support those words.'

'Willingly, monsieur, the moment I have attended to my master.'

'Now, monsieur,' Guerchy shouted, and Geneviève heard the rasp of steel as he drew his sword. My God, she thought, he will kill me yet. Worse, he will kill Adam as well. She summoned all her strength, drew a long breath; she could hear it wheezing into her lungs.

'Put up your sword, monsieur,' she whispered. 'It is my wish that Captain Menzies attends me, and none other.' She turned her head, with an equal effort, to look at him. He met her gaze for a moment, and then stepped back.

'Yet will my honour be satisfied, Chevalier. When you are well again.'

'Be sure I shall be ready, my lord,' Adam said, and carried her from the room and up the stairs. He frowned at her as she would have spoken, and she gathered they were being accompanied. 'I will need the Chevalier's manservant, Jules,' he said.

'I am here, monsieur. My God, is the Chevalier ill?'

'He will be well. But we shall have some more of that mustard compound, and I wish an enema prepared. You'll see to it, Jules.'

The door to her bedchamber was opened, and an anxious valet gaped at her.

'Outside,' Adam snapped. 'And stand guard. No one is to be admitted except Jules.'

'My dear Captain Menzies,' Nivernais was protesting. 'I feel I should remain in attendance. After all, it has happened in my house . . .'

'If I am to cure the Chevalier, My Lord Duke, I must have complete privacy.'

'Witchcraft,' Nivernais muttered. 'I will have no witchcraft.'

'Would you rather answer for the Chevalier's death?' Adam laid her on the bed.

'Well . . .'

'Believe me, my lord, I can cure him, but I need to be left alone.'

'Hum. Very well, Captain. But if you do *not* cure him . . .'

The door closed. Geneviève realised she had been holding her breath, that the room was still revolving round and round her head.

'Adam,' she whispered.

'Hush, my darling,' he said. 'Don't attempt to speak. You will need all your strength.'

She lay still, and allowed her eyes to close. Immediately the sensation of spinning through space redoubled, and she was only half aware of being undressed, of hearing Jules' voice, of having towels placed beneath her, of again vomiting as liquid was poured down her throat at the same time as her bowels were also emptied, time and again. She wanted them to stop, because of her agony, but her brain continued to flicker; if she was feeling pain, then she was feeling, and the poison was being extracted from her. And at last she slept, and awoke to a raging thirst and a tumbling headache and a great void where once she had possessed a stomach, and saw Adam asleep in his chair by the bed.

The candle had burned low, and the room was almost dark. She could not see Jules. But she was awake, and alive, and . . . she watched the door move, for it was that sound which had awakened her. She moved her hand, seeking her poniard, but it was not there. The door swung inwards, and for just a moment the intruder was silhoutted against the light outside.

Geneviève sucked air into her lungs. 'Adam,' she screamed.

Adam raised his head, and Guerchy struck at him with his drawn sword. But the main force of the blow was taken by the chair, and Adam was on his feet, swinging the cushion to hit his adversary across the head and tumble him against the wall, while drawing his own weapon.

'You first,' Guerchy snarled, and drove a deep thrust, which Adam avoided by throwing himself to one side, before lunging in turn, but Guerchy was too quick for him. He stumbled against the chair, kicked it to one side, and drove the Scot back with the fury of his assault. My God, Geneviève thought, attempting to roll across the bed. Adam was a soldier, not a fencing master. He would hardly sustain such an attack for very long. She found herself on her face on the far side of the bed, and there on the table was her swordbelt and rapier. She gasped, rose to her knees, siezed the hilt and drew the blade.

Adam was against the far wall, pressed against the wash basin, knocking over the ewer and spilling water with his left hand as he desperately parried thrust after thrust with his right.

'You stand in need of practice, my dear Captain,' Guerchy smiled. 'Shall I kill you, I wonder, or merely maim you for life?'

'Neither, my lord,' Geneviève gasped. She wrapped her left arm round the bedpost, thrust her right hand forward; the sword point just touched Guerchy's shoulder. 'Drop your weapon or die.'

Guerchy hesitated, and Adam looked past him. 'Chevalier,' he shouted.

But it was too late. Guerchy had turned, his mouth slowly opening as he gazed at the woman kneeling on the bed; Geneviève had not realised she was naked.

'By all that is Holy,' Guerchy whispered.

'Now you *have* to kill him,' Adam said.

Geneviève stared at her enemy. The effort of moving had brought waves of nausea back up from the pit of her stomach, and she knew that in a very few moments she was going to faint. But she could not kill a defenceless man; however many her crimes they had never included cold blooded murder.

'You'll pick up your sword, monsieur,' she said.

Guerchy shook his head.

Blows hammered on the door. 'What is happening in there?' Nivernais was shouting. 'Chevalier? Are you all right?'

'Let me,' Adam said.

'No,' Geneviève said. 'Fetch my robe.'

She kept her sword presented to Guerchy's breast, while Adam stepped round him and picked up her undressing gown. Geneviève wrapped herself in the robe, lay down; indeed she half fell down. The room was going round and round.

'What's to be done?' Adam asked.

'Open the door,' she said.

'But . . .'

'Open it.'

A last hesitation, and he turned the key. Nivernais pushed in, followed by Jules and several other servants.

'Chevalier? Monsieur de Guerchy? What is happening here?'

'There is your assassin,' Geneviève said. But was it her speaking? The voice seemed to come from very far away.

'De Guerchy?' Nivernais was amazed.

'Aye.' She was too exhausted to think any more. 'Arrest him, and send him back to France.' And do not listen to what he has to say, she thought. It is all lies. Lies . . . lies.

She opened her eyes, discovered she had been dreaming. Because she *had* to have been dreaming. She lay in her bed, and the drapes were drawn to allow the sunlight to stream into the room. Jules sat in the chair by the bed, reading a book. Jules? Watching over her as Bertrand had watched over the King. But she felt perfectly well, except for a slight weakness. And the persistent memory of bad dreams.

'Jules?' Even her voice was weak. But it was her voice.

His head came up, the book snapped shut. Monsieur?' he cried. 'Oh, monsieur. Oh, dear, sweet mademoiselle.' He seized her hand to kiss it.

'Really, Jules. What time is it?'

'Approaching noon, monsieur.' Jules regained his composure.

'Then I have slept too long. Where is my chocolate?'

'Chocolate? Captain Menzies has said you are to drink nothing like that.'

'Captain Menzies? Stuff and nonsense.' She attempted to push herself up, discovered to her horror that she could not move. And her dream was hammering at the back of her memory. 'Jules. Last night . . .'

'Last night, monsieur?'

'That drink. Jules . . .'

'Six days ago, monsieur.'

Slowly she subsided back on to the pillows. 'Six days?'

'Indeed, monsieur. Your life has been in grave danger.'

'But . . . my God, six days. Where is Captain Menzies?'

'Sleeping, monsieur. We have taken turns at watching you.'

'But . . . six *days?* Can you wake him, Jules? I must see him.'

'I am instructed not to leave your side for a moment, monsieur, until relieved by the captain.'

'I am all right again now, Jules. Do as I ask. It is very important.'

'So is your life, monsieur,' he said, as he opened the door. 'To me at the least.'

Dear Jules. She had never done more than dislike him, as her father's creature, as a constant reminder of the unnatural sham she was forced to support. She had never considered what his true feelings might have been, towards her. And now he had sat beside her for six days, twelve hours a day. Could there be truer devotion?

Save from Adam. She watched the door, heart pounding, watched it open, watched him standing there, only half dressed. Then he entered the room, closed and locked the door behind him. Jules thoughtfully remained on the outside.

'Geneviève?' he asked. 'Are you really speaking?'

'I owe you my life. And Jules.'

He shrugged. 'We have but done our duty, Chevalier.'

'A moment ago you called me Geneviève.'

'I have called you Geneviève often, as you lay there sleeping. Lying there, you are, Geneviève.'

'I am still lying here, Adam.'

'But your brain is awake again, and that brain belongs to the Chevalier d'Éon.'

She sighed. 'Then you will not hold me in your arms, kiss me, love me?'

'That would be unnatural, Chevalier.'

Oh, damn and blast you, she thought. I hate you, hate you, hate you, for a Calvinist rogue.

'No doubt you are curious as to what has been happening,' he said.

She shrugged in turn. 'Is it important?'

'Very. How much do you remember of that night?'

'I remember drinking, and then falling down.'

'Do you not remember Guerchy breaking in here?'

She frowned at him. 'I remember a dream.'

'No dream, Chevalier.'

'But . . .' She sat up again. 'My God . .'

'Oh, indeed. He saw you, naked.'

'And . . . ?'

'Said nothing.'

'Where is he now?'

'Nivernais sent him back to France, under arrest. And do you know what he has done? Immediately instituted proceedings again you, for libel.'

'Libel?'

'Well, slander. For accusing him of poisoning you.'

'My God,' she said. 'Can it not be proved?'

He shook his head. 'I have been able to discover none.'

'But he was discovered in my chamber. How does he explain that away?'

'He was seeking me. He had challenged me, remember?'

Geneviève thrust both her hands into her hair; it needed cutting, as usual. 'And what is the outcome?'

'Who knows? We only received notice of his action in yesterday's mail. The case will take some time to go to court. But surely the man is clutching at straws.'

'You think so? Pompadour's creature. Oh, she put him up to this. She'd not dare harm me in France. But in England . . . my God, she must be cursing me for not killing him.'

'I'm not sure I understand.'

'Well,' she explained. 'It is Pompadour's doing. She must have been certain that he would either succeed, or be killed. Instead of which we let him go, accused of poison. For her to have him eliminated on his return to France would only have compounded her guilt. So she must take me to court, and prove to the world that I am a liar.'

'Then why has he not also accused you of being a woman?'

'Oh, he is saving that to prove just how much of a liar I am.'

'Then you must go back to France and fight him.'

'He'd never accept a challenge from me.'

'I meant, in the courts.'

Geneviève chewed her lip. 'Either way,' she said, half to

herself, 'they will gain the advantage. My mission is vital to French security. To give it up for a personal matter would hardly please the King.'

'Your mission,' he said bitterly. 'To suborn one or two English ministers? To seduce a princess? That is a mission?'

She glanced at him. If only she could think clearly.

'I will tell you all, when I can,' she said. 'But I beg you to understand that my mission *is* vital to the security of France. I cannot go back to Paris until it is completed.'

'You'd allow Guerchy to win his case by default?'

'A much greater case would go by default were I to return to France empty handed. Either way I would be lost. And you too.'

'I doubt I am important enough, for you to worry about my fate, Chevalier.'

She gazed at him. Oh, Adam, she thought, if you could only unbend, for but a moment . . . you unbent once, and what a spendid summer that was. But she was not going to beg him.

'I worry about all of my people, Captain Menzies,' she said. 'Now I must make haste to regain my strength. Food. And wine.' she smiled at him. 'You may taste it for me.'

He bowed. 'I shall see to it. Shall I inform the Ambassador that you have recovered?'

'You may. Not that I wish to see him immediately. But I would like those interviews he promised me arranged as soon as possible. Is my illness noised abroad?'

'Oh, indeed, Chevalier. London speaks of nothing else.'

'Damnation. Well, we must work with what we have. Oh, there is one thing more, Captain. I am expecting a visitor.'

'Chevalier?'

'I cannot tell you his name, because I do not know it. But I imagine he will be a seafaring man, by no means well to do, you understand. He has information of great importance for me.'

'Why, such a fellow was here two days ago.'

'Adam.' She threw back the covers. 'Where is he now?'

'I have no idea. I sent him away again. I did not suppose you could possibly have any business with such an uncouth rogue.'

'Oh, my God. But . . . you must find him.'

'He will be coming back, Chevalier. I told him you were ill, well, he could have learned that by listening to any street corner gossip, but that you would be well again, and that he could return in a week.'

'A week,' she muttered. 'From the day before yesterday. Pray God he comes.'

'I am sure he will, Chevalier,' Adam said coldly. 'How could any man resist your charms?'

Silly wretch. She wondered she did not send *him* back to France. As he had said, he was not the least important to anyone. So Richelieu supposed he mattered to *her,* well, why should he? He had given her the best tumbling of her life. She had enjoyed the six months they had spent together, sleeping every night in each other's arms. But she had never made the mistake of falling in love with him. Or, if she had supposed she might do so, she had very rapidly pulled herself back from the abyss. As he so truly said, the Chevalier d'Éon could never love, any more than could his sister. They were twin stems of but a single branch, and it was absurd for her ever to suppose they could be separated. If Adam intended to be a total fool, then she must allow him to be a total fool. She had been given a task to perform, and if she succeeded the entire world would be at her feet. She could buy as many Adams as she chose.

So damn Adam for sending the seafaring man away. But surely he would come back, and meanwhile she could regain her strength, as if even eating was a simple matter with her stomach turning somersaults.

'We have been invited by Mr Fox to a supper party,' Nivernais informed her when she was finally able to dress and sit down at table. 'For next Wednesday evening. By then hopefully you will have recovered your entire health. And may I say, my dear Chevalier, how dreadfully sorry I am that such a mishap should have overtaken you under my roof.'

But there was no truth in his words. He would just as soon have seen me die, Geneviève thought. He regards me as · parvenu, even as a rival, and he is quite right. Once again the dreadful loneliness which was her constant companion threatened to overwhelm her.

But she merely smiled at him. 'Next Wednesday will be very fine, thank you, Your Excellency. I am well on my way to regaining my best health.'

'I can see the bloom in your cheek, Chevalier. What do you think of the news from Paris?'

Once again she produced a smile. 'I think you were too lenient with the Seigneur, Your Excellency. I had supposed you would send him back in chains.'

'My dear Chevalier, how could I do such a thing? The scandal ... and it was not proved. It has not been proved. I do not see how it can *ever* be proved.'

This time her smile was icy. 'It matters very little, I do assure you. I have powerful friends at Versailles, and they will attend to this upstart. Certainly they will make sure that nothing interferes with my purpose here. I look forward to meeting Mr Fox.'

But where, oh where, was the seafaring man? 'Tell me of him,' she begged Adam.

'An ill favoured lout.'

'A Frenchman?'

'Partly. He claimed to hail from one of the islands in the Channel. Alderney.'

'I have seen it,' she said, recalling the carefree days when she had strolled the cliffs of Jobourg. 'Then is he playing the traitor. Alderney is subject to England.'

'Oh, he would play the traitor, Chevalier,' Adam agreed. They walked in the garden of the Embassy, watching the flowers fade and the leaves come drifting down. Occasionally their hands brushed. But they both wore gloves, as they both wore breeches and boots. 'I said he was an ill favoured lout.'

'Necessity requires some strange bedfellows,' she remarked, and turned to him. 'Adam ...' Now why, she thought? Have you not resolved never to beg him? But how can I not, when my body cries out for his? Then you are, after all, nothing but a weak willed woman, anxious for surrender. 'Adam. Can you not soften your heart just a little? I do what I do, because I must. But I do it for us, for our future, for a lifetime of happiness. And that can only come from wealth and security.'

'Happiness, Chevalier, is where a man and a woman find each other and love each other. It matters naught whether they are wearing satin or sackcloth, whether they eventually lie on the grass or in a gilded bed.'

'Oh, you . . .' But she kept her temper. 'Then by your own words, Captain Menzies, as we have known happiness, we should be able to find it wherever we are standing, whatever we are wearing, whatever guise we may be forced to assume.'

He flushed. 'I have no skill with words, Chevalier.'

'I am not seeking words, Adam.'

They stood facing each other, their lips only six inches away from each other. Love me, she willed with her eyes, here and now, love me. Come with me to my bedroom, and love me there. Send away all these groundless fears, these senseless objections, these meaningless rules you have made up for life. Love me, and I will love you. I will love you, Adam, and follow you to the end of the earth. Only do it now. Now. Now …

'Ahem,' Jules said.

'Oh, Jules,' she snapped. 'Have I no privacy?'

'I beg your pardon, Chevalier. But there is a gentleman to see you. A seafaring man, by the look of him.'

Chapter Eleven

The seafaring man turned out to be tall and cadaverous, with a deeply lined mahogany brown face, but surprisingly lively blue eyes. He wore a faded blue smock over canvas trousers, held his cap in both hands, frowned when Geneviève appeared in the doorway.

'The Chevalier d'Éon?' His words rolled out of the corner of his mouth.

'I am he. You'll remain outside, Adam.' She closed the door. 'You saw my signal?'

'I did, your Honour.' He looked embarrassed. 'I had expected an older man.'

'My age is no concern of yours, monsieur. Are my goods in England?'

He nodded. 'Aye. There's a small problem.'

'You'll explain?'

'Well, your Honour, my people don't like it. Those barrels. 'Tis devilment, they say.'

'Have they never smuggled before?'

'It's a living, your Honour. But wine, or perfume. They're asking what's in that cargo.'

'Gunpowder. There's no devilment in gunpowder.'

'No, your Honour, there ain't. But that stuff ain't like any gunpowder I've ever seen.'

Her turn to frown. 'You have looked at it?'

'Well, your Honour, my people wanted to know.'

'But now they are no wiser. Believe me, it is nothing more *than* gunpowder. A form of gunpowder.'

'I doubt they'll accept that, your Honour. And even if it is true, 'tis not the sort of stuff one wants lying around, so to speak.'

Geneviève took a turn up and down the room. 'Where is it now?'

'Well, your Honour, it's in a house in Dorset. A house I've used these ten years, with never a complaint from the owners. 'Till now.'

'Dorset? Have you no storage facilities nearer to the Solent?'

'Well, I have your Honour, but naught so good. You'll understand that it ain't easy to bring the stuff ashore so close to a big seaport.'

'Then that will have to do.' She found herself smiling. 'I do not even know your name.'

'Skillett, your Honour. Joseph Skillett.'

'Well, Captain Skillett, the barrels will have to stay where they are for the time being. Where is your vessel?'

'Well, your Honour, she's lying in Poole, in Dorset. We're a fishing craft, you'll understand, and after doing our little bit of business we're away to a proper port to sell our catch. And maybe, I thought, we've sprung a plank and needs to lie up for a while while we looks at it.'

Geneviève nodded. 'Very good. But you can get her to sea?'

'Oh, aye. I can float her on any tide. But the fact is, your Honour, my lads won't have that stuff back on board again, not for nothing.'

'It's quite harmless unless you hold a match to it, Captain Skillett.'

'They'll not believe it, your Honour.'

Geneviève stopped her perambulating, slapped her hands together. Richelieu and his damnable plans. There could be no question of abandoning the enterprise, with Adam's life at the end of it. Yet nothing could have been more dogged by misfortune. No, not misfortune. Never misfortune. Guerchy had been planted by the Pompadour, and Richelieu had just been overelaborate. But she could combat all of that, with her own courage and skill.

She turned to face him. 'Would your men be prepared to transport the gunpowder by sea if I sailed with them, Captain?'

'You, your Honour?'

'If I am on the vessel, they can hardly suppose anything will happen to them, at least from the gunpowder. I am not about to blow myself up.'

'True.' Skillett scratched his chin. 'True.'

'You will remain with your vessel in Poole Harbour until I come to you.'

'And when might that be, your Honour?'

'I do not know. It may be several weeks, or it may be two or three days.'

Skillett's fingers moved to his hair. 'And the powder has to be stored that time?'

'I'm afraid so, Captain Skillett. You are being well paid.'

'Well paid,' he muttered. 'I ain't received nothing yet.'

'I shall see to it before you leave, Captain. Now all you have to do is give me the name of your craft.'

'The *Alderney Rose,* your Honour.'

'Lying in Poole. The *Alderney Rose.* I shall look forward to seeing her.'

He will do anything you tell him to do, Richelieu had said. God damn and blast Richelieu. Or had he known all along? Captain Skillett could be led, but he certainly would never be sent.

'Secrets,' Adam said. 'Do you know, for a moment there this afternoon, I thought you were going to share them with me, Chevalier?'

He need not have added the title. He was again angry. And how I want to share my secrets with you, Adam. But what would your reaction be? She had no doubts at all. He would insist upon heading the raid himself, and equally he would insist that she remain behind. And he would be killed.

The other way they would both be killed. What a choice. I seek fame and wealth and position, she thought, and I am more certain of finding a coffin. She found herself smiling. Not even a coffin. If she was anywhere near that explosive when it went up, there would be nothing left of her at all. Just the memory, and the question, was she a man or a woman? Those who knew the answer were unlikely to divulge it.

'Am I that amusing?' Adam asked.

'I love you,' she said. 'So I am entitled to find you amusing, my dear Adam. But I was not smiling at you. A thought had crossed my mind.' She held his hands. 'I have secrets, because I must. Believe me, my darling, I shall be straight with you whenever I can. And in the meantime I am most grateful for your presence, and for your support. You have saved my life. Therefore my life is yours.'

'Then throw off those breeches and come away with me.'

She sighed. 'It is not possible.'

He freed himself. 'You do not wish to. This unnatural life you lead is too attractive.'

She bit her lip. She wanted to take him in her arms, to swear to him that it was not so, that the moment her mission was completed she would do anything he asked. But she could not make herself tell the lie. Could she *ever* give up the excitement of being the Chevalier d'Éon, the freedom of being a man, the heart swelling pleasure of being famous, or even infamous?

'I love you,' she said again. 'I had never thought to be able to love any human being, but I love *you*. I know that now. Can that not suffice?'

'No, Chevalier,' he said. 'It cannot possibly suffice until I know, until *you* know, whether you love me as a man or a woman. You'll excuse me.'

'Adam . . .' But she hesitated. She could make no promises, and she dared not tell him what she was about. She allowed the door to close and could then throw herself across her bed and give way to tears. Because at the end of it all she was a woman. And because she was the loneliest creature on this earth.

'It is a private party, you'll understand,' Nivernais explained. He tapped his nose. 'But there is more business done at private parties than at public ones, eh? I beg you only to remember what I told you, that there is no greater rogue in all England than this man Fox.'

Who turned out to be a large, jolly looking man with fat red cheeks and heavy eyebrows. 'Why, Chevalier,' he said, taking Geneviève's hand between both of his. 'Your reputation scarce does you credit. Allow me to present my wife.'

Geneviève kissed Caroline Fox's hand. 'The pleasure is mine, madame.' But as with most English women, she found her rather plain and quite lacking in elegance.

'Our guests are impatient to make your acquaintance, my dear Chevalier,' Mrs Fox said, tucking her arm under hers. 'It is only a small party, you'll understand, but the dear Duke of Nivernais told us you wished to meet England's leaders in an informal atmosphere.'

'Admirably put, madame,' Geneviève agreed, and was introduced to several men and their ladies, none of whom really interested her at all, as they did not include Mr Pitt.

'Well, what would you,' Fox explained over dinner. 'He'd not come. Believe me, Chevalier, he is the most confoundedly stiff-necked man I know.'

'He does claim to be ill, Harry,' said the gentleman one removed from Geneviève.

'He is always claiming to be ill,' Fox huffed. 'But we shall save such talk until after dinner. Do you intend to explore England, Chevalier?'

'Perhaps,' Geneviève agreed. 'When my business is completed.'

'You must allow me to be your guide,' said the man on her right. 'I have estates in Yorkshire, and know the north very well.'

She could not even remember his name, but he was distinguished looking, with somewhat severe features which he could relieve by the most brilliant smile, and a tall, lean, slightly stooped body. Apart from herself – she was wearing blue satin – he was the best dressed man in the room.

And to her surprise she discovered that the entire table had fallen silent, as if awaiting her reply.

'That sounds very attractive, monsieur,' she said. 'I should be delighted to accept. Whenever I can.'

For a moment longer the table remained silent. Then the man said, 'Capital. We must talk of it later,' and immediately the conversation broke out with renewed vigour, far more excitedly than before. Geneviève attempted to catch Nivernais' eye, for he was seated obliquely opposite, but he was deep in conversation with the woman next to him, although she could have sworn he was well aware that she was looking at him.

'Is it true, Chevalier, that an attempt was made to poison you, last week?' inquired the lady on her left.

'I'm afraid it is, madame.'

'But . . . how terrible. The villain was taken?'

'He was returned to France, madame.'

'And is now suing you for slander,' Fox said. 'Ha ha. What a rum world it is to be sure, Chevalier. In England we'd have turned him off.'

'Turned him off?'

'Hanged him,' her new friend said.

'Ah. But the Seigneur de Guerchy has powerful friends. In France it is all a matter of whom you know,' Geneviève pointed out.

'Justice by rank, what? Ha ha,' Fox shouted, and then suddenly stood up. 'Ladies?'

His wife obediently also rose, and stepped away from the chair hastily pulled back by one of the footmen. The other ladies followed her example, and filed from the room.

'Thank God for that,' Fox declared. 'My belly is bursting.'

Instantly two of the footmen came forward, each carrying a large porcelain chamber-pot. The gentlemen released their breeches.

'Will you not, Chevalier?' asked her friend.

'I have no need, thank you very much, monsieur.'

'Then I shall not either,' he declared.

'Ha ha,' Fox shouted. 'Do you suffer from the same complaint, Ridingham?'

'I beg your pardon?' the Earl of Ridingham inquired.

'Ha ha,' Fox shouted again. But now he was busy himself, uttering a great sigh of relief as he half filled the pot.

'Do I have a complaint, monsieur?' Geneviève asked.

One of the other gentlemen sat himself opposite. 'You have no idea the rumours that are spread of you, Chevalier.'

'Tell me.'

'Why, sir, I dare not, or you would call me out. One of the rumours is to the effect that there is no finer swordsman in France.'

'I have some skill, monsieur. But I do not fight my friends.' She smiled at them. 'And we are all friends here, are we not?'

'Oh, indeed.' The footman had placed an enormous decanter in front of Fox, and from this he now filled his own glass with port before passing it to his nearest neighbour on his left. 'Well, then, Chevalier, tell us true. Did you conduct a series of duels last summer dressed as a woman?'

'Why, monsieur, I did.' Geneviève continued to smile. 'Times were hard, just at that moment. And I do assure you, properly dressed, I can pass for a woman.'

'I have no doubt of it at all,' Fox agreed.

'You are the most handsome devil I have ever laid eyes on,' Ridingham murmured, removing himself to sit next to her, and filling her glass with port.

'I suppose that is where the rumours began,' observed the other gentleman, whose name, Geneviève now remembered, was Clossett.

'You still have not told me what the rumours are, monsieur.'

'Well . . .' Clossett went very red in the face, busied himself with producing an ornate box from which he poured a quantity of snuff on to the back of his hand, before inhaling vigorously.

'Ha ha,' Fox shouted. 'That you are indeed a woman,

Chevalier, who prefers to masquerade as a man.'

Still Geneviève smiled, while Nivernais appeared to have swallowed some of his port the wrong way. 'That is hardly likely, messieurs. I hold the rank of captain in the De Beauffremont Dragoons, and indeed have seen service with them. They'd soon wheedle out a cockless wonder, I assure you.'

'Besides,' Nivernais pointed out, having recovered his breath, 'the Chevalier holds the Cross of St Louis, as you can see from his sash. The most prized order in all France, messieurs.'

'You could never be a woman, my dear Chevalier,' Ridingham murmured, refilling her glass, although she had taken no more than a sip. 'They are detestable creatures, and you, you are magnificent.'

Now Geneviève did drink some port, although her own bladder was indeed feeling fairly full. Suddenly she understood the reason behind the interest in her acceptance of his invitation. The English vice, Richelieu had called it.

'To say truth, Chevalier,' Fox remarked, 'whether you are a man or a woman, you are a damnedly handsome fellow, but damnedly young, too, for such a mission. I am informed you have plenary powers.'

'I do, Mr Fox, and would greatly appreciate a word with you in private.'

'Oh, speak up, man, speak up. We are all friends here. All politicians. And all capable of keeping our secrets, eh? Speak up.'

'Well, monsieur, my mission is a very simple one. To discover whether it is not possible to end this silly rivalry between our nations. Surely four hundred years of enmity is sufficient.'

The table fell silent. Then Fox drank port, noisily.

'Well said, Chevalier,' Ridingham remarked. 'I can think of no greater boon to mankind, than for England and France jointly to face the world, rather than each other.'

'And how will this miracle come about?' Fox demanded. 'Not by us five sitting here drinking port.'

'I have certain proposals to make,' Geneviève ventured.

'Ha ha. Now we get down to the nitty gritty.'

'And these proposals could easily be incorporated into a general treaty of peace and friendship between our two nations.'

'There would have to be certain adjustments,' Fox pointed out. 'We should certainly have proposals of our own.'

'You may put them, monsieur.'

'India. America. The West Indies. Safeguards for Hanover.

All of these things have ever been a bone of contention between us. I do not see, Chevalier, with the best will in the world, how they can be resolved to the satisfaction of all.'

'We can try, monsieur.'

'I doubt even that, sir,' Clossett remarked. 'Are not our colonists already at each other's throats in the Americas? Your people keep building forts, following the line of the Ohio River, as I understand it . . .'

'Clossett is an expert on American affairs,' Fox said.

'Well, sir, it is outrageous, nothing less than an attempt to confine our people within the limits of the Allegheny Mountains and the sea. There's a place I would like to see adjustment.'

'India,' Fox said dreamily. 'This fellow Dupleix is leading us a merry dance. Why, sir, he is arming the princess with European muskets and cannon. That can forbode nothing good, I tell you that.'

Geneviève was taken quite by surprise; Richelieu had suggested nothing of such strength of feeling about colonial matters. 'Why, messieurs, I had supposed we would commence by discussing European affairs.'

'A pox on Europe,' Fox declared. 'Enough English blood has been spilled on European soil, sir. You are interested in Europe? Should we give you a free hand on the continent, would you give us a free hand elsewhere? Withdraw your people from Canada and the Ohio Valley, from India, from Martinique and Guadeloupe?'

'You ask the world,' Geneviève objected, 'in exchange for a quarter of it? Would you withdraw from Hanover?'

'Why, sir, how can we do that, as we never occupied it in the first place? Hanover is Hanoverian.'

'And you happen to have a Hanoverian king, so there is an English enclave in the heart of Germany.'

'Or a German enclave in the heart of England, what?' Clossett remarked, trying to lighten the atmosphere.

'It is a misfortune,' Fox insisted. 'For England at the least. But it is there, and we must make the best of it. I am sorry, Chevalier, but I find it impossible to see an end to Anglo-French rivalry, and that being so, I doubt we shall ever find ourselves upon the same side when it comes to blows. We must content ourselves with praying that it does *not* come to blows.'

Geneviève realised that there was no hope here. But she was determined to persevere. Her life hung on it. 'Surely what is really required is good will on the part of a few leading men of each nation, monsieur,' she said. 'Men such as yourself, and ...' She glanced around the table. 'And your friends. I may say, Mr Fox, that my powers include the authority to inform you that the French government would be eternally grateful were it possible to arrive at a peace treaty between our two nations, and that you would find such gratitude expressed in the most concrete fashion.'

She paused, hating herself, and hating herself even more as she watched the expression on Fox's face. A rogue, Nivernais had called him, who worshipped only money. But he worshipped patriotism more.

'Bribery, sir?' he inquired, his voice hardly a whisper.

'I doubt it should be expressed in that blunt a fashion, monsieur.'

'Blunt a fashion?' Fox was on his feet. 'You would seek to bribe a minister of the crown, Chevalier? Out, sir. I ask you to leave. Leave my house, sir, this instant. You ...' He pointed at a thunderstruck Nivernais. 'Are you a party to this . . . this excrescence?'

'Why, I ... I ... I ...' Nivernais flushed crimson, looked from Fox to Geneviève.

Who realised that she also was flushing. She stood up. 'His Excellency knew nothing of my plans or my intentions, Mr Fox,' she said. 'I am sorry to have insulted you. It was not my intention, to be sure. You'll make my apologies to your wife.'

'Chevalier.' Ridingham was also on his feet. 'I'll come with you.' He glanced at Fox. 'I am afraid these gentlemen have drunk too much port.'

'Ah, begone with you,' Fox shouted. 'You're a right pair. Oh, aye, sodomities all.'

'You'll answer for that,' Ridingham snapped.

'Leave him be,' Geneviève said. 'My offence is far the greater.' She went into the hall, where a footman was already waiting with her cloak.

'You'll ride in my carriage.' Ridingham was also calling for his cloak.

'Why, my lord ...'

'I insist.' He winked. 'I would carry this discussion further.'

'Are you in the government, my lord?'

'But of course I am.' He winked again. 'I am in charge of His Majesty's privy purse.'

'Which means he controls all the secrets of the realm,' Clossett pointed out, having followed them in an endeavour to heal the breach.

Geneviève hesitated. That Ridingham intended more than a mere continuation of the conversation could not be doubted. But as commander of the English Secret Service he would wield immense power. And certainly he could be no different to the Prince of Conti. But that would mean revealing her secret.

On the other hand, he was very drunk. And he was her very last hope.

'It will be my pleasure, my lord. I'll bid you goodnight, Mr Clossett.'

Ridingham threw his arm round her shoulders as they descended the stairs. 'You should have come to me first, my dear Chevalier. I'd have known how to go about it. Fox fancies himself as a patriot, in the worst possible sense. For how may a man express his patriotism in a more worthwhile fashion than by securing peace for his country, eh? Answer me that?'

'Indeed, my lord, I agree with you.'

'Of course you do. Wait there.' This to his coachman, for as they were now outside the house he proceeded to relieve himself into the gutter. 'Will you not join me?'

It was most certainly necessary, with a difficult evening in front of her. Geneviève got behind a stone effigy of Cupid firing off an arrow and lowered her breeches as quickly as she could. But even so she only just managed it before Ridingham was standing above her.

'You are modest, Chevalier. I like that. But not too modest, I trust.'

'That depends upon my company, my lord,' she said, allowing herself to be assisted into his carriage; the blinds were drawn, and they were completely private.

'We shall to my home,' he said. 'It is not far from here. And there we may discuss your proposals. And sundry other matters I have in mind.' The door was closed and the carriage started to rumble over the cobbles. And immediately Ridingham's arm was round her shoulders again. 'Because you are a dear, dear fellow, my dear Chevalier . . . or may I call you Charles?'

'You may call me anything you please, my lord,' Geneviève agreed, her brain tumbling. He was not yet sufficiently drunk for her to avoid telling him the truth. She had not expected so immediate an assault, had counted on another couple of glasses of port to assist her.

'Then I shall call you Charles. Oh, Charles. Charles . . . He was kissing her cheek, and now he sought her lips. These she allowed, readily enough, bringing up her hands to protect her chest as his own hands were wandering all over the place, but mostly concerned with her breeches. 'Charles, Charles, where have you hid the dear fellow? My dear Charles, say you are a big, big . . .'

'I wear a strap, my lord,' Geneviève whispered. 'That I might not thrust in an unseemly fashion.'

'Ha ha,' he shouted. 'Spoken like a man. You are the most delightful fellow, Charles. So young, and so strong. Why, I have not been so excited in years.' He released her. 'I shall show you.'

'My lord? Would it not be better to wait until we are safely within your house?'

'Bah. It is a long drive. I cannot wait. I am impatient. Impatient, my dear Charles.' He was tearing at his breeches, and now he slid them down round his knees, lurching to the movement of the coach. 'Charles, my dear Charles . . .'

The coach stopped, with a suddenness which sent Ridingham tumbling across on to the seat opposite, while Geneviève had to hang on to the window to stop herself joining him.

'What in the name of God,' the earl demanded, trying to sit up. 'By God . . .'

The door was pulled open, and a lantern thrust inside, seeming to hang immediately above Ridingham's exposed penis.

'By God, the man said; he wore the distinctive red waistcoat of a Bow Street Runner.

'Eh? Eh?' Ridingham at last got himself sitting, dragged up his breeches.

The lantern was held to Geneviève's face. 'You are under arrest, Chevalier.'

'On what charge?' Geneviève demanded.

'Sodomy, Chevalier. And you too, sir.' Obviously he did not recognise the earl, which – as Ridingham's reputation seemed well known – meant that he had been tipped to follow the Chevalier d'Éon, and no one else.

'You cannot,' Ridingham cried, his voice rising. 'My dear fellow, there is a mistake.'

'No mistake, sir. I have my men at my back.'

'And what made you stop *this* coach?' Geneviève inquired, her brain a seethe of anger.

'Information received,' the runner said.

'I am sure this can be decided in a civilised fashion,' Ridingham said. 'You'll accompany me to my home, and there we'll have a glass of wine, and there'll be more, you may be sure, my good man.'

'On the contrary, sir. You and this French gentleman will accompany me to Newgate Prison, and there we'll take statements.'

'You'd seek to have me hanged.' Ridingham declared.

'Indeed, sir, that is my understanding of the law.'

'Oh, my God, my God,' Ridingham cried. 'What's to be done? What's to be done?'

'Why, it becomes necessary to convince this man that he has made a mistake,' Geneviève said, keeping her fury under control.

'Mistake, Chevalier?' the runner inquired. 'Two men alone in a carriage, and one of them baring his all? There is an open and shut case.'

'There is no such thing as an open and shut case. My lord, would you leave the carriage, and permit me five minutes alone with this . . . gentleman?'

'Leave the carriage? Leave the carriage? I say, what . . . ?'

'If you would be so kind, my lord, I think I may be able to save us both a great deal of embarrassment.'

'Well . . .'

'I'll take no bribes,' the runner pointed out.

'I would not waste a sou on one such as you, monsieur,' Geneviève pointed out. 'I am but seeking to save your reputation and possibly your neck. Perjury is also punishable by hanging, is it not?'

'Why, you . . .'

'My lord?'

'You'll not . . . ah . . .'

'I shall take your identity with me to my grave, my lord.'

'*Can* you reason with him? Can you persuade him?' Ridingham's fright was pitiful.

'I think I can, my lord. But it must be done privily.'

'Then I shall get out.' Ridingham scrambled down the steps.

'And remove that lantern,' Geneviève said.

'You plan murder, monsieur,' the runner said. 'I know your reputation.'

Geneviève drew her sword, being careful to keep the hilt towards the runner. 'You may take this as well.'

He hesitated, then passed the weapon to his aide.

'Now, will you remove the lantern and close the door?' Geneviève said. 'What I have to say is for your ears alone, monsieur.'

The interior of the coach was plunged into darkness, and the door was closed. The blinds remained drawn.

'Now, monsewer,' said the runner. 'I'll have no treachery.'

'I plan none,' Geneviève said. 'What I am about to tell you is of the most utter confidence. Do you swear to honour that confidence?'

. 'If it is consistent with my duty, monsewer.'

'It is your duty I am thinking of. I would save you from a ghastly mistake.' While she had been speaking she had been unfastening her clothes. 'Give me your hand.'

'Monsewer?'

As he hesitated, she reached out and took it, brought it towards her, inserted it inside her opened shirt.

'Monsewer?' he gasped.

'I am not done.' Still holding his hand, she removed it from her shirt, and pushed it down the front of her breeches. 'You may find what you will.'

His fingers sifted through her hair, discovered her slit, and jerked out as if burned.

'Monsewer!'

'You gave me your word,' Geneviève said, 'that his would remain our secret.'

The runner had recovered his equanimity, and realised he was alone in a darkened carriage with a very beautiful woman.

'If I could make absolutely sure, monsewer . . .'

Geneviève sighed. 'You may.'

He fondled her breast, investigated her breeches again.

'Oh, monsewer . . .'

'And you will keep calling me monsewer,' she said. 'It would embarrass me greatly were my true sex to become known. On the other hand, were you to force, I should reveal all in court and as I mentioned earlier, you would be under arrest for perjury and false arrest.'

'I should not dream of embarrassing you, monsewer,' he protested.

'Then you can do me another favour,' she said. 'I should

prefer, in the circumstances, not to accompany my friend to his home. Will you take me back to the Embassy?'

'Monsewer, I would take you to the ends of the earth.'

'The Embassy will do, for a start,' she assured him, and kissed him on the mouth. 'I can see we are going to be very good friends.'

'But depend upon it,' she told Adam next morning over breakfast, 'There is some tremendous conspiracy directed against me. What possible reason could the runners have had for stopping Ridingham's coach, had they not been following me from the beginning?'

'And were you not guilty?' he inquired. 'As you were on your way back to his house with him? What would you have done when you got there?'

'I was studying that very fact,' she admitted. 'But don't you see, Adam, he is immensely powerful. And my instructions are to open some sort of negotiations with Englishmen of authority. Not that I am making any progress whatsoever. I really am in a mood of despair, and having you criticising me is no help at all.'

But then it was necessary to face the Ambassador.

'Because I am afraid, Chevalier,' said Nivernais, looking very severe, 'that I am going to have to make a report of all that has happened to Paris. My Embassy has not been the same since your arrival, and it is being brought into disrepute.'

'I was given a task to perform, Your Excellency, and this I am attempting to do.'

'Ha. To accuse a member of your staff of poisoning you? I can tell you, that is the talk of Paris already.'

'Do you suppose it was one of your own people here, Your Excellency?' Geneviève commenced to grow angry.

'Of course it was not.'

'Yet was I most definitely poisoned. But for the prompt action of Captain Menzies I should now be dead. I can assure you, that would have caused even more talk in Paris.'

'Harrumph,' he remarked. 'And then, attempting to bribe the Secretary of State at his own table. Outrageous, monsieur.'

Geneviève nodded. 'Perhaps I was a little too forthright, Your Excellency. I am new to this sort of diplomacy. But as Mr Fox would not take the bait we have lost nothing; from what he said I do not suppose he would have accepted my offer in any event. He is the sort of Englishman we are going to have to fight. He wants all of America, all of India, all of the West Indies. I do not see us ever gaining any accommodation from Mr Fox.'

'I could have told you that, Chevalier. And then, going off with that known sodomite Ridingham . . .'

'He was at the least willing to listen to my proposals,' Geneviève pointed out.

'He wanted to get his hands on you,' Nivernais said, and flushed. 'You do not know sufficient of the ways of the world, Chevalier. Unless . . .' He hesitated, blew his nose.

'Unless I am already that way inclined,' Geneviève remarked.

'I did not say it, monsieur.'

'But I have no doubt you have heard tales to that effect,' Geneviève said. 'Well, it came to naught.'

'I have heard of that also,' Nivernais said. 'To be with the man is bad enough. To be concerned in an arrest, why, I am amazed to find you here this morning. No doubt you bribed the runner?'

'No doubt I did, Your Excellency.'

'And now, the final straw,' Nivernais said. 'Have you heard that there is a wager made in London, concerning yourself?'

'I have not, Your Excellency. May I ask about what aspect of myself it concerns?'

'Well, monsieur, to be perfectly frank with you, it concerns your . . . ahem . . . your sex.' Nivernais flushed scarlet.

Geneviève frowned at him. 'There is a wager concerning my sex?'

'There is, Chevalier. Some fellow has taken odds of fifteen to one that you are a woman.'

'And how does he propose to collect his bet?'

'I have no idea, Chevalier. Although I may suspect that he may summon you to Court over the matter. Think what a scandal that will be.'

Geneviève stroked her chin. 'Do you know his name?'

'I do. 'Tis a surgeon named Hayes. Do you know him?'

'I have never heard of the fellow.' That runner, she thought. The wretched scoundrel.

'Does the bet concern you, Chevalier?'

'Concern me, Your Excellency? Why should anything so foolish concern me? This fellow is obviously deluded by the reports of my having fought some exhibition duels in France, dressed as a woman. It was a necessary subterfuge at the time, and one I regret most heartily. May I ask the amount of the wager?'

'One hundred English pounds. There is a considerable sum.'

'Then the fellow is a bigger fool than he appears. But I should be obliged, Your Excellency, if you *would* discover his address for me. I do not really appreciate being made the object of irrational bets.'

'That you may challenge him and despatch him, you mean.'

'That I may prove to him that I am a man.' Geneviève bowed.

'I shall see what can be done,' Nivernais agreed. 'Meanwhile, you continue to attract the curious. Her Royal Highness the Princess of Wales has invited you to call.'

Another chance? A very last chance. Geneviève was more upset than she dared admit even to herself. It seemed to her that her troubles were gathering. First the poisoning, then the arrest, and now this outlandish bet, all coming one on top of the other. For who would bet a hundred pounds on such a subject unless he, or she, possessed inside knowledge? It had to be the runner. The alternative, that it was someone from the Embassy, was too disturbing for consideration. Although she preserved her privacy with the greatest of care, admitting only Jules and Adam to her rooms, yet was it possible that *someone* had seen her in déshabille, or noticed Jules secreting her menstrual pads, or observed some other telltale aspect of her behaviour. And while it was entirely possible that whoever it was had merely decided that here was a chance to make some money in a hurry, coming on top of the other two episodes it was all too suggestive of a plot, and who would inspire such a plot, but the Pompadour?

But what was to be done about it? She knew so little. The Pompadour seemed set on sabotaging her mission. But *which* mission? Could it be possible that the King had kept the attempt on the English fleet a secret from even the royal mistress? The Pompadour certainly wanted war with England, and she also wanted the destruction of the Chevalier d'Éon. Therefore she would be killing both birds with a single stone were she to engineer a diplomatic failure by either murdering or entirely discrediting her rival.

But that took her no further, Geneviève realised. The mere fact that Guerchy had not been imprisoned on his return to France, but had indeed been permitted to bring a legal action against his intended victim, showed that to accuse the Pompadour, without irrefutable evidence of her guilt, would be a waste of time. And even with irrefutable evidence, she was not at all sure how Louis would react.

It seemed that every time she aspired to climb a little higher, she actually found herself deeper in the bog that was the French court. But this time there was no escape, nowhere for her to run away to, no one for her to run away with. She was French, and she was working for the French government, and Adam's life was the hostage to which her success or her failure must be related. Therefore her only hope was to succeed, despite the Pompadour. Succeed one way or the other. But pray heaven it might be possible to succeed without involving the mighty engine of destruction with which she had been armed.

And the Princess Augusta was the only remaining ray of hope of doing that. She dressed with the greatest of care, took her place in the carriage for the ride out to Richmond. She could not even make a plan, until she actually met the Princess and her Scottish lover, decide whether she must act the man or reveal herself as a woman, and to which of them.

The journey was interminable, and a fine November rain was falling to make the coach at once damp and chill. She wrapped her cloak around her and brooded at the grey afternoon. This was definitely her very last chance. Certainly King George would discover this visit – if not by his own spies, she did not doubt the Duke of Nivernais would see that he was informed – and therefore her credit with the British Government would be reduced to nothing. And they were signing their own death warrants, the poor fools, without even understanding it.

The drive was lined with sodden oaks, the drip drip of water sounded even above the rumble of the wheels as the carriage slowed to a halt before the Italian style portico of Richmond Lodge. The door was opened, and a footman rolled down the steps while another unfurled an umbrella to shelter her from the downpour. She hurried beneath the shelter of the porch, and was greeted by a young man, who gave her a most elaborate bow.

'Chevalier. This is indeed an honour. London is ringing with your name.'

'You flatter me, monsieur.'

'On the contrary, sir, there has been no such source of…ah… interest for years.'

'You were going to say, gossip,' Geneviève remarked, as she was escorted into a surprisingly small entrance hall, richly enough decorated, from which a curving stairway led to the first floor.

'I would hesitate to say anything which might cause offence to so renowned a swordsman.' he pointed out with unashamed candour. 'I am Sir Peter Frankle, equerry to Her Royal Highness.'

'My pleasure,' Geneviève agreed.

They had reached the next level, and footmen were opening double doors into a delightfully warm and cosy withdrawing room, large enough, but furnished with upholstered chairs and settees, and mahogany wood tables, and containing a huge glowing fireplace at each end. After the chill of the afternoon it was like entering a bedchamber.

'His Excellency the Chevalier d'Éon,' Frankle announced, bowing.

Geneviève followed his example, sweeping her hat so low it brushed the floor, and only slowly straightening to regard the woman in front of her. Augusta of Saxe Gotha was in her middle thirties, a slender, somewhat sombre-looking woman, dressed in strangely oldfashioned clothes, with a pointed stomacher and an obviously tight corset beneath which the hoop ballooned her skirt to give her a perfect figure, according to the fashion of the time. But again, in a strangely outdated mode, her low cut gown contained only the most irrelevant of fichus, and her constricted breasts – which Geneviève estimated were not very large when left to themselves – swelled with every breath. As she had a long neck and an equally long face, the expanse of white above the pale blue of the gown was dazzling, broken only by an equally oldfashioned sarsenet of pearls. Her features were perfectly regular, but again a long nose and a high forehead, combined with a small mouth and very wide set eyes, made her seem ill proportioned. Her fair hair was pulled back in a neat bun, from which descended a coif. She wore no rings, Geneviève discovered as she kissed her knuckles, but this was no doubt deliberate; her long hands and even longer fingers were her only real claim to beauty.

'Cheavlier,' she said, and for all her German origins she had managed to accumulate a much better English accent than her father-in-law. 'It is good of you to call. No French ambassador has visited this house in ten years.'

'It is a privilege, ma'am,' Geneviève said. 'I can only apologise for the carelessness of my predecessors.'

Augusta gave an amazingly girlish giggle, indicated the man standing beside her. 'You have not met the Marquis of Bute.'

Geneviève straightened, well aware that there was another man in the room, or rather, a boy, who could only be the Prince of Wales. But his mother preferred to introduce her lover first. Here was something to be remembered.

'Marquis?' She bowed. Bute was a tall man, in his forties, she estimated, with a somewhat off putting face, for it was very thin, and while the bone structure was fine, and the nose as sharp as the eyes, yet it gave her an uneasy feeling that she was looking at an animated skull.

'As Her Royal Highness has said, Chevalier, ye're welcome in this house, whatever they say of you.'

Geneviève raised her eyebrows. 'Monsieur?'

He smiled, and greatly relieved the gloom of his expression. 'A jest, Chevalier. But your reputation extends before ye like a team of horses. Ye'll wish to meet His Royal Highness the Prince of Wales.'

Another bow, while Geneviève took in the young man. He was tall for his seventeen years, slender, and quite handsome in a Germanic fashion, for he had the popeyes and the bobbing Adam's Apple she remembered from the Grand Duke Peter Feodorovich. But his eyes were much better than the Grand Duke's, brilliant and intense at the same time; they suggested a very active mind, only just offset by the petulant droop of his lips. Yet there was no suggestion of resentment at his being last to be introduced as he gave a brief bow, and said, 'I can only echo my mother's and the Marquis' greeting, my dear Chevalier. Dare we hope that it may herald a new era of relations between our two countries?'

'It is my earnest wish that it should do so, Your Highness,' Geneviève said.

'Good. Good. Then I will leave you to speak with the Marquis. He is more learned in these matters than I. You'll excuse me, Mama.'

He kissed his mother's hand, bobbed his head to Bute, and left the room.

'A good boy,' Augusta remarked. 'He will make a good king. He knows his own mind, and also his own limitations. He is capable of listening to the advice of those who know better than himself. You'll sit down, Chevalier.'

'Ma'am.' Geneviève sat on a straight chair, while the Princess seated herself on a settee, and Bute took his place before the fire.

'We have heard that you possess exceptional powers, Chevalier,' the Princess said, and smiled and blushed together. 'I mean as an ambassador, not in yourself, although there also we have heard the most remarkable tales.'

'I have been forced to live a somewhat unusual life, ma'am,' Geneviève confessed. 'But as to the powers which I have been given for the purposes of this embassy, they are unlimited, providing I bring about peace between England and France.'

'Oh, well said,' Bute agreed. He came across the room, pulled a chair close to Geneviève's, and sat down. 'That the two greatest nations in Europe, in the entire world, should ever be at each other's throats is an abomination. Would you not agree?'

'I am here in that belief, my lord,' Geneviève said, wondering how Frederick of Prussia or the Empress Elizabeth Petrovna would react to his estimation.

'But there are difficulties,' Bute pointed out. 'Mainly in the field of the colonies.'

'I understand that, my lord. And Hanover.'

'Hanover. My God, that is an open wound in the side of Britain. That a single Englishman or Scotsman should lay down his life in defence of such a principality is abhorrent to me, but what will ye, the King will never give it up. And he will expect us to defend it. On the other hand,' he said, with another of his charming smiles, 'no king lives forever.'

'My dear Marquis,' Augusta protested, very quietly. 'I think we should take tea. Do you drink tea, Chevalier?'

'I have done so, ma'am,' Geneviève said cautiously, remembering the scalding glasses of Russia.

'It is a very civilised habit,' Augusta said. 'I approve of taking tea.' She rang a little golden bell on the table beside the settee, and immediately two footmen entered, carrying trays on which were several china cups and saucers and a matching china pot, from which the Princess herself dispensed the thin brown liquid. To Geneviève's surprise it contained lemon, and had a completely different taste from the Russian drink.

'So,' Bute said, 'if we accept that Hanover must remain, our differences must be settled in the colonies.'

'Indeed, my lord? What of the Americas?'

'Bah. A country of forests and rivers, and wild Indians. And I may say it, my dear Chevalier, wilder colonists.'

'Then what would be your consideration regarding them?'

'America is a large continent, as I am informed. Surely there is room for us both?'

'The West Indies?'

'You have islands. We have islands. It is a large world.'

'And India?'

'You have clients, we have clients. India is an even larger world, Chevalier. Competition. Peaceful competition. There is the key to affairs. Our nation prospers by trade, not by spilling blood. This is the eighteenth, not the seventeeth century, Chevalier.'

'Why, my lord,' Geneviève said, heart swelling, 'I had never hoped to hear a politican admit it.'

'Ah, but my lord of Bute is not a politician,' the Princess pointed out. 'He is a philosopher, a man of learning, a man of sense.'

'Indeed, ma'am,' Geneviève agreed. 'But alas, a man without power.'

Augusta and Bute exchanged glances.

'I certainly desire to speak evil of no man, or no woman either, Chevalier,' the Princess said. 'But nothing in this world endures forever. By the very nature of things, change is inevitable. Old men die, younger men take their places. There is no force on earth can alter that simple fact, just as there is no force in England, at the least, can alter the law that when the head of a family dies, he is succeeded by his eldest son, and should that son be unhappily already dead, then by his eldest grandson. That is the law, from the humblest peasant to the King himself.'

'It is the same in France, ma'am. But it sometimes occurs that eldest sons, or eldest grandsons, are obliged to inherit their patrimony while still very young, and it is impossible to decide what course a young man's thoughts, ideas, determination, may take. What advice he may accept.'

Augusta's head came up. 'In my house, Chevalier, my son will always accept *my* advice, adopt my politics. It therefore follows that he will follow the advice of those I choose should advice *me*.' She stood up without warning. Geneviève hastily put down her teacup and also rose. Bute was already on his feet. 'I should like to walk in the garden,' she decided. 'Will you accompany me, Chevalier? The rain has stopped.'

'Of course, ma'am.'

Augusta inclined her head and swept past them. A lady in waiting was already holding her pelisse, and she tucked her head away inside the hood. A footman brough Geneviève's cloak, and she followed the Princess down the stairs and through a glass door into a small rose garden; but the plants were bare of flowers and although the rain had indeed ceased, the drops continued to drip most dolefully from leaf and branch.

'An English autumn,' Augusta remarked. 'Can there be a more dismal time of year? And yet, one knows that after autumn will come winter, and then the spring of a new year. Is that not always a cheering thought, Chevalier?'

Geneviève walked at her side. 'Indeed it is, ma'am.'

'Even a young widow must believe in a new year, some time, Chevalier.' Augusta herself opened a little gate set in a privet hedge, and they passed through and down a much longer path, again bordered with empty flower bushes, backed by another privet hedge, and ending in a gazebo about a hundred feet away. 'And her lot is harder than most.'

'Is it not possible for a young widow, even in a postion of great prominence, great responsibility, to discover some solace, ma'am?'

Augusta gave her a quick glance. 'You have been listening to gossip, Chevalier. The Marquis is my friend, and indeed my mentor. He has one of the most profound brains I have ever discovered. And he is my son's tutor.'

'Ma'am, I ...'

'I respect him more than any man I have ever known,' Augusta continued as if Geneviève had not spoken. 'But one needs more than respect.' Another glance. 'Would you not say, Chevalier?'

'Indeed one does, ma'am.'

They had reached the summer house, and here the Princess paused. Geneviève's heart commenced to pound. Crisis was rushing at her. And, most disconcertingly, for the first time in her life she found herself liking the person she must bedevil.

'It is damp, is it not?' Augusta remarked.

'Allow me.' Geneviève opened the door, and the Princess stepped into the gloom, her arm brushing Geneviève's as she did so.

'I suspect you are but agreeing with me out of politeness, Chevalier.' She seated herself on the wooden bench which ran round the octagonal walls. 'What can a man like yourself, young, handsome, famous, know of loneliness? How can you feel the slightest sympathy for a dowdy woman several years older than yourself?'

307

'Ma'am.' Geneviève sat beside her, seized her hand, and kissed it. 'You have also been listening to gossip.'

'Is it gossip?' She did not withdraw her hand, left it lying in hers. 'Are you not the finest swordsman in France?'

'I doubt that, ma'am. One of them, perhaps.'

Her head turned so that she could look directly into her eyes. 'Have you not, on occasion, masqueraded as a woman?'

Geneviève heaved a sigh. 'The exigencies of my duties, ma'am. You see before you one who was employed by his country in the most devious tasks before he was even due to leave his school.'

Augusta moved her other hand, rested it on Geneviève's cheek for a moment. 'You would make a superb, a beautiful woman, as you are quite the most handsome man I have ever seen.'

'You choose to flatter me, ma'am.'

'Chevalier, we are alone in this gazebo. And I have sufficiently indicated that I would be your friend. Can you not manage to call me by name?'

'I . . . I would deem it an honour.'

'Then do so.'

'Augusta,' Geneviève said. 'Augusta.' She took her other hand as well, kissed that also, and discovered that the Princess's eyes were shut. My God, she thought. But here at last was the possibility of success. She leaned forward and very gently placed a kiss on the small mouth presented to her. Instantly the lips parted, and the hands were moved from hers to rest on her sleeves and bring her closer. Geneviève allowed her own hands to slide round the Princess's shoulders and hug her close, felt the lips leave her.

'Chevalier,' Augusta whispered. 'Oh, Chevalier. How I have dreamed . . . would you be my friend, Chevalier?'

'I could think of nothing more delightful,' Geneviève said, not altogether untruthfully, and found her lips again, while allowing her hands to slide round in front and gently hold the small breasts. Augusta gave a little wriggle of pleasure, and her own hands moved, but stopped short of an exploration of Geneviève's breeches, to her relief.

'You will call again?' the Princess asked.

'I shall indeed,' Geneviève said. 'But you will understand, my dear, sweet Augusta, that my sojourn in London depends entirely upon the success of my mission.' How she hated herself.

How she hated everything she was forced to do, at the whim of people like Richelieu and Conti, and even Louis himself. And discovered she was shocked. All of her life she had hated others, had been concerned only with her own progress; never before could she remember hating herself. Because she was making the mistake of liking this rather helpless little woman. But she was discovering that she liked a great many things about England. Even the mob in Covent Garden had been friendly, once they had discovered she did not mean to defy them.

'I understand that. And I want you to stay. What do you want of me, Chevalier?'

'An understanding, Augusta. I am sure that will suffice.'

The Princess clung to her, resting her head on her shoulder. 'I cannot answer for the King, or for his ministers. He is too dependent on his ministers. There is half the trouble. I can answer for my son. He will be *King*. I promise you this. He will rule. But he will also take advice, from those he can trust. He trusts me. He trusts the Marquis. Does that meet your needs?'

Geneviève kissed her on the lips. 'My needs are peace between England and France.'

'My happiness also indicates that there should be peace between our two countries, Chevalier. I give you my word that all my efforts will be directed to attaining that end.' For a moment longer she clung to her. 'Now we must return, or suspicions will be aroused. But when next you call, Chevalier, my dear dear Chevalier, be sure I shall arrange it that we may be alone, and in more pleasant surroundings than these. Be sure of that.'

Geneviève was so happy she could scarce stop herself from breaking into song as the carriage rumbled back through the streets of London. Only the necessity of hoodwinking the Princess, the looming problem of how to satisfy her as a man, suggested that life was not an endless panorama of the most perfect joy. But it could be done. She was sure of it, one way or another, even if it meant revealing herself as a woman. Augusta sought friendship more than sex.

But the most important thing was that she had secured a stay of execution. It was nothing more nor less than that simple fact.

'I have letters to write,' she announced to Nivernais. 'A very urgent despatch which I would like to send by special messenger to the Duke of Richelieu. And Your Excellency,' she said, 'this man must be entirely trustworthy. I shall use my own valet, Jules Hoggonet'

'My dear Chevalier,' Nivernais protested. 'That is entirely irregular, and quite unnecessary.'

'Nevertheless, I will have it so, Your Excellency. And Your Excellency, I will hold you personally responsible for the safe arrival of Jules in Versailles. Be sure that the Duke would take a serious view of any mishap, or even delay, in a journey of such importance.'

'If you do have news of such importance,' Adam remarked as she sat at her desk, 'then Jules is hardly the fellow, for such a task. Why do you not send me?'

'I wish you here.' Geneviève's pen raced over the paper.

'For, as you yourself said, My Lord Duke,' she wrote, 'His Majesty is very old, and cannot be long for this world. To go to war now, with the prospect of peace looming so close, would be folly. Her Royal Highness is entirely upon our side in this matter, and although there may be certain problems ahead regarding our relationship, I am confident I can resolve these also to our advantage. So, my lord, may I counsel a certain patience? No more than a year at the outside, I am sure of it.'

'You still require a bodyguard,' Adam said bitterly.

Geneviève sanded the sheet of paper, blew it clean, placed it in the envelope and affixed her seal. 'There. I need you here, my dear Captain Menzies, to assuage the desires of a poor girl's heart.'

'You know my feelings on this matter, Chevalier.'

'I do. And I think I have been patient for too long.' She went to the door, where Jules waited, already booted and spurred. 'Now, all haste, Jules. And remember, that despatch is the most urgent message you have ever carried for me. Return with Richelieu's reply at the very earliest moment.'

'Of course, monsieur.' He bowed. 'I shall be back in four days.'

She saw him down the stairs, went to the window to continue watching him as he rode out of the yard. 'You will have to perform the duties of valet, for four days.'

'I?'

'You were happy enough to be my nursemaid when I lay dying of poison.'

'That was different. I would have done as much for anyone.'

Jules was out of sight, lost in the mist. She turned away from

310

the window. 'Would you, Adam?' She went towards him, taking off her coat and wig as she did so. 'Don't you understand? I have succeeded in my mission. There will be peace, between England and France.'

'And that is a cause for celebration? That means Scotland will be entirely subject to English law, and for the rest of our days.'

'It means there will be less bloodshed than otherwise, and that can never be a bad thing.'

'Now you are talking like the woman you are, and not the man you pretend to be.' But he could not keep his gaze from straying as she removed her shirt. He wanted as much as she wanted him.

'As the woman I am. As the woman you know me to be, my darling Adam. Forget all else. Once I have succeeded, I can do what I like. I have been promised the most magnificent rewards should I succeed in this task, and I *have* succeeded.' She stood against him, put both her arms round his neck, kissed him on the mouth.

'Geneviève,' he said. 'Geneviève. And how do I know that when the offer of another scandalous assignment, with another set of rewards, is asked of you, you will not don your breeches without a moment's hesitation?'

'You don't,' she said, and kissed him again. 'But if you love me, Adam, and you do love me, then it will not matter.'

'Geneviève...' He reached behind his neck to move her hands, but she had clasped them, and her strength was not greatly inferior to his. She leaned against him, and as they were only a few inches from her bed, he found himself pushed against it. 'Geneviève...'

'Love me, Adam,' she begged. 'Love me as only you can love me, as only I can love you. Love me, Adam, in spite of what I am, in spite of my crimes, my follies, my senseless ambitions. I doubt I will ever change, Adam. I doubt I can ever change. But love me, *because* you love me, Adam.'

As he did love her. As he would always love her. There could be no doubt. For how long, she wondered, as she lay beneath him and enjoyed the ecstasy of his surging thrusts, has he wanted to surrender? Why, for just as long as I have been too preoccupied to beg him. He is a man, and he wished nothing more. And now, surely, there could be no more problems.

Save of their own making. He had raised himself on his elbow, his face crimson; she could feel his heart thudding against hers. 'You did not come.'

311

'I am too happy,' she said, 'for orgasm. Would you have supposed such a thing could be possible? Listen. You will tell His Excellency that I have caught a chill, and must spend the next four days in bed. Then you will come back up here and minister to me. I wish to see no one until I hear from Richelieu that he approves my plans. I wish to see only you.'

Only Adam. They had never honeymooned before. Even the previous summer, after their one glorious night together, they had been constrained by the necessity to discover a means of livelihood. But now there was nothing to do save wait, and lie in each other's arms, and love. But this was all they would ever do, in the future, she was determined on it. They were the four happiest days she had ever known in her life, a small eternity of smiling love, for Adam, having resisted her for so very long, was as eager as herself, and as contented as herself. She wished Jules would never return, that they could just wait here forever, without even the necessity of moving on to something even more pleasurable.

But Jules did return, on the fourth day as he had promised, splashed to the waist with winter mud, his fifth horse falling beneath him as he entered the Embassy courtyard. And in his wallet was a sealed letter from the Duke of Richelieu.

Geneviève sat at her desk, her hands trembling as she ripped the envelope, her eyes seeming to lose their power, so that she had to blink again and again, as she read the words.

'... matters naught, for the decision has been taken. Therefore on receipt of this letter, which you will immediately burn after committing its contents to memory, my dear Chevalier, you will at once proceed to implement the main part of your plan, which as you will know, involves a visit to the seaside. As hostilities cannot be delayed more than a matter of days, perhaps even hours, I cannot express too strongly the urgency of this step. It must be carried out within forty-eight hours of your receiving this communication. I need also hardly remind you, Chevalier that your entire future depends upon a successful completion of this task. But should you remain in any doubts, should you conceive any idea that by delaying you may improve your situation, I must inform you that there is a warrant for the arrest of both Captain Menzies and yourself, waiting for you here in France. The warrant for Captain Menzies concerns his folly in antagonising the Empress of Russia several years ago and will certainly mean his imprisonment for life; the warrant for you is a result of a legal case which has just been heard here, and in which it has been adjudged that you slandered the Seigneur de Guerchy by falsely accusing him of an attempt to murder you by poison. There is also in possession of the Duke of Nivernais a sealed envelope, which he is instructed to open and execute immediately on receipt of a code word from me. This envelope contains instructions to abrogate the diplomatic immunity granted to Captain Menzies as a member of your staff, and to surrender him to the English authorities as a traitor who fought for the Stuart cause at Culloden, and also to hand you over to the English government as he will have become aware of your design to destroy the English fleet.

'I trust you will reflect upon these measures which I have been forced to take for the good of the country we both honour as our own. I give you my most solemn word as a Frenchman and as a minister of His Majesty the King, that the moment you have completed your mission both of these warrants will be destroyed, and in addition, I wish you to be in no doubt as to the rewards awaiting you upon a successful return to France. Succeed, my dear Chevalier. Succeed for the good of France. Succeed for your own future. You cannot afford to fail.'

Chapter Twelve

Geneviève gazed at the letter for several moments, while its import slowly sank into her brain. She had hoped, she had *believed* – but entirely because she had so desperately wanted to believe. Because had she not known all the while that Richelieu's objective was war?

'What would he have you do now?' Adam inquired, sitting on the edge of the bed.

'Carry out my original instructions,' she said, and bit her lip. She had not meant to tell him.

He was frowning. 'Original instructions?'

'Another assignment.' She got up. 'I must leave London for a few days.'

'That will make a pleasant change.'

'You will stay here.'

His frown deepened. 'Why? Are you on your way to seduce yet another politician?'

'Yes,' she said. 'Yes, that is what I am going to do.'

Adam got up, went to the door, closed it, and leaned against it. 'You are an unsuccessful liar, Geneviève. This instruction has nothing to do with seduction.'

'Indeed?' she demanded, cursing the flush she could feel in her cheeks. 'What other talents have I?'

'That is exactly what I am considering. Swordsmanship. By God. There is an assassination planned.'

'Now, really, Adam . . .' But she hesitated, helplessly.

'And you would leave me behind. I have ever carried your sword for you, Mademoiselle Geneviève.'

'If only there were swords involved.' She sat down again, rested her head on her hands.

'So tell me.' He stood at her shoulder.

How she wanted to tell him. How she had wanted to tell him from the very beginning, to share with him the dreadful burden which was overtaking her.

Adam sat beside her. 'Tell me,' he said. 'If it involves your life, then does it also involve mine.'

Richelieu's instructions were committed to her memory; now it was necessary to implement them. She drew five hundred English pounds from a scandalised Nivernais, then she and Adam made their way first of all to Portsmouth, stopping for the night in Guildford, and finally riding into the seaport at night. Throughout the two days the November drizzle clouded down, and they arrived at their destination soaked and eager only for supper and bed. They clung to each other, but there was no sex involved. Their minds were too consumed with the enormity of the task that lay ahead, the catastrophe of public success being balanced against the catastrophe of personal failure. Even Adam, who conceived himself still to be fighting a war on behalf of his beloved Prince Charlie, was numbed by the thought of destroying fifteen or twenty ships – virtually an entire fleet with a single charge.

'It is not possible,' he had said.

'It is,' she had insisted. 'I have seen it work. It is the most terrifying thing I have ever witnessed.'

'It will revolutionise warfare,' he had said, half to himself, his soldier's brain encompassing all the possibilities.

'It is what it will do to us that concerns me for the moment,' she had pointed out.

The inn belonged to one of Richelieu's people, long settled in England, and available to French agents as they needed him.

'We are going further west for a couple of days.' Geneviève explained over breakfast. 'But when we return, we shall require horses. We shall also leave a change of clothing with you here.'

'Of course, Geneviève,' he agreed.

'It is possible that we shall return privily, in the middle of the night.'

'Of course, Chevalier.'

Geneviève hesitated. 'We may also be wet, and pursued.'

'Of course, Chevalier. I cannot help you outside, but if you can gain my premises unseen, you will have nothing more to worry about.'

'Then I thank you most heartily.' Geneviève squeezed his hands and joined Adam, waiting by the door.

'You told me you could not swim.'

'I cannot. I am relying upon you.'

'And yet you did not wish me to come, in the beginning. Were you contemplating suicide?'

'Hopefully it will not even come to swimming, if all goes well.'

Certainly there was no point in considering anything except success, at this moment. Before leaving Portsmouth they went down to the hard to look out of the harbour, past the forts, at the calm waters of Spithead, where the fleet lay at anchor, nearly a hundred giant three-masters. All was a bustle, with bum boats going to and fro, luggers and cutters sailing up and down; introducing one more into the middle of that armada was not going to be difficult.

As Adam also realised. 'There is some method in Richelieu's madness,' he remarked. 'It could succeed. By its very boldness, it could succeed.'

'But think of the lives,' she muttered, and turned her horse away. That evening they rode over the shallow Hampshire hills and looked down on the harbour of Poole; the town waited at the inner end of a vast area of enclosed water, dotted with islands and entered by half a dozen creeks – the outlet to the sea consisted of a narrow passage hardly a quarter of a mile wide, and bounded to either side by banks of sand. But beyond were the whitecaps of the English Channel, driven by a fresh easterly wind, and in the far distance, some thirty miles away, Geneviève could just make out the shadow of the Isle of Wight, the island which lay off the English coast and enclosed the even larger area of sheltered water known as the Solent. Spithead was at the far end of that. Her stomach rolled. But perhaps it was the thought of crossing those thirty miles of open water.

Adam leaned across to squeeze her hand. She gave him a quick smile, urged her horse down the slope. Poole was a more rugged sister to Dover. Geneviève and Adam, both far too well dressed, attracted a goodly number of whistles and catcalls as they walked their exhausted mounts down the narrow streets, making always for the masts which towered above the chimney pots.

'The *Alderney Rose*?' The customs officer scratched his chin. 'Sprang some timbers, she did. She's over there on the hard.' He looked Geneviève up and down. 'Interested in her, are you?'

'I have business with the master,' Geneviève said. Adam led the horses, and they walked along the cobbled pier, past ship after ship, very reminiscent of Cherbourg – and what memories that brought back, for had she not been betrayed by her instincts on that occasion she would not be here now. But then, she would never have regained Adam either.

The tide was out, and most of the vessels were either on the mud or close to it; at the end of the dock the harbour was even shallower, and here there were two vessels high and dry, leaning against the quayside and secured there by large warps from bow and stern as well as round the masts. Two men sat on the deck of the *Alderney Rose,* mending nets; another was standing on the sand and banging away at the hull in a desultory fashion.

'Good afternoon,' Geneviève said. 'We seek Captain Skillett.'

'He's ashore.'

'Can you tell me where?'

The man pulled a face. 'Maybe the Dorset Arms.'

Geneviève nodded. 'We have some things with us we'd like to leave aboard.'

The man became interested. 'Aboard here, your Honour?'

'We intend to take a short voyage with you.'

'By God, your Honour.' He scrambled to his feet. 'You'll be the gentlemen we was told to expect.'

Geneviève nodded.

The seaman was looking at Adam. 'We was told to expect but a single gentleman.'

'I am he,' Geneviève said. 'But I will not travel without Captain Menzies. Now, would you stow our gear and we shall find the captain. What time will she float?'

316

'Three hours.'

Geneviève looked up at the overcast sky; there was no moon possible. 'And will Captain Skillett be able to find his way out of the harbour in the dark?'

'Oh, aye, your Honour. Captain Skillett sails as well drunk as sober.'

And as she had suspected, and feared, Captain Skillett was most definitely drunk. He sat in the corner of the tap room of the Dorset Arms, sprawled across one young woman while another sat on his lap. Clearly Richelieu was paying him too well, Geneviève thought, as she surveyed him from the door.

'That fellow is of no use to anyone,' Adam remarked.

'At this moment,' she agreed. 'We shall have to sober him up.'

'We shall have to extricate him from here first,' Adam pointed out. For the tavern was full, of sailors and whores, so far as Geneviève could gauge. The air was thick with tobacco smoke and rum-filled breaths, laden with curses and giggles.

'Well, we'd best set about it,' Geneviève decided, and went down the stairs, pushing men and women to each side as she shouldered her way through the throng to stand before Skillett. 'Well, Captain.'

He blinked at her. 'Chevalier,' he said. 'My pleasure, monsieur.' He attempted to rise, which deposited the girl on his lap on to the floor.

'In the name of God you stupid man,' she shouted, spilling her beer.

'And watch your tongue, you idiot,' Geneviève snapped.

'Monsewer?' inquired mine host, leaning on his counter. 'A Frenchman is it?'

'Does that thought concern you, sir?' Geneviève inquired, dropping her hand to the pommel of her sword.

'I fought against you, monsewer,' said the publican. 'Lost these fingers, I did.' He held up his left hand to reveal only the forefinger remaining.

'I apologise, sir,' Geneviève said. 'No doubt you left one of my countrymen in a similar state of disarray.'

'I did,' he shouted with a roar of laughter. 'By God, I did. You'll take a glass, monsewer.'

'It would be my pleasure, sir, but I must catch the tide. With this gentleman.'

Adam was gently urging Skillett to his feet.

'Ah, just one more glass, your Honour,' the captain begged, swaying to and fro and leaning against him.

'Not even one, Captain Skillett.' Geneviève raised her hat. 'You'll excuse me, host. There's the tide.'

'And right you are, monsewer. They're not to be missed. You want me to sober him up?'

'We shall take care of it,' Geneviève decided, not at all sure what Skillett might say next. What indeed he might already have said. Between them she and Adam bundled him up the stairs and into the drizzle.

'Brrr.' He shuddered. ''Tis no night to be abroad, your Honour. There'll be wind behind this rain. Oh, aye, you may mark my words.'

'We shall,' Geneviève agreed. 'So there is the more cause for haste.'

'This is the man we are trusting with our lives?' Adam whispered.

'Picked by Richelieu,' she said. 'What would you?' They had got Skillett down a side street, away from passers-by. 'Where are the barrels, Captain?'

'Barrels,' Skillett said. 'Barrels,' he bawled. 'I dream about them barrels,' he shouted.

'Hush your trap,' Adam snapped. 'You'll have the watch on us.'

'Or the customs.' Geneviève pointed. 'There's the docks. Let's get him aboard.'

It took a struggle, but once they reached the dockside the crew were able to climb up and help them.

'Sea?' Skillett demanded at the top of his voice. 'I'm not going to sea. We've a stove timber. I'm for my bunk.'

Geneviève gave him a push and he tumbled down the ladder, to be caught by his mate. 'Do we float?'

'Oh, aye, your Honour. We can be off any time. But without the skipper . . .'

'You've been in and out of this harbour often enough,' she pointed out.

''Tis not easy. And where might you want to be going?'

'Powder,' Skillett shouted at the rain. 'Powder. We're after the powder.'

'I'm going to have to silence him,' Adam said.

'Get him below,' Geneviève said. 'And make ready a bucket of salt water.' She lowered her voice. 'It is the powder we're after, Mr Lucas. You'll know where it went ashore.'

'Oh, aye, monsewer. It went ashore at Lulworth Cove.'

'Where's that?'

'Just round the headland. Matter of twenty miles west.'

'Twenty miles?' she cried. 'West?' The Solent lay to the east.

'Aye, well, that's where the skipper has his friends.'

'And do you know how to contact them?'

'Aye, well, we makes signals with our lamp. But the fact is, your Honour, they won't deal with nobody but him.'

'We'll have him sober by the time we get there,' Geneviève promised grimly. 'How long?'

'Well . . . tide's with us. Matter of four hours, I reckon.'

'Then cast off, for God's sake.' She went to the hatch, nearly retched at the stench arising from the cabin, and the ship was still alongside. 'Can you get him sober, Adam?'

'Leave him to me,' Adam promised. 'Send down that water.'

One of the hands was waiting with the full bucket. Geneviève removed herself from the vicinity of the action, listened to Lucas giving the orders. The mooring warps were cast off, and the foresails set. The little ship drifted away from the dockside, Lucas gave full starboard helm, and she gathered way as the sail filled. But the whole thing seemed terribly slow.

'Can't we set more sail?' Geneviève asked. 'This will take much more than four hours.'

'Oh, we will, your Honour, we will. But right now we're beating into it, see. There'll be a fair wind once we gets outside. And then, there's the sandbanks. We wants to be careful. You'll go forward, Tom Adams, with the line.'

'Aye aye,' said the sailor, and he clambered into the bow to commence swinging his leadline.

The lights of the town faded into mist, and they ghosted through the darkness.

'How can you tell where you're going?' Geneviève asked in sudden alarm as the last of the land disappeared.

Lucas tapped the compass. 'This little fellow here.' He unfolded his chart, held it under the lantern by the binnacle. 'I've laid a course, see, from the dock to the southern edge of Brownsea – that's the island with the fort on it – and from there to the Swash. That's the exit channel. Course, it's only practical to do that at high water; there's a lot of mud between us and there when the tide's out. But it should work. Visibility ain't too bad.' He tilted his head. 'But we're going to have to tack. Set that mainsail there, Jeb.'

The second member of the crew heaved on the halliard, and slowly the big mainsail climbed up the mast, immediately commencing to flap to and fro and take the boom with it, so that Geneviève was forced to duck. But a moment later it filled with wind and the cutter heeled as she responded.

Geneviève peered at the compass. It did not read anything resembling the pencilled figure on the chart.

'We're not on course.'

'Aye, your Honour. That's because the wind is dead in our teeth. We has to tack, to and fro, like, for as long as the sails fill.'

'Then how can you tell where you are?'

He winked at her. 'You feels it, your Honour. But soon enough we'll catch a sight of something we recognise. Or we'll run into the mud.'

Geneviève did not find that the least reassuring, wrapped her cloak round herself, and leaned against the taff-rail. The drizzle had ceased, but the wind remained light, and there was scarce a sound above the swish of the water away from the hull and the chanting of the leadsman in the bows. Even Skillett had fallen quiet, and now Adam rejoined her on deck. 'Sleeping,' he said.

'But will he be awake by the time we get to Lulworth?'

'We shall have to get him up,' he said. 'Where are we?'

'I wish we knew,' she said. But a moment later they heard the rumble of surf, and saw the hump of the land close to their starboard side. They were in the Swash Channel, running down with the falling tide, the bows suddenly plunging into the little waves kicked up by the easterly breeze. 'Ugh,' Geneviève said, and knew she was going to be sick.

'You'd best lie down,' Adam recommended.

'I'll not go below.'

'Here on deck.' He found a tarpaulin for her to sit on, took off his own cloak to add to hers.

'You'll freeze,' she pointed out.

'The wind will be behind us, once we come about,' he said. A moment later the ship altered course to run down to Anvil Point, and the breeze did seem to drop as it went astern. The motion eased off as well, but Geneviève decided to remain where she was; she couldn't afford to be feeling sick when they arrived at Lulworth.

'Young gentleman not feeling well?' Lucas inquired with a smirk.

'The Chevalier will be good enough for you, Master Lucas,' Adam said. 'When the time comes.'

Geneviève slept as the little ship curtseyed through the gentle waves. At one time the rain started again, and she awoke with a start, but the sight of Adam sitting beside her, of Lucas on the helm, reassured her and she dozed off once more to awake fully as the anchor plunged into the water and the ship brought up. She scrambled to her feet, saw that the mainsail had already been lowered and the foresail was at that moment being handed, and that they lay in a splendid natural harbour formed by two curving headlands which permitted only a narrow exit to the sea.

'Haste,' Lucas said. 'We don't want to be here when the wind gets up. That entrance can be a death trap.'

'There is no wind,' Geneviève said.

'There's going to be, your Honour. It's been raining now for twelve hours, and the breeze is already starting to back. You mark my words, by midday there's going to be a right gale piping up the Channel. There's an old saying amongst sailorfolk: "Wind before rain, soon make sail again, but rain before wind, sheets and halliards mind".'

'Hum,' Geneviève said. 'Then we'd best get the captain up.'

'Ah, can't a man sleep?' grumbled Captain Skillett. 'Christ, me head. Christ . . .'

Adam squeezed a wet cloth on his face, and he sat up with a start. For pity's sake, your Honour . . .' He peered at Geneviève. 'Cannot a man sleep?'

'Not when he has work to do. You'll come ashore, Captain. We need that powder.'

'Powder? Powder?' He clapped his hand to his forehead and gave another groan. 'Where are we?'

'Lulworth.'

'Lulworth?' His mutter became a bellow. 'How'd we get here? Who sailed my ship without me knowledge? I'll have the lubber's guts, that I will.'

'You'd best explain, your Honour,' Lucas said from the hatchway.

'It was on my instructions, Captain Skillett,' Geneviève said. 'This ship is under my orders, is it not?'

'Well . . .' Skillett rubbed his head some more. 'It ain't right, your Honour, taking a man's ship to sea without him being on the helm. It ain't right.' He glared at Lucas. 'All ship-shape?'

'You'll find naught to complain about, Captain. Saving we're here come daybreak. There's a blow on its way.'

'Haste,' Skillett bawled, scrambling up the ladder. 'Haste, your Honour. Make haste.'

321

It was four o'clock in the morning and the coldest Geneviève could remember since leaving St Petersburg. She wriggled her fingers inside her gloves to restore feeling to them as the boat approached the shore. Apparently the signals had been received and understood, for there were two men on the beach.

'Is that you, Captain Skillett?'

'It is. I've come for the stuff.'

'Well, thank God for that. 'Tis no sleep I've had this past fortnight.'

The boat grated on the sand as it thrust its way thought the gentle surf, and two of the crew, wearing thigh boots, and armed, as were Skillett and Lucas, with cutlasses and pistols, jumped over the bow to hold her steady.

Skillett followed. 'You've transport?'

'It's arranged.' The man peered at Geneviève as she dropped to the sand, followed by Adam, inspecting their cloaks and hats and boots and swords. 'Who might these be?'

'My principals,' Skillett said. 'We're in haste, man. The weather is pooring.'

'I'll say Amen to that. Powder, is it?' He came closer to Geneviève to stare at her.

'Powder,' she agreed.

'It don't look like powder to me.'

'Is it your custom to open other people's goods?'

'Aye, when it smells.'

'I shall be pleased to relieve you of it, sir,' she said, keeping her temper, 'if you would be good enough to lead me to where it is stored.'

He continued to look at her for some seconds, almost as if he was memorising her face; then he nodded, and turned away, to lead them up a steep path cut into the side of the hill. As they ascended the wind began to grow in strength, and Geneviève and Adam had to hold their hats on to their heads. They were out of breath by the time they reached the top, and could turn and look back down at the almost perfect oval of water beneath them, where the *Alderney Rose,* showing no lights, was resting motionless, in some contrast to the sea outside the entrance, where the whitecaps were already starting to show.

'Haste,' Skillett growled. 'Make haste.'

'The farmhouse was only a quarter of a mile from the cliff top. Here too there were no lights, but the horses stamped in their stables and the cows lowed in their barns at the approach of humans.

A window opened on the upper floor. 'Is that you, Peter Harris?' a woman asked.

'Go back to bed, Martha,' Harris growled.

'They'll be taking the powder, then?' his wife inquired.

'Bed, woman.' He led them across a straw-littered yard, splashing in and out of muddy puddles, to reach a shed.

'In there?' Geneviève demanded.

'I'd not put that stuff in me cellars,' Harris said. 'It could come to no harm here.'

Geneviève pulled her nose. The door was swinging open, and there were the twelve barrels, neatly stacked. 'And supposing the excise had come to the farm?'

'They didn't' Harris pointed out. 'There's a cart. We'd best get moving.'

The sailors fell to with a will, helped by Harris and his hand. Geneviève and Adam overlooked the proceedings, Skillett at their side.

'He's a good man, really, your Honour,' Skillett said.

'I doubt that, Captain Skillett, Geneviève said. 'Still, if we regain the ship I shall not complain.'

'How do we get the barrels down the cliff?' Adam inquired.

'There's a rope and pulley.'

'But ... if one were to slip ...'

'Oh, aye, your Honour. 'Tis a dangerous business. We brought them up. But as I told the Chevalier, we'd not take them down again without himself standing underneath.'

Adam glanced at Geneviève, who shrugged. The cart was loaded, the two horses waited patiently. 'Let's go,' she said, and wondered what she was doing at all. Why, oh why, was she not tending the tap in some pleasant Savoyard inn? Surely she had enough memories of adventure and sudden death to satisfy even her restless spirit. And whatever their shortcomings, she liked these people. She had no desire to harm a single one of them. There was the simple truth of the matter. But the other simple truth was that she had no alternative. She was absolutely damned, and there was an end to it. She could only aim to succeed, and afterwards to discover some slight solace in the arms of Adam.

They had reached the cliff-top, and the wind was plucking at their hats and coats. The windlass was made ready, and the first barrel placed in the sling. Geneviève and Adam climbed down, together with Skillett and one of his men. Lucas remained at the top with Harris and the farmhand. Once they reached the sand, Skillett gave a shrill whistle, and the barrel was thrust over the edge. They listened to the windlass squealing even above the rising note of the wind, and Geneviève supposed it could be heard for miles. She wondered what would be heard for miles if the rope were to break and drop that barrel from a height? Well, she thought, it will not matter to any of us.

Down it came, slowly but surely. At the foot they lifted it out, and turned it on end. It would take them all to get it into the jolly boat. Up went the sling to repeat the performance. By now it was just threatening to get light, but she reckoned they still had about an hour before sunrise, and that should just be sufficient. As indeed it was. The last barrel was rolled out of the sling, the sling was returned to the top, and Lucas and Harris and the farmhand came scrambling down the cliff path just as the first true daylight flickered across the beach.

'Thank God for that,' Geneviève said. 'Now let's get them aboard.'

She led the way down to the beach, where the remaining crew member held the jolly boat steady, and checked at the sound of a shout.

· 'Hold there!'

Geneviève looked up the beach, watched half a dozen red-coated soldiers debouching from the shelter of a gully, not a hundred yards away.

'Turned in, by God!' Harris shouted, and ran for the cliff path. A musket exploded, and then another, followed by an entire fusillade.

My God, Geneviève thought, looking from right to left as the bullets seemed to buzz around her like bees. Suppose they hit the barrels?

And indeed one did, but no doubt the range had been too great, for the lead merely crunched into the wood. She realised that her heart was pounding fit to burst – apart from the fear of an explosion it was the first time she had ever been under fire. She was the only one of the shore party still on her feet; even Adam had dropped for shelter behind the jolly boat, while Harris appeared to have been hit and was moaning at the foot of the cliff.

'We have them, lads,' shouted the officer in charge of the excise party. 'Load.'

'Come on,' Geneviève shouted, and drew her sword.

324

'Where?' Adam scrambled to his feet.

'We'll charge those fellows. Come *on.*' She slapped Skillett across the shoulders with the flat of her weapon.

'Charge soldiers?' the captain demanded, plaintively.

''Tis that or hanging,' she pointed out. 'And their pieces are empty. Follow me.'

She hurried forward, not running, so as to maintain her breathing at a steady level; feeling her boots crunch into the sand.

'Stop there, sir,' shouted the officer, and presented his pistol. But before he could aim Adam fired his, and he gave a shout and fell to one knee. Without their officer, and with their pieces only half loaded, the soldiers hesitated. One or two hurriedly fixed bayonets, the others dropped their muskets and used their bayonets as swords. But their thoughts were already turning to flight; it had apparently not crossed their minds that the smugglers might assault them. Geneviève touched blades with the first man, brushed his aside with the greatest ease, and drove into his shoulder. He gave a howl of pain and ran along the beach. Adam had wounded another, and Lucas's flailing cutlass had hurt a third. A moment later the beach was cleared save for the officer, who was trying to regain his feet.

'We'll do him for a start,' Skillett said; he had remained at the back of the fight, but was now brimming with ferocious courage.

'There'll be no murder,' Geneviève snapped. Not here, at the least, she thought, and knelt beside the stricken man. 'You'd best see to Mr Harris.'

The officer had been hit in the chest, but at too great a range to be killed; he was losing a lot of blood, however, and Geneviève used her cravat to stuff the wound and bind it in place with his belt.

'Who are you, sir?' the wounded man muttered.

'An enemy, alas, monsieur,' she said. 'Your men will return for you when the beach is emptied. We shall be as quick as we can.'

'Be sure you will hang,' he said.

'You are probably right,' she agreed, regaining her feet. 'And no doubt deservedly.' She returned along the beach, to where Harris was on his feet. He had been no more than grazed by a spent ball, although from his groans and sighs it would have appeared he was close to death.

'Come along, Mr Harris,' Geneviève said. 'We must load those casks. Haste now.'

Geneviève said. 'We must load those casks. Haste now.'

'Load the casks?' he demanded. 'And what of the excise?'

'They'll not come back while we command the beach. Their muskets are on the sand.'

'And if they've been tipped, don't you suppose they'll know where the stuff's lain this past week?'

Geneviève chewed her lip. She could not deny his reasoning. And who had tipped? Another example of the sinister ill-fortune which was trailing her like a shroud.

'No doubt they do, Mr Harris, but it was their decision to wait until we started loading, to catch us all. Once the powder is on board, there's no evidence against you, is there? No one has recognised you. That officer is too far away. So keep your voice down and help us load, and you'll be safe the more quickly.'

He muttered some more, but did as he was bid. They heaved and sweated, loaded first one and then another cask into the jolly boat; it would only take two at a time. Then the powder had to be hoisted on board the *Alderney Rose,* using the main halliard, before the boat could return to the beach for the next load. It was growing steadily more and more light, just as the wind was steadily increasing, even inside the cove.

'At least it's gone round to the west,' Adam pointed out. He had taken off his cloak and doublet, despite the cold, and was sweating with his exertions. 'We'll have a dead run all the way back to the Solent.'

Geneviève shuddered. It was not something she wished to contemplate. She felt she was living a long nightmare, with only disaster there when she awakened. But at last the twelfth cask was stowed in the cutter's hold, partially hidden beneath the pungent remains of the last catch of fish, and she could give Harris his bag of coins. 'My thanks, Mr Harris. I doubt we'll meet again.'

'Aye,' the farmer agreed with satisfaction. 'Saving it's on the gallows. Don't blow yourself up,' he said as the jolly boat pushed off for the last time.

'Now there's a thought,' Skillett was on the tiller. 'Just what *are* we supposed to blow up, your Honour?'

'Time enough for that,' Geneviève told him. 'Your business is to navigate me into the Solent.'

The anchor was winched aboard, and under foresail only the *Alderney Rose* stood for the entrance. Now the sun was high, as the clouds had started to break overhead, and Geneviève caught her breath as she looked at the whitecaps racing past the entrance.

'We'll not make it,' Skillett muttered. 'It's too late.' He turned the helm up into the wind, and the cutter lost way, bobbing on the swell which was finding its way even into the shelter of the cove.

'What do you mean?' Geneviève snapped. 'We can't stay here.'

'There's no other way, until the wind drops.'

'And when might that be?'

He shrugged. 'Two, three days, maybe. Prepare to anchor,' he bawled.

'Anchor?' Geneviève shouted. 'We must get out. We *must*.'

'We ain't going, your Honour. I'm the captain of this ship, and I says there's too much wind.'

'Balderdash,' Adam snapped. 'You've not set sufficient sail.'

'Now you listen to me . . .' Skillett began.

'You,' Adam shouted. 'Stay away from that capstan or I'll bring you down.' He rested his hand on the pistol at his belt. 'I'll have the mainsail up, Mr Lucas.'

'Mutiny, by God,' Skillett shouted. 'Why . . .'

'Be quiet, Mr Skillett,' Geneviève said, and drew her own pistol to present it at his breast. 'Just stand still.'

Lucas looked from Geneviève to Adam. 'Who'll con her?'

'I will,' Adam said.

Lucas hesitated only for a moment longer. Then he shouted, 'Come on lads.'

The hands swarmed over the boom and the mainsail climbed the mast. From the shore there came the sound of an explosion, and then another. The soldiers had managed to reload and were firing at them. But the range was too great for any harm to be done, and so far as Geneviève could see none of the bullets even reached the ship. Then the mainsail was filling, and the cutter was turning back to the entrance, and gathering speed with every moment. Geneviève clung to the rail and watched the narrow entrance, the seething surf beyond. If they were swept on to the rocks they would certainly drown, but it was too late to worry about that now. She glanced at Adam. He stood with his feet well apart, swinging the wheel to and fro to keep the ship as far to the windward side of the channel as he dared, biting his lip and frowning. She inhaled the biting air, heart seeming to slow . . . they were in the entrance and crashing through, the bow plunging into the first of the rollers, rising up so that she nearly slipped, and then thudding down into the trough beyond, while Adam swung the helm. 'Harden those sheets,' he bawled.

Hands seized the ropes holding the foot of the sail and pulled them taut, and the cutter, about to pay off and lose way, came

327

closer to the wind and regained her speed. Adam was a superb seaman, Geneviève realised. And Skillett's crew were hardly inferior, properly led. Men she must take to their deaths, unless she was unnaturally lucky.

But she had always been lucky in the past.

Now the cutter was turning downwind, having gained some distance from the shore. The waves were bigger than anything Geneviève had seen before, but the ship rode them beautifully, with Adam's strong hands on the helm, twisting to and fro, looking aft to see where the next roller was likely to hit his ship, ordering the sheets to be freed so that the sails would balloon and fill, to send the *Alderney Rose* crashing onwards.

'How long to the Solent?' she shouted.

'With this breeze? No more than eight hours.'

And it was nine of the morning now. Nothing could be better; they would enter the sound just on dusk. Her heart began to pound again. After all, they would fulfil their mission. They would triumph. *She* would triumph, if she lived to tell the tale.

She stood beside the wheel, hugged Adam against her. 'It goes well.'

'Aye.' He kissed her ear. 'You'd best lie down. 'Tis a long night we have ahead.'

Remarkably, she slept. As the day grew warmer the wind seemed to drop a little, and as they rounded Anvil Point once again the seas became more even, the movement more regular. She was even able to eat some bread and cheese and take a glass of wine at noon, by which time the Isle of Wight was large and clear in front of them. She then wondered if they would arrive too soon, but now the tide, which had been sweeping them along, turned, slowing their progress and kicking up a fierce short sea against the gusting wind. The *Alderney Rose* plunged and heaved, and rolled as well, for every trough knocked way off the ship, and she threatened to broach in the big following seas. Skillett and Lucas took turns on the wheel, while Adam kept an eye on them, ordering sail to be shortened to relieve some of the burden on the helmsmen. The ship hardly seemed to move, the white cliffs in front of them seemed if anything to be receding rather than advancing, and to top Geneviève's discomfort her stomach once again rebelled against the unusual motion, and she heartily regretted her lunch.

'Not too far now,' Adam said, holding her against him. 'When do you reckon to tell the skipper your plan?'

'Not until the last possible moment,' she said.

'And what will happen then, do you suppose?'

'There's money enough for him to buy a new vessel. And he'll not be in a position to refuse my commands, with his hold full of that powder. Besides, once we light the fuse he'll be in haste.'

'We'll all be in haste,' Adam said with a grim smile. 'I still think it would be more sensible for you to leave first, and get ashore. I am perfectly capable of handling this lot.'

'And what do you suppose I should do were you to be killed, save blow out my own brains?' she inquired. 'We fight this one together, Adam. It will be our last, I promise you.'

He smoothed her hair back from her face. 'You promised me that once before.'

'This time I mean it. And you'd best not be so attentive; Captain Skillett is taking you for a catamite.'

For indeed the captain was casting them inquisitive glances. But he was soon too preoccupied with conning the ship as they approached the Needles Channel, so called because several large rocks had broken off the closing headland, to jut out of the sea like a row of needles, while to the left the seas were breaking upon the shingles sandbank, leaving only a narrow gut of green water, streaked with white foam, boiling in front of them.

'We'll not make it against the tide,' Skillett decided. He had regained a good deal of his nerve, did not seem to bear Adam any ill will. 'We'll just heave to out here and wait. It won't be more than a couple of hours.'

'A couple of hours?' Geneviève cried. But there seemed no alternative, not even Adam could drive the ship against the fast running tide. The cutter was turned into the wind and the sheets pulled hard, the foresail to port and the mainsail to starboard, so that every time the ship attempted to move off in one direction she was brought back by the other sail. Thus restricted she curtseyed to the waves, tossing showers of spray over her bows to soak the decks and those on them, losing ground slowly to the ebb, but holding her own against the wind and sea.

'And to think that these men spend their lives doing this,' Geneviève said, feeling violently sick. But at last — and the wait seemed an eternity — the tide turned, the sea immediately went down, and the sheets were freed to commence the run up the Solent. By now the sun was low in the western sky, and by the time they drew abreast of Hurst Castle it was quite dark.

'What ship is that?' came the hail from the watch.

Skillett glanced at Geneviève. 'Those cannon would blow us clear out of the water first time around, Chevalier. They're trained on the centre of the Channel, and there ain't nowhere else to go.'

'Then tell them the truth,' Geneviève said. 'You're a fishing smack.'

'So I am,' Skillett agreed, and got out his speaking trumpet. 'The *Alderney Rose*,' he bawled. 'With a cargo of mackerel. Bound for Lymington.'

There was no reply, and Geneviève anxiously watched the lights flickering on the castle battlements; she could just make out the ugly muzzles of the twelve pounders through their ports. One shot from one of those and that would be the end. There would be a bang heard in London, no doubt. But the guns remained silent, and a moment later they were out of the narrows and in the broad, quiet waters of the Solent. Now the curling whitecaps of the Channel were forgotten, the heaving and the pitching and the rolling, the stomach churning plunges from crest to trough. Geneviève found herself actually enjoying the breeze playing on her face, even as the blood began to pound in her arteries. They would be at their destination by midnight.

Captain Skillett handed over the helm to Lucas, and came to stand beside her. 'Lymington is over there,' he said, pointing to some lights on the port bow. ''Tis a creek with a village at the head. They builds good ships in Lymington.'

'I'm sure they do,' Geneviève agreed.

'But you're not going there,' he said.

'I wish to sail up to Spithead,' she said.

'Spithead? That's where the fleet is anchored.'

'There'll be room for us, Mr Skillett.'

'No doubt there will, but begging your pardon, your Honour, them's all navy ships. If we was to be boarded, and with twelve barrels of gunpowder in our hold . . .'

'There's no law against conveying gunpowder.'

'Maybe there ain't, monsewer. But there'd be questions asked, in the middle of a fleet and all. There'd be those saying we was a fireship.'

'Oh, come now, Mr Skillett. How can one vessel, laden with one cargo of gunpowder, be regarded as a fireship? What damage could we cause, save to the vessel immediately alongside us? Just do as I ask. We'll anchor there for the night, and I will give you your instructions.'

'Can't say as I likes it, your Honour. There's many a tidy little bay in which we could anchor, well before Spithead. If we was to be challenged ...'

'You'll give the same reply as you did to the castle, Mr Skillett. I'd be obliged if you'd carry out my instructions. Or there can be no payment.'

He glared at her for a moment, then returned to take the helm himself. Only the occasional gust of wind reached them under the shelter of the land, and they ghosted through the calm water with hardly a sound. Now there were more lights to either side as they approached Egypt Point to starboard, with the growing port of Southampton away to their left. And now, like a swarm of fireflies on a tropical night, they could see the lanterns of the anchored fleet. Geneviève caught her breath. Never had she seen so many lights. And these were real, with real, living men on board, not a collection of models in a stagnant pond.

'Half an hour,' Adam said. His voice was quiet, but she could tell he was excited. 'And after ...'

'Don't think of after,' she said. 'Only *now* matters, Adam. After is there, if we live to enjoy it.'

He said nothing, and she kept staring forward, into the darkness. There was no moon, but the myriad lights made the water seem almost bright. Beyond the ships were the lights of Portsmouth itself. Their ultimate destination, if they could make it.

'What ship is that?'

The hail took her by surprise; she twisted her head to and fro in an endeavour to identify the voice, and discovered a small sloop approaching from their starboard side.

'Done for,' Skillett muttered. 'There's the patrol.'

'Answer him straight up, man,' Geneviève snapped.

He gave the wheel to Lucas, went to the taffrail. 'The *Alderney Rose*,' he bawled. 'Bound for Portsmouth with a cargo of fish.'

'Heave to,' came the command.

'Christ, oh Christ,' Skillett muttered.

'Give us those smocks,' Geneviève said, and she and Adam dropped the fishy smelling seamen's smocks over their shoulders, discarding their hats for woollen cloches, and then moving forward away from the binnacle lantern. Meanwhile Lucas had put up the helm and the cutter swung into the wind, losing way and lying almost dead in the water.

The patrol sloop came alongside with a rattle of heaving lines, dropping her mainsail as she did so. An officer wearing the blue coat and white breeches of the Royal Navy jumped over the side, and Geneviève loosed her sword in its scabbard.

'Fish you say? From Alderney?'

'Caught in the Channel, your Honour,' Skillett said. 'Open those hatches there.'

The hatches were thrown open, and the officer peered into the hold, sniffed, and stepped backwards. 'Fresh caught?'

''Tis only a day old, your Honour. We was delayed by the weather.'

'Bah. You'd have done better to put into Poole,' he said. 'That catch is off. You'll get naught for it.'

Skillett tapped his nose. 'You'd be surprised, your Honour.'

'I would. Well, I'll not detain you or you'll stink out the fleet. But you'll mind how you go, there's a deal of cable out. Foul a royal ship and I'll have you in irons.'

'I'll not, your Honour. Good night to you, your Honour.'

The lieutenant glanced along the deck, to where the crew, Geneviève and Adam in their midst, were gathered by the mast. Then he climbed back on board the sloop, and the lines were taken in. The patrol boat fell away, and they listened to the creak of the mainsail being set.

'Christ,' Skillett said. 'Oh, Christ. It's running down me legs.'

'You did well, Captain.' Geneviève took off her smock. She wondered if she'd ever smell clean again. 'Now let's be away.

'You have to tell me what you're about, your Honour,' Skillett said. 'Or I won't budge an inch.'

'You're drifting down on the fleet, Captain,' Adam pointed out. 'You'd best get her sailing.'

Muttering to himself, the captain returned to the helm.

'We'll have that mainsail down,' he said, and Lucas went forward. The sail clouded on the boom and was secured, and under single foresail the cutter slipped into the middle of the great ships. Geneviève looked to left and right, her belly rolling. The men-of-war towered above them, gunports secured, varnished hulls gleaming gently in the light from their neighbours They were still, as it was near midnight, but the anchor watch was on deck, looking down at her, it seemed.

'You spoke about anchoring,' Skillett said.

'We'll go in a way yet,' Geneviève said, attempting to gauge numbers. But once they were sailing through the middle of the fleet they were entirely surrounded by the masts and it was impossible to decide where they were in relation to the land.

'They'll send a message to that patrol boat,' Lucas remarked. 'They'll not leave us anchored here for long. Oh, aye, there'll be a to do.'

'I know that,' Geneviève said. 'But an hour will do the trick.' She felt as if she had known these men all of her life. And now they were following her into the very pit of hell itself, still without understanding what they were doing. 'Are you ready, Captain? No shouting. I'll let you know when. Adam?'

'Ready.' He carried the bag in which her fuse was.

'Well, Mr Skillett, you'll prepare your boat, before we anchor. We'll have no time to lose.'

'We're going ashore?'

'That's right. Adam?'

He nodded, climbed down into the hold, the bag slung over his shoulder.

'You're going to explode that powder, here?' Skillett's voice rose.

'Hush.'

'You'll not. We'll be killed.'

Geneviève backed against the taff-rail, drew her pistol. 'You'll be killed if you disobey me.' She faced them all, for the crew had come aft to free the jolly boat, and could overhear the conversation.

Lucas scratched his head. 'Twelve barrels of gunpowder? What d'you hope to do, your Honour?'

'Just explode the powder. Do as I say, and no harm will come to you. Adam?'

He scrambled out of the hold. 'It's alight. Thirty minutes.'

'Bring up and anchor,' Geneviève said.

Skillett hesitated, chewing his lip, looking from her pistol to Adam, who recognised the situation, and also drew his weapon.

'Twenty-nine minutes now, Captain.'

Geneviève jingled the bag at her belt. 'There's more than enough money here to buy you a new ship, Captain Skillett. A better ship.'

'Twenty-eight minutes,' Adam said. 'We don't want to be around here when she goes up, Captain.'

Skillett glanced at Lucas, who shrugged. Then he snapped his fingers. 'Drop that foresail. Let go.'

The men hurried forward, the foresail came down as Skillett brought the ship up into the wind. The anchor rasped through the hawespipe, plunged into the still water, and the *Alderney Rose* came to rest, slipping back as the cable paid out, until she was no more than thirty feet from the nearest battleship.

'Now lower your jolly boat,' Geneviève said. 'Haste now.'

'Ahoy there,' came the call from above them. 'You'll not rest there, you damned lubber?'

''Tis a sick man we have aboard,' Adam shouted. ''Tis haste we need.'

The jolly boat splashed into the water. But time was passing so very quickly.

'I don't give a God damn what you have there,' shouted the officer above them. 'Get that vessel moved.'

'Into the boat,' Geneviève commanded, and the crew climbed over the side.

'It'll not work,' Skillett moaned. 'We'll be hanged.'

Geneviève pushed him over the side and followed.

'You'll move, God damn it,' bawled the officer. 'Or I shall fire into you.'

'Good enough,' Geneviève muttered, sitting on the transom. Adam alone remained. 'For God's sake hurry,' she begged.

He dropped beside her. Now they could hear the fuse sizzling.

'Load that gun,' the officer was bawling.

'Give way, for God's sake,' Geneviève commanded.

'Musketeers,' came the shouted command from the warship. And now the interest was communicating itself to the others, and bugles were blowing as the alarm was sounded.

'Row,' Adam bawled, and the sailor dug their oars into the water. All around them was seething noise. But they would not be in time, Geneviève thought, her mind singing with the enormity of what they were doing. While if the British were so careless as to fire into the fishing smack . . . she dared not think what might be the result.

'Anchor chain ahead,' Adam sang out from the tiller, and they altered course.

'There they are,' someone shouted from above them, and a shot was fired, but where it went Geneviève had no idea.

'Run out that gun,' came the dwindling voice of the officer on the first ship.

'Row,' she shrieked, 'or we shall be blown to bits.'

The oars dashed into the water, spray scattered across her face, and behind her there came the report of a cannon.

'By God.' Skillett stopped rowing, stared aft. Geneviève

twisted in her seat, gazed at the *Alderney Rose*. The cannon had been depressed as far as possible, the shot had entered almost at the hatchway, had plunged through the hold, and through the gunpowder, and the cutter was already sinking. But there had been no explosion.

'In the name of God . . .' Adam said.

Geneviève just stared. She could not believe her eyes, or her senses.

'There,' came a shout as another ship identified them.

'Fire,' the order rippled through the night, which promptly exploded into sound. There was a balloon of water all around them, a wild shriek from Skillett, and Geneviève's lungs filled with water as the dinghy capsized.

She stared at the sky, at the stars, felt the wind on her face. I am dead, she thought, and ascending slowly into Heaven. No, no, her mind reacted in sudden alarm. I am drifting slowly down to Hell. There can be no Heaven for the Chevalier d'Éon. That I am freezing is merely a payment on account of the horrors I have yet to suffer.

Fingers biting into her ribs, reaching through even the terrible cold that gripped her limbs, making her lungs work – at every squeeze and thrust she expelled air, and instinctively sucked it back in as the pressure was taken away.

'Adam,' she whispered. 'Adam.'

'Oh, my darling.' He kissed her neck. 'My dearest girl. Are you alive?'

'If you are.' She endeavoured to sit up, but fell back with the effort, exhausted on the shingle.

'Hush,' he begged, and lay beside her.

She twisted her head to and fro, realised that she could see nothing, although there was a great deal of noise and light beyond her immediate vision. 'What happened?'

'The dinghy was struck and capsized. I got you ashore, and we are in a gully on the beach.'

'What of the others?'

'I do not know.'

'My God, those men . . . Adam, why did the ship not explode?'

'I wish I knew. But had it, we would have been dead men.'

'I know it. But . . .' Skillett had said. 'that don't look like no gunpowder to me.' She had never inspected the contents of **Beaucamp's** barrels. *That* had been explosive, sure enough, explosive of an immense power. But there had been none on board the *Alderney Rose*. *That* was why the bullets crunching into the casks had not set it off on the Lulworth Beach. Someone had substituted a harmless material for Beaucamp's deadly formula. But who? Richelieu? It did not make sense. Pompadour? Would she allow her personal enmity to go so far? Pompadour. Of all the women in the world, Geneviève thought, you alone do I truly hate. Pompadour. But it had not exploded. However much she might have to bear the guilt for Skillett and his crew, she had not become a mass murderer. Whatever the future held, she could thank God it had not exploded.

'I reckon we can make a move,' Adam said. 'The noise is dying. They must suppose we all drowned. And we shall certainly freeze if we do not gain shelter.'

She sat up. Her limbs seemed to have a life of their own, as did her teeth, chattering away. When she endeavoured to stand, water flowed out of her boots.

'You must have pulled me a long way.'

'I'm a strong swimmer.'

She kissed him on the cheek. 'You are making a habit of saving my life. Or attempting to do so. I must endeavour to reciprocate.'

He held her arm, helped her up the sloping, crumbling shingle.

'By cooking my meals?'

'I shall do that,' she said.

His head turned in surprise. 'We have failed in our task.'

'Yet are we not entirely lost. I shall have such a tale to tell...'

'They'll not permit you.'

'They?' She smiled. '*They* have twisted my tail for too long, Captain Menzies. *They* have sent me to my death on at least three occasions. That I have survived, to be used by *them* again, is to our credit, not *theirs*. Now *they* will discover that I can be as dangerous an enemy as useful a friend.'

'You'd tilt against Britain *and* France?'

She squeezed his hand. 'And win, I promise you. Get me back to London before word of this can reach there.'

They were in town in thirty hours, by riding throughout the night. The innkeeper had been waiting for them, having been alerted by the hubbub in the harbour. He asked no questions, but showed them to a private chamber where they could change their sodden clothing. Horses were ready, and they were in the saddle before dawn broke over the distracted seaport. The following evening they rode into London, splattered with mud and once again soaked with rain, having stopped only for a bit of supper, but sure that no one could have reached the capital in front of them.

'The Embassy?' Adam asked as they crossed London Bridge, hooves striking sparks from the roadway.

'I have a call to make first,' she said. 'You return to the Embassy, and have Jules pack our things. We shall not be staying.'

She had drawn rein, and he reached for her hand. 'What do you plan? What call? Had I not best stay at your side?'

'It won't be necessary, believe me. And it is something I had best do by myself. I shall be with you in an hour.'

Still he hesitated, so she squeezed his fingers and turned her horse down the next side street. In a remarkable fashion, after the endless terrifying exhilaration of the last few days, her brain had cooled as her body had relaxed. For the first time in her life she was able to see life in its entirety, to see her own place in it. I am a woman, she thought. The terrified child who lay in her bed with blood dribbling across her leg had been too confused to understand, could only continue muttering to itself, I am a man. I have been brought up as a man, therefore I must be one. That single fact had bedevilled her throughout her life, had dominated her thinking. She had enjoyed it, every aspect of it, the absurd as much as the sinister, the romantic as much as the exciting. But it was behind her now. Her relief at having failed to murder several thousand men was like a drink of cool water after a month in a desert. It permeated her being, with a throbbing sense of happiness. It was the greatest thing she had ever done, merely to fail. She was not going to fail again, because she was never again going to risk failure. It was only necessary to play the man for one last occasion, to secure her future and Adam's future. She had no conscience about what she was would do. The men who ruled this world had sought only to use her; it was necessary only to remember that.

She turned her horse through the ornate gateway, walked it down the drive. Footmen waited in the drizzle, and there were several carriages.

'Sir?' The groom peered at her, held her stirrup for her to dismount.

337

'The Chevalier d'Éon. You may announce me.'

'But . . . his lordship is entertaining.'

'Then you will request him to see me privily.' Geneviève led the bewildered troupe up the stairs and into the hall. 'It is an urgent matter.'

'But Chevalier . . .'

'Oh, whisper in his ear,' Geneviève said. 'But bring him to me.'

The butler hesitated, sighed, opened a door into a small antechamber. 'If Your Excellency will be good enough to wait?'

'For a brief while,' Geneviève said. She would only succeed by presenting her most formidable exterior, her most confident, insufferable arrogance, her most absolute certainty of what she was about. She took a turn up and down the room, kicked mud from her boots, faced the door as it opened.

'Chevalier? My God.' Ridingham came into the room, closed the door behind him. 'You must be mad, coming here. Suppose . . .'

'Suppose who, my lord?'

'Well, that Bow Street Runner . . .'

'Ah, the runner. It was he I was going to discuss, my lord.'

Ridingham sank into a chair. 'He has come back for more?'

'I did not bribe the gentleman, my lord.' Geneviève stood above him. 'I . . . shall we say, I hoodwinked him.'

Ridingham sat up, frowned at her. 'Hoodwinked him?'

'I managed to persuade him that I was actually a woman, my lord, and that if he took us both to Newgate he would be the laughing stock of London, as well as liable to a severe sentence for false arrest, and of a peer, as well.'

'My God,' Ridingham said. 'My God. He believed it? But of course he did. Then this wager that is the talk of the town . . .'

'Is based upon his belief, I have no doubt.'

'My God,' Ridingham said again, and mopped his brow. 'The case is to come to court?'

'Indeed it may. But not for a while. Not until after we have discussed certain matters.'

'My dear boy,' Ridingham said. 'You are as handsome, as entrancing as ever, but in the circumstances, I do not see how I can continue my invitation to travel with you.' He seemed to notice her mudstained clothes for the first time. 'What in the name of God have you been doing?'

'Riding non-stop for virtually forty-eight hours,' she explained.

'To see me?'

'Indeed my lord, I have decided to seek political asylum in England.'

He goggled at her.

'It would appear,' Geneviève went on, 'that I have very powerful enemies in France, enemies who are determined to bring me down. I would thus prefer not to return there.'

'Why are you telling me this?'

'Because I felt that in you I would find a sympathetic listener. In all the circumstances.'

Ridingham gazed at her for some moments, then got up, went to the sideboard, and poured himself a glass of claret. As an afterthought he poured one for Geneviève as well.

'You are an agent of the French government,' he said. 'Whose backstairs intrigue is the talk of London. It is well known how you managed to closet yourself in a summer house with the Princess of Wales for nearly an hour. I had thought you a man of taste, Chevalier.'

Geneviève shrugged. 'Duty demanded, my lord. I am a faithful servant, when I am allowed to be.'

'And you would become a faithful servant of England?'

'No. A faithful *resident,* to be sure. But I seek only to retire into private life.' She smiled at him. 'I am contemplating writing my memoirs.'

His head came up. 'What do you want?'

'Well, my lord, I possess nothing, save for my wits. I have nothing to sell, save myself and my memories . . .'

'You shall have a pension. But you will write not a word.'

'Not a word about *us,* my lord. But there is another matter. I have a faithful servant, by name of Adam Menzies, who is a Scot, as you will understand, and had the misfortune to be on the wrong side at Culloden. To put it in a nutshell, were his diplomatic immunity to be withdrawn, he would be hanged. This I could not permit.'

'You expect me to save another man for you to bugger? You are the most wretched scoundrel I have ever encountered, Chevalier.'

'You may well be right,' Geneviève agreed.

'And do you not suppose that you will very soon be found out? There'll be no persuading the runners a second time. And I will be involved. I absolutely forbid it. By God, *I'll* have the fellow hanged.'

'My lord,' Geneviève said, 'you are concerning yourself needlessly. But I will agree my affairs, and yours, are rushing to a crisis. As you say, there is a wager, and that will certainly involve my appearance in Court. Once I am proved to be a man, I will certainly be forced to confess who are my ... friends, and they will be after you as well as me. We may share the same gallows.'

'My God,' Ridingham said. 'Oh, my God. What a fool I was ever to interest myself in you.'

'As I have said, should you be willing to cooperate with me, you have naught to fear.'

'Cooperate?'

'Give me an authority to prove that Captain Menzies is and always has been a secret agent of your own, and is therefore immune from arrest. Over your signature, as controller of His Majesty's Secret Service, that should suffice. Although it would be more convenient were you to take steps to ensure that no one even tries to arrest us. Him, at least.'

'In addition to a pension?'

'If your lordship would be so kind. Oh, and somewhere for us to live until we can plan our future. I shall have to leave the Embassy.'

'And what do I obtain in return?'

'In return, I will undertake to prove, by means of affidavits subscribed by faithful servants, that I am a woman. In the circumstances, I do not see any English judge requiring me to undress in Court.'

Ridingham was shaking his head. 'It may work for a while, but afterwards, especially with you living with this damnable Scot ...'

'I am not finished, my lord. I will also undertake to wear women's clothing for the rest of my life, and to write my Memoirs claiming to be a woman.'

He scratched his head. 'That will set the world by its ears, if all the tales of your exploits are true.'

Geneviève smiled. 'The world has had *me* by my ears for long enough, my lord. It is time we changed places.'

He chewed his lip, paced the room. 'I suppose it is the only solution that holds out any hope.'

'It is the only solution, my lord. And it will work, I promise you. I promise you more, that I shall be nothing more than a nine days' wonder, soon to be forgotten.'

'Providing you are discreet.'

'I shall be discreet, my lord. Providing I neither find myself starving nor deprived of my dearest friend.'

He glared at her. 'Why can you not become my housekeeper, as you are going to be playing the woman?'

'Because I do not love you, my lord.'

'Ha.' Another pace up and down the room. Then he stopped, and faced her. 'Very well, Chevalier. A pension, and immunity for your Scotsman. But so help me God, if I am ever indicted for sodomy, I will have him hanged, drawn and quartered, and you beside him.'

'And a home?'

'By God, but you drive a hard bargain, Chevalier. Very well. I have a house some distance up the river. It is very lovely there. You may use it until I can find you a place of your own. And now, Chevalier, my dear Charles, as you *are* here, and as we are to be partners, so to speak . . .' He reached for her hand. 'I care naught whether you love me or hate me, so long as you grant me the use of your sweet body.'

Geneviève avoided his hand. 'You will never be taken for sodomy with *me,* my lord. I can swear to that. As to your other friends, I can offer you no protection there. But if we have reached an agreement, and as I know you are in haste to rejoin your party, why, there is a desk, and paper. You have but to sit down and write.'

It was nearly midnight when she regained the Embassy. But time no longer mattered. She had secured her own safety, and her own future. And even more important, Adam's future. Why, they could get married. Me, she thought, Geneviève d'Éon de Beaumont, becoming Mistress Adam Menzies? Geneviève Menzies? But that would be too risky, too public a proclamation of either her femininity or her unnaturalness.

But they could live together, forever and ever and ever. There would be happiness. But the future had suddenly become so full of prosperity she dared not think of it. It was a time for living, not for planning. And her first task was to regain Adam, and take them both, and Jules, away from the poisonous intrigue of Richelieu and Pompadour.

She threw her reins to the groom, went inside, found the butler waiting for her. 'His Excellency requests your company, Chevalier.'

'At this hour?'

'Urgent despatches from France.'

I am sure there are, Geneviève reflected. But she would have to have an interview with Nivernais in any event; it might as well be now.

She climbed the stairs to the Ambassador's office; a footman opened the doors for her, and she smiled at the Duke, who was seated behind his desk, regarding her, as usual, as he might have regarded the Devil himself entering the room.

'Where have you been, Chevalier?'

Geneviève continued to smile. 'I was paying a private call, Your Excellency.'

'Upon completion of your mission?'

'In so far as it could be completed, yes.'

'Hum. Well, no matter. I have a warrant here for your arrest.'

'Indeed, Your Excellency?'

'So I would be obliged if you would surrender your sword, and prepare yourself to return to Paris tomorrow morning.'

'And if I am not prepared to do that?'

'Then I should be obliged to use force. But I would beg you, my dear Chevalier, to avoid any such unpleasantness.'

'I see,' Geneviève said. 'May I ask what has happened to my aide de camp?'

'Captain Menzies was arrested the moment he entered the house.' Nivernais permitted a smile to flit across his features. 'He made the mistake of resisting.'

'You have killed him?' Geneviève cried.

'No, Chevalier. But it was necessary to hit him on the head.'

'Oh, my God. I must go to him.'

'You will go nowhere, Chevalier.' Nivernais stood up. 'Your sword.'

'You will have to take it, Your Excellency.'

'Then I shall,' Nivernais agreed. 'You have an acquaintance with Monsieur Shirér, I believe?'

Geneviève turned. The swordsman had waited in the shadows at the back of the room. Now he stepped forward.

'Chevalier.'

Geneviève glanced at Nivernais, who had remained behind the desk. 'Do you propose to come at me together?'

'I am sure Monsieur Shirér will be sufficient.' Nivernais sat down again. 'I have no skill with foils, Chevalier. But Monsieur Shirér is unequalled in all France. I beg of you not to be foolish. There is no death sentence at present involved, merely a term in the Bastille. But for you to draw on Monsieur Shirér would be the same as putting your head upon the block. Have some sense.'

Geneviève's heart had slowed, but it was a reaction of anger, that Adam should have been struck down, and anxiety for him, not of fear. That the Pompadour should have sent her tame assassin to see to her arrest was an equal cause for anger; the fishwife would be well aware that Geneviève would never surrender, and that this time Shirér would have no compunction about killing her. Well, then, she thought, let me die. But by God I will scratch his face for him.

'Monsieur will permit me?' she asked, and took off her hat and unbuttoned her coat.

Shirér wore no hat, but he removed his own coat, then drew his sword and discarded his baldric. Geneviève followed his example, tested the floor with her boots. It was parquet, and inclined to slip.

Shirér smiled at her. 'Would the Chevalier care to disrobe further?' he inquired, no doubt remembering their earlier encounter.

Geneviève considered the matter, decided against it. He was wearing leather shoes, and was at least equally liable to miss his footing. 'I am content, monsieur.'

'Then let us set to, Chevalier.' He kissed the hilt of his sword, and Geneviève did likewise, was reminded of the sunlit rose garden- in Tonnerre, with Monsieur Lannes facing her. Monsieur Lannes had feared Shirér. But that had been thirteen years before, and the swordsman's reputation already established. Let us suppose he was twenty-five then, she thought, he is thirty-eight now, possibly older. And far too confident, as he has enjoyed nothing but success. But I am twenty-seven, about the same age as he must have been when he reached the peak of his career. Therefore I have no cause to fear him; he has far more cause to fear me.

And when I have killed him, I shall be the greatest swordsman in Europe.

Because I *must* kill him, as he has been sent here to kill me.

Shirér's point flickered towards her. But he had not yet grunted. She retreated slowly round the room, keeping her eye on the door. But she was fairly confident that Shirér would have insisted upon settling this by himself, to avenge himself for his defeat in October.

'Ha,' he said, and his point whipped at her. But she was

already out of range, using her speed rather than her sword to evade him, and immediately countering. He avoided her riposte easily enough, but she watched his chest swell as he reached for breath. There was her answer. Not a greater skill? That too, hopefully, but it would be stupid to risk her life, and Adam's life, for they would not keep him alive were she to die.

'Ha,' Shirér said, and moved towards her again. Once again she parried and returned the assault. He retreated across the room, clearly seeking to conserve his breath. She charged immediately, performed a passado, legs scarcely brushing as they crossed and spread again, and lunged at his belly. He parried with expert skill. Her sword was swept aside, but she recovered before he did, regained her balance and thrust again. Once again his parry was the result of consummate ability, but he was tumbling across the room in an effort to regain his breath.

Her own was laboured and she had an instant decision to make; attack again, and risk running out of breath altogether, or give herself a few seconds to recoup and hope that he would not do as well. She opted for the break, lowered her sword, sucked air into her lungs, watched him regaining his balance. But his gasps were still greater than hers. She moved forward, watched him react, and jumped back again. He followed, unable to break his rhythm. This time, as she had anticipated, there were no grunts, just a deadly flurry of steel and purpose. She met him with frantic defence, retreating all the while, found her back against the wall and turned, while his sword drove past her and ripped paper.

'Ah,' she shouted, and drove at him once more. He turned, parried, panted, parried again, and forced her retreat by his exquisite combination of defence and attack. But his breath was becoming ever more laboured. Geneviève, temporarily off-balance, realised that he lacked the immediate determination to counter-attack. Summoning the very last reserves of strength she possessed, she launched herself forward yet again; their blades clashed and slithered along their lengths so that their faces almost crashed into each other as their bodies thudded together. Shirér's lips were pulled back in a twisted smile, and Geneviève knew that he realised he was beaten, by the sheer speed and agility of his younger apponent. She used her left hand to push him away, and then hurled herself forward again; still he parried, steel tinkling against steel as he retreated, face

344

horrible to behold, mottled white and purple, reaching for breath, fighting now from sheer instinct and memory rather than conscious technique. But Geneviève, rivers of pain running down her arms and legs, her own throat dry and her own lungs desperately empty, would no longer give him a respite. Their swords clashed for a last time, and once again he endeavoured to maintain contact while he drove his blade the length of hers. But now she was the stronger, and disengaging herself she leapt to her left, leaving his sword following only feebly. His entire right side was exposed as he turned, almost in slow motion, knowing that he was about to meet his master. And his death.

'Ah,' Geneviève gasped as she lunged to the full extent of her arm, as her sword point pierced the white shirt and the pink flesh beneath, to be immediately clouded in a rush of blood. Shirér's knees gave way and he hit the floor. Geneviève withdrew her blade, and the swordsman fell forward, dead before his face crashed into the parquet.

'My God.' Nivernais mopped his brow. 'He is the greatest swordsman in France.'

'He *was,* Your Excellency,' Geneviève panted.

The Ambassador seemed to realise he was alone in the room with her, and attempted to get round his desk and reach the door. But Geneviève, still gasping, was in front of him and he checked as her red dripping point was presented to his chest.

'I wish my people, Your Excellency,' she said. 'And should you attempt treachery you are a dead man.'

'My God,' he said again.

Geneviève went behind him, allowed her point to touch the middle of his back. 'You may open the door.'

Nivernais hesitated, and then turned the handle, stepped into the corridor. An anxious footman watched them from the head of the stairs.

'You'll not approach if you'd save the Ambassador's life,' Geneviève said. 'Now go and tell your people the same. Haste, Your Excellency.'

Nivernais led her up the stairs and along another corridor to her own chambers. Here there was another footman on guard, armed with a pistol.

'Drop it,' Geneviève commanded, and the weapon clattered to the floor. A moment later she was inside, and giving her weapon to Jules while she took Adam in her arms. He had been given little chance, had apparently been struck from behind by a club.

'Geneviève,' he said. 'My God, have you rescued me again?'

She kissed him. 'Tit for tat,' she said, and straightened to face the Ambassador. 'We are now going to leave your house, Your Excellency. You will accompany us for a short distance, then you will be set free. But always remember that I am ready to kill you should you attempt to escape me.'

'You would compound crime upon crime?' Nivernais said. 'You have no hope of survival, Chevalier. Do not suppose I am ignorant of your true purpose in England. I was advised of it but yesterday. Once I· give that document to the British government . . .'

'He is right, Geneviève,' Adam said. 'They will hang us both.'

'Geneviève?' Nivernais asked in bewilderment.

Geneviève smiled at him. 'I have decided to become a woman, Your Excellency. Manhood is a tiring business, and a dishonest one, as well. As for French justice, it cannot touch me here, while English justice . . .' She tapped her breast where the precious papers were concealed, 'is prepared to overlook my peccadilloes. You may inform His Majesty that I have decided to retire, from politics, from diplomacy, and from treachery, and become instead a devotee of the art of love. But tell him also, that as a poor young woman must make her way, I shall be writing my memoirs. What I put in them of course depends on whether His Majesty continues to pay my pension as a Chevalier of the Cross of St Louis. I shall await his answer with interest. But not for too long.'

Nivernais goggled at her as she took Adam's arm and assisted him to the door. Jules stood immediately behind the Ambassador, his poniard pressed against Nivernais' back.

'I must confess I do not understand your confidence at all,' Adam remarked as the door opened. 'Where are we going now? Where can we live?'

Geneviève squeezed his hand, waved away the anxious footmen who clustered the corridor. 'We are going to a house by a river,' she said. 'And there I am going to be what you have always wanted, my darling: A woman.'

Conclusion

The Chevalier did write her Memoirs, although as King Louis did continue her pension she omitted some of the more remarkable episodes of her life. She did not, however, succeed in retiring, but remained one of the leaders of English society, the target of every ambitious hostess.

While the rumours and the gossip grew and multiplied, despite a High Court ruling that she was indeed a woman, delivered at the conclusion of the case of Jacques versus Hayes, in which Dr Hayes received judgement in his favour. The stories persisted until her death, when the doctors who examined her body claimed they had discovered some characteristics of *both* sexes, an opinion which has been disputed often enough since, whenever scholars have investigated the facts of her remarkable career.

Certainly Geneviève d'Éon lived happily for the remainder of her long life – she did not die until 1812. And equally certainly she must have been happy to have turned her back on the tinsel that was Versailles. She may have supposed, when Madame du Pompadour fell from favour only a few years later, to be replaced by Madame du Barry, that had she remained near the King she might have achieved that exalted position, but before her death she had seen the entire society she had known and loved turned upside down by the Revolution, and du Barry herself, the last survivor of the great era, mount the scaffold.

Nor was her judgement less sound at the other end of Europe, for on the death of the Empress Elizabeth Petrovna, which was not long delayed, it took only another year for the Grand Duchess Catherine Alekseeyevna to have her husband Peter murdered, and ascend the throne herself as the Empress Catherine the Second, the greatest of all the rulers of the Romanoff dynasty.

As for the attempt to destroy the English fleet, since it failed, and the barrels of gunpowder are no doubt still at the bottom of the Solent, we shall never know the true cause of the fiasco. Was it treachery by the Pompadour, or did Monsieur Beaucamp really discover an early form of high explosive? Certainly the looming war between England and France, and their various allies, was not long delayed; it was a war which, carelessly embarked on by the petticoat government of France, was to raise Great Britain to her greatest power and begin the rapid decline which was to topple the French monarchy forever.

The Chevalier could afford to smile.